"Meet Detective 8 Ballo. H[e]
describes the hugely ente[rtaining]
debut. His beat is New York ~~~~~ ... the 1920s, the Jazz Age, the era of
speakeasies and flappers and bootleggers battling for turf. He's trying
to find a girl named Velma. Before he does, he'll find a mountain of
trouble, make plenty of enemies, and meet all the big names in town,
from Dorothy Parker to Babe Ruth to Bugsy Siegel. Before you're done,
you'll find a mountain of entertainment, a book filled with action,
suspense, plot twists, and a sense that you're actually living back there
in the fantastic world that author Matt Cost brings so vividly to life.
Velma may have gone awry. But don't let her get away. Read the book."

—William Martin, *New York Times* Bestselling Author
of *Back Bay* and *December '41*

"*Velma Gone Awry* is a smooth, captivating, twist-y mystery from
Matt Cost—blending his penchant for history, crime, and observations
on changing social attitudes. Set in the 1920s in New York City and
Brooklyn, the tale includes an intriguing mix of actual persons,
historic events, and places as well as a series of conundrums that keep
the reader guessing: Whodunit? What's at stake? What's the truth?
8 Ballo, the gutsy investigator, is a grand combo of brawn, intellect,
empathy, and fast wit. He's a sleuth worthy of hire, and this
reader is looking forward to his next adventure."

—Jule Selbo, screenwriter and author of five award-winning novels
including the Dee Rommel Mystery Series (*10 Days*, *9 Days*,
and the upcoming *8 Days*)

"Readers won't anticipate the blend of historical and social inspection
of the times that permeates *Velma Gone Awry*, but this strength is just
one of the pleasing surprises of the vivid story... a powerful tale of
intrigue, redemption, and discovery that comes full circle...
Libraries looking for full-bodied mysteries that display equally
captivating elements of historical and social intrigue will find
Velma Gone Awry just the ticket for a more literary and complex
inspection than a simple whodunit alone."

—Diane Donovan, Senior Reviewer, *Midwest Book Review*

Novels by Matt Cost
aka Matthew Langdon Cost

The Goff Langdon Mainely Mysteries

Mainely Power

Mainely Fear

Mainely Money

Mainely Angst

The Clay Wolfe / Port Essex Mysteries

Wolfe Trap

Mind Trap

Mouse Trap

Cosmic Trap

Historical Fiction

I Am Cuba: Fidel Castro and the Cuban Revolution

Love in a Time of Hate

At Every Hazard

Velma Gone Awry

A Brooklyn 8 Ballo Mystery

MATT COST

Encircle Publications
Farmington, Maine, U.S.A.

Editor, Encircle Publications: Cynthia Brackett-Vincent
Cover design by Deirdre Wait
Cover photographs © Getty Images

Published by:

Encircle Publications
PO Box 187
Farmington, ME 04938

info@encirclepub.com
http://encirclepub.com

Chapter 1

8 Ballo was sitting in his dingy office, feet up on the desk, reading *The Brooklyn Daily Eagle*, when the outer door opened with a bang.

The man who strode through the opening was a large fellow, a bit under 8's 240 pounds, with a square chin, blue eyes, and carefully combed blond hair slowly turning to gray. He had a pencil-mustache that crawled across his upper lip, oddly gray-black and not matching his hair.

It did not escape 8's attention that a rangy lad with the alert look of a gunslinger filled the door momentarily before turning his back to stand guard. 8 would've been more impressed if the kid had checked the empty inner office before retreating to stand watch. There could've been a pack of assassins in there.

He, of course, knew Fritz Hartmann, as the man was one of the wealthiest in Bushwick, having a factory and storefront for the custom wallpaper that he shipped all over the country. 8 believed that the man also had his fingers in a sweatshop for women's clothing, a sugar refinery, and several slaughterhouses.

"You're 8 Ballo, private detective?" Hartmann's tone was more an accusation than a question.

"That's why I'm here."

"What's that?"

8 slid his feet to the floor and stood with an agility rare for a man of his size. He waved to the door. "Was coming down the stairs this morning and the door had my name on it, so I came on

in. Seemed like the thing to do."

Hartmann turned to look at the dark-wooden doorway with the smoky glass that held the inscription, *8 Ballo, Private Detective*. He laughed. "I suppose that was wise Mr. Ballo, I suppose it was." He held out his hand. "Fritz Hartmann."

8 took the proffered hand. It was firm, but not trying to impress, and the grip relaxed promptly. "Please sit, Mr. Hartmann."

As Hartmann gingerly sank into a creaky wooden chair, 8 followed suit, sitting forward with his elbows on the desk that, given his bulk, looked as if it were more fit for a child. He waited for the man to break the silence, an affair that lasted nearly a minute as they sized each other up.

8 knew that Hartmann saw a rumpled bloke in a worn suit that he seemed to be bursting out of, though none of the weight was excess. He'd been born big, grown big, and matured big. He had a round face and blue eyes that could go from warm sky to cold ocean at the drop of a hat.

"I need you to find my daughter, Mr. Ballo," Hartmann finally said.

8 nodded. That sounded more exciting than investigating insurance fraud. "Tell me about your daughter."

"Like what? Velma's missing. I need her back."

"How old is your daughter, Mr. Hartmann?" 8 asked.

"Twenty-five."

This surprised 8, but he kept that emotion from reaching his face. They were sitting across from each other on either side of a cluttered desk in the drab outer room of his office. He'd rented this space with the idea that eventually business would allow him to hire a secretary, and he'd move into the inner office. Besides, he lived upstairs on the third story, and there was a grocery, cigar shop, and tavern just downstairs. Of course, the tavern had been converted into a restaurant ever since the passage of the Prohibition Bill on January 16, 1920. Meaning, the tavern no longer served alcohol due to prohibition... unless you went through the coatroom and were let through the doorway that led to the basement juice joint.

"Do you think Velma was abducted?"

"You know who I am?"

8 nodded.

Hartmann sighed and settled back into his seat, his squared shoulders slumping in what appeared to be an uncharacteristic posture. "She's been missing for three days, and there's been no request for money."

"What, then, do you supposed happened to her?" 8 asked.

"I've been assured that you're very good at finding people. That you're a private investigator with an emphasis on *private*."

8 gave the man his no-bullshit stare. "I'm a professional," he said.

"She might just be off on a bender," Hartmann said. "She fancies herself as one of those modern women, what is it they're called?" He looked up at the hanging lamp that clearly illuminated the room before looking back down and snapping his fingers. "Flappers."

"In which case, you'd be wasting your money hiring me."

"Do you know, Mr. Ballo, why these young women are called flappers?"

8 knew of two possible answers. He decided to not go with the original meaning from across the pond, which was a loose woman or prostitute. "It's the rubber galoshes they wear as some sort of fashion statement," he said instead. "They don't fasten them, causing them to flap when they walk. Like a bird."

"Ah, I see. I thought it was because they run their mouths so much. Don't know their place."

8 winced but tried not to show it. "Have you been to the police?"

"Yesterday. They weren't much help as there's been no hint of foul play." Hartmann's piercing blue eyes flashed in anger.

"Other than being off on a bender, do you have any other thoughts on why your daughter might be missing, Mr. Hartmann?"

"I fear that Velma is not always wise where her safety is concerned.

She often doesn't come home until a new day has dawned. God knows where she spends her time, but she'll reek of rum or gin and can struggle to walk a straight line."

"And when did you last see her?"

"It was Friday. I got home promptly at six, and, as is her wont, she was just preparing to go out. With far too much paint on her face for my liking, but that was nothing new. Lipstick, rouge on her cheeks, soot on her lashes—'putting on her munitions,' she called it." Hartmann sighed wearily.

"Did she say where she was going?"

"No. She never told me what her plans were. Probably a cluster of speakeasies, would be my guess, from the way she'd come tripping home."

"I guess the logical place to start would be with her friends," 8 said. He picked up a pad and pencil. "Can you tell me who her friends are?"

"I don't know a great many, I'm sorry to say," Hartmann said. "She did mention one day that she'd had dinner with that woman, Zelda Fitzgerald, you know, the one married to that playboy who wrote a book?"

8 nodded. "I have read Scott Fitzgerald."

"I'm told that the one about paradise or something like that wasn't half bad," Hartmann said. "But his second one, *The Beautiful and Damned*, I hear, is nothing more than wastrels pissing away their privilege."

"Vocation," 8 murmured. "It's about what a person does when they have nothing to do."

"You don't say? That'd be my Velma. Never had to do a damn thing in her life."

"Do you know of anybody else your daughter was friends with, Mr. Hartmann?"

"The only other name that sticks with me is she used to have lunch with that Dorothy Parker gal, you know, the wisecracker?"

"I've read her reviews in *Ainslee's*," 8 said. *Ainslee's* was a literary periodical that he enjoyed perusing on occasion for the fine writing. "She has quite the sharp tongue. Was Velma joining the group at the Algonquin Hotel?"

"I don't—wait, she did say something about going to *The Gonk.* That'd be the same thing, I presume."

8 wrote this down on the pad, noticing that Hartmann was twisting his thin mustache idly between thumb and finger where it curled just past the corner of his mouth. "Do you have a picture of Velma?"

Hartman took a Kodak photograph from the breast pocket of his tailored suit and handed it over to 8. Velma Hartmann was a waif of a girl, a gamine. She had fragile shoulders from which hung pin-thin arms. A long neck rose to a pixie face with smoldering eyes, mysterious eyes that promised intrigue at the very least, if not trouble. She had on a cloche hat, a bell-styled cap made of lace, from which a few dark curls escaped. *Yep,* thought 8, *she was definitely the kind of dark beauty who probably attracted men who liked danger.*

"Can I keep this?" 8 asked.

"Of course."

"Is there anything else you can tell me?"

"Like what?"

"Where did she attend school? What does she like to do?"

"She graduated from Barnard College up in Morningside Heights just about three years back." Hartmann drummed the table and looked up in the air. "Like to do? She reads everything she can get her hands on. Fiction. Garbage. Philosophy. More garbage. Poetry. Not a practical bone in her body."

Interesting, 8 thought, *very interesting indeed.* He, too, had a penchant for reading fiction, philosophy, and poetry. "Is that what she studied at Barnard?"

"English and the Classics. Rubbish." Hartmann snorted, but then smiled. "She does play the piano wonderfully. And the mandolin, as well as the harp."

"She sounds quite accomplished," 8 said.

"Frivolous, you mean."

"I will start immediately."

Hartmann twirled his mustache. "Bring my daughter home to me, Mr. Ballo."

"I'll find her, Mr. Hartmann, of that you can be certain." 8 leaned back and studied Hartmann. "We need to discuss finances. I charge $20 a day plus expenses."

"Money is no object. Find my daughter. Find Velma."

8 filled in the fee on a piece of paper with his Gordon's ink pencil and slid it across the desk. "I need you to sign this. Can I ask how you heard about me?"

"You did some work a bit back for a colleague. Said you were very effective for him. Never had a problem with you Hungarian fellows." Hartmann signed the paper with a flourish. "Ballo is a Hungarian name, no?"

"Yes. My grandparents fled after the failed revolution of 1848. Came to New York, ended up here in King's County."

"If you don't mind me asking, how did you acquire the moniker of 8?"

"My mother was certain that I was going to be a girl. There were four older brothers and three older sisters, so I guess she just thought it right to even the scales. My name was to be Margit." 8 shrugged. "When I turned out to be a boy, she was at a loss. My dad was out to sea at the time, so she just wrote down the number 8, as I was the eighth child. She said she meant to change it once my father got home, before it became official, but that never happened."

"It's certainly unique," Hartmann said. "And I've been assured that you *are* one of a kind."

"I do what it takes to get the job done."

Hartmann looked as if he might rise, and then settled back,

blowing a huge gust of air out with a whistling sound. "There might be a third explanation for Velma going missing, and I'm afraid it involves foul play."

8 had guessed that Hartmann was holding something back. "Go on."

"You know something of me, it seems, so you know that I've been very successful in my business enterprises. This doesn't happen without—how shall we say?—making certain enemies along the way."

"Such as?"

8 was not one much for dancing around a topic. It seemed a colossal waste of time the way so many people took so long to get to the point of what they were saying.

Hartmann cleared his throat. "I've stepped on many toes climbing to the top."

"If somebody took your daughter, Mr. Hartmann, you did a bit more than step on a toe or two," 8 said. "So, who'd you tick off?"

"There's some Jewish boys down in Brownsville, came to me a while back when I was having some issues with my employees at the abattoir I own in Gravesend. The one who does all the talking isn't a lick over five feet tall, mind you, tells me they'll take care of the problem for a price. The other one has a face as smooth as the day he was born, not a hint of a whisker anywhere, but he just kept staring at me with his bug eyes." Hartmann cleared his throat. Drummed his fingers on the table.

"What happened, Mr. Hartmann?"

"Nothing. Nothing at all. I told them to run along and that I'd handle it myself."

"And did you... take care of the employee problem at your slaughterhouse?"

"Wasn't nothing at all," Hartmann said. "I removed the outspoken workers, and the others shut up real quick and got back to work without any more belly-aching."

8 waited but there didn't appear to be any more forthcoming information. "Spill it, Mr. Hartmann. Are you telling me that two adolescents took your daughter for no reason?"

"I had them looked into. They run an outfit between the Lower East Side and Brownsville called the Bugs and Meyer Mob. The kid who didn't say anything is Bugsy Siegel. The short one was Meyer Lansky."

8 rolled his tongue over his teeth. He knew them well. Hell, everybody knew of them. Bugsy had started extorting money from pushcart vendors when he was twelve, and now, at age seventeen, he'd killed more than a few men and was climbing up the ranks of the gangster mobs through sheer brutality. Meyer was the brains of the outfit, a short Jewish kid who was absolutely ruthless, but had the accounting skills of an adding machine.

"They took offense at you dismissing them," 8 said after a minute.

"First and only time the little snot-nosed kid spoke, the one I now know is Bugsy Siegal. He looked at me, his eyes all shiny and crazy, and told me I was making a mistake. Then they walked out."

"They've been making a considerable bit of noise as of late," 8 allowed. "Lads they might be, but they certainly shouldn't be underestimated. Rumor has it that it was Bugsy who killed those three fellows in Brownsville last week. Seems one of the gents was impolite to Bugsy, called him boy or some such thing, so he killed them all. Just because they called him boy."

Hartmann jerked his thumb over his shoulder at the doorway. "That's why I have Mouse out there."

"Not a very big fellow to be a bodyguard."

"The boy is a wizard with a gat and not afraid to use it," Hartmann said. "The muscle is down with the automobile. Bull. He makes you look tiny."

8 stood up. He was considering telling Hartmann to get the hell out of his office. Nobody in their right mind got on the wrong side

of Bugsy Siegel. Lansky kept the youth on a tight leash, but when let off? A bloodbath was sure to follow. 8 could use the money but was fine without it at the same time. It was the missing woman that kept his tongue in check.

Just last fall, 8 had stopped into a shop down Bushwick Avenue toward Brownsville to find the proprietor, an old friend of his father's, on crutches and with half his face bandaged up. Seems he'd missed an 'insurance payment' to the Bugsy and Lansky gang, and Bugsy had paid him a visit. He'd taken a baseball bat to the man's legs, breaking one of them and badly bruising the other. In his wanton rage, he'd also taken the man's eye out and broken a cheekbone. Bugsy Siegel was a psychopath and not to be messed with.

But, there was something terribly alluring about the girl and the mystery that lay within her eyes.

"To be clear," 8 said, "I will find your daughter for you, Mr. Hartmann. If she's being held against her will, I'll get her back. If she doesn't want to be found, I'll report back to you that she is safe, but not where she is. Is that acceptable?" He did not raise scenario number three, which was that she might already be dead. "And the price is now $25 a day."

Hartmann stood up and held out his hand. "All I want to know is that Velma is safe. Perhaps if she has a reason to stay missing, I imagine there might be a man involved. You'd be able to get a message to her?"

8's enormous paw enveloped that of his newest client. "That I'll do. A hundred bucks should get us started." He handed Hartmann one of his newfangled business cards with the office address and telephone number on it. They made him feel like a very serious man indeed. He fought back a smile at his own pretentiousness.

Hartmann took out his wallet and counted out the money. "Keep me abreast of what you find out, Mr. Ballo. Here is where you can find me." He handed over the money and address and walked out the door.

8 went back and sat down, putting his feet up into the very pose he'd been in before Hartmann had arrived. *Very interesting,* he thought, *very interesting indeed.* He pulled open a drawer and tossed the money inside and pushed it shut. He plucked the photograph of Velma from his desktop. She was a beautiful woman, that was for certain. *A bit thin,* 8 mused, her shoulders barely wider than his hand. It was Velma's eyes that intrigued 8. Though in this photo they were intelligent and slightly mocking, he could see that they were also but a moment away from sad, tortured even.

What real troubles could a rich, gorgeous, and intelligent lass have come across in just a quarter century of life? 8 had grown up with seven older siblings who smothered him with attention, often making it hard for him to breathe. He knew that they cared for him, but he'd been happy to go off on his own, live his own life, and have his own space. Sure, he had some friends he ran with, and had met some nice dames, but always, he was happy to have his solitude at the end of the day.

Velma Hartmann looked as if she could be alone in the middle of a crowd. She'd most definitely be worth finding. Then, he could ask her about the melancholy behind those brown eyes.

Chapter 2

The Algonquin Hotel was at West 44th Street and 6th Avenue just up from Times Square. 8 figured this was as good a place as any to start. From what he'd read in the society pages, Zelda Fitzgerald was most likely not awake until afternoon, and he figured that he needed a better grasp of the lay of the land before facing Bugsy Siegel and Meyer Lansky. Besides, it was no secret that Dorothy Parker had her midday meal at The Gonk, the Round Table luncheon slowly becoming as famous as the theater reviews she wrote for *Ainslee's*.

8 had no idea what kind of reception he would get. He was nervous about walking unannounced up to a table of sharp-tongued wits, but as of yet, he'd found words didn't hurt nearly as much as a punch in the face. He thought there might be some sort of hotel security, but there was none. The round table was in the center of the hotel dining room. Smaller tables circled it like pilot fish around a whale.

There were eight chairs. Seven were filled by five men and two women. It was obvious who Dorothy was. She was speaking, and the others were listening with rapt attention. Her flat-black hair fell to just below her ears, the cut straight. Her chin was strong, and her eyes flashed with disdain. 8 slid his way into the eighth and only empty chair.

Dorothy was finishing up speaking as all eyes swung from her to 8. "Billie Burke is the new Maude Adams like I'm the new Theodore

Roosevelt." She turned her piercing eyes toward 8, who now sat two seats to her left. "You're a large one, aren't you?" she said.

"Hello, Mrs. Parker. 8 Ballo."

"And tell me, my dear number 8, are you a critic, a publicist, a writer, or a producer?"

"I'm none of the above, Dorothy."

"Oh, leave that at the door. My friends call me Dottie. What is it that you *do* do?"

"This luncheon is by invitation only." The man who spoke had a receding hairline and hound dog eyes.

"Shush, my dear Benchley. I'm curious to hear about our new friend," Dorothy said.

"I'm a private investigator," 8 said. "And a great fan of your writing."

"Ah, I knew I liked something about you. And pray tell, what of my writing interests you?"

"You recently published a short fiction piece, *Such a Pretty Little Picture*, that seems spot-on as to why I've never married. Your wit is only matched by the depressive narrative of the institution of wedlock, it would seem." 8 judged by the look in her eyes that he'd passed a test. "I never thought I'd get the opportunity to ask you but wanted to at the time. If Mr. Wheelock had all but disappeared, what was to keep him from actually doing so?"

Dorothy narrowed her eyes, first looking out, and then inward. "Appearances, I suppose, my dear 8. Life is all about creating a pretty little picture, true or not."

The host came up and whispered in Dottie's ear. She waved him away. "The institution of wedlock, as you put it, 8, certainly sounds extremely confining, or at the very least, tedious. That, I can attest to first-hand." She flicked ashes from her cigarette and took a puff. "Has my husband hired you to follow me?" The table laughed, if somewhat nervously.

"I'm looking for a woman I believe you know, Dottie. Velma

Hartmann." A waiter handed 8 a glass which looked to be water but tasted like gin.

"Ah, you just told me that marriage is not for you, yet you look for a young woman. What are your intentions, 8? Take her or leave her; or, as is the usual order of things, both?" Dorothy tittered and those around her broke into guffaws.

8 smiled. "She is indeed a winsome young lass," he said. "But the problem seems to be that she is missing, and her father is worried about her."

"Ah, the jailer of her existence. The ass who believes himself to be her caretaker. I'm sure that our dear little Velma is having herself a bit of fun outside the prison of her home."

"I, too, have my reservations about Fritz Hartmann," 8 said with a grin. "I've told the warden that I'd ensure his daughter was safe and not in harm's way, but that if she didn't want to be found or returned, her location would remain unknown to him."

The host came up and again whispered in Dorothy's ear. She turned to face him and said loudly, "Tell him that I am fucking busy, or vice versa."

The table guffawed gently, and the waiter retreated, red-faced.

The man with hound dog eyes by the name of Benchley cleared his throat. "We don't go in for private investigators coming in and snooping around. Why don't you be a good chap and scoot along?"

8 looked the hound dog in his mournful eyes and smiled. "If I scoot, Mr. Benchley, it will be with one hand wrapped around your ample neck as I take you outside to have a conversation about your manners."

This caught the attention of everybody at the table. They didn't normally travel in circles where people offered to drag somebody outside and beat them to a pulp. Their weapons were words and not brawn.

Dottie snickered. "You seem to have started a beef with a big six, my dear Benchley. What now?"

Benchley's face had gone from rosy to sallow in a split second. "I assure you, sir, that we don't go in for that sort of behavior in here."

8 ignored him and looked back to Dottie. "I give you my word that I'll do nothing to harm or interfere in the chosen life of Velma Hartmann. But there are some circumstances that suggest that she may be… unsafe. Anything you can tell me would be helpful."

Dottie took a puff of her cigarette and looked down her nose at 8. "I could use a wisp of fresh air. Do you think that you might step outside with me for a moment? Without dragging me by the nape of my neck?"

8 nodded and stood up. He took a step, stopped, and stood awkwardly, wondering if it was offensive to the flapper culture to pull out the chair for a lady. He was saved from this indecision as Dottie also rose and led the way toward the exit. He noted that she did *not* have galoshes on, was more modestly covered up than the picture of Velma. She wore a frock of mauve velvet with a circular flounce that reached just to the top of her calves, with silver lace and brown grosgrain-ribbon trim. 8 sometimes liked to read the fashion magazines, mostly to look at the pretty models. He followed Dottie through the lobby and out the front door.

The sidewalk was crowded as people spilled out looking for lunch, mixing in with delivery men, businessmen, shoppers, and those just getting up for the day. Pedestrians wended their way through the automobiles clogging the street. It was a general chaos that hadn't yet reached Bushwick in Brooklyn where 8 lived and worked.

"Ah, the Big Apple," Dottie said. "Don't you just love the hustle and bustle of it all?"

"The Big Apple?"

"New York City."

"Why the Big Apple?"

Dottie snickered. "A name coined by Black stable hands in New Orleans referencing that our racetracks here are the 'big time.'"

"Gotcha," 8 said. "Bit busy for me, truth be told. I run at more of a Brooklyn pace."

"I dare say you did look a tad out of place in The Gonk. Although you seem to be well-read and well-spoken."

"Came up this way to go to Washington Square College and then hustled home as fast as possible."

"And do tell, what did you study there?"

"I received a degree in liberal arts."

"Hmm. How about that? What were some of your favorite areas of study?"

8 wondered how this conversation had become about him, but figured he was being sounded out more deeply as worthy of her trust. "Philosophy. American literature. And a bit of French literature."

"You speak French?"

"You sound surprised?"

"I suppose it is the… I guess you being a baby grand is what surprises me, that and you seem to be bursting out of that suit you're wearing. Tell me, are you on the up and up?"

"In regard to the suit?" 8 chuckled. "I can't afford a tailor, and off-the-rack is hard to come by in my size. But yes, I don't much see the point in hedging the truth. If people don't like the facts… well, I can't much help them now, can I?"

"No, I suppose that's not your concern."

"Tell me about Velma. Who is she?"

Dottie snickered. "She comes off as a party girl who likes juice joints and men, but underneath that façade, she's one of the most brilliant people I know. She doesn't let on, mind you, but if you pay attention, you'll realize she knows something about everything."

"I promise I won't do anything to harm her," 8 said.

Dottie lit another cigarette. She was standing very close to him but turned her head to blow smoke sideways. "Okay, here's the skinny. Velma has a guy she hangs out with who plays for the Dodgers. Hank something or other. You follow baseball, 8?"

"I manage to go to a few games a year and check the scores during the season," he said. "Played stickball as a kid, like every other boy in Brooklyn."

"Bet you could hit that thing several streetlights, now, couldn't you?" Dottie grasped his bicep and squeezed. "My, you are a big six," she said. "So, you know the Hank I'm talking about?"

"I'm thinking there's just the one on the team."

Dottie kept her hand clasping his arm, her face turned up to him. "She also loves that blues music up Harlem way. Pretty friendly with a lady named Mamie Smith."

"The one who sung 'Crazy Blues'?" 8 asked. "About having a man who don't treat her right?"

"My, Mr. 8, you do continue to surprise. You follow baseball *and* Black singers. Anyway, I think Mamie took her band barnstorming across the country and might even be in Oregon now, but she left behind her saxophonist, a fellow by the name of Hawk. He decided the road was no more for him and took a job with an orchestra. Velma could be up with him."

"Coleman Hawkins?" 8 was starting to feel extremely jealous of Velma Hartmann.

"That's his name, but they usually call him Hawk or Bean."

"Fritz mentioned that Velma was quite musical."

"She loves music. Especially jazz. You can tell she feels it right down into the marrow of her bones."

A woman who loves jazz and *baseball*, 8 thought with a whimsical smile creasing his face. He might start to really like this Velma Hartmann.

A man bumped into Dottie, pushing her the last few inches into 8's body. The man turned with an angry expression, took one look at 8, and quickly apologized before moving on. 8 had wrapped his left arm around Dottie to stop her from stumbling further.

"Those sound like two great promising places to start," he said. "Maybe I'll take a trip up to Harlem this afternoon."

"Might find him hanging around up in Harlem at Black Swan Records."

"Then, I'll take my leave and get started right off, if you don't mind."

"Oh, the best place to begin is right upstairs," Dottie said. She looked up the outside of the Algonquin Hotel.

"Upstairs?"

"Zelda and F. Scott Fitzgerald are in from Long Island for a few days. Got a room upstairs, and they should be rising from the dead in about an hour and descending to find some nourishment, most likely in the form of a cocktail to ease their way back to the living. Velma and Zelda are thick as thieves, those two are."

As they made their way back into the hotel, Dottie's group was on their way out, a presence that could be heard before seen. It seemed that most of the group had been working on gin or some other alcoholic beverage, and they were in fine spirits. They gathered Dottie in their wake like a large wave crashing out the door and onto the sidewalk. There was mention of cocktails at Nyesa's.

8 looked at his timepiece. According to Dottie, he had an hour to kill before the Fitzgeralds descended from their lair. He decided to take a walk around Times Square, seeing as he'd crossed the bridge into the big city. He rarely ventured out of Brooklyn, and this would be an opportunity to see what he was missing.

Times Square was crisscrossed by trolley tracks swooping in every direction, and if he worried that riding in the taxi had been dangerous, making his way from corner to corner here was almost a death sentence. He noticed that *Lady Butterfly* was no longer at the Astor Theater and mentally kicked himself for having missed it. He'd heard that it was well worth braving the trip to the hectic city.

Several policemen were in the road trying to stop automobile traffic for pedestrians, and 8 took advantage of this to cross the street. It was still a harrowing experience as the automobiles came rushing at him before he was safely over. A woman in a slinky dress asked him if he was interested in having a good time. A pack of boys surrounded him asking for nickels.

This all reminded 8 why he chose to stay on the other side of the East River. Not wanting to chance crossing the Rubicon again, he continued on down the block until he found a quieter intersection and worked his way back to the Algonquin Hotel, stepping into the lobby with a sigh of relief. Crowds weren't really his thing.

8 made his way back to the Rose Room in search of the Fitzgeralds. As Dottie claimed, they were indeed sitting at a small table in the corner nursing drinks and looking a bit worse for the wear. 8 recognized F. Scott immediately, the man now quite famous. He had large round eyes, unruly hair, and a broad mouth above a pointed chin. Zelda, he thought, could've been Dorothy or Velma for that matter, as she followed the trendy bob cut, short, dark hair swirling around her head. Her cheeks may've been a bit puffier, but her eyes glinted in their sockets with a piercing intelligence.

"Mrs. and Mr. Fitzgerald? Do you think I might have a moment of your time?" 8 asked, standing over them like a grizzly bear in the civilized space of the Rose Room.

"Let us finish two more of these before hearing what you have to say," Zelda said. Her husband did not bother to look up from the table that he was intently staring at.

"It's about your friend, Velma Hartmann."

"What about Velma?"

"She's missing, and her father fears foul play."

Zelda snickered. "Foul play, indeed. What did you say your name is?"

"8. 8 Ballo. I'm a private detective." He grabbed a chair from the next table and slid it over, settling himself in as if asked.

The waiter came by with three glasses of water, but again, 8's tasted like gin. There must be a standing rule to bring a drink to any patron every ten minutes, he figured.

Fitzgerald looked up. "Scott." He held out his hand. "My first published work was about a detective," he said. "In the school paper when I was thirteen."

"Perhaps his best work to date," Zelda said and laughed.

"If my work falters, it is the fault of my muse burning too dimly," Scott said.

"Don't mind his grumpiness," Zelda said. "He took a beating upstairs at the Thanatopsis Literary and Inside Straight Club last night. I shouldn't wonder we might have to curtail our trip to the city, he lost so much money."

"The cards were as fickle as you, my dear," Scott said.

"The contemplation of death," 8 murmured. "A fitting name for a poker game, I suppose."

"It *was* last night." Scott groaned and put his face in his hands.

"You know the Greek word *thanatopsis*?" Zelda's eyes shone with interest.

"I know the work of William Cullen Bryant," 8 said. "*She has a voice of gladness, and a smile and eloquence of beauty.*"

Zelda cast him an appraising look. "*And she glides into his darker musings, with a mild and healing sympathy, that steals away their sharpness, ere he is aware.*"

"I would say his best work," 8 said.

"Do you think that death is welcoming?" Zelda asked.

"I suppose that when the time is right, it just may be." 8 took a tiny sip of the gin. "But first we must accomplish what we were meant to do in this life. What is it that you wish from life?"

"I want to be very young always and very irresponsible and to feel that my life is my own to live and be happy and die in my own way to please myself."

"The alternative to growing old is a grim prospect." 8 wasn't sure how the conversation had shifted so far from the intended topic. "And that brings us back to the safety of Velma Hartmann."

"I haven't seen Velma in ages," Zelda said, lighting a cigarette.

8 wondered how long 'ages' actually was. "Do you have any idea where she might be?"

"I haven't the foggiest. I'm sure she's fine."

"She's not been home in three days. Her father says that that's not normal."

"*I don't want to live, but love first, and live incidentally.*"

8 figured there was a hidden implication in there somewhere. "Are you suggesting that Velma is in love?"

Zelda laughed loudly and slapped the table with her hand, causing Scott to groan again. "My dear Velma is in love all of the time, rarely with the same man twice."

"I've been told that she spends time with a fellow named Hank, and another called Hawk." He paused, contemplating the young woman in front of him. He couldn't quite get a grasp on Zelda. There seemed to be a disconnect between her and the world.

"I do believe that Hank has been let go as a beau," Zelda said. "Not sure about Coleman. You are most certainly well informed, my dear 8."

8 thought it odd that she'd not commented or inquired about his name. "Knowing things," he said, "or more accurately, knowing people who know things, that's my business."

"What about those two gents she brought out to the cottage a few weeks back?" Scott interjected, raising his head from his hands. "The two good-looking lads who we thought might've been together?"

"They certainly were fine-looking specimens," Zelda said with a sly smile. "But I don't think they showed much interest in myself or Velma, if you know what I mean."

"*Phish*, they were tight as thieves. What were their names?" Scott drummed the table with his fingers. "They were Russians, weren't they?"

"The one was Peter, 'like The Great,' he said to me." Zelda seemed to think this was all great fun, trying to track down Velma, and now, Scott had joined in as well. "The other was more arcane."

"Arcane?" Scott took a large swig of gin. "Arkady. That was it."

"Yes, Peter and Arkady," Zelda said. "Two large Russians with blond and brown hair and fair skin."

"Do you know where I might find them?" 8 asked.

"I heard them say they lived just off the Bowery over in Coney Island," Zelda said.

"That's right," Scott said. "There's a saloon they frequent there called Diamond Tony's or something like that. Said we just had to give it a go sometime."

"What can you tell me about Velma?" 8 asked. "What kind of a gal is she?"

"I don't know if there's a book she hasn't read," Zelda said.

"She showed me a short story she wrote once," Scott said. "It was magnificent. She brought the tale to life. I wanted her to publish it, but she refused, said that it wasn't for public consumption."

"What was it about?" 8 asked.

"A troubled girl in Brooklyn."

Chapter 3

8 stepped out of the Algonquin onto 44th Street. He checked the time on his Elgin pocket watch, a gift from a former client, a woman whom he remembered fondly whenever he looked at the time. It was just past three o'clock. Plenty of time to get up to Harlem and pay a visit to Coleman Hawkins.

Dottie didn't know where the man lived but had heard he was doing some recording work at the Pace Phonograph Company for Black Swan Records up in Harlem. It seemed like a good place to start. He planned on taking one of the elevated cars, but as he reached 6th Avenue, one of those new yellow cabs was parked on the corner. He figured, what the heck, he had an expense account, and Hartmann didn't seem very concerned about money.

8 had never taken a yellow cab before. His buddy, Pearle, owned a Nash 681 Touring automobile, and he often rode in it with him. It seemed a fine way to travel, even if they had a few harrowing experiences as they rumbled their way uptown. It appeared to be a tossup as to which automobile had the right of way at the cross streets. The driver assured him that that was what the horn was for. After a twenty-minute ride, they pulled up in front of a building beside whose wide front doors hung an impressively large, handsome sign in the shape of a record with a swan in gold against a black background.

As he entered the business, a ruckus was taking place in the front lobby. A woman with a broad set of teeth and a high forehead was angrily yelling at a light-skinned Black man with a stoic expression. 8 barely had enough time to step aside as she turned and stormed past him and out the door.

"She's right, you know, Harry." The man who spoke was sitting on a couch next to another fellow against the wall to 8's right side.

"I got to make business decisions that's best for me, Smack. I got to record some white folks if I want to keep the business alive," Harry, the man who'd taken the brunt of the yelling, replied.

"If you think that losing Ethel Waters is a wise decision, then you're one crazy son-of-a-bitch," Smack said.

"I won't be treated like that in my own studio," Harry said. "Not even by Ethel Waters."

8 cleared his throat. "I'm looking for Coleman Hawkins."

Harry swung his gaze over to settle on 8. "And who are you?"

"Just got a few questions for Mr. Hawkins."

"You're not the police," Harry said.

"Looks like a Pinkerton," Smack said.

"Big fellow, aren't you?" Harry said.

"I'm a private detective, but not a Pinkerton." 8 stepped further into the room. "Was that really Ethel Waters?" he asked.

"That was her. You looking for her, too?" Smack asked.

"Nope. Just a fan. As I am of Mr. Hawkins."

"What's your business with Hawk?" Harry asked.

8 paused, considered prevaricating, then settled on the truth. "I'm looking for a young lady," he said simply "I believe he's acquainted with her."

"Who?" the third man asked. He had a thin mustache that crested like a wave directly under his nose.

"*You're* Coleman Hawkins," 8 said. "I saw you play with Mamie Richards last summer."

"That's me," Coleman said. "Who you lookin' for?"

"Velma Hartmann."

"What makes you think I know some broad named Velma?" Coleman asked.

"Hey, buddy, maybe you just better move along," Harry said, taking a tentative step towards him.

8 looked at the thin fellow. He let his glare take the wind out of the man and then turned back to Coleman. "Heard from someone downtown that the two of you been hanging out."

"Man, I don't know no flapper white woman named Velma." Coleman stood up. "The man over there just asked you to leave."

"Somebody say that this Velma was a flapper? And white?"

The other man also stood, the three of them crowding around 8 with hostile stares. "You best be leaving and heading back downtown and let us get back to our business."

8 leaked out a half-smile. He rolled his shoulders to loosen them, a movement that was like sand dunes shifting. "Why they call you Smack?" he asked. "Aha, I know who you are. You're that piano player, Fletcher Henderson. Your fingers certainly dance over those ivories. Never heard you called Smack, though." At these innocuous words, the tension seemed to drain out of the room like the air out of a balloon.

"Okay, so you got our names, man. Who're you?" Coleman asked.

"8 Ballo, private detective," he replied, sticking out his hand. Coleman took it grudgingly, then Smack, and finally Harry. "Velma's father hired me to find her. Afraid there's been foul play."

"So you run up here trying to pin the blame on a Black man," Coleman said.

8 shook his head. "Friend of Velma's told me you been hanging out with her, is all. Thought maybe you could point me in a direction."

Coleman sighed. "Velma, she's like, what you call it? A will-o'-wisp. She flits in and out as she pleases. Ain't seen her in a couple of weeks. She done gone awry."

"Gone awry?" 8 asked. "What's that mean?"

"Ya know, headed in the wrong direction, all twisted up and askew."

8 tucked that away. Velma gone awry. "Anything you can tell me would be of help."

Harry snorted. "I'll be back in the recording room," he said, walking through an inner door.

"I don't know about gone awry," Smack said, "but that woman has some real talent on the piano. She spent a little more time practicing with a real band than at the speakeasy, she might find herself a place in this business. But no. Said she just plays for herself. Guess if you got money, you can do that."

"That's not the only thing she plays well," Hawkins said.

"Look, I don't know anything about Velma other than she got some talent, real natural-like. Such a shame, you know?" Smack said. "But I got to get back to work." He followed Harry through the inner door.

"She say anything to you about a fellow named Hank?" 8 asked Hawkins. "Ballplayer for the Trolley-Dodgers."

"Didn't hear nothing about no ballplayer," Coleman said. "She friendly with that theater critic, the witty one, Dorothy Parker. She'd quote things that woman said that would have us both rolling on the floor laughing." He turned and sat down on the couch.

8 went behind the desk and sat facing him. "She mention anybody else she rustled around with?"

"I only saw the woman a half-dozen times," Coleman said. "She came up to me one night after an engagement I had at a juice bar. Bought me a drink. We hit it off."

"No idea where she might be?"

"One night she told me something funny a guy named Benji had told her. Something about how he told his tailor to make sure his pockets were quart sized."

"You get any other name to go with Benji?"

"No, man. What you trying to run that Sheba down for? Damn, man, she hates that flat tire who calls himself her father."

"That seems to be the consensus," 8 said. "At least amongst her friends. She happen to mention why that is, 'zactly?"

"Not so much. Might've had something to do with her mother but I couldn't say for sure."

"Her mother, huh?"

"She got real pensive when I asked about her mother. Said she was dead, and Velma blamed her father for not treating her right while she was alive, or something like that."

8 salted that thought away to be revisited at a later time. "How about the names Peter and Arkady? Couple of fellows who live down to Coney Island."

"Don't believe I heard of them. Arkady? Imagine I'd remember that."

8 handed the man one of his business cards. "You think of anything, you give me a ring. Got a phone in my office down in Bushwick."

Dusk was descending as 8 got off the newly-minted nickel train in Coney Island. He hadn't been over this way since he was twenty. Him and a couple of his friends had come over for a few days of debauchery, betting on the horses, going to Steeplechase Park for the rides after entering through the rolling barrels. They'd drank, caroused, and a few of them had visited the ladies of the night.

Much of that neighborhood was gone now, burned down in fires, but the Bowery still raged along. Illegal speakeasies, burlesque dance revues, gambling joints, freak shows, rides, food, music, bathhouses and beach clubs—and above it all, spinning lazily through the sky, the Dip-the-Dip, a 150-foot-high ride that promised 'the thrill of a scenic railway, the fun of a Ferris wheel, and the excitement of the Chute-the-Chutes'.

It's a fine time to be alive, 8 thought with a detached whimsy. Tanned men and women ambled through the streets fresh off the beach. There was a vibrant current of hot-blooded youth, money in their pocket, out for a good time rippling through the neighborhood that put a bounce in his step and a lightness to his mood. Coney Island was much less serious than Bushwick, Harlem, or Manhattan.

Zelda had said that Velma had often met up with Peter and Arkady at Diamond Tony's Saloon after seven for a cocktail or two. 8 thought that Bowery Lane had been loud. It was tame compared to the saloon. As he entered the tavern through the hidden door, down the stairs, and through a second door, he was met with a blast of piano music and a medley of horns. There were five people blowing trumpets, saxophones, and bugles walking through and around the crowd spilling back from the bar and tables.

On stage were boys in their teens dressed as women and in full makeup, all doing the shimmy or some variation of it. Men and women were catcalling, hooting, and hollering in appreciation of their efforts. 8 thought this a bit risqué for a bar, but obviously, things were different here than in Bushwick. He looked around the crowd and judged that very few of the patrons were actually gay, just out for a good time, and boys dressed like women doing the shimmy seemed to fit the bill.

8 decided that he might as well get a drink and maybe some information. He fought his way to the bar. A few men started to complain, looked at his barrel chest, and carefully moved out of the way. The bartender was an Italian with flat-hard eyes that suggested he didn't put up with any shit.

"Old Fashioned Carolina," 8 said. The drink was a quarter. He put a five spot down. "And point me in the direction of a couple of fellows named Peter and Arkady."

The bartender made the drink and set it down, all the while rolling a toothpick in his mouth. He took the five-dollar bill and slid it into his pocket. "Table at one o'clock, all the way back against the wall."

8 turned and viewed the room. The two men at the table at one o'clock fit the description Zelda and Scott had supplied. The last number came to an end, and the room erupted in cheers. It was no

easy feat crossing the crowded floor, but he carved a path through the sea of people without incident.

There were no extra chairs at their table but 8 nabbed one on his way over and set it down. It looked a bit flimsy, and he eyed it dubiously before gingerly sitting down.

"Phew," the larger of the two men said. "Thought you might be busting that thing into matchsticks."

8 chuckled. "I won't feel safe until I return to standing. Name's 8 Ballo. You'd be Peter and Arkady?"

"I'm Arkady," the man replied. He had blond hair and a wide face with a friendly smile. "This here is Peter. We know you?"

"I'm looking for a woman you know," 8 said. "Velma Hartmann."

"What has our Velma done now?" Peter asked. He had a narrow face, was thinner than Arkady, but had massive forearms.

"Disappeared," 8 said.

"I can't think that that is unusual," Arkady said. "She's quite the free spirit."

"Her father is concerned."

The men laughed. "Fritz Hartmann has been worried about Velma since she turned fourteen," Peter said.

"Right after her mother died," Arkady said. "It's quite possible that our lovely Velma began acting out due to that sad event."

"How'd her mother die?" 8 asked.

The two men looked at each other. Peter shrugged. "Not sure. Might've been consumption?"

Cheers and catcalls rippled throughout the room causing 8 to look at the stage. There seemed to be a dance competition going on, the teenage boys dressed as women taking turns doing the shimmy on stage, as the audience roared and cheered. A waiter suddenly hovered over them. Arkady and Peter both ordered another drink. Yet, the waiter still loitered.

"Any of you blokes need a woman?" he asked. "Clean. Pretty. Cheap. Right upstairs."

Arkady looked at 8. "We're fine. How about you, Mr. Ballo?"

8 shook his head and waved the man off. "Seems to be a full-service venue," he said.

Peter laughed. "Drinks, music, whores, and boys dressed like women. Now, all we need is a sailor with his shirt off up on stage."

"What's that?" As if on cue, a sailor stopped, having apparently overheard the statement as he was walking by. "What are you? A table full of fairies?" He was dressed in the traditional white sailor's uniform with a round hat, square-cut collared shirt, and a dark neckerchief crooked around his neck. With the Brooklyn Navy Yard just around the corner, sailors were a large presence in the city.

"We don't want no problems," Arkady said. "We're just enjoying a drink and some music. Same as you."

"I don't like pansies like you drinking in the same place I do," the sailor said. "You best be leaving. Me and my buddies need your table." As if on cue, four other sailors came up behind him.

8 stood up, towering over the man who was maybe just a few inches over five feet. "Why don't you go find another table? We're not going anywhere."

"Whoa, they sure make fairies big here in the Bowery," the sailor said. But he took a step back, jostling the others behind him.

"Let's get a drink, Patrick. They ain't no skin off our teeth." A sailor pulled on his arm.

"I got my eye on you," Patrick said, turning and allowing himself to be pulled away.

"I bet you do," 8 said. Patrick paused, but then continued walking away. 8 sat back down. "I don't think Patrick would be all that enticing with his shirt off up on stage," he said.

Arkady and Peter laughed. "Wasn't quite the sailor I had in mind," Peter said. "The tall one behind him, maybe." They laughed again.

"When'd you last see Velma, if I might ask?" 8 asked.

"Think we met her here a bit more than a week ago. It was on a Saturday," Arkady said.

"That's right. Mae West was here," Peter said. "That was one helluva of an act. That woman can shimmy."

"She seem strange at all? Anything different about her?"

"Mae West?"

8 chuckled. "No, Velma."

"Nope," Arkady said. "She was just Velma. Was feeling pretty good. She even climbed up on stage at one point and was doing the shimmy alongside Mae. The crowd loved it. There's something intoxicating about that girl. Men love her. I even get a little jealous when she's chatting with Peter."

Peter punched him lightly in the arm. "If either one of us has a thing for Velma, it'd be you."

Arkady laughed. "Anyway, men were mobbing her afterward. Think that might've been why she left early."

"She leave by herself?"

"We walked her out and put her in a cab about midnight."

"She going home?"

Arkady laughed. "Doubt it. Not that early."

"Think she told the driver she was going somewhere in Williamsburg," Peter said.

"Williamsburg?" *Now that was interesting*, 8 thought.

"That's what it sounded like. I remember thinking the same thing, what the hell is in Williamsburg?" Peter said. "No place for a woman alone at night, but weren't nobody gonna tell Velma that. Hell, I'd worry about walking around there after dark. A guy could get his throat cut."

"You hear from Velma, or of her, can you let me know?" 8 leaned over with his new-fangled business card. Fourth one today he'd given out.

"What if she don't want to be found?" Arkady asked.

"I told her father that I'd make sure she was safe. If she doesn't want to be found, then she stays gone. I'm just to make sure she's okay."

"Okay," Arkady said, taking the card.

"You gentlemen have a good night," 8 said, standing up.

"Good to meet you, 8 Ballo," Peter said.

8 walked across the crowded room. He noticed Patrick eying him from a group of four or five other sailors. On the street it was dark out but no less crowded than before as he emerged from the basement speakeasy. The fresh air coming in off the Atlantic Ocean felt fantastic, though, and he gulped it in to wash out the thick fog of cigarette smoke that had assaulted him inside.

He cut down an alleyway, as much to get out of the crowd as it was a shortcut to the station. Unfortunately, it was a dead end, and he was forced to turn around. Coming toward him was the group of sailors with Patrick in the lead.

8 counted six of them. There was nowhere to run. He wasn't really of the running persuasion, anyway. He'd grown up scrapping with older boys. His size seemed to intimidate them into wanting to fight him, to prove their toughness, and he'd lost many a fight early on. It'd been quite some time now, since he'd lost a fight, though. Of course, he didn't usually throw down with six men at once.

"Hey, there, big fellow. We don't like fairies around here." Patrick had a stick or club in his right hand that he was slapping into the palm of his left.

"Depends on how long you been out to sea, I imagine," 8 said.

"What'd you say?" Patrick stepped forward, leading the surge of sailors.

"You heard me," 8 said. "You want to get the hell out of my way?"

Patrick swung the club, and 8 caught it in his hand, pulled it free, and struck him across the chest with it. Patrick fell backward into the arms of the others and then they surged forward like a tidal wave. 8 jabbed the stick into a man's throat. Hands grasped at it, and he was forced to let go.

He picked up a man with bowlegs and threw him into a wall. A club crashed across the back of his head, and he staggered forward into another man. He put one enormous hand behind the man's neck and crashed his forehead into the sailor's nose and felt the satisfying crunch of breaking cartilage.

8 felt an arm encircle his neck from behind, and he leaned forward, throwing the man into a pile of trash. A fist slammed into his chin and the coppery taste of blood filled his mouth. He roared in anger and struck the man in the forehead, and he dropped as if shot. The club crashed into 8's cheek, and everything went shadowy. With blood in his eyes, he grasped a man, picking him up, and hurling him into the ground.

A man wrapped his arms around 8's legs and two others jumped on him, and he toppled to the ground like a felled redwood tree. A mass of humanity swarmed over him, and he gouged his thumb into what felt like an eyeball, bit somebody's arm, and tried to wrestle his way free.

Suddenly, he felt bodies pulled from him, and looked up to see two figures throwing men left and right. He was able to regain his feet and stumbled forward to help Arkady and Peter, who were battering the remaining sailors, who had had enough and began to make their escape. 8, Arkady, and Peter allowed the sailors to slink away carrying their wounded.

8 stood tottering in the alley, bleeding and gasping for breath, watching them stumble off.

"We saw them follow you out of the saloon," Arkady said. "Figured you might need a touch of help as there was a whole passel of 'em."

"Appreciate that," 8 said. "Looks like you two know how to scrap."

"You softened them up for us," Peter said.

"I suppose I owe you fellows a drink, but I'm not really up to it right now."

"We'll hold you to that another time," Arkady said.

Chapter 4

8's battered and bruised face barely drew a second look on the train. There were far stranger sights to be seen than a bloodied man leaving Coney Island. As a matter of fact, he'd sat next to a bearded lady for the first part of the ride who was on her way home from her day at the freak show. She was very nice and helped straighten his clothes and clean the worst of his tattered visage.

It'd most certainly been an interesting evening, 8 thought. Velma Hartmann had an interesting circle of friends. She often lunched with Dorothy Parker at the Algonquin. Visited with Zelda and Scott Fitzgerald out at their place on Long Island. Slipped into speakeasies and juice joints up in Harlem where she ran with Coleman Hawkins and got up to God knows what with him in the early morning hours. Then she was off to Coney Island, shimmying on stage with Mae West while having drinks with a gay couple. Arkady and Peter seemed like swell enough fellows and tough as nails to boot. They all seemed to be good people.

This Velma Hartmann was becoming more alluring to 8 by the moment. She was admired for her intelligence by no less than Dorothy Parker. Scott and Zelda Fitzgerald were impressed with her breadth of reading *and* writing. Coleman Hawkins and Fletcher Henderson were bowled over by her musical abilities. Arkady and Peter suggested she could hold her own dancing on stage with Mae West. What an eclectic range of people she interacted with. He was, in fact, a bit jealous of her. Of course, she was missing, possibly mixed up in some bad business, but he somehow doubted it. He was starting to conjure a picture of her as a savvy, energetic intellectual with a backbone. She liked to read the classics, enjoyed music, baseball, and seemed to take life by the horns. Even if, perhaps, a bit lost in its complications. What had Hawk said? Velma gone awry.

As the elevated cars rocked their way through the darkness, 8 looked down at a lit-up Brooklyn some thirty-five feet below. 8 wondered about all the people, the automobiles, the hubbub of the city below as so many people went about their business. They passed through neighborhoods of distinct ethnicities, Germans, Russians, Irish, and others, but much of the area was mixed, a true melting pot of the world.

8's thoughts drifted back to the trenches during the Great War, but not the violence and killing, but rather the comradeship he had discovered there. It was a place where 8 first began to see the world as bigger than Bushwick, Brooklyn, or even New York City. This was due in no small part to the friendship he developed with a Brit by the name of Oliver Harvey.

The man had emigrated to the U.S. from the U.K. after the second Boer War in which he'd participated as an eighteen-year-old youngster fresh from rural England. The atrocities there had made an impression on Oliver, and he'd become an activist against Imperialism, a teacher of philosophy at Washington Square College, and a friend of 8's.

The two of them had spent countless hours in the trenches talking of Kant, Descartes, Hume, Locke, and even Marx, with Oliver lending 8 his books. The world of ideas had been thrust open for 8 during those months in the trenches. They spoke of Social Darwinism, the White Man's Burden, and Colonialism. Oliver had signed up for the war against his better judgement, suggesting that both sides were wrong, but a powerful Germany scared him more.

It was in these trenches, between the business of killing, and the practice of exchanging ideas, that 8 had grown into the man who had come home to Bushwick. The unsure naïve young fellow he'd been was quite gone, and he carried with him a new set of principles. Concepts such as empathy, self-analysis, reflection, justice, and moral values formed the bedrock of who he was.

Sadly, Oliver Harvey had been killed by a bullet at the end of October 1918, just weeks before the armistice.

His closest station was east of Woodward Avenue. The tracks grumbled underneath as they came into the terminal, churning and shuddering underneath them. He got off along with a smattering of others. It was almost a mile walk to his apartment, and he set out with determination, looking forward to reaching his destination and sitting down in the comfort of his own home.

Somewhere, he had the issue of *Collier's* magazine that featured the Fitzgerald story, *The Curious Case of Benjamin Button*. 8 thought that might be an interesting read now that he'd met the man. He wondered if Velma had read the story and what her take on it would be. This made 8 think of her musical tastes, which seemed well-aligned with his own. Though he wasn't able to go out to jazz clubs every night, not if he wanted to get up and go to work in the morning, but he still liked his music. Not for the first time, he told himself he should build one of those crystal radios that seemed to be so popular lately. It'd be nice to have music at home.

The streets of Bushwick were much less busy than Coney Island, and while the crowds had been fascinating there, they'd also been exhausting for 8. He didn't mind going to visit busy places like Diamond Tony's Saloon, but it was always nice to get back to peace and quiet and possibly a good book.

His body ached as he dragged himself up to his third-floor abode. It'd been a busy day even before he'd gotten the shit kicked out of him. When he turned on the light in his kitchen, two men were sitting at the table. 8 figured that it was about time to start packing his .38 Special.

"Could've turned on the light," 8 said. "Instead of sitting here in the dark."

"I don't much mind the dark." The man stood up and held out his hand. "Meyer Lansky."

8 reckoned the tiny fellow was under five-feet tall and slight of frame. He was probably no more than twenty years of age but had an old face. If the man hadn't been sitting in the dark in his kitchen in a threatening manner, he might've worried he was going to crush the fragile fingers of this child-like old-man. As it was, he hoped he did. "8 Ballo," he said shaking hands vigorously. "Sorry about the blood."

"You look like you've had a rough night," the other man said. He also seemed no more than a boy, his face innocent of the touch of a razor. "Ben Siegel. Blood doesn't much bother me." He too stuck out his hand, his grip firmer than Lansky's. He was also taller, stronger, and more handsome.

"Been a little trying," 8 said. "Looks like the night isn't improving much."

"Sorry to intrude like this, Mr. Ballo," Lansky said. "But we thought it might be good to have a conversation with you."

"As I understand it, a conversation with you often ends up with broken bones," 8 said.

Siegel smiled, the gleam of his teeth lighting up his face, but not reaching the chill in his eyes. "I bring a baseball bat for those conversations." He spread his arms wide. "As you can see, no lumber."

"Perhaps we could sit down," 8 said. "Would you fellows like something to drink?"

"You got any of that Cuban rum?" Lansky asked.

8 opened a cabinet over the oak refrigerator and pulled out a glass decanter. It was about a third of the way full. He'd taken it as payment from a young lady for helping her track down her husband, who'd run out on her and their five children. 8 had

persuaded the man to provide some financial support, which she'd been very grateful for. He still visited with her on occasion. "How about an Irish whiskey?"

"Why not?" Siegel said and Lansky nodded.

8 took down three of the crystal glasses that'd come with the decanter and poured two fingers into each. He motioned for the two men to sit and brought the whiskey over to them, sitting down opposite them. "So, what is it you want to talk about?"

"I hear that you had a visit from Fritz Hartmann this morning," Lansky said.

"Who'd you hear that from?" 8 asked.

"Did you have a visit from Hartmann this morning?" Siegel asked.

"Don't see how that is any of your business," 8 said.

Siegel stood up. His eyes bulged in anger. "The baseball bat is downstairs in the automobile. Don't make me go get it."

8 chuckled. "If you'd like to bring it up to me, I'd be happy to crack it over your noggin."

Siegel pulled a pistol from his jacket pocket and pointed it at 8's head. "Guess I could just shoot you in the face."

"Even so, it still won't be any of your damn business," 8 said. He took a drink. He could tell why people called the boy Bugsy. On account of him being bug-eyed when mad.

"Take it easy, Ben," Lansky said. "We're just here to talk."

"Then this gent better start singing like a canary, or we're wasting our time," Siegel said.

"Mr. Ballo, we know that Hartmann came to see you," Lansky said. "We just wonder what the nature of his business was?"

"Got nothing to do with you fellows," 8 said. "He's looking for his daughter."

Siegel put the pistol back in his pocket. "Velma?" he asked.

8 took another sip of the whiskey. It tasted good. Too good. "You know her?"

"We had a bit of a falling out with Hartmann," Lansky said. "So, we know a lotta guys, did some asking around is all."

"You telling me you never met her?" 8 asked.

"Hartmann was rude to us," Lansky said. "And perhaps has strayed too far from home."

"We don't take all that kindly to rude people," Siegel said. "Some people make that mistake on account of our age and all. They don't make it twice—I'll tell you that."

8 nodded. They hadn't answered his question. "So, you didn't abduct her to get even with the old man?"

"No, Mr. Ballo, we didn't *take* her," Lansky said. "We're businessmen, and sometimes we play rough, as all businessmen do, but we have our principles. We don't abduct nor harm women."

"Why are you here?" 8 asked.

"We heard that Hartmann came to visit you and thought that he might be hiring you to look into our... business. I can see now that we were mistaken," Lansky said.

"I'd appreciate it if you let me know what you find out about that tomato," Siegel said.

"Velma?" 8 asked. "The lady you don't know?"

"Yeah, that's the one. Let me know what you find out." Siegel pointed his finger at 8 with the thumb up, mimicking a pistol, and play-acted taking two shots at him. "Don't make me come looking for you."

"I wouldn't suggest working for Hartmann." Lansky stood and put his tan Fedora on his head. "Don't make us come back."

8 noticed for the first time how large his ears were. "Next time, I'd appreciate if you knocked."

Chapter 5

Velma sat at the bar, a cloche hat pulled low over the curls of her hair, her hand tapping in time with the music. It was 2:00 a.m., and she was in a shabby speakeasy in Williamsburg listening to some of the best music she'd ever heard—and she'd been privy to some mighty fine beats. Velma was all dolled up and sipping a sidecar, and she thought about getting out on the floor to hoof it with an air-tight gent who'd been giving her the once over.

She'd been staying with a fella at the Hotel Albert up in Greenwich Village, but he'd become a bore. Tonight, when he wanted to call it quits before midnight, Velma had given him the ole' heave-ho. She'd simply stepped up to a yellow cab, climbed in back, and told the driver to drive. The poor fella never even turned around to see that she was gone. He was like that, a bit caught up in himself, thinking that the paint splatter art he made was earth-shattering.

The guy on the piano certainly knew his onions, Velma thought, as the notes tumbled across the room. He was the man of the band, she knew. He was the Clarence of the "Clarence Williams' Washboard Five." Two of the fellas wore washboards around their front, beating and scraping at them with metal thimbles on their fingers for a sound Velma had never heard before. A Black woman with a beautiful voice belted out notes. Clarence referred to her as 'Evie'. As compelling as the music was, she knew she'd best be finding another place to stay before too long. Finding a room became harder after the sun came up.

When the band took a break, Velma asked Clarence if it'd be okay if she played a song. It'd been days since she'd played the piano, and she was feeling a bit rebellious, and the music had gotten her juices flowing. He said that'd be okay.

Velma sat down, testing the keys. It was a fine piano. Perhaps nicer than her Daddy's. The thought of Daddy cemented in her mind the piece she was going to play. "Ain't Nobody's Business." The patrons of the juice joint had broken into raucous banter when Clarence and the band had gone on break. Therefore, the first notes she played only were heard by those closest. Gradually, like the tide receding, the noise descended, and all eyes turned to the beautiful young flapper producing the haunting sound. And then she sang.

> *There ain't nothin' I can do nor nothin'*
> *I can say, that folks don't criticize me*
> *But I'm gonna do just as I want to anyway,*
> *I don't care if they all despise me*

She sang to the end of the song, and when she finished, the room broke into applause. She stood, bowed, did a slight shimmy, and walked back to her seat where the bartender slid a complimentary sidecar in front of her. The men on either side of her tried to engage her in conversation, but she had her eyes on another and brushed them off with the ease of one who'd done it before.

It wasn't that Velma was broke. She had plenty of dough. She'd been skimming from her dapper for years. Putting aside part of Daddy's excessive allowance. Selling items from the house she knew he'd never miss. Taking sawbucks from his wallet when he left it lying around. After all, the man deserved it. He was responsible for the death of her mother. The doctors had said otherwise, but Velma knew. He was the monster responsible for murdering her.

Fritz Hartmann thought that he could control his daughter with money, Velma mused, a caustic grin creasing her face. Men always thought they could control her. Lock her in a glass jar to be brought out when they fancied. Her daddy wanted her to go around sipping tea and talking about gardening and housekeeping. He'd sure been surprised at her sweet sixteen debutante ball when she'd gotten drunk and ended up in his bed with Danny Weber. They'd both passed out naked and were awakened by an enraged Fritz Hartmann. Poor Danny had run into the street without a stitch of clothing on.

After that incident, Daddy had been cold to her for months, refusing to speak to her or even acknowledge her presence. She'd made it up to him. She always did. And then things had been good for a bit, until she wanted to go off to college. They compromised by her staying in the city, so that she slept at home, his chauffeur driving her back and forth.

They hadn't had another real fight until she went off to Florida with that fellow who had business down that way and asked her along. Velma had been gone for two weeks, and when she came home, Daddy was awful angry with her. She wondered if he'd started sleeping with her friend, a girl from college, just to get even with her. It'd been the third time that she brought Idina around the house that her father began acting strange around her. So, she stopped bringing the girl around, but Daddy must have pursued her, because next thing Velma knew, her best friend was sleeping in *her* house in *her* father's bed. Not that Velma was surprised.

The girl's parents must've gotten wind of something because they whisked Idina off to Paris for an extended visit with some aunt. Then it'd just been Velma again. Until she met Colleen just last year at a dance competition up in the Village. It'd come down to the two of them as finalists, and the judges couldn't pick a winner between them. So they'd shared the trophy and cash prize.

After that, they became best of friends. Two peas in a pod. Sometimes they'd dress alike, and people couldn't tell them apart. They had so much fun running through the city, giggling at every stop, wowing the crowds as they climbed onto stages to shimmy, and turning all the boy's heads. Velma felt as if she'd fallen through the rabbit hole and entered a world of incredible beauty and creativity. And then it happened again.

It wasn't Colleen's fault, Velma thought. The poor girl had grown up practically a pauper and had never known any sort of luxury. She'd had a couple of bit roles in the moving pictures but that didn't really provide any money, now, did it? It couldn't have taken much to get Colleen to give her vital young self to Velma's old and wrinkled father. Perhaps it was the diamond bracelet or the pearl necklace that did the trick. Velma had smiled gaily and pretended it didn't bother her a whit, but inwardly, she was seething. First, he'd neglected her mother, driven away her first friend, and was now bedding her soul mate. Daddy was insufferable.

At least that was now over, Velma thought grimly. Even if things had ended badly for Colleen. How did the girl think things were going to go with a monster like Fritz Hartmann for a lover?

"Hey, doll, your voice is as beautiful as you. Can you dance as well as sing?" The man who'd been giving her the eyeful had finally worked his way over. He was about five years older than her, had a wiry frame, and intense dark eyes.

"Depends," Velma said taking a drink. "You look like you got two left feet. You a heeler?"

"Don't worry, doll, I can Oliver Twist with the best of 'em."

She liked his grin and his confidence. Those were good signs. "Let's see what you got." It didn't hurt that he was the cat's pajamas in the looks department.

As they stepped onto the dance floor, the band broke into the song, *I Wish I Could Shimmy Like My Sister Kate*.

"What's your name, doll?" the man asked, taking her hands in his.

"Call me Sister Kate," Velma said, and began to shimmy, her shoulders vibrating and sending the tassels on her short, tight dress to shaking in wild abandon.

"You sure are keen, Sister Kate," he said, mirroring her movements as they wheeled around the dance floor. "I'm Tomas."

Chapter 6

8 made himself a cup of coffee to bring down to his office. He was an hour later than his normal seven o'clock rising time, but to be fair, the day before had been long and difficult. He'd lain in bed tossing and turning trying to make sense of all that was going on. It was a simple missing person case, but Velma seemed to be a will-o'-wisp. Gone awry, Hawk had said, and that seemed most apt.

It was almost like she was some ghostly apparition flitting from place to place in the blink of an eye. Was this the modern woman, 8 wondered? Whatever the case, he was becoming quite intrigued with Velma. She was an enigma, both charming and disturbing, light and dark—a mysterious soul who intrigued him with her provocative lifestyle and elusiveness.

The office door was solid wood, so he left it open when inside and not with a client. Unless he was napping, in which case he pulled it shut. It also made the twenty by fifteen-foot space feel a bit roomier. He did have one window that looked down onto Bushwick Avenue that he pulled open to introduce a bit of fresh air to the stuffy room. His desk was a solid affair made of oak, as was the chair. The room was well-lit. That was one thing that was important, which is why 8 had installed a large milk jug pendant lamp overhead and two spherical wall fixtures.

Feet up on the desk, coffee in hand, 8 set his mind to the events of the day before. There was an arrogance to Fritz Hartmann that rubbed him the wrong way, but that was true of many wealthy men and persons in positions of authority, like politicians and policemen. The man was paying good money and simply wanted to find his daughter. He professed to be happy enough to simply find out that she was safe and didn't demand that she be returned against her will.

Coleman Hawkins had been a dead end, other than supplying yet one more name, one more man, to search out. Not that this one would be easy, as it was simply a first name. Benji. Other than pulling his bacon out of the fire when he got jumped in the alleyway, Arkady and Peter hadn't brought much to the table.

Dorothy Parker had seemed to be the genuine article and the most helpful so far. He liked her deadpan wit and sardonic expressions. Perhaps it was that he sensed a kindred spirit in her personality. 8 was not given to effusive displays of emotion but did quite enjoy a clever caustic comment, even more so if it went flying above the head of an intended target lost in self-absorbed oblivion. He felt comfortable that, if Velma got in contact with Dorothy, she would hear of 8's concern.

While it'd been fascinating to meet Scott and Zelda Fitzgerald, they didn't seem to know much. 8 did have a sense that Zelda may've been holding something back, and he guessed that she wore the pants in that particular relationship. It was something that he wouldn't have thought prior to meeting them, but now had the distinct impression that she was the brains of the outfit. It made him wonder how much she helped him with his writing, or if she was actually the author behind the books? It wouldn't be the first time a man had taken credit for a woman's work.

8 sighed, finished his coffee, and pulled his feet off the desk. He jotted a few thoughts down on paper about each of the people he'd spoken to the day before in connection with the case. There were still a few dangling threads. Like, what did Bugsy Siegel know about Velma that he was hiding? It'd been clear that he knew her but had lied about it. 8 didn't believe that the man had

been involved in her disappearance, but Velma was certainly no stranger to him. Why not just say so?

8 wrote down a note to learn more about Bugsy Siegel and Meyer Lansky. The others might ignore, avoid, lie, or pander to him, but those two might very well break his legs or kill him. 8 didn't really want either of those things to happen, and he idly wrote another name on the paper. Pearle. Not yet, but he'd have to consider contacting him to see if he wanted a bit of work. It was starting to look like this case was going to require somebody watching his back.

8 was shaken from his thoughts by a shadow crossing his desk. A man stood in the door opening with his hat in his hands. He seemed nervous. "Are you Mr. 8 Ballo?"

8 looked up and surveyed the man. His nose was crooked as if broken a few times but was set upon an open and guileless face. "That's me."

The man stepped into the room. "I heard you was looking for Velma."

8 motioned to the straight-backed wooden chair across from him. "Have a seat, Mr...."

"DeBerry. Name's Hank DeBerry."

"Same DeBerry who's the catcher for the Robins?"

"That'd be me. One of the Trolley-Dodgers."

"Your Brooklyn Base Ball Club has more nicknames than... than I've got socks." 8 almost had said wins, and then realized that might be offensive.

"That we sure do. I like Trolley-Dodgers myself, seeing as I'm doing that on a regular basis. Lucky to be alive, I am."

8 chuckled. "Ain't that the truth. You hear that R.E. Peary said dodging street cars in Brooklyn is more dangerous than an Arctic expedition?"

Hank laughed in return. "That might just be the case."

"Can't be any scarier than catching for Dazzy Vance. That fellow can throw the ball," 8 said.

"That ain't no problem at all," Hank said with a serious expression. "I stick my glove out somewhere, and that's where he throws it. Pop. Every time."

"You fellows going to have a better year?"

"Sure hope so. We'll do our best, that I'll tell ya."

"What can I do for you, Mr. DeBerry?"

"Well, call me Hank, for one." He was nervously wringing his hat in his hands.

"What can I do for you, Hank?" 8 wondered how the fedora would ever fit back on the man's head.

"Heard ya was looking for Velma. That she went missing."

"Somebody mentioned that you occasionally were stepping out with her," 8 acknowledged.

"That young woman is some fun but not one the likes of me is ever likely to hold onto," Hank said. "Haven't seen her for over a month."

"When'd you last see her?"

Hank scrunched his hat even tighter. "That's the thing. Last time I saw her, she was going off with the Bambino."

"The Bambino? As in Babe Ruth?" 8 wasn't easily shocked, but this man was larger than life.

"Yep. That's him. Babe Ruth."

The way Hank said the man's name made 8's teeth hurt. "Don't sound like you much like the man."

"He gives ballplayers a bad name, with all his carousing and womanizing. We ain't all like that, is all."

"Tell me about Velma going off with the Babe."

Hank rubbed his forehead in one powerful hand, smoothing his hair back on his head. "We was having an exhibition game with them Yankees at that new stadium they got built. That's a pretty nice place, that is. Well, anyway, Velma came by to watch. Got her a seat right above our dugout, I did."

8 waited for the man to continue, but when he didn't, prompted him along. "And?"

"Well, the Bambino, he hit one of those monster home runs that he hits, right out of the ballpark in right field, stands there in front of me, posing like somebody might be making a marble statue of him, he does, and then breaks into that waddle jog of his like he was the second coming of Jesus himself. He sure took his time getting around them bases, and he was just rounding second when I looked over at Velma in the stands and saw the look on her face, and I knew right then and there that was the last I was going to be seeing of that little whirlwind."

"You're telling me that Velma vamoosed with the Babe after the game?" 8 asked, thinking that this was one very good reason why Hank hated the fellow.

"Yep. Last thing I saw of her. She went sashaying over to the Yankee dugout. Next thing you know, they're gone."

"Why are you here, Mr.… Hank?"

Hank wrung his hat and sighed. "Guess I'm worried about her, is all. Want to make sure she's safe. I don't trust that Babe Ruth at all, no sir, I don't. I heard he went down to Havana last year and lost more on the horse races than I make in two years. And who knows what else he spent his money on down there? If you know what I mean."

"Where'd you hear that I was looking for Velma, if you don't mind my asking?"

"I was up to a place in Harlem last night, and Bean was playing. He's the one who told me."

"Bean?"

"Yeah, man, Coleman Hawkins."

Ah, that's right, 8 thought. *Dottie had also called the man Bean.* "You got any idea where Velma might be off to?"

"Other than Ruth has her locked in a room of his mansion?" Hank let a few seconds pass before cracking a thin smile. "She don't much like her father. Told me once she thinks he killed her mother. Then he took up with one of Velma's friends."

After Hank DeBerry departed, 8 looked at the sheet of paper on his desk.

Babe Ruth.
Hartmann killed wife?
Affair with Velma's friend?

Nine words was all, but a virtual treasure trove of information, 8 thought, trying to untangle their deeper meaning. His thoughts drifted back to his first ballgame, when he was just seven years of age. His father had taken him and his four older brothers over to Eastern Park to see the Brooklyn Base Ball Club play. It wasn't until years later that 8 realized that this was their official name.

The papers called them the Robins, Ward's Wonders, the Grooms, the Trolley-Dodgers, and his dad called them the Superbas. It was also years later that 8 understood that this was most likely due to their ineptness at this time in the mid-1890's. This nickname was associated with a traveling circus of performers who were famous for their 'knockabout' comedy routines, where they stumbled, fell, tripped, and acted as buffoons.

Nonetheless, 8 had been entranced by the players and the game and had wanted to be a professional ball player for many years after. He didn't think the Trolley-Dodgers were all that bad that year as he carefully followed their scores in the *Brooklyn Eagle*. They were 71-60. Not great, but not terrible. 8 had dreamed of playing first base and hitting the ball like Candy LaChance, or maybe being a pitcher like Brickyard Kennedy.

It was also that day that he learned more of his father's thoughts, why he called them the Superbas.

8 walked into the ballpark in awe, that day in 1895. His father led the way through the crowds to their six seats. As the youngest, he was graced with the worst seat, as far from the batter as possible,

but he didn't care one whit. The pitcher on the mound was a tall blond-haired fellow who threw the baseball like a bullet. 8's brother, Markos, three years older, told him that his name was Brickyard. 8 was unable to take his eyes off the fellow when he was pitching. Brickyard would wind his body up, and then unleash, releasing the ball as his arm and torso came hurtling toward the batter and the ground. And then almost instantly, the ball would pop into the catcher's glove. 8 would try to imitate that motion for the next ten years playing stickball in the streets.

In the third inning, Candy LaChance hit the baseball over the fence in center field, and 8 had himself a new hero. In his teenage years he'd tried to mimic the great bushy mustache that Candy sported, but it'd been a terrible failure and he'd never tried to grow any sort of facial hair again. Not because he couldn't, but because it made his face look like a buffoon, or a Superba. The newspaper the next day recorded the statistics, the Grooms, as it was currently calling them, having won 4-2. Brickyard was the winning pitcher, and Candy had three hits including the homer.

Mr. Ballo bought each of them their own bag of large roasted peanuts for a nickel apiece. 8 had never tasted anything so delicious. Afterward, walking home, 8 told his father that he was going to be a professional baseball player.

Mr. Ballo stopped in the middle of the street and gripped 8's shoulder. He told 8 that he'd do no such thing and explained that baseball players were a lower class of people. They were there to provide entertainment for those who worked hard, had families, and contributed in a meaningful way to society. He went on to say something about the gladiators who fought in ancient Rome and slaves who fought bare knuckle for the amusement of Southerners. 8 didn't hear the rest as he was daydreaming that he was the one pitching, throwing the ball by the batter in a great sweeping motion, and then he was the batter, swinging the stick of wood and connecting with the ball to send it soaring over the fielders, over the fence, out of the park.

8 hadn't known that his father had a first name other than Mr. until he was fourteen years old. His mother usually called 8's father dear, but on that day in 1902, when his brother, Albert, died from consumption, she kept crying out, *Miksa, Miksa, Miksa.*

8 never brought up his dream of playing professional baseball to his father again. He never shared his stickball exploits and how many lampposts he'd hit the ball or the number of batters he struck out. It was also at stickball that he met Pearle, his best friend, and he did make the mistake of bringing this new acquaintance home. This is where he learned something more about his father. Ballos did not consort with Black people.

Chapter 7

8 picked up the *Brooklyn Eagle* to check when the Yankees were back in town, or up in the Bronx in that fancy new stadium of theirs. They'd gone out to Cleveland on the 7th, two days before Velma came up missing, and weren't back until they hosted the Sox on the 31st. He wondered what it was like to travel around the country playing baseball games in different cities every few days. He'd heard rumors of players, like the Babe, who had a woman in every town.

8 silently vowed to save enough money to go on a road trip like the ball players did and stay in a different place every three or four days. Cleveland, Detroit, St. Louis, Chicago, Philadelphia, he said to himself, the cities rolling off his tongue like delicacies off the gilt-edged menu in a fancy restaurant. The Yankees had really done a job on the Tigers, putting up sixteen runs, even if the Bambino only had one hit, and not even a home run, at that. Pipp, the first baseman, had four hits including a dinger. 8 imagined that it was he playing first base for the hated Yankees.

No, it'd be better to be a Trolley-Dodger and to play against them. Perhaps he'd pitch and strike out the Babe time and again, and the fans down to Ebbets Field would scream and cheer for him. 8 had been there on April 5th, 1913, for the first game ever played at the newly-built ballpark, a loss to the dreaded Yankees in an exhibition game. He'd cheered valiantly along with 30,000 other fans who'd jammed into the stands to become part of history.

He'd gone to the game with Oliver Harvey. They'd first met

during 8's second year at Washington Square College, some seven years before that first game in Ebbets Field, and twelve years before they would spend so much time in the trenches together. 8 was outside sitting on the bench on that fall day waiting for his first class with Professor Harvey to begin. He was going over the designated reading for the day, *Society Must Be Defended*, by Michel Foucault.

"What's your take on that?" the man asked. 8 wasn't even yet aware that it was Professor Harvey.

"I suppose that the winner gets to write the history books."

"Does that make it real?"

"Make it real?"

"If they win, write down their version, and hand it on generation to generation, does that myth in fact become reality?"

At the time, 8 didn't have an answer for the man. When the man went inside and to the front podium to prepare for the class, 8 realized that he'd been talking to Professor Harvey.

Enough daydreaming, 8 thought, standing up. It was time to go pay his buddy in the 83rd Precinct, Stephen McGee, a visit, and see what they were doing about the missing Velma Hartmann. He'd just reached the door when he heard steps on the stairs. This reminded him that he best be taking his pistol with him, now that Bugsy Siegel was in the game, and was stepping back to his desk to retrieve it from the locked drawer as Asta Holm appeared in the doorway.

He'd met Asta a little less than a year ago at a Trolley-Dodger game. 8 had gone by himself on a whim, as had she, and they'd struck up a conversation. It turns out she was moving into a new apartment the next day, and he offered to help. They'd gone for dinner after the game before tumbling into bed together. They'd been casually seeing each other ever since. He liked her ironic sense of humor and wit.

"Hello, 8," she said. "Are you coming or going?"

"Hello, Asta. I was on my way out the door. You need something?"

"That's why I'm here."

Asta was short for a Danish woman, barely five feet, with the typical blonde hair and stunning blue eyes of her nationality. There was a tousled look to her that was normal, and her eyes, if stunning, were sleepy and content, like the cat who'd got the cream.

"Have a seat," 8 said. "I can certainly make time for you."

"Thought maybe we could go upstairs."

That was a loaded statement, 8 thought, trying to hide his smile. Sometimes Asta came over for sex. Sometimes she came over to ask for his help with something else. That could be anything from fixing a door, changing a light, or paying an unwelcome suitor a visit to tell him to lay off. Upstairs seemed to suggest she was here for the first reason. But he didn't want to be assuming anything.

"What can I do for you, today?" he asked.

"Woke up cranky this morning," Asta said. "Couldn't rightly see going in and connecting people on the telephone switchboard, so, called in sick."

"You look far from sick," 8 said. "As a matter of fact, you look exquisite."

"*Tak*," Asta said in appreciation of his compliment. "Nonetheless, I think I need some... 8... below, if you know what I mean." She fluttered her lashes as she looked down below her waist.

8 let the grin slip out this time. "I suppose I have an hour or so."

"Might be a bit more than that," Asta said with a sly smile. "I was hoping we might start with that French thing. You know, with your tongue and lips?"

"But of course," 8 said, taking her hand and leading her out the door and up the stairs.

It was most certainly longer than an hour, but less than two, when 8 stepped out onto the street, holding the door for Asta. He pulled it shut, taking a moment to enjoy the sign above that proclaimed that '8 BALLO, PRIVATE INVESTIGATOR' was on the second floor in suite C.

"I do believe that was just what the doctor would've prescribed, you know, if I'd gone to visit and paid the fee," Asta said. "My mood is much improved."

"You enjoyed yourself, then?" 8 said with a satisfied chuckle.

"Ja. Very much, Mr. 8 Ballo. I always do when I'm with you. I don't suppose you'd consider marrying me?"

8 put his hand on her shoulder. "I don't believe we'd enjoy ourselves quite so much if we married."

"Ja. You're probably right." Asta looked left and right, and then rose up on her tiptoes to give him a deep and passionate kiss. "Hmm. I love your mouth," she said and walked quickly off.

8 watched her sway away with a broad smile. She was quite a woman. Maybe he should marry her. He wasn't getting any younger. Thirty-five was working its way to confirmed bachelor for life status. It wasn't that he was opposed to the institution of marriage or had a fear of commitment. Just the opposite. He believed in true love. Love at first sight. A deep and unsettling emotion that would tear through his mind and body with an exhilarating abandon. And while he enjoyed Asta Holm very much, both with her clothes on and off, she did not send that particular freight train racing through his veins. Not like Camila Morales had. Of course, he wasn't sure if that had indeed been love or just the foolishness of youth.

With a sigh, 8 turned the other way to walk up Bushwick to Dekalb which he followed down to the 83rd Precinct on the corner of Wilson. The building was of the Romanesque Revival style, the structure having the look of a medieval castle, standing out in stark contrast to the tenement buildings around it. 8 knew that this was the intent of the architect, a fellow by the name of Tubby, to create a beacon of safety and protectiveness for the neighborhood. All this, he'd read on the plaque beside the front doors one day waiting to meet his friend. From blocks away, he was able to see the crenelated tower that rose high above the three-story fortification, and the clock, which suggested that he was two hours late for his meeting. Not that he was overly concerned with his reasons for being late.

8 went up the steps between two of the massive columns, reading the inscription above the entrance before pulling the door open, *"Eendraght Maakt Magt,"* the Dutch motto of the city of Brooklyn, meaning "Unity Makes Might." *A simple three-word phrase*, 8 thought, *but quite powerful and correct.* He wished that he could commit to a unity with Asta, but that was not to be. The Dutch had settled the area some years ago, from which Bushwick itself got its name, 8 knew, meaning "town in the woods." *It sure has changed*, he thought.

The man at the desk told him that McGee had gone out on a call. 8 found him down by Cooper Street talking to an angry man standing by the embers of what had recently been a newsstand but was now a smoldering pile of ash. 8 got himself an apple at a nearby grocer while he waited for the statement to be taken. He was pretty sure he knew what had happened.

After about ten more minutes, McGee came strolling over. "You stood me up," he said with an attempt at irritability.

"My reasons were very good," 8 said.

"Mm, I know that grin of yours, like the cat who ate the canary, or more apt, the PI who diddled an *álainn* lass." McGee was not yet thirty, had dark brown hair shaved on the sides and waved on the front, pale skin, was short and wiry, and claimed to be one-hundred percent Irish.

"I take it that is a compliment?" 8 asked.

"Aye, that it is. It means she's a fine thing, it does. Am I right?"

8 nodded. "I did have a visit from a beautiful woman around the time I was supposed to meet with you. Sorry about that."

McGee shook his head and laughed. "You got to tell me your secret, sometime, on how you get so many stunners *visiting* you all the time. It's certainly not your sense of fashion."

8 chuckled. "It's simple, really. The more you give, the more you get." He nodded back to the charred remains of a man's livelihood. "Fellow not pay up his insurance?"

"Yeah, some local hooligans probably working for Bugsy. Three of them came up and bought a soda pop each, must've been squirting gasoline on the papers on display as they paid, lit a match, dropped it on the shelf, and ran off, laughing the whole way."

"Say who they were?"

"Claims he didn't know them."

"Which is a complete lie."

McGee nodded. "You don't pay your insurance, you get burned out. You finger somebody, and you get your legs broken. Or worse."

"Bugsy and Lansky paid me a visit last night," 8 said.

McGee whistled. "And you can still walk?"

"It was just a misunderstanding."

"Even worse. That usually gets you killed."

"They thought I'd been hired to investigate them. I straightened them out on that account."

"And who'd they think hired you to do that?"

"Fritz Hartmann. Know him?"

"Yeah, I know him. Not much gets done in Bushwick without his say so, hell, that could be true of most of Brooklyn." McGee spit on the sidewalk. "Did the guy hire you for something?"

"Sure, just not to investigate those two Jewish leg breakers."

"He retain your services about the girl?"

8 furrowed his brow. "Yeah. Velma."

"Velma? Who in hell is that?"

"His daughter. Who are you talking about?"

"Colleen Brooks." McGee looked around nervously. "Young woman who was playing house with Hartmann. Went missing about a month back, or at least, that's what her father said. Hadn't heard from her in a few weeks, so he came looking for her. Lives over in New Jersey."

"How young we talking?" 8 asked.

"Nineteen. She told her parents she was living with friends in Brooklyn. In reality, she moved in with a fifty-year old man because he was showering her with gifts."

8 looked up Wilson Avenue. Automobiles clogged the street. Pedestrians filled the sidewalks. Street vendors plied their wares. "What'd Hartmann say about her up and disappearing?"

"Said she left about a week earlier. Mind you, I wasn't on the case, but one of the lads in the Precinct was telling me. I think he said that Colleen was friends with Hartmann's daughter. That must be the Velma you're talking about. You saying she's gone missing now?"

Chapter 8

Martin Hoffman hadn't been able to meet with 8 until the following day at ten in the morning. He was an up-and-coming reporter for *The Brooklyn Daily Eagle*, a second-generation Jew from the banks of the Rhine River in Western Germany. At five inches over five feet and slight of frame, he wasn't very imposing, but once he spoke, he could tear down any obstacle. His soft brown eyes and honeyed words could somehow make the most polished politician, corrupt contractor, or savvy businessman give up the story to be told.

The offices of the *Eagle* were located over by the Brooklyn Bridge, and from there he would continue into Manhattan and have another conversation with Dorothy Parker and/or Zelda Fitzgerald on the whereabouts of their friend, Velma. 8 took the elevated cars, thinking it probably would've done him good to walk. It was about five miles, and he could've used the exercise. Maybe on the way back.

Marty was clattering away on a typewriter at a corner desk at the end of a long row of journalists all doing the same when 8 walked up. "Give me a minute," he said. "How about you buy me a coffee and a pastry across the way at the bakery, and I'll be right down."

8 had already eaten, but could always use another cup of the mud, and dutifully bought Marty a pastry with glazed sugar on top as well. There were a few small tables out front, empty at this pause between mealtimes, and he settled into the small wooden chair tentatively just as Marty came striding across the street. He had the gait of a man

much taller, his legs gobbling up real estate with each step. He also seemed impervious to the automobiles whizzing past him.

"Sorry about that," he said, gliding into the chair across from 8 and grabbing the pastry to bite off a large chunk. "Goddamn son-of-a-bitch of an editor spills this story on me that he wants in tomorrow's edition. And he wanted it done immediately so he could proof the facts himself. Shit for brains." Marty washed the half-chewed chunks down with a huge swig of coffee. It was good that it'd gotten a chance to cool.

"Hello to you," 8 said with a grin. He was used to the high-energy and frantic pace of his friend. They'd met each other his last year at Washington Square College, and they'd been tight ever since.

"Yeah, shalom, 8," Marty said. "*Guten morgen, bonjour.* What's up?"

8 chuckled. These were just three of the six languages that Marty was fluent in. "Thought I'd check in with my good friend and see what he's up to."

"Writing stories for a paper that people pay three cents for, probably so they can start a fire or wipe their ass with it, because nobody seems to pay any attention to the news. The real news. Not whether the Superbas won or lost or whether or not the modern girls' college is an old maid's factory or not." Marty stuffed the last of the pastry into his mouth and swallowed, possibly without chewing. "Goddamn it, 8, I'm a busy guy. What do you want?"

"What do you know about Fritz Hartmann?"

Marty paused his cup on the way to his mouth, and then set it back on the table, suddenly silent. "Why?"

"He hired me to find his daughter."

Marty raised his eyebrows, then said, "He's got a host of legitimate businesses where he pays slave wages and expects fourteen hours of work a day for that pittance. The wallpaper place, of course, textiles, sugar, and several abattoirs."

"Sounds about the same as any wealthy businessman in this city," 8 said.

"You know who Arnold Rothstein is?"

"Yeah, the fellow who fixed the 1919 world series."

"Well, I have it on good authority that Hartmann was one of the money men behind that particular play."

"That would put him in slightly more unsavory company."

"Ya think?" Marty leaned forward, drumming the table with his hands. "I'm not sure, but Rothstein is behind that Luciano bloke who's into heroin and runs most of the gambling in lower Manhattan. Wouldn't surprise me to find Hartmann knee deep in that shit as well."

"According to Hartmann, he got on the wrong side of Bugsy and Lansky at one of his sweat shops. I imagine if he was bankrolling Luciano, he'd be able to squash that particular problem."

"Why's that?"

8 also leaned forward, the chair groaning underneath him. "My people tell me that Lansky and Luciano are like kissing cousins, only tighter."

Marty furrowed his thick eyebrows so that they almost met across his forehead. "An Italian and a Jew? Not likely."

"Way I heard it—Luciano was shaking the Jew kids down for protection money at ten cents a week. Lansky refused to pay it, even after he got the shit kicked out of him. Salvatore thought that was pretty plucky and befriended the boy. Hell, I think Lansky was fourteen at the time."

"Okay, okay, whatever the case. Get to the point."

8 carefully eased back and crossed his legs. "Think I already did. Wanted to know how dirty Hartmann was."

"You mean, would he kill his own daughter and hire you to find her?"

"No. I think he truly wants to find Velma, safe and sound. But I think she's hiding from him for a reason. Maybe she's scared of him."

"Other than the obvious, why would you think that?" Marty asked.

"The obvious?"

"Yeah, the fact that he's knee deep in criminal enterprises. You got any other reason to think that?"

"You ever hear of Colleen Brooks?"

"Sure. She's been in a couple of moving pictures and does a hell of a shimmy. I saw her dancing up at the 300 Club on 54th Street. That doll could really shake it."

"Rumor has it that Hartmann became her sugar daddy, and then about a month back she disappeared."

Marty whistled, a low keening sound. "Shit. You're thinking Hartmann killed the doll, Velma knew about it and ran, and he wants her back to make sure she keeps her mouth shut."

"Thought had crossed my mind."

"What do you want from me?"

"Put your ear to the ground. You're a reporter, you're curious, and you try to do what's right when the rich abuse the poor. And you're Jewish. You could get a rock to talk and have it roll away thinking you'd done it a favor. And then I'll owe you one. Okay, pal?"

"Seems that all I ever do is collect more debts you never pay."

8 chuckled. "You know I'm good for it."

Marty looked skeptical. "Sure thing. Is that all?"

"You know where I can find Bugsy and Lansky?"

Marty looked over toward the Manhattan skyline across the East River. He sighed. "Most likely to find them at their place in Brownsville these days."

"Got an address?"

"They call it the Candy Store." Marty scribbled on a piece of paper and handed it over. "Be careful."

"Don't worry. I like my legs just as they are. Intact."

Marty stood up. "Got to get back to work. Poker game at your place on for Friday?"

"McGee said he'd be up for it. I can check in with Pearle. One more'd be nice."

"'I'll ask around." Marty set off back across the street with his unnaturally long stride weaving through the traffic.

8 took the BMT elevated cars across the Brooklyn Bridge and worked his way up to the Algonquin. He figured he was right about on time for the daily luncheon of the Round Table but wasn't sure he'd be welcomed. That fellow Benchley hadn't cared for him much, or perhaps that was just the man's demeanor.

The group was known for the brutality to each other, in wit if not physicality. 8 made a note to himself that he shouldn't threaten the man with violence, but should rather, meet him with caustic verbal parries. This was more likely to raise his esteem with the group. Not that he really wanted to see himself welcomed in, not after he'd found Velma and moved on, anyway.

Dorothy Parker seemed a nice enough sort, even if a bit sad. There was a forlorn air about her that seemed to match Zelda Fitzgerald's troubled countenance. 8 wondered if that was because it was a man's world? He'd read the same article that Marty had referred to in the *Eagle*, about the popular notion that the modern women's college was just creating highly educated women destined to become unhappy old maids as they didn't fit the more traditional role of mate, helpmeet, and mother. This seemed to be the prevailing opinion in society.

It was a sorry state of affairs, 8 thought, that much of society thought that a woman's sole purpose should be to get married and start a family, unless, of course, that is what they truly wanted. He suspected this was not true of Dorothy Parker or Zelda Fitzgerald. At the time, he'd discounted the story as balderdash. Of course, women were every bit as smart as men. There was no reason for them to not become educated, vote, and have careers, while still having marriage and family if they so desired. But was that the reality? It was certainly a fact that much of society was busy constructing roadblocks preventing that possibility. Perhaps this was why these two brilliant young women, Dorothy and Zelda, looked so melancholy?

Dottie was again holding court, the table crowded today, about eleven people, 8 judged. The man, Benchley, was there next to her. 8 plucked a chair with one hand as he walked through the room, wedging it into the space between them. "My dear Benchley, will you be so kind as to allow me to squeeze in?" he said.

Benchley looked up, his disdain oozing, but he scooted his chair over. "Ah, the gumshoe returns," he said. "Or, are you just a grifter, Mr. Five?"

"8 is the name, Bench. The trick is you have to use both hands to count that high."

Dottie snickered. "Welcome back, 8. We've missed you. I'd have to say the company has been rather tedious today."

"Sometimes the palate does demand a new flavor," 8 agreed. "Or the Socratic irony becomes unintended."

"You *are* most certainly a refreshing breeze, startling for our immured conclave," Dottie said.

8 chuckled. "I believe this may be the least secret gathering in the entire world."

"Touché, 8. How goes your search for our lovely Velma?"

"Pretty much shooting blanks," 8 said. "Velma is proving to be very elusive."

"The rumble is that she doesn't want to be found. Not by you. Not by her father."

"Have you seen her?"

Dottie took out a cigarette and lit it. The others at the table were engaging in desultory conversation with one ear aimed toward them. "Might've seen her up to the Cotton Club last night with some Italian mug. She was perfectly healthy."

"Did you mention I was looking for her?"

"I did." Dottie took a drag and blew out a ring of smoke. "She said she's fine. Doesn't want to be found, is all."

"What'd you think?" 8 asked, staring into her eyes and wondering what thoughts were flitting through her brain. "Is she really fine?"

Dottie sighed. "She looked scared. You ask me, that gal is behind the eight ball. Stuck in a difficult place."

"You know where to find her?"

Dottie shook her head. "Told her your name, and she could find you down in Bushwick. If she wanted."

"Who's the fellow she was with?"

Dottie shook her head. "Looked like a two-bit Bruno for somebody. Not so much a bruiser, but a mug who carries a knife or a gat. Had that look like he'd been in the big house. Velma, she never cared much for who she hung around. Liked fellas of all sorts."

"Let me know if you hear anything else," 8 said. "I'm trying to help her. Honestly."

"You got somewhere I can find you?"

8 handed her a business card. He was fairly certain that he'd given her one the last time he saw her. "My office is on the second floor. I live on the third."

"Mm, Mr. Ballo, I will make sure to come by late."

8 decided to walk downtown and cross over the Williamsburg Bridge. Stretch the legs a bit, get a little fresh air, and do some thinking. The first order of business was to try to figure out if Dottie Parker had been flirting with him for real, or was just having a bit of fun. She was a fascinating woman, if a bit dark. He'd just have to see how it played out. 8 was not one to rashly rush into anything, especially a relationship with a married woman.

It was hard to formulate much of anything behind a desk, but out in the open, moving, thoughts percolated more freely. He figured it to be about five miles to Williamsburg and thought that'd be a fine place to catch a trolley.

If Dottie could be believed, Velma was healthy, just not wanting to be found. Not by 8. Not by her father, whose motives he was beginning to question. Although, if she hated the man for some perceived wrong he'd committed, true or false, well then, being her father, he might still be interested in her safety.

Relationships with fathers could certainly be difficult. This, 8 knew from first-hand experience. Your father was not always the shining knight that you created in your mind as a young child. His thoughts turned to the time that 8 was told that Ballos did not consort with Asian girls, along with baseball players and Black people. He'd been fourteen at the time. As was his wont, for many years after that incident, if not so much recently, he would fantasize about being a hero, making a difference, and breaking the pattern his father had tried to instill in him. His reverie was interrupted by the cry of a woman.

It came from an alleyway, but between the shadows and the car blocking the limited visibility, he couldn't make out anything. Perhaps he'd been mistaken? Maybe a cat had screeched? 8 paused, took a tentative step down the alley, and the cry of a woman came again followed by the curse of a man, and a thwack that had to be sound of a hand striking flesh. His last trip down an alleyway hadn't been all that great, but there was no turning away now.

"Hey, what's going on down here?" he asked, easing his way toward the car that was about twenty feet into the darkened access. "Is everybody okay?"

"Get lost, buddy." A male voice came out of the shadows.

8 stepped around the car and saw a man straddling a woman on the ground while two others held her arms. 8 cursed silently, having again forgotten his pistol. It was probably time to start carrying the

thing, just to be safe in this crazy city, if not for the case he was working on. "Don't think the lady likes the smell of your breath, fellow. Why don't you get lost?"

The man looked over his shoulder from his knees. His face was sallow and sported a brush-like mustache. "I'm not going to tell you again, buddy. Get lost."

8 took two steps and kicked the man, aiming for the mustache, but slamming into his chin and clamping his brown-stained teeth together. He toppled off the woman, his hands coming to his face in shock. The other two men came to their feet, one pulling a long slim blade from inside his belt. 8 dealt with him first. He feinted with a left jab, and when the man slashed at his arm, withdrew it and followed with a looping right that crashed into his cheekbone and sent teeth clattering sideways against the wall.

The third man bum rushed him, but he was a small fellow, and probably should've also been carrying a knife. 8 put one massive hand around his neck and another in his crotch and threw him into the wall with a sickening clump. The first man lunged at him from the ground, his mouth streaming blood, and 8 met his face with a knee, this time missing high, smashing into his nose, above the mustache, with an unsettling crunch.

Two men lay without moving while the third was staggering deeper into the alleyway. The woman had pulled herself to a sitting position with her back against the brick wall. She sobbed once, took a deep breath, and steadied herself.

"Are you okay?" 8 asked. "Did they..."

"I'm fine. You came before they could... hurt me." A bit of blood dribbled from a split lip, and she adjusted her ruffled skirt and blouse.

8 figured her to be no more than fourteen years old. This was always the age of the damsel in distress, for the past twenty some years, ever since his first kiss. "Can you walk? We should be moving on." He held out a hand without stepping too close, offering, but not threatening.

"Yes. I will be okay." She went to stand, whimpered slightly at a scraped knee, and then held out her own hand.

8 stepped forward and let her tiny hand slide into his enormous paw. "My name is 8. 8 Ballo," he said, pulling her to a standing position.

"I am Min Siniang." She looked up at him with dark eyes. Her hair was shiny and cut flat across the front and tied into a single braid at the back. "Thank you very much, Mr. 8, for saving me from those bad men."

They took two steps, drawing even with the automobile. 8 asked her to wait just a moment, went and retrieved the knife from the ground, and punctured the four tires. He dropped the blade into the pocket of his suit jacket and stepped back to Min.

She slid her hand into his once again, and they walked down the alleyway to the street. "I was walking home, and this car came up next to me, and the next thing I knew I was in the back seat between two of those beasts pawing at me." Min said this in a very matter-of-fact and clipped tone. "They think I am a prostitute and can do what they want with me."

"Where do you live?" 8 asked as they emerged onto the street.

Min nodded her head to the left. "Chinatown."

8 turned in that direction. "I'll walk you home."

Min looked at where the sun had descended behind the buildings. "Just to Canal Street will be fine. It is not safe for you after dark in Chinatown with the Tongs."

"I'll be fine."

8's mind drifted back to when he was fourteen years of age. It was then that his father got strike three, as far as 8 was concerned. Strike one was the baseball game when his father had told him ballplayers were a lower social class and that he was not to aspire to being part of such rabble. Strike two came a few years later when he brought his friend, Pearle, home, and was told unequivocally that he was not to consort with Black people. Strike three came when his father came upon him in the midst of his first kiss.

Klara Winkler was the daughter of the grocer on 8's childhood block. Her father was a thick-set German with a friendly smile. Her mother was a Chinese woman who spoke little English. 8 never knew how they'd come to be married, but at fourteen, it wasn't a concern. Klara had a beautiful smile and ripe red lips that he spent many an hour thinking about.

One day he got up the nerve to say hello to her. That was the first time he saw her sunrise of a smile. 8 began to find excuses to hang around the grocery. After a few weeks, he asked her for a kiss. Klara agreed to meet him in an hour around the corner. It was the longest hour of his life. When she came walking up, he was ready to tell her that he'd just been joshing with her, and that they didn't have to kiss. Luckily, he couldn't get the words out.

As he stood there, mouth agape, struggling to speak, Klara tilted her head upward, her Cupid's-bow lips quivering ever so slightly, and then he was kissing her delicious and succulent mouth. Her lips were so soft and wet. It was as if the earth stopped turning and everything went suddenly silent.

8 never saw his father walk past. When he got home, however, he got the back of a hand across his cheek. Mr. Ballo told him that he was never to see that... well, 8 had erased that insult from his brain, but he was told that Ballos did not speak with, consort with, nor kiss Chinese women. His father must've had a similar talk with Herr Winkler, because Klara was not let out of his sight, and 8 was no longer allowed into the grocery.

8 realized he was standing alone at the entrance to an alleyway and had been for some time. There was no Min. No automobile with flat tires. No men lying beaten in the dust. He'd imagined the entire incident, a fugue state he very occasionally experienced starting just after he was demobbed in 1918. For years after his father had broken off his friendship with Klara Winkler, 8 had fantasized about coming to her rescue in just this way. Saving her from society's racist beliefs.

It must be Velma who'd thrown him back into disturbing fantasies of being a hero. Once again, in real life this time, he'd been tasked with saving the girl. He didn't mean to fail.

Chapter 9

The ringing of the phone jarred 8 from his musings. It was Thursday afternoon, and he again had his feet up on his desk and his head tilted back staring at the ceiling. He was so lost in contemplation that a pack of squirrels could've run in the window, and he wouldn't have registered it. This was how he spent most of his time while in the office.

"Hallo," he said into the receiver.

"Is this 8 Ballo?"

The voice was faintly familiar. "Yes. Who's this?"

"This is Arkady Bortnik. We spoke the other night."

And a bit more than that, 8 thought, *including chucking sailors off walls and busting skulls.* "What can I do for you, Arkady?"

"Me and Peter, we'd like to talk to you. There's a few things we didn't tell you about Velma."

"Yeah, like what?"

"Something that Velma told us."

"So spill it."

"Not on the telephone. Too many prying ears."

"You want to come here to my office on Bushwick Avenue?"

There was a pause on the line. "Better not. There might be prying eyes there."

"Where you want to meet, then?"

"You got a blind pig near you? Not a clip joint, but a juice bar out of sight? Where the patrons are too drunk to remember our faces?"

"Got a place on Broadway, under the elevated tracks, called Walter's. Corner of Green Street. Tell the man you need to use the John and would prefer to use the Hylan one."

Arkady laughed over the phone. "Probably not a good idea to mock the mayor of New York City when you're running an underground speakeasy."

"Probably not," 8 agreed. "It's up on the third floor. Bottom two floors are deserted. Unless the whores are using it on the side to not share the money."

"Nine o'clock," Arkady said. "We got a couple of things to do first."

"I'll be there."

8 hung up the phone to see a man step through the doorway. It was the slender gunslinger who'd accompanied Hartmann on Monday. He had a brown newsboy hat on that matched his too-big suit jacket. His eyes flickered around in their sockets like agitated goldfish in a bowl and when he spoke, 8 realized he had buck teeth with a sizable gap between them.

"Boss wants to see you."

8 surveyed the man with curiosity. He wasn't much more than a boy, too young to have gone to the Great War but most likely had already shot a fellow or two, and that made him think he was tough. 8 had attended Kaiser Bill's War. He knew what terror, death, and killing was, and what it did to you. Fellows like the toothpick in front of him were the first to die.

"I said the Boss wants to see you. Best be getting your ass out of that chair."

"Who's your boss, again?"

The boy started to speak, spluttered, and put his hand in his jacket. "You remember me from the other day. People don't forget my face. It may be the last thing they ever see."

8 moved his feet to the floor. "Ah, yes. You're Hartmann's shoeshine boy."

"Don't think I won't shoot you right in the face."

"Don't think Fritz would like that much." 8 stood up and stepped around the desk. The boy was unsure whether or not to pull the gun out. The indecision cost him as it was only two steps to crowd him against the wall.

"Hey, get away from me."

"Just grabbing my hat." 8 reached over the boy's shoulder and grabbed his bowler from the peg. "We're going out, aren't we?"

The boy led him to an automobile that was red with a soft top. "Is that a Durant?" 8 asked.

"Sure is. The A-22."

A chauffeur held the door, and 8 climbed in the back while the boy sat up front. "Where's the boss at, anyway?" he asked.

There was no answer as they pulled into traffic. It turned out to be only about a mile, over to Wykoff Avenue and the industrial sector of Bushwick. The building had a large sign that proclaimed: HARTMANN WALLPAPER.

The boy led him into the building and to an office located to the right. They passed by two men with fedoras and Tommy guns. Fritz Hartmann was inside with his jacket off and sleeves rolled up behind a large mahogany desk.

"You can go, Mouse," Hartmann said.

8 watched Mouse exit and close the door behind him. "Nice joint you got here. People over this way must really like their wallpaper."

"Why's that?" Hartmann asked.

"Figure that's what the chopper squad out there is protecting. Stopping people from stealing your wallpaper."

"It seemed a good idea to have some protection after my trouble with Bugsy Siegel."

"Can't you have your boy Arnold Rothstein put Bugsy off your tail?"

Hartmann flinched. "What do you know about Arnold?"

8 stared him in the eye. "Only that you put up some of the dough

to get the Black Sox to fold like a house of cards in a windstorm."

"That's a lie." Hartmann held his stare.

"But you know the man? Do business with him?"

"Did." Hartmann cleared his throat and looked down. "We have parted ways."

"That's too bad. Hopefully it was amicable, and he didn't set that murderous syndicate on you," 8 said.

"Me and Arnold are on fine terms," Hartmann said haughtily.

"Not fine enough to tell his stooges to lay off, it would seem."

"What have you found out about my daughter?"

8 sat down. "She was seen up to Harlem at the Cotton Club couple of nights back."

"Seen? By whom?"

8 saw no reason to keep Dottie out of this. "Dorothy Parker."

Hartmann snorted. "And you'd believe a woman who runs her mouth as much as that one does?"

8 was starting to not like Hartmann very much. Still, he checked his bridling irritability. "I believe that she was telling the truth, yes."

"You got anything else?"

"Couple of gents from over Coney Island are meeting up with me later tonight. They said they had something for me. Something Velma had told them. I was planning on hearing what they had to say before checking in with you, but then Mouse showed up. That boy is a bit impatient."

"Who are these men?" Hartmann narrowed his eyes and leaned forward.

8 shrugged. "Couple fellows she used to run around with."

"You mean sleep with?"

8 chuckled. "No. Just drinks and laughs."

"They got names?"

"Sure. Most people do."

Hartmann tried to stare him down. It did not work. "They live out to Coney Island?"

"That's where they're coming from."

"Velma's got a photograph on her bureau in her room. Her with two blokes. Said they were… homosexuals. She was always trying to get a rise out of me. Throw that all in my face. I take it those are your sources?"

8 didn't waver his eyes nor answer the question.

"So, you'll be able to track her down and bring her back to me?"

"I believe that our agreement is that I'd ensure her safety."

Hartmann waved his hand. "I ask that you'd pass on a message to her."

"What's that?"

"Tell her that I hold no grudge against her. That I love her. That the house is empty without her. And that it needs a woman's touch and presence to ward off the cold."

8 thought that this sounded a bit strange. Most women were off and married by the time they were twenty-five. Correction, he thought, in this day and age, many were staying single longer and getting a job, but very few were still living at home with their father at that age. "Why would she think that you hold a grudge against her?"

Hartmann stood up and walked over to a painting that hung on the wall and stood in front of it, back to 8, hands clasped behind his back. It was of Velma, seated sideways at a desk, wearing a yellow dress that was hiked midway up her thighs, one strap off her shoulder, a cigarette in a long holder draped casually between her fingers, and a string of black pearls around her neck. 8 thought it to be quite a sexy painting.

"My wife died eleven years ago. It was very difficult for Velma. I did my best. But she was very headstrong. Over the years I've had several lady friends. Velma always hated them. Thought I was cheating on her mother. Her dead mother."

He let that last part settle in the air between them. After a bit, 8 figured he was supposed to say something. "That must've been challenging for you."

"The most recent lady friend was the most difficult for Velma."

"Because Colleen was her friend and younger than her?" 8 asked. "I can see how that may've been awkward for Velma."

Hartmann turned around. "It seems that I'm paying you to investigate me. I believe our arrangement was to find my daughter."

"It's important to know all of the information. You seem to have left that particular piece out when we first spoke."

"I suppose so. Yes, I suppose so. Anyway, Velma came to hate Colleen very much. And then Colleen came up missing."

8 realized that Hartmann enjoyed dropping nuggets of information and then standing back to see what impact they had. This time, he kept silent, waiting Hartmann out. It took only a minute.

Hartmann cleared his throat. "I fear that Velma believes that I suspect her of... having had something to do with Colleen's disappearance."

"And is Velma, indeed, guilty of that?"

"I've no idea and do not care a whit. I just want my daughter back."

8 stood up. "I'll find her and tell her, Mr. Hartmann. But I'm going to need more dough."

-+⟶◉〇⟵+-

It was dark when Arkady and Peter got off the elevated cars at the station. It took a moment for Arkady to get his bearings, as he hadn't been to Bushwick but maybe twice in his life. He was comfortable in Coney Island, so why would he leave? Him and Peter got up to the Village once in a while, but that was the extent of their travels. Except for the time Velma dragged them over to the Fitzgerald's on the North Shore.

Prior to leaving their apartment, he'd looked at a map and knew it wasn't far. Sometimes a train station got you all turned around, though, and he wanted to make sure to go in the right direction. He didn't notice the two men who'd been idly lounging but now stood with interest at the bottom of the stairs. Being gay in a foreign neighborhood was usually enough reason to keep a close eye on his surroundings, but Arkady was preoccupied with which way to go. And it was passing from day to dark, a dusky gloom in the air.

"Down this way," Arkady said, setting off.

"You sure about this?" Peter asked.

"We knew her. It wasn't right what happened."

"I expect you're right." Peter didn't sound as if he believed it.

"That 8 Ballo seemed to be a real square shooter." Arkady also wasn't certain that they should be sharing this information with the man. He was merely trying to dispel his own disquiet about the situation.

"It's not really any of our business."

They turned left onto Broadway. Arkady weighed whether it was any of their business. What was the right thing to do, he wondered? He certainly didn't believe that the law was a simple, unequivocal statement of right and wrong. He broke the law every day he was with Peter. He didn't regard the church as being the arbiter of morality either, for the same reason.

Was it wrong to break the confidence of a friend, he wondered? Not that Velma had sworn him or Peter to keep mum about what she had told them. It certainly seemed like a good reason for her to not go home and see her father. Arkady could only imagine how awkward it must've been to sit across the table from each other and have a conversation or even be in the same house with the man after what'd happened.

Arkady had left home when he was sixteen and couldn't imagine why somebody Velma's age would still be living with her father. His own father wouldn't have understood Arkady's sexual inclination, and when he realized it himself, he began to make plans to leave his home and Russia behind. Perhaps that had been the stimulus to him packing a seabag he'd bought from a second-hand store and signing onto a steamer for the trip across the Atlantic. He'd not even known where in America he was going, only that he was going to the land of promise.

A cat yowled, startling Arkady from his reverie. The neighborhood was strangely quiet, nothing like the hustle and bustle that was Coney Island. Streetlamps dotted the avenue sending flickering shadows. Automobile traffic had become sporadic, with the occasional horse and wagon trundling by on some night errands. The few pedestrians walked furtively along, no doubt bent on some mischief, many likely on their way to a speakeasy.

Arkady figured that the next street corner was Greene, and that the three-story brick building would be Walter's. He grinned to himself in the darkness, thinking about the code words for admittance mocking the mayor of New York City. Arkady had heard that John Hylan had a home here in Bushwick and wondered if it was true. Maybe the man would be at Walter's? This thought made him laugh, and Peter looked at him strangely.

There was a deserted lot next to Walter's, overgrown with shrubs and small trees, and as they passed this desolate spot, Arkady suddenly felt an arm encircle his waist from behind while something sharp was pressed against his neck. He thought about prying the blade from his throat but didn't like the chances much. Better to hand over what money he had and hope to be left alive.

"Right in here if you know what's good for you," a voice growled.

There seemed to be little choice but to allow himself to be steered into the bushes of the empty lot, dimly aware of Peter alongside of him. "What do you want?" he asked, the movement of his throat causing a prickling pain from the knife held there.

"Shut your mouth. Over by that tree."

"My wallet's in my pocket."

"Like a poor sap like you would have any money."

"What do you want?"

"I'm here to make sure you keep your mouth shut."

Arkady felt the knife saw and slash across his neck. He went to take a breath and couldn't get any air. He sank to his knees. Peter was lying on the ground beside him. He toppled over onto him. He felt the men rifling through his pockets and taking his wallet. Then everything went dark.

Chapter 10

Thunder was crashing. The waves were smashing the shores. The gods in heaven roared. No, 8 realized, it was somebody pounding on the door. He looked at his bedroom window. It was not yet light out. He pulled on a pair of trousers and tucked his pistol into the back of the waistband. Barefoot, bare chested, he trod silently over to the door.

If they were here to harm him, the door would be easy enough to break down. 8 made a note to himself to get a more solid door installed. He turned the lock and jerked it open with one hand behind his back grasping the butt of the .38 Special.

"8, how ya doing, hey?" McGee stood there in his blue uniform with the gold buttons shining. A second policeman stood a few steps back behind him. "Mind if we come in?" He stepped past into the room.

"Sure, come on in," 8 said. He stepped aside and gestured the second officer inside.

"Might want to put a shirt on, lad, *ye* might have to go for a walk."

8 went back into the bedroom and put a shirt on, and then, on second thought, added his socks, shoes, and grabbed a jacket. He came out to find McGee pouring a finger of whiskey into a glass.

"Little early for the sauce, isn't it?" 8 asked.

"Late for me. Home to bed for me soon, so I can get back over here to relieve you of your money at cards." McGee sat down at the table and motioned for 8 to join him. The second officer stood by the door with his hands clasped behind his back.

"What brings you by, other than my brown liquor?" 8 asked.

"Found a lad with his throat cut a couple of hours back. No identification on him."

"What's that got to do with me?"

McGee pulled a business card from his pocket and dropped it on the table. "Only thing on him was your card. Thought maybe you could help us out."

8 had a sneaking concern that he knew who it was. "Where'd you find the fellow?"

"Empty lot on Broadway. Next to that juice joint, Walter's."

"Just one body?"

McGee looked strangely at him. "Just the one. Had a bit of blood on his back that didn't appear to be his own, which was pooled underneath him. Could've been from his assailant or another victim. Why you ask?"

"Was supposed to meet a couple of fellows down that way last night around nine. They never showed up."

McGee finished the dram and stood up. "Suppose we should take you down and have a look at the lad."

8 followed him down the stairs. "Had he been there long?" he asked.

McGee turned his head slightly to be heard. "Not so long that it couldn't have been around nine last night. What were you meeting with them lads about?"

"They said they had some information on the Velma Hartmann disappearance." 8 figured it couldn't hurt to share.

"What'd they have?"

"Don't know," 8 said. "Didn't want to tell me over the phone." They walked out onto the street. The sky was just starting to lighten, promising a gray day.

"What are their names?"

"Let's see if the fellow is one of them, first."

"Suit yourself."

There was a small gathering at an empty lot next to Walter's. Behind some bushes a body was lying inert on the ground. People parted way as McGee led 8 through. The man lay on his back, blood coating the front of his jacket, crusty and brown in the early light.

"He was face down when we found him," McGee said. "Rolled him over to get a look at his mug."

"That's one of 'em," 8 said. "Peter. Don't think I have a last name for him."

"You say you were meeting two lads. Who's the other one?" McGee asked.

"Arkady. Arkady Bortnik. I think. They hail from Coney Island." 8 nodded back to the street. "Can we go out there and talk in private?"

McGee led him out onto the street. "What gives?"

"Arkady and Peter were a couple," 8 said. "They were friends with Velma Hartmann, and I interviewed them a few nights back. They didn't have much for me, but afterward, I had an altercation with a ship full of sailors and they came along and helped out. Seemed to be real decent fellows."

"And they contacted you because they had more information about Velma, and you planned to meet them over there at the juice joint?" McGee nodded his head at Walter's.

"That's about all I have for you. I sat and waited about two hours for them, and they never showed. Went home, and the next thing I know is you're pounding on my door."

"Probably be best if we keep the part about the dead guy being queer between us," McGee said. "Hate to say it, but half the lads in the department won't bother looking very hard for the murderer if they know that."

"Yeah, that's why I dragged you out to the street," 8 said.

"That should do for the time being. I'll probably have more questions for you, but you can scram for now."

"Okay," 8 said. "See you at nine."

"I'll be there. I'm feeling the luck of the Irish. Conor needs a new pair of shoes and Aine wants a new dress."

Conor was his middle child, a six-year-old with the red hair his father lacked, and Aine was the wife. "How's the family, anyway?" 8 asked.

"Great. You'll have to come over to dinner sometime."

"That'd be great. I could use a home-cooked meal."

McGee snorted. "You could use to take a week off of eating, is what you could use."

"All muscle, my friend," 8 said, thumping his belly. "See you tonight."

"Yep. Best be watching your back. If somebody killed that lad to keep him from talking to you, then your name's not too far down the list."

"Yeah, especially when word gets out that only one of them died. Could be coincidental, Peter getting killed on his way to meet up with me, but I don't really believe that. Somebody killed him to stop him from speaking to me, plain and simple."

"Who knew you were meeting up with them?" McGee asked.

Who indeed, 8 thought? Fritz had guessed at their identities. It was possible that Arkady and Peter had shared the information with somebody, the wrong somebody. But 8 didn't think so. "If you find the other one, Arkady, let me know. I need to find out what he was gonna tell me. Something worth killing over, evidently."

"Yep. And you do the same. If you find him, steer him our way."

"Doubt he'll want to talk to you."

McGee nodded to indicate he figured as much. "Where you off to now?"

"Thought I'd go find somebody to watch my back for me so I don't have to."

"Good idea. And tell Pearle to bring plenty of cash tonight. Shoes and dresses aren't cheap."

Pearle Hill, whom 8 had known since he was ten, lived in a home just off Fulton Avenue in the area that was starting to be known as Bedford-Stuyvesant. Not just an apartment, but an entire home. He'd done well for himself and owned a string of grocery stores and restaurants.

It was twenty-five years earlier when they'd first met, a thought that was hard to comprehend. 8 had taken to finding stickball games away from his own block to lessen the chance that his father would see him. He figured it was easier to ask forgiveness than permission if he were caught. This was still four years before the kiss with Klara that had gotten 8 the back of his father's hand. In this case, he knew what his father's reaction would be if he were caught. Mr. Ballo had made it quite clear that ballplayers were below their social class, a concept that he still did not understand at that young age. Not that he understood it now, he thought with a sardonic grin as he walked.

On that spring day of 1898 he'd wandered over to the Bedford neighborhood. He'd asked if he could join in on a game, and been taken in, possibly because they had an odd number and he evened things out. There were no Black boys in his school and few in Bushwick, a thought that hadn't yet crossed his young mind. It hadn't registered yet that the Trolley-Dodgers were all white. And it didn't even occur to him that the stickball game he joined into was all Black. All he knew was that it was a good group of boys. And they played the game well.

He went back the next day and the one after that, and for many years he was a regular. It wasn't until a few months after that first game that he first brought Pearle home. They came through the front door to grab a snack before dinner, and 8 thought that somebody must've certainly died by the look on his father's face. He didn't say anything, much like he'd not interrupted his first kiss with Klara

Winkler, but later that night, after another "we don't associate with those people" speeches, he got the belt out and tried to reinforce his twisted, racist lesson on 8's bare ass.

It took almost a full year before 8 told Pearle why he no longer invited him over to the house, and they decided together that adults were very strange people and left it at that.

Pearle opened the door on the second knock, and even at this hour, looked like he'd been up for some time. He was almost as thick as 8, but shorter, and not as muscular. He had a mustache that merged into a goatee on his chin and he had round spectacles. Pearle flashed a large grin when he saw 8, an expression of friendliness that was never too far from the surface. He was also the coolest cucumber 8 had ever seen in a tight situation and could handle a gun or knife with the best of them. They'd gotten into their fair share of scrapes growing up and trusted each other implicitly.

"Brrr, it's chilly out here," Pearle said. "Almost like the temp is eight below." His grin erupted into a mouthful of chuckles.

After one of those early scrapes when a couple older guys thought that the two of them would be fun to bully and had found out how wrong they were, Pearle had looked at 8, and said, "Man, you were cold, kicking the shit out of that big country boy. That must be where you got the name, cold as hell, freezing cold, like you was 8 Below." It'd been a constant source of enjoyment to him for the past twenty-some years.

"Glad you're up. Was afraid I might be waking you."

"You know I'm always up before sunrise."

"That was back before you got rich and retired."

"I still got to manage all them places, you know."

8 snickered. "You mean you got to count your money once a month, is what you mean."

"Nah, I got somebody to do that for me." Pearle stepped back. "Come on in before the neighbors call the police because there's a white man out on the street."

The area had a burgeoning Black population, but there was still a mixture of white people scattered in. "Probably just figure I'm your chauffeur." 8 followed him into the house.

"Coffee?" Pearle asked.

"Yes, absolutely," 8 said.

Pearle's home was not one of those supposedly esthetically pleasing but incredibly uncomfortable places filled with Victorian furniture. Rather, the living room had several comfortable armchairs and a sofa that was filled with goose feathers. There was a billiard table and a fireplace. A bar with four stools filled one corner. Pearle claimed to have no desire to ever get married but would remain a bachelor for life. While 8 was currently in the same boat, he did hope to find the perfect somebody someday.

"What brings my esteemed private investigator friend over this morning? Are you going to try and beg your way out of the poker game tonight?" Pearle handed him a cup of coffee and gestured for him to sit down.

"Not at all. As a matter of fact, McGee told you to bring plenty of sawbucks tonight as Conor needs a new pair of shoes."

"Ha. That Irishman is like a mirror. You can see his hand right in his eyes every time."

"Ain't that the truth," 8 said. "You been good?"

"Always, my friend. Business is booming. Got a couple lady friends who I visit with. Good whiskey. Cuban cigars. What more could a man want?"

"Perhaps a bit of excitement."

"What do you mean?"

"You know, something to get your blood racing."

"Yeah, well, I currently got two somebodies that get my blood racing and got my eye on another one."

"Was wondering if you might want a job?" 8 set the coffee cup down. "Got a little work that might interest you."

"Yeah? You need a bodyguard for a lonely and wealthy wife?"

"Not quite. Thought you might watch my back."

Pearle's eyes went from gentle humor to hard in a blink. "Somebody messing with you?"

8 told him about the missing Velma Hartmann, the Bugsy and Meyer connection, and the death of Peter, last name still unknown.

"You think he was killed to keep him from telling you what he knew?" Pearle asked.

8 shrugged. "Good possibility."

"You think it was that Bugsy Siegel?"

"No idea. He usually breaks legs or shoots people, as I understand it, but slashing a throat isn't beyond that mug's expertise. Don't have any other leads."

"You tell Hartmann you was meeting with them?"

"He did seem most interested in them. Guessed at who they may've been. Guessed right. Possible he sent some fellows out looking for them with a picture in hand. He knew they lived in Coney Island and were coming to meet me. Watch the train station. Could be. Just could be."

Later that afternoon, 8 was back in his office, doing his best work, namely his feet were up on his desk, and he was lost in contemplation, when the phone again interrupted him. There was a certain convenience to the things, he thought, but they were sure a damn nuisance. He managed to pluck the receiver from the cradle without putting his feet down. "8 Ballo."

"Hello, 8. This is Dottie Parker."

"Why, hello, Dottie. What can I do for you?"

"I thought maybe we could get a drink?"

"Now?"

"Around nine?"

"I'm actually busy at nine," 8 said, regretting it. "Is this something to do with Velma?"

"I just thought I'd like to get to know you better. What are you doing at nine?"

"I, uh, have some friends coming over to play poker."

"Well," Dottie said, "I quite enjoy a bout with the aces and eights."

8 cleared his throat. "Would you like to come join in?"

"Oh, that'd be the bee's knees. You got any hooch?"

Chapter 11

"Aces and eights," Dottie said, laying down her cards.

8 looked over his cards at her. Was she cheating, he wondered? She'd made the crack about enjoying a bout with aces and eights, and now, here, on just the third hand of the game, she was laying them down and raking in the pot. And what's more, she was grinning wickedly in his direction.

She was wearing a black dress, open shockingly far down the front, perhaps to distract the other players, 8 wondered? Her face wasn't particularly pretty, he mused, with a square chin and a hardness to the corners of her eyes, but this was overcome by her sparkling wit and intellect.

Pearle threw down his cards with a curse. "Dammit, woman, you must be Lady Luck herself."

"*Fortuna caeca est*," Martin said. The *Brooklyn Eagle* journalist had arrived with no further information for 8. "Luck is blind."

"She sure don't play like she's blind," McGee growled.

"It's been three hands, you palookas," Dottie said. "Calm yourselves."

"Who you callin' a palooka?" McGee asked.

"Hey, what can I say, I'm lousy with good cards," Dottie said.

"Lousy with as in bad or lousy with as in you got all good cards?" Pearle asked.

"Ask the gumshoe over there," Dottie said. "I told him I like the aces and eights."

"I'd suggest checking her for hidden cards," 8 said.

"You be my guest," Dottie said, spreading her arms wide.

"Same game," McGee said. "Different outcome." He dealt the cards around.

"Anybody need a whiskey topper?" 8 asked, holding up the bottle.

Dottie pushed her empty glass his way. "Be a good egg and put a bit more in this time."

The cards flitted around the table, money went back and forth, brown liquor, gin, and rum were consumed, and conversation bounced from topic to topic.

"Superbas took a drubbing yesterday," McGee said.

"DeBerry got a triple," Pearle said.

"Met him the other day," 8 said. "He's one of the fellows who was hanging around Velma Hartmann."

"Sounds like the lady swings a wide circle," Martin said.

"Left him to run off with the Bambino," 8 said. "After an exhibition game. Hasn't seen her since."

"You don't think they're shacked up together, do you?" Pearle asked.

"Velma and the Babe?" Martin asked.

"Nope," 8 said. "Dottie saw her up to the Cotton Club the other night, and the Babe's on the road."

"Now, that's a real ball team and one swell fellow," Dottie said.

"The Yankees?" McGee asked. He spluttered. And said it again. "The Yankees?"

"You got it," Dottie said. "Beat the Browns in St. Louis 9–2 yesterday while your Trolley-Dodgers were getting wiped up in the same city by the Cardinals. The Babe hit a home run in the ninth, and the Yankee's went to 18–8 on the year."

"Yeah, but—"

"She's got a point," Martin said.

McGee didn't speak for three more hands as he worked at losing his money and drinking his gin. When Dottie won the third hand

and yelled home run, he cracked a smile, and they all laughed loudly.

"What do you know about Lansky and Siegel?" Pearle asked, looking at Martin. "Being a journalist and all up in Williamsburg, you must know something about them."

"Lansky is all brains," Martin said. "Tough as hell but not gonna beat anybody up by himself. That's why he's got Benji."

"Benji?" 8 asked. *That sounds awful familiar,* he thought.

"Yeah, Benji Siegel," Martin said. "If you want to call him Bugsy to his face, you best be friends with him, or ready to throw down. You run into him, make sure you call him by his given name. Benji."

"Also ran into Coleman Hawkins the other day," 8 said.

"You saw the Hawk and are just telling me now?" Pearle asked. "That man can blow the sax. I saw him up to Harlem with Mamie Smith and the Jazz Hounds last year, and I haven't been the same since."

"Well, anyway," 8 said. "He mentioned that Velma spoke about some fellow named Benji that made her laugh. Something about pockets big enough to hold a quart. Of liquor, I figure."

"Not the only Benji in the world," McGee said.

"No, but everything seems to be linking up like the cars on a train," 8 said. "And I don't much believe in coincidences. Like that guy Occam said, the simplest answer is most likely the correct solution to your problem."

"What's that?" McGee asked.

"Occam's Razor," Pearle said. "The Principle of Parsimony."

"He's a thirteenth-century English Franciscan friar," Martin added.

"Occam is," 8 said. "The razor part is a rule of thumb philosophers apply to discount unlikely explanations. Basically, the logical proof that has the fewest number of propositions is more likely to be correct."

"Sometimes you lads make me glad I never went to a whole lot of schooling," McGee said. "They sure taught you some messed up *shite.*"

They all laughed. Dottie won another hand.

"So, what are the police doing about Arkady Bortnik?" 8 asked.

"Not much," McGee said. "Put in a call to the precinct in Coney Island. They went by his place. Nobody there. Place looked like it'd been searched already. That's probably the end of it."

"What about the murder?" Martin asked.

McGee looked at him with chilling blue eyes. "Can't imagine why I'd sing in front of a two-bit journalist."

"That just means you got nothing, and nothing is being done," Martin said.

"Yeah, that about sums it up." McGee laughed and held up his glass. "Dead Russian ends up in an empty lot next to a juice joint, and we're supposed to get our knickers in a bind?"

8 knew that this was not McGee's personal philosophy. If it was up to him, he'd dig and dig until something turned up. His superiors had differing views, though. The poor were buried and forgotten. Resources were best spent on the wealthy and the living.

"Did you go out to the Fitzgeralds' cottage?" Dottie asked.

"What's that?" McGee asked.

"That's right," 8 said. "That's where Arkady and Peter met Velma."

Dottie nodded. "Arkady and Zelda got on fabulously, and Scott didn't mind so much, because, well, you know. He wasn't a threat in that way."

"Are they out of The Gonk?" 8 asked.

"The manager told them to scram yesterday. Something about skipping through the halls at four in the morning singing some silliness. Guess the guests complained."

"They're out at the *cottage* in Great Neck?" 8 asked.

"This flatfoot ain't going out to the North Shore," McGee said. "Hell, they'll arrest me and deport me to Ireland."

"All the more reason you should go," Pearle said. "You go home and tell Aine how much money you lost tonight, and you might as well climb aboard a boat back to the homeland."

"And to a flapper at that," Martin said, looking glumly at the stacks of cash in front of Dottie. "What's the world come to?"

"Nobody is going to be telling Aine anything about no Sheba being here," McGee said. "And not a word about me losing any money."

"I got a warehouse over on Wykoff," Pearle said. "Meet me there tomorrow around five? I'm thinking we can rustle up a dress for Aine and shoes for Conor."

"You want to swing out to Great Neck tomorrow?" 8 asked, looking at Pearle.

"Sounds like a plan. A Saturday drive in the country," Pearle said.

"I figured if our fellow, Arkady, is out there, I'd try to persuade him to meet up with you, McGee. Either way, I'll let you know what he has to say."

With that, the game broke up. Pearle offered rides in his automobile, his Nash fitting four comfortably. Martin and McGee took him up on the offer. Dottie declined. She and 8 stayed up talking and drinking until the sun was breaking in the east. There was a sexual tension rippling between them, but both were hesitant to act upon it. Perhaps it was because she was married or that he was becoming infatuated with Velma. Instead, they entertained each other with their minds, telling stories and drinking into the early hours. At some point—8 was a bit bleary on the details—she gathered herself into a yellow cab and went home.

Benji 'Bugsy' Siegel tapped the bat with a steady cadence on the concrete floor in the warehouse out back of the Candy Store in Brownsville. *Bang-bang-bang-bang.* The shelves were lined with crates of alcohol in sections for gin, rum, and whiskey. They were full-service providers. A dim light provided the only illumination.

Two men with Tommy guns loitered in the shadows. Meyer Lansky sat in a chair. Across from him was a man tied to a chair who had blood on his face.

"I'm going to ask you one more time, and then I will turn it over to my associate, Mr. Siegel," Lansky said. "Where is Fritz Hartmann stashing his hooch?"

"I don't know. I just drive for him." The man was known as Shaggy Dave.

"We've been over that. Where do you pick up the hooch? That would be where he stashes it."

"I meet them up by the shipyard. There's an empty lot there. I leave my automobile and get in the truck and away I go."

Lansky stared at him. "I don't believe you."

Bugsy looked at the chopper squad. "Why don't you boys go check on the lookout."

He kept tapping the bat. *Bang-bang-bang-bang.* Bugsy had turned seventeen just a few months back. Already, in his young life, things were starting to look glorious. He'd started out running a protection scam with Moe fleecing street cart vendors and was now standing in a warehouse full of hooch worth millions.

Bugsy had no false illusions about his success. It was because he was willing to do whatever it took. Often, that meant inflicting pain and killing. He had no problem with that.

He stopped banging the bat and stepped forward to the man tied in the chair. "Who you think you're protecting? Fritz don't give a shit about you."

The man said nothing, but his breathing and eyes spoke plenty about his fear.

Bugsy started slapping the bat against his hand. *Slap-slap-slap-slap.* "Ya see, Williamsburg is our territory. I was born there. That will always be my home."

Bugsy was starting to get very angry. This man was standing between him and the dream that he had envisioned since he left school and joined a gang. He wasn't going to be a bum like his father working three different jobs just to put food on the table. No, Benji Siegel was going to be rich. He was going to marry a movie star. He'd be respected by men, and women would swoon in his presence.

Slap-slap-slap-slap.

"How about a fellow named 8 Ballo? Ya know him?"

"8?"

"You lying sack of shit." Bugsy swung the bat, putting his legs into it, just like his buddy Al Capone had taught him. Snorkie, as they all called him then, had played two years of professional ball and knew what he was talking about when swinging a bat.

Bingo. He made clean contact with the man's elbow, and he could feel it crunch before the chair toppled over. Shaggy Dave screamed. Bugsy grabbed the man by the hair and jerked him back upright. "You need a haircut, ya fucking bum."

"Please. I don't know nothing." The man was a blubbering mess.

"Don't lie to me."

Bugsy hated it when the man's voice climbed to that particular high pitch of abject terror. This just made him angrier. This time he brought the bat in a high arcing motion down on the man's knee. Crack. Screaming. But Bugsy barely noticed. His ire was up now. He did the other knee. Then he went for the fence and put good wood on the fellow's noggin. Bugsy loved that sensation. It was like hitting a pumpkin and watching it explode. It excited him. It aroused him. After a minute of beating the already dead man on the floor, Bugsy paused to take a breath, panting, a wide grin on his face.

"I don't think he'll be telling us where the warehouse is," Lansky said drily.

Chapter 12

8 didn't feel so bad sleeping until noon. It was Saturday after all. When he finally rolled his way out of bed and down the stairs, he called Pearle to ask him if he still wanted to go visit a famous author. Five minutes later, Pearle was outside laying on the horn. 8 had only had time to splash some water on his face and get a cup of coffee.

It was a stunner of a May day. Pearle had the top of the turquoise automobile down for the almost hour-long drive out to Great Neck.

"I thought we were going out at ten?" Pearle said.

"I thought about it but remembered that it was too early for the Fitzgeralds," 8 said. "They might've had one of their lavish parties last night, and, anyway, they don't get up until noon."

Pearle pulled into the street. "Bullshit," he said. "You was up late with that wisecracker who took all our money, weren't you?" He looked over at 8. When he didn't answer, Pearle leaned his head back and roared in laughter.

"She's a fascinating lady," 8 said.

"I bet," Pearle said. "I 'd be willing to wager that she has more than cards up her sleeves."

"She was quite the woman," 8 said. "You know? To hold her own with our group?"

"That she did, and then some. Knows the theater, poker, and baseball. What more could you want?"

"Somebody that's not married?" 8 asked. His thoughts turned to the mysterious Velma. "Interesting that Hawkins said Velma was hanging out with Bugsy Siegel. And, at the same time, her father was having problems with the man."

"You don't know that for sure," Pearle said.

"I'd be willing to place a wager on it right now," 8 said. "A sawbuck?"

"You're on. How about a double sawbuck?"

"Ten is good with me. I'm not a wealthy businessman. Just a poor schmo trying to make an honest living."

"Speaking of wealthy businessmen, I imagine you charged Hartmann a good price to find his daughter. What do you know about him?"

They'd left the buildings of Brooklyn behind for a more rural scenery with trees, bushes, and green grass. Pearle had taken the speed of the automobile up, but the rutted dirt road forced him to slow down. At least there weren't any horses and carriages passing them, 8 thought as he watched the countryside float by at about twenty miles an hour.

"Owns a wallpaper business, a few sweatshops in the garment industry, and probably some other businesses. His wife died about ten years back," 8 said. "Most recently, he was carrying on with a young woman named Colleen Brooks who has disappeared. Had a tiff with Siegel and Lansky and has a gunslinger following him around and a couple guys with Tommy guns protecting his office."

"Doesn't much sound like the actions of a legitimate businessman," Pearle said.

"What do you know?" 8 asked. He was used to how his friend eased into sharing any important information.

"I asked around this morning about him, while you were sleeping or doing lord knows what," Pearle said. "None of this is substantiated, mind you, and you know how I hate spreading rumors and gossip."

"Understood."

"Hartmann has a legitimate façade. He's also running hooch, has several brothels, and might be dipping his fingers in the heroin trade."

"So, he's competition for Bugsy and Meyer, and it wasn't just some labor problem like he told me."

"Not just them, but the Italians. Lansky is tight with Luciano. Shapes up to a be a major conflict. Both sides are bringing in brunos and button men with enough guns to fight a small war."

"The Italians and Jews versus the Germans. Right in my own neighborhood."

"Remember that run-in with that Italian gang we had back when we were, what was it, maybe fifteen years old?" Pearle asked.

"All over some girl you liked," 8 said. "What was her name?"

"Elisabetta."

Pearle had asked 8 to go up to Williamsburg one night. He'd run into the girl coming out of a shop in Stuyvesant earlier in the day, and they'd exchanged flirtations while Elisabetta waited for her mother to come out of the store. She'd given him her address and promised to sneak out and meet him if he came up to her neighborhood that night at ten. But, she wanted to bring a friend, and hence, 8 was invited along.

They never made it to meet up with Elisabetta. Walking up the block, they'd suddenly found themselves surrounded by a group of Italian boys, maybe seven or eight of them, who were heckling Pearle about the color of his skin and lumping 8 into the mix.

"What was it that you said to that one fellow?" 8 asked. "You asked him—"

"Ha. I asked him if he'd been milking cows, and when he didn't answer, I said that I figured that was how he got the cowlick on his forehead."

8 shook his head. "It was a lot funnier at the time."

"Yeah, you got that right. Taught them boys a lesson, though, didn't we?"

It was not the first time that 8 and Pearle had been accosted for being places together, Black and white, where one or the other was considered an outsider, and it wouldn't be the last. Already, at fifteen years old, they were savage fighters who reveled in the occasional altercation, getting out the misery of their home life in a good, wholesome brawl. Sharing that and a fierce need to fight injustice in the world, 8 and Pearle had become fast friends. It was still a few years until they started carrying guns.

"You got stuck with a blade pretty good, if I remember," 8 said.

Pearle rubbed just below his shoulder. "Yeah, had to sew that one up."

"Never saw that girl again, did you?"

Pearle grinned. "I might've gone up and hung out with her in a park a few days later. She was quite impressed with my wound."

"Well, it was worth it, then," 8 said.

"We supposed to turn here?" Pearle asked. They were in Great Neck.

"Yes," 8 said. "Should be right up here. Before we get to the old money on the water, Dottie said."

And, indeed, they found themselves pulling into a driveway that led to what was more than a cottage but perhaps less than a mansion. There were grand, arched windows and lots of ornate millwork. The lawn was expansive and the flower beds in bloom. 8 banged the knocker on the door several times, but there was no answer. After a bit, they wandered around the side of the house and found Zelda Fitzgerald reclined in a chair in the back, reading a book. She had on a wide-brimmed straw hat, a man's long-sleeve shirt, and had an iced drink next to her.

"Well, well, well," Zelda said looking over the top of the book. "The big six and a pal. What brings you to our tiny cottage?"

"Hello, Zelda. You remember me, 8 Ballo. This is my associate, Pearle Hill."

"Of course, I remember you," she said. "You're the one looking for our lovely Velma."

"Have you seen or heard from her?"

"Not since I last saw you a few days back."

"After I spoke with you on Monday, I followed up with a few others." 8 sat down at a long, wooden table and Pearle sat across from him. "One of them was Arkady Bortnik and his partner, Peter." The only tell on her face was a slight tic to her left eye as she picked up her drink and took a sip.

"Arkady? How brilliant. How is he?" Her voice was a bit faint.

"Peter was found dead in an empty lot in Bushwick next to a joint I was supposed to be meeting them at."

"That's horrific," she said after a long pause. "I quite liked them. Did the coppers pinch anybody for cutting his pipes?"

8 had not said anything about his throat being cut. But the news could've made it out here to Great Neck by now. "What do ya know about all of that?" he asked.

"First I'm hearing the scoop." Zelda set down her book, pulled on a pair of sunglasses, stood, and joined them at the table with her drink in hand. "And Arkady? Is he okay?"

"He's disappeared," 8 said. "Thought you might know where I could find him."

Zelda shook her head. "At his place in Coney Island, I suppose."

"Is he here?"

"No. Why would he be here?"

"How'd you know Peter had his throat cut?"

Zelda flinched. "You told me, I suppose. Yes, you must've."

"I didn't." 8 looked around the manicured backyard backed by trees. It was a nice spot. "How many bedrooms you got in this place?"

"What? Uh, seven, I believe."

"Is your husband here?"

"He's writing in his office up over the garage. Some new project about eggs. West eggs and east eggs or some such thing. A fella by the name of Gatsby who wants what he can't have."

"Yeah, what's that?" Pearle asked.

Zelda looked with surprise at him. "The American Fucking Dream, I suppose."

"Would you mind giving us a tour of your house?" 8 asked.

Zelda sighed. "He's not here. He came by last night with another gent, didn't get his name, and asked to borrow some money. I gave him what I had, and they flew the coop."

"Was he injured?"

"He had a bandage around his neck. Said the fellow must've had a dull shiv. I told him I didn't want any of that business around here and to get on."

"Did he give you any idea where he was going?"

"No."

"Zelda, listen to me. I think Peter was killed because of what they had to tell me. Something important they didn't want to share over the telephone. Something about Velma and where she is."

"I feel like I can trust you," she said.

"I only want what's best for Velma."

"The fella he was with? I think he works at The Nest, place up on Bedford Avenue."

"I know the place," Pearle said. "What's his name?"

"Arkady called him Nikos. Don't know him otherwise. Scott and I were in there a bit back, and he caught my eye."

"Yeah? What caught your eye?" 8 asked.

Zelda flickered her eyes to the garage. "He was a real sheik, okay? Dark hair and eyes. A jaw that was carved out of marble. Shoulders that you could rest a drink on. Suppose if he's running with Arkady it doesn't matter much." Zelda took a drink, looked toward the garage again. "Not that it mattered much anyway as I'm married."

"You think they were heading back that way?" 8 asked.

"Don't know," Zelda said. "I think it'd be for the best if you stayed away from him. Just leave him alone, won't you?"

8 pondered that. It was possible that he'd get the man killed. It was most likely his fault that Peter was dead. "I think it's too late for that," he said. "Once the people who killed Peter find out Arkady is still alive and may be able to finger them? They gotta knock him off.

If you want him alive, you best tell me what you know. I'm the only chance he has." *That might've been laying it on a bit thick,* 8 thought, *but I do need to speak to the man.*

Zelda finished whatever she was drinking, her eyes crossing, suggesting that it was alcoholic in nature and quite strong. "The man, Nikos, told Arkady he could lay low at his place until things blow over, but that he had to work tonight. That's all I know."

Chapter 13

Velma had on a new trimmed hat that she'd just purchased at Bedell's on Fulton just to wear to this ballgame. That was because she'd lost her hat the night before. She wasn't sure how that had happened, but it wasn't the first time. She'd considered stopping at Oppenheim, Collins & Co. for a dress but was running late. Maybe she'd go back later.

Yesterday she'd bought herself an automobile. It was a used 45-B Oldsmobile but sure did the trick just fine. She wasn't sure it had been a wise move as her money wouldn't last forever. And then she'd have to go back to Daddy. This wasn't something that she wanted to think about. She was tired of being his boob tickler. Laughing and flirting with his clients. No more, she vowed, but wasn't sure how that was going to work without getting hush money.

She was late to pick up Tomas, his pal and that fella's gal, a woman who Velma thought was a bit of a Dumb Dora. Velma admitted that she was kinda goofy about Tomas, and at the same time, realized that this infatuation wouldn't last long. There hadn't been a man yet who'd kept her attention. Either they became boring, possessive, or bossy.

The other night at the Cotton Club, Velma had run into Dottie, who told her there was some private investigator looking for her, hired by Daddy. She said that he seemed to be a square shooter, even if he was a Father Time, probably five years over the age of thirty. She was thinking about paying him a visit, just to see what he was all about, if nothing else. It wasn't like Daddy could force her to come home. She was an adult woman. Then Velma thought about Mouse and Bull. She didn't much care for how Bull looked at her when Daddy wasn't around, the idea making her shudder slightly.

Tomas was standing outside his place in Williamsburg when she pulled up. He looked angry. Velma didn't much care for men who got angry with her.

"Where ya been?" he asked, clambering into the passenger seat.

Velma checked her own ire. She needed him. "Where's Tito and what's her name?"

"I sent them on with their tickets. *Cazzo!* The game is half over already."

She didn't think his Italian was a compliment. Velma had never quite figured out why anybody need bother watching the first seven or eight innings of a baseball game. She mostly went to see the players. "Relax, Tomas. We'll get there."

"Where you been?"

"I had to buy a hat. Not that you noticed."

"You had to buy a hat?" Tomas gripped her arm. "You're late because you had to buy a fucking hat?"

Velma, making a point, almost ran over a pedestrian who'd thought it was safe to pass in front of her speeding automobile. Less than one goddamn week with Tomas and already he was trying to control her. Like all men did. Like her Daddy did. They'd had some fun over the past week. He was a handsome devil, but she wasn't about to put up with his need to dominate her. No, best to nip this in the bud, as she had need of him.

"I *don't* like to be yelled at. Especially by men. So get your goddamn hand off of me and check your tone or get the hell out of the car."

Tomas started to speak, stopped, and removed his hand. "I'm sorry, V. I'm just looking forward to this game, is all."

"My father would yell at me. All the time. After he killed my mother."

"What's that? Killed your mother?"

Velma didn't look at him, wheeling around a corner and almost hitting a parked car.

"C'mon, V, I'm sorry. Tell me what happened."

Velma pulled the Oldsmobile to a shuddering stop with Ebbets Field just off to the right and ahead of them. She turned to look at Tomas. A single tear was running down her left cheek. "I was thirteen when my mum got the consumption. One day, she was healthy and fine, and suddenly she'd lost twenty pounds, and her skin was clinging to her like she was a scarecrow."

When she didn't continue, Tomas did. "That ain't the same as your father killing your mother, V. People get sick."

"I'm not fucking done," Velma said in a whisper. "I came home from school one day a bit early to find my dad standing over my mum with a pillow pressed to her face. He said she asked him to do it. That she couldn't take it anymore. So he did. It was the merciful thing to do, is what Daddy said. It was out of love, he said. But that didn't bring her back, now, did it?"

"I'm sorry, V. I know you hate your father, just didn't quite know why. You want I should kill that pig-fucker for you?"

Velma looked at him with narrowed eyes. It wouldn't be easy to murder her daddy, she thought. Then she blinked her coal-blackened lashes, shook her head, and gave a slight giggle. "You're so sweet, Tomas. Let's go watch the game."

It was the bottom of the eighth inning and Zack Wheat was up with the Trolley-Dodgers holding a 4–3 edge over the St. Louis Cardinals.

"He had an inside the park home run in the first inning," Tito told them excitedly.

Tomas groaned but didn't say anything. This time, Wheat wasn't up to it, lining out to right field, and two more outs quickly followed. Which didn't matter, as they had the lead going into the ninth. That is, until two hits and an error led to a Cardinals lead going into the bottom of the ninth.

Hank wasn't on the field, but Velma thought she might've seen him wave over to her from the dugout, which was in shadow, and she couldn't tell for sure. She looked away and leaned into Tomas.

"Isn't this the best part?" Velma asked, squeezing Tomas' arm. "People are always saying to be on time, but who really cares about the first eight innings. The ninth and final inning is what it's all about."

"Sure, babe."

And when Jimmy Johnston hit a double off the left field wall to score two runs and win the game, she reached over and kissed him hard and long. "Told you," she murmured into his neck. "The end is always the best part."

Chapter 14

8 had always liked that Pearle didn't feel the need to talk just to fill space, and figured his friend thought the same about him. They'd pondered aloud the information that Zelda had shared about Arkady possibly staying with a man named Nikos who worked at a joint called The Nest. That seemed to be the best lead to follow up on right now.

They decided it'd probably be best to pay him a visit there a bit later that night. 8 agreed to join Pearle and stop by the warehouse on the way back and meet up with McGee for the promised dress for the wife and shoes for the boy. Pearle liked to bust the balls of the Irishman, but at the same time, was always helping him out. It wasn't easy supporting a wife and three kids on the salary of a flattie.

As they came back into Bushwick, on that border avenue between it and Ridgewood, where the warehouse was located, 8 looked over at the Evergreen Cemetery and a wave of emotion swept through his body. At age sixteen, when his father died and was buried there, he hadn't felt the slightest bit of sentiment.

At the time, he'd believed his father had effectively struck out as far as being a capable and trusted parent. First, claiming that baseball players were a lower social class, second, suggesting that Ballos did not hang out with Black people, and finally, ending his first love with Klara Winkler because she was Asian. Strike three. 8 had barely spoken to the man for the two years before he died. He now regretted that.

His father, Miksa Ballo, had worked at the Welz and Zerweck Brewery, occupying the triangle formed by Wycoff Avenue, Myrtle Avenue, and Madison Street, a spot they were now passing—the empty forlorn building a casualty of prohibition. He'd switched to this job after 8 was born, giving up a more lucrative career on the sea to be, presumably, home with his family more.

It wasn't until 8 was in his mid-twenties that he finally started to forgive his father. The man was a product of his own upbringing and struggled every day to provide for a family of ten mouths. He'd drink once a week, on Saturday night, bringing home a case of beer, Gambrinus Bock being the usual choice, and work his way steadily through as many as he could, before stumbling off to bed. He was not an angry drunk. Just a forlorn one.

Miksa Ballo had done the best he'd known how to do. Perhaps his own youthful experiences had led to some of the misgivings that 8 had in committing to and creating his own family. Never far from the center of his mind was the question, would he be able to provide the basic necessities for his own clan, much less shoes and nice clothes? Would he be able to take them to ballgames?

What prejudices would he have that would offend the sensibilities of his children? 8 couldn't imagine his daughters out in public doing the Charleston, much less the Shimmy, wearing next to nothing and shaking everything they had. 8 didn't want to become his father. But he didn't blame his father. Mr. Ballo had done the best he could to provide for his family in the only way he knew how.

"You going to sit in the car or come in?" Pearle asked. He was standing on the sidewalk looking at 8 sitting lost in thought in the automobile.

8 shook his head to clear the cobwebs of memories and stepped out of the car. "You ever think about having children?" he asked.

"I imagine once I'm done shopping the field, I might be willing to have a couple little Pearle cherubs running around," Pearle said. "But that time isn't yet."

"Thought you weren't ever going to settle down," 8 said.

"Things change in life, don't they?"

That they do, 8 thought, *that they do.*

The building took up half the block. It was made of red-brick and had no sign over the entrance. Pearle led the way inside. The space was cavernous, high ceilings supported by steel girders. Tables filled the floor, busy with women packing boxes with various items. Dresses in one spot, shoes in another, and what looked like bathing suits down the way.

McGee was just inside the doorway waiting for them. "Quite an operation you got here, Pearle," he said.

"You paying these women a fair wage?" 8 asked.

"More than the competitors," Pearle said. "But not out of the goodness of my heart. Found out they work harder and don't send little Johnny around to say they're sick nearly as much if you're fair with 'em."

8 laughed. He knew that behind the swagger Pearle hid a big heart.

"Some of these broads aren't bad looking," McGee said.

"Aren't you married and here to get a dress for your wife and shoes for your kid?" Pearle asked.

"Sure. A guy can look, can't he? You two lads got the Life of Reilley, now, don't you, while I'm tied down. All I can do is look."

"Who is this Reilley?" Pearle asked.

"You know, *Is That Mr. Reilley,* about the lad who sings about what he'd do if had a fortune."

"I think that's called, *Is that Mr. Pearle Hill,*" 8 said, chuckling.

The three men strolled through the warehouse, McGee picking out the dress and shoes with advice, good or bad, from the other two. 8 told McGee about Nikos, maybe hiding Arkady, working over in Bedford and promised to keep him in the loop.

As they emerged back on Wycoff Avenue, Pearle paused. "Isn't that Hartmann over there?"

8 looked down the street. "That's him. That's his wallpaper company he's out in front of. And that looks like a couple of the fellows standing guard outside his door."

"Looks like they're going out on a hit," McGee said.

Sure enough, there were two cars, and five men packed into each one, and it looked likely that they were carrying Tommy guns under their trench coats, or at least some of them were. Hartmann gave terse orders, and then the cars pulled out, driving past them.

"C'mon, let's follow them," 8 said.

Pearle was already climbing into the driver's seat as 8 opened the door. McGee started to say something, sighed, tossed the dress and shoes in the back, and followed suit.

"What's the play here?" Pearle asked. "We going to watch, or we getting involved?" He had his pistol out and lying on his lap.

"Let's see what happens, first," 8 said. "Maybe they're just going to guard a bootleg shipment." He pulled out his .38 Special and likewise, checked the rounds.

"Lot of firepower for running some hooch," Pearle said.

"I'm not wearing iron," McGee said.

"Got a Tommy gun in the back," Pearle said. "When we stop."

8 looked at Pearle and wondered what a legitimate businessman might need with a Tommy gun.

"Where ya think they're going?" McGee asked.

"We're in Williamsburg now," Pearle said. "Maybe they're crossing over into the Lower East Side?"

"Both places are heavy with Italians and Jews," 8 said.

Pearle looked sideways at him. "You thinking Siegel and Lansky?"

8 shrugged. "They seem to have a beef with each other."

"Ya think this has something to do with his daughter?" McGee asked.

"Velma," 8 said. "Could be. Can't—hey, turn left." He pointed.

Pearle had to cut across traffic, losing ground. "Not going over the bridge," he said.

"Look out!" 8 said.

A boisterous crowd spilled out into the street, and Pearle was forced to slam on the brakes. There were about twenty people carrying beers, flasks, and even whole bottles of liquor.

"So much for Prohibition in Williamsburg," Pearle said.

"Looks like they came from the game," McGee said. "The Trolley-Dodgers won in the bottom of the ninth."

"They're going to the right up there," 8 said.

Pearle sat forward in his seat with his pistol pointed at the pack of jubilant fans. "Get the hell out of the street!" He honked the horn. "Move!"

A few of the crew caught sight of him and pulled people out of the way as he hit the accelerator, brushing past a few of the more inebriated partiers.

"Right here," 8 said.

They turned onto the street, busy with automobiles and pedestrians, but no sight of the men they were following.

"What now?" Pearle asked.

"They gotta be around here somewhere close," 8 said. "Between here and the river. Let's go up and down the streets looking for 'em."

It took five minutes. They turned onto a quiet street not far from the East River, and there were the two cars. A driver sat in each, with two men by the cars, and two at the door of a three-story apartment building. There were no pedestrians on the street. Most likely because the men now held Tommy guns in plain sight.

Pearle pulled over at the end of the street, about a hundred yards away. "They sent four trigger men inside," he said.

McGee hopped out the back. "Let me in the boot."

"This isn't our fight," Pearle said. "And there's ten of them." Still, he got out of the automobile, opened the boot of the automobile, rummaged through various items, pulled a Tommy gun out, and handed it to McGee.

McGee pulled out a fifty-round drum that looked like a moving picture film cannister and wound it back, *click-click-click*, eleven times, before snapping it onto the bottom of the Thompson Machine Gun. "You going to just stand around and watch?"

"The thought had crossed my mind," Pearle said.

"I'm a policeman," McGee said. "It's my duty."

"You don't even know what's going on," 8 said. The three of them stood at the back of the automobile talking in hushed tones. "Maybe they're picking up drugs. You want to get yourself killed to stop some dope peddlers?"

"Them lads are hatchet men, I bet my tin on it." McGee pulled his badge out and stuck it to his suit jacket lapel.

As if on cue, gunfire erupted from inside the building.

"You lads get in the car and drive around the block and come out the other side," McGee said. "Slow them down if they try and leave that way. I'll defend this end of the block." He stepped behind a parked car and took up position. "Go, now. More cops will be coming soon. We just got to pen them in."

The quick rat-a-tat of shots died away. 8 looked at Pearle, shrugged, and they both hurried back into the car. Pearle pulled a U-turn with a squeal of the tires and drove back around the block. As they rounded the corner, they heard a single burst of three or four shots, and then silence. As they sped down the parallel street, they passed a man and woman running out of an alleyway, apparently avoiding the gunfight that now seemed over.

Pearle pulled his automobile across the end of the street and joined 8 on the far side from the gunmen. "If my Nash gets shot up, that Irishman's going to pay," he said.

"That's only if you live through it," 8 said.

The four men that'd gone inside the building came streaming out of the building yelling, though their muffled words were indistinct. It was most likely some version of 'let's go', as they piled into the two cars, revved the engines, and came racing down the street.

Other traffic had disappeared, as if the people of Williamsburg had some signal that mischief was afoot. Such as gunshots. The two cars pulled abreast of each other as they came whizzing toward 8 and Pearle and the Nash.

"You got the right, and I got the left," 8 said, aiming his .38 Special over the back of the motorcar. "Take the tires and then the driver."

"I'm not sure we should be getting involved in a war when we don't know what it's about," Pearle said. "We shoot the tires out— ten guys get out with Tommy guns and kill us. We shoot them, we're killing people for what we know not why."

That makes a certain amount of sense, 8 thought. "Agreed. Best duck, then." The two of them went to the ground and rolled under the automobile as the approaching cars split and passed them on either side. 8 caught a glimpse of a submachine guns protruding from the side windows and shadowy faces behind, but no shots were fired, as no danger was perceived.

It was two hours later that McGee came back down the stairs and outside and told them they could go. A good ten to twelve coppers had shown up, two of them taking statements from 8 and Pearle and then telling them to wait.

"What happened?" 8 asked the Irishman.

"Dead guy inside," McGee said. "Took four bullets to the chest and then one in the head. Name of Tito Cattaneo. Mean anything to you?"

Pearle shrugged and 8 shook his head no.

McGee turned to go, paused, and turned back. "Why'd you let the two motorcars go without firing a shot?"

"Why the hell would we?" Pearle asked. "We didn't know what happened, and they outmanned and outgunned us five to one. So, I guess the answer is, we aren't goddamn stupid."

"Could've been a simple robbery with warning shots." 8 added. "Hell, we don't even know what it's all about. What are you buzzers gonna do about it?"

"I guess, first thing I'll be doing is having a chat with your client, Fritz Hartmann," McGee said. "He'll be lucky to see the sunshine for quite some time, I'd think, so you best start looking for work elsewhere. Don't think he'll be paying you anytime soon."

Pearle snorted. "If you get Fritz Hartmann down to the station at all, he'll be walking free within an hour. Wealthy men don't sit in jail."

"For murder, they do," McGee said.

Pearle laughed aloud this time. "No. No, they don't. But even if they did, what do you got? He talked to some people on the side of the street, and then they went and killed somebody. If it was me, I'd say they asked me for directions to the candy store, is what'd I do, and that I didn't know them from Adam."

"Shite. You're probably right," McGee said. "But I'm gonna keep after this one."

Chapter 15

8 didn't have a telephone in his room. He figured it was easy enough to go down to his office if he wanted to make a call. He didn't much like the idea of people being able to bother him at home by just giving a ring. Plus, it was hard to justify the expense.

Therefore, he'd cleaned up and changed to go out for the night, and was down in his office waiting for Pearle, when the telephone rang.

After he said hello, there was empty air for a few seconds as the operator went to connect them, before Pearle said, "You really need to get a home telephone."

"Why? What's up?" 8 asked. "You about on your way over?"

"Yeah, that's the thing. I got a little problem."

"What's up?"

"I, uh, forgot I was supposed to go out with Clarissa tonight."

8 could hear the discomfort in Pearle's voice. Clarissa didn't take kindly to being stood up. Yet, his friend, 8, needed somebody riding shotgun with him as they searched for a man who might have information to share that people were willing to kill for to prevent that sharing. "Hey, don't worry about it. Arkady seems to be harmless. I imagine that Nikos is just your average joe. I'll be fine."

"Or," Pearle let the word hang for several seconds, "we could all go to The Nest together. Didn't you say that you ran into Coleman Hawkins the other day?"

"Yeah, sure, why?"

"It seems that he's playing at The Nest. Clarissa loves the Hawk."

"I can't much see that playing third wheel to you and Clarissa would be all that dandy for me." 8 had wondered if Black people were even allowed into The Nest but hadn't brought it up. He knew that many clubs allowed performers only, and not patrons, who were Black.

"The Hawk is off the reservation with Ethel Waters and Smack Henderson," Pearle said. "They left the orchestra to go maverick at The Nest tonight. It's going to be wild."

"Been meaning to ask, don't take this the wrong way," 8 said. "Do they let you into The Nest?"

There was an awkward and heavy silence. "Yeah, they'll let Black people in who have money. Drop a sawbuck here and there in the right hands. Just the poor Black people they keep out. Look, here's the thing. I mentioned I was supposed to go with you to The Nest. Clarissa said, fine, we'll all go. Why don't you ask that flapper Dottie Parker to come along?"

It was 8's turn for an awkward and heavy silence. "Not sure that her husband would appreciate me giving a ring and asking," he said.

Pearle laughed. "How about Asta? She and Clarissa get along great."

"I'll see what I can do," 8 said. "How about I just meet you two up there at nine?"

"Sounds like a plan. We'll have some drinks. Listen to some music. Brace Nikos and have him take us to Arkady. Sounds like we're a couple of swells who know how to show some dames a good time."

Arkady sat at the table in a rickety chair staring at the worn and scarred wall. It was awful nice of Nikos to let him hide out here until he figured out something better. But the place was a pigsty. Arkady had no idea how anybody could live like this. It was depressing enough that the man lived in one room—bed, table, armchair, and kitchen all combined. His undergarments along with the rest of his clothes fluttered from a rope across the alleyway out back. It was on the second floor, so his wardrobe could be glimpsed with the smallest amount of effort by anybody passing underneath. The trick was, Arkady supposed, to not have anything nice that somebody might want.

These elements of Nikos' life were understandable, as the man's income was not large, working part-time as a bouncer down at The Nest. The true problem was that dishes clogged the sink, clothes littered the floor, and something was rotting in the cabinet. Arkady knew that beggars couldn't be choosers. He'd found the decaying food—apples and moldy bread—and thrown them out. Arkady piled the dirty clothes in a corner, but was reluctant to wash them both to avoid offending Nikos and because he could hardly bear to touch them in the first place.

Peter was dead. Arkady couldn't quite wrap his mind around this. The man who he loved. No more. He'd never touch or be touched again by Peter. No more kisses or caresses. No more would they enjoy a cup of coffee, a laugh together, or a conversation of a serious or a frivolous nature. Never again would they enjoy music or a drink or a quiet joke at somebody's expense. Their intimacy was a thing of the past. Arkady wasn't even sure what was being done with the body.

The knife had rasped across his own throat and darkness crossed his eyes and his knees crumbled and he fell facedown, but not to the ground, onto another person. Peter. He might've blacked out, for how long he had no idea, it could've been seconds or hours, but he'd come to with a sore throat and an incredible thirst. His first thought was for Peter. Their assailants had done a better job on his lover. The knife had cut deep, and the pool of blood underneath was all from his beloved.

Arkady's own throat had been slashed, but his attacker had done a poor job of it, breaking the skin, but not the jugular, nothing to bleed him out, not much more than a discomfort really. His blood had colored the back of Peter's suit jacket, darkening and wetting the material, no more than that. Arkady had fought back the nausea, because to vomit would be incredibly painful, and not at all helpful. He'd refused to break down and cry for his Peter. But he'd let panic take hold and had fled the scene. What if the assassins came back? And Arkady had no doubt that they'd been targeted, not merely for mugging, but because someone wanted to keep them quiet, permanently.

He'd run. Or staggered. Once he was certain that Peter was, indeed, dead, Arkady had slunk his way down the quiet and dark street. He couldn't go home. Most of the people he knew lived in Coney Island, all the way across Brooklyn, too far to travel in the wee hours of the morning. Nikos was the answer. He lived in Williamsburg, just a stone's throw from Bushwick, a distance that took him two hours to cover, and the morning light was creasing the horizon before he'd arrived. Nikos had generously taken him in and offered up his meager living space for as long as needed.

With a shake of his head to banish these painful memories from his mind, Arkady stood up and got a glass of water. His timepiece said that it was 2:00 a.m. His eyes flickered to the door. Nikos should be home soon. It was just about twenty-four hours since Arkady had regained consciousness, lying atop the lifeless corpse of the love of his life.

Nikos had borrowed an automobile and driven him out to the North Shore to see if Zelda would let him hide out in her country mansion. It was huge, out of Brooklyn, and well-hidden amongst the wealthy. She'd been adamant that Scott wouldn't put up with it and that he couldn't stay, trying to buy him off by pressing money into his hand. Money that he didn't need. He had money in the bank. Enough to flee the city. Perhaps go down to Miami. Or over to Chicago.

But, no, he wasn't going anywhere. Whoever was responsible for Peter's death was going to pay. They were going to suffer. Russians were vengeful people. And patient. Arkady was going to ensure that somebody paid for the death of Peter. For cutting his throat. And he didn't believe for a second that it'd been any sort of arbitrary attack.

It was possible that they'd simply been targeted for being gay. Or it was a random attack by some depraved individual. Or for their money. But Arkady knew that to not be true. Peter was dead because of what they were going to tell that big fellow, the private detective, the one looking for Velma, 8 Ballo. Their throats had been cut to keep them quiet. To silence them. That meant that Arkady most likely knew who was responsible for the death of his dear Peter. And that person must pay for their transgression. For ripping the heart right out of Arkady's chest.

There was a knock at the door. Arkady thought that was strange —Nikos had the key.

8 and Asta found Pearle and Clarissa at a table so far in the back it was almost on the street. The Nest was filling up fast, but was not as packed as it would be later on. Nine o'clock was relatively early for the place.

Ethel Waters was up on-stage crooning "You Can't Do What My Last Man Did," a song 8 knew as a dirge to a woman who took abuse once, but not again. *Listen, daddy mine.* 8 pulled the chair back for Asta and sat down as Waters' words caressed his senses. *So, daddy, there's the gate.*

"Nice table," 8 said drily.

"Son-of-a-bitch took the green from my hand and sat my Black ass back here where nobody would see us," Pearle said.

You've lost your nest, go east or west, but go, just go, now that last cruel papa, he blacked my eye, then left me alone to sigh and cry, but you can't do what that last man did.

Coleman Hawkins played a few more notes on the sax in accompaniment with Fletcher 'Smack' Henderson on the piano, and the crowd started clapping and hooting and hollering.

"Easier to talk back here, anyway," 8 said.

"That man was just angry because he don't ever get any pussy," Clarissa said.

Asta laughed and slapped the table. "That does seem to make a man uptight," she said.

8 found himself flushing. "It wasn't our friend, Nikos, was it?" he asked.

"No," Pearle said. "I asked him, and he said he was John. Probably a Brit."

"Nikos is Greek?" Asta asked.

"Yep. Dark eyes and hair and the shoulders of a god, or something like that," 8 said. "According to Zelda Fitzgerald, the writer."

"I thought it was the husband who wrote," Clarissa said.

"Zelda writes as well. She might even be the creative brains to his books," Pearle said. "Or so people whisper."

Ethel Waters finished another song, and after the clapping subsided, announced that they were going on break, and worked her way in their direction. Coleman Hawkins and Smack Henderson followed. They made their way to the table next to them where a long-legged Black woman sat by herself.

Hawkins was about to sit down when he caught sight of 8. "Hey, you're that fella who was looking for Velma. You ever find her?"

"No. Not yet," 8 said. "Still looking."

Clarissa cleared her throat. "You going to introduce us?"

8 fumbled his way through introducing Clarissa, Asta, and Pearle, and they ended up pushing their tables together, perhaps out of solidarity as being the only Black people in the speakeasy. The long-legged woman was a dancer named Ethel Williams and appeared to

be with Ethel Waters. This they confirmed in conversation after the other three went back to do another set.

Their waiter pointed out Nikos when asked and said that the bouncers started to go home just before two, after the crowd had dissipated. As Clarissa was completely enamored with Hawkins and Ethel Waters, they decided to put off approaching the man until the music was all done, sometime after one and before two. The musicians came back for another break at eleven, and then ended their night just after one.

"Can I buy you all a nightcap?" Pearle asked.

This didn't seem to be an offer that the band would consider refusing. Once the drinks had been delivered, 8 said, "Look, we got some business to attend to." Asta and Clarissa had already agreed to stay a bit longer, and if Pearle and 8 didn't reappear, take a yellow cab home.

"Don't you worry none," Hawkins said. "We'll keep an eye on your ladies."

Pearle shot him a dark look. 8 looked at Asta and saw that she'd barely registered they were leaving as she was caught up in conversation with Smack.

"You boys go do what you gotta do," Ethel said. "We should be here for at least another hour. My pipes need some lubrication."

They worked their way toward the door which Nikos now stood inside of next to another man, their hands clasped in front of them, eyes watching the crowd for any disruptions. The man did indeed have a rugged physique to match his jawline. He was only about six inches over five feet, so 8 figured he still had the man by sixty pounds, give or take a few.

"Mind if we ask you a question?" 8 said.

Nikos looked at him, judging his danger, a somewhat wary look at 8's bulk and Pearle at his side, not a small man either. "What'cha need?"

8 looked at the other bouncer next to him. "In private?"

Nikos stared hard at him. "What's this about?"

"Zelda told us you might know where to find somebody," 8 said.

Nikos showed surprise and then masked it. "I don't know what'cha talking about."

"Look, he was coming to see me the other night when he ran into some trouble," 8 said. "I just want to help."

"You're the gumshoe?" Nikos asked.

"8 Ballo. This is my associate, Pearle Hill."

"Arkady said you seemed like good people."

"We're just trying to help."

Nikos appeared to contemplate this. "Hey, Jake, I'm going to step outside for a minute." He led them down the stairs and outside to the sidewalk which was relatively barren. It was after all, a speakeasy, even if it was well known to everybody, including the police.

"Thank you for talking to us," 8 said. "We're here to help."

"What can I do for you?" Nikos lit a cigarette, the orange ember glowing in the darkness. The Nest was positioned equally between two streetlights, giving the entrance some anonymity.

"Arkady was supposed to meet me with some information the night Peter was killed," 8 said. "I'd like to find out what that was. I'm thinking that was the reason they were attacked."

Nikos nodded. "They cut his throat, too, just not deep enough. He won't tell me why, just that he's gotta hide out or disappear."

"We can help," Pearle said. "With either of those things."

"How can I trust you?"

8 shrugged. "What choice you got? If Arkady had a better option, you wouldn't be out here on the sidewalk talking to us right now."

"I don't got room for him to stay with me much longer, that's a fact," Nikos said.

"Where's your place?"

Nikos stared at 8 with his dark eyes, seemingly finding the answer he was looking for. "Just around the corner. Give me a minute, I'm pretty sure I can leave as the joint seems to be winding down for the night." He went back inside and up the stairs, leaving them outside on the sidewalk.

"You think Clarissa and Asta are okay?" Pearle asked.

"They seem to be doing just fine," 8 said drily. "Not sure Asta even noticed we left."

"It'd be a shame to kill a man who makes such beautiful sounds," Pearle said, "but he best be keeping his hands off my woman."

8 chuckled. "I think your concern should be whether she can keep her hands off him."

Pearle cursed at him and looked blackly down the street. They said no more until Nikos reemerged and led them in the direction Pearle had been staring. True to what he'd said, at the next street they took a right, and it was the fourth building on the left. They went up one flight of stairs and down a hallway.

"What the hell?" Nikos asked. His door was cracked open slightly. 8 went to grab his arm, but he was already pushing his way forward.

8 and Pearle drew their pistols, giving each other a look, and followed him through the entrance. The place was a mess. And quite empty.

Chapter 16

8 stared at the German businessman across the mahogany desk in his office at the wallpaper plant. Was it possible, he wondered, that this man had Peter killed and was trying to hunt down the surviving Arkady and finish the job? There had been no sign of violence at Nikos' apartment. No blood. Even though the place looked like an altercation had taken place, it turned out, that was the normal state of his bachelor pad. Arkady was gone, either willingly, or taken at gunpoint, but gone he was.

What was it that Arkady knew? What information might he possess that put his life in very mortal danger? Last night, they'd been close, oh so close, to finding out. But now, 8 was back to step one, no closer to finding Velma, no closer to uncovering the secret, and with no real leads to follow.

Pearle had been in a sour mood when they got back to The Nest and 8 had to keep a careful eye that he didn't crack Coleman Hawkins upside the noggin for having kept Clarissa company in their absence. 8 had to admit that he wasn't overly happy at the shine in Asta's eyes from conversing with some fellow named Smack, but he knew he had no call to jealousy. And the fact was, that Asta had gone home with him and spent the night, and it'd proven to be quite a pleasurable frolic.

"So, out with it," Hartmann asked, looking up from his papers. "What've you found?"

"I'm surprised to find you here, and not at church," 8 said.

"Been already. St. Paul's on Knickerbocker. Are you a religious man, Mr. Ballo?"

"Sure am," 8 said. He could've added that he just didn't know which one. None of the religions he'd heard of so far made much sense, but he was hoping that he would come across one that did sooner or later. It'd be nice to believe. "I see you got a few more fellows outside, loitering, with not much to do." He'd taken a careful look at their faces, trying to discern whether he'd seen any of them the previous day on their way to murdering a man, but he couldn't be certain, as it was a fleeting glance and from a distance at that. "Something happen?"

"I don't see how that has anything to do with you finding Velma."

"The other day when I spoke with you, I told you I was meeting up with a couple of fellows that might have information on where Velma is," 8 said. He looked around the spartan office, the sole portrait of Velma adorning the wall. Not for the first time, 8 thought how sexy the young lady was.

"The *homosexuals*." Hartmann said the word with distaste. "I remember. What of it."

"Before they could meet up with me, these *gentlemen* were attacked, and one was killed. Had his throat cut. The other one disappeared."

"And what?"

"As far as I know, you were the only one who knew I was meeting them."

Hartmann glared at him. "Are you suggesting that I slashed the throat of a fancy man?"

"Did you?"

"No."

"Did you send some of your goons out to bump them off?"

"I'm a businessman, Mr. Ballo. I do not have people bumped off."

"I have a pal who owns a place just up the street from here," 8 said. "I was over there yesterday late afternoon and saw you speaking with a couple carloads of men toting heavy artillery. Thought I'd follow them, see where they went. Seems they went up to Williamsburg and whacked a guy. An Italian. What do you know about that?"

"You, Mr. Ballo, are the reason that the police came and spoke with me?" The only indication Hartmann gave of his anger was the flaring of his nostrils and the steeliness of his eyes. "I'll tell you the same thing I told them. A car pulled over as I was walking, and asked me directions, which I gave them, and that was all there was to it."

Son-of-a-gun, 8 thought, *Pearle hit the nail on the head with what the cover story was.* "Where were they going? The candy store?"

"My daughter, Mr. Ballo. What are you doing to find her?"

"I believe finding this man—the *gentleman* that got away—will help in that pursuit." 8 watched Hartmann's features closely, but, if the man did have a tell, he couldn't see it. He almost believed that the man had had nothing to do with the attack upon Peter and Arkady. "I tracked him to an apartment in Williamsburg last night, but he was gone before I got there."

"Can I help you with… resources?" Hartmann asked. "I have men that could be put to use."

"I'll let you know." 8's eyes flickered to a photograph on the desk in a frame. "Was that your wife?" The woman was blonde-haired and fair of skin.

Hartmann's eyes softened. "Yes. Petra. She was the candle guiding me through life."

"How did she… pass away?"

Hartmann's mouth twitched, a kink of the upper lip. "Consumption killed her." He stared down at his desk. "I thought she was getting better. She'd lost so much weight, but her cough was improving, rarely blood and less mucous, and then one morning she didn't open her eyes."

"I'm sorry for your loss."

"I will know her again upon the eternal return," Hartmann said softly.

"Nietzsche," 8 said. Nietzsche had been a favorite of Professor Harvey, both during 8's college days and later in the trenches of the Great War. In those last days before he died, Oliver Hardy had talked much about meeting 8 again in some future universe in which he hoped he might be a little less foolish.

Hartmann looked up with surprise. "You know of his belief in eternal reoccurrence?"

"I'm not sure that I believe it myself, but yes, I know of it. The universe repeating itself."

"You continue to surprise me, Mr. Ballo."

"Last time we spoke, you suggested that Velma may've had something to do with the disappearance of Colleen Brooks," 8 said. "Would you care to expound on that?"

"I would not."

"You said that Velma might've run away because you thought her guilty of foul play regarding Colleen. What did you mean by that?"

"You are a persistent man, Mr. Ballo." Hartmann sighed and leaned back in his chair. "I didn't say that I thought her guilty. I said that *she* may believe that I thought her guilty. A distinction."

"And why would she think that?"

"Velma hated any woman I was with, especially Colleen, as she was the same age as her. She would sometimes, when angry, tell me that she was going to kill—excuse my language—kill that bitch and dump her in the East River."

"And then Colleen disappeared?"

"And then Colleen disappeared."

8 sifted this through his mind. "And do you think that Velma had something to do with Colleen's... vanishing?"

"I think that Colleen got tired of me and moved on. She talked about wanting to go to Hollywoodland and be in the moving pictures. She'd been in a few small roles here, but that is where the real deal was happening, or so she said. I suspect that one of these days we'll see her in a film, is what I believe."

"She got tired of you cuz you were too old and couldn't keep up?" 8 asked.

Hartmann's eyes flashed irritation. "She got tired of me because she was a silly little thing who didn't know what she wanted."

"Why am I really looking for your daughter, Mr. Hartmann?" 8 asked. The man was paying well, so he didn't want to look a gift horse in the mouth, but the question had to be posed. "I mean, she is an adult, and she appears to be living her life as she chooses, however much it may not be to your liking."

"She's an adult in years only," Hartman said. "Her mind has the fragility of an adolescent. She flits from thing to thing with the attention span of a small child."

"Velma is, was, a regular at the round table at the Algonquin Hotel, Mr. Hartmann. That group is considered to be one of the great intellectual gatherings in all of the city. She calls writers and musicians of the highest caliber in the world friend. I don't think your assessment of your daughter is all that accurate, or perhaps not that honest?"

"That group you refer to is frivolous, with little thought to anything of merit. Fashion and entertainment, idols of the foolish they are."

8 weighed this carefully and found it wanting. "The fact is that Velma seems quite capable of taking care of herself."

Hartmann stared at 8 with unflinching eyes, and then he broke, his glance falling back to his desk. "I accused her of murdering Colleen," he said. "In anger when she came into the house in the middle of the night falling down drunk. I fear that is why she's flown off in the wind."

8 waited. He sensed that there was more.

Hartmann cleared his throat. "Your assessment of my troubles with Bugsy and Lansky is correct. I bootleg some hooch and have other endeavors that have crossed over into what they consider to be their territory. Things have, become, shall we say, tense. I'm afraid that they might abduct or harm Velma to get to me."

"But they haven't."

"If Velma is here, I can protect her. If she's out on the streets doing God knows what? I fear those Jew boys will get their hands on her to get at me."

Pearle picked 8 up outside the wallpaper plant at exactly one o'clock. "Where to now, boss?" he asked as 8 climbed into the motorcar.

"Hartmann allowed that he does participate in some unsavory business practices," 8 said. "Dealings that have caused friction with the Jews and Italians in Brooklyn."

"You mean Bugsy and Lansky?" Pearle asked.

"That'd be the Jews I'm referring to," 8 said. "I understand that they are working in association with Salvatore Luciano. Marty said they got friendly after Luciano beat Lansky bloody, or something like that. Seems a strange way to start a friendship."

"Lansky and Luciano were in the Five Points Gang together," Pearle said.

"I don't think Hartmann's dumb enough to take on Luciano, but he doesn't hold much respect for the Bugsy and Lansky gang. Seems his bootlegging business is overlapping theirs."

"Not to mention the heroin and the whore houses," Pearle said.

"He failed to mention those but did allow there were a couple of other endeavors that might be adding to the problem. I sort of got the impression that you might be right that he's into those as well."

"And this is pertinent to finding Velma how?"

"Hartmann's afraid that she's in danger," 8 said. "That Bugsy might snatch her or harm her to get to him."

"What do you think?"

"I think we should go ask them."

Pearle laughed a deep rumble. "You do take the bull right by the horns, don't you?"

"Don't want the damn thing sneaking up behind me."

"We going to the Candy Store?" It seemed that Pearle also knew that Bugsy and Lansky had made their headquarters in the back room of a candy store down in Brownsville.

"That was the thought."

Pearle hit the accelerator and squealed out into traffic. 8 was glad to have the man watching his back but wasn't sure how much he trusted him as a chauffeur.

The Midnight Rose Candy Store had an awning over the nondescript brick and glass façade that said, CANDY-SODA-CIGARS. The owner, Rose Gold, was a wisp of an elderly lady with sharp eyes. The shop was open twenty-fours a day, hence the name. As they parked, a train rattled its way overhead on the elevated tracks.

Rosie gave them a no-nonsense stare when 8 asked to see Siegel and Lansky. He knew enough to not call him Bugsy, a name over which Siegel had reportedly broken several legs. There was a man to the rear of the shop sitting in a chair reading a paper next to a door. Rosie's eyes flickered in his direction.

The man rapped on the door three times when they asked access. A small panel at the top slid open. The man gathered their names and a few minutes later he asked them to place their guns, except he said gats, in a box on a table next to his chair. He then patted them down, knocked twice more, and in they went.

They went through another small room past several men who cast them dark looks. The next room had a long table at which Bugsy Siegel, Mayer Lansky, and two other men were seated. There were no windows and smoke swirled through the air of the dimly lit room.

Lansky was reading something and didn't look up, but Bugsy stood with a wide smile on his face. "8 Ballo and sidekick. Welcome." He wore a gray chalk-stripe flannel suit with a wide silk tie and a white handkerchief in the breast pocket.

8 nodded. "Benji Siegel. This is my associate, Pearle Hill."

"Sit. You two," he waved at the two other men, "get up and give up your seats. Can I get you something to drink?" When they responded to the negative, he sat back down, and they followed suit. "What can we do for you?"

"As you know, I've been hired to find a young lady. Velma Hartmann." 8 could feel his neck prickling with the two men standing behind him.

"That's what you said."

8 didn't know any way to dance around asking what he wanted to know. So he didn't try. "Fritz Hartmann says that bad blood has developed between you and him."

Bugsy's smile never wavered. "Hartmann has been straying out of his neighborhood."

"He's afraid that you might've taken or hurt his daughter to get at him."

Bugsy slammed the table with an open hand. He leaned forward, his eyes bulging dangerously. "We might operate outside the edge of the law. But we do not *take* or *harm* women."

"I believe you," 8 said as calmly as possible. "I just thought it best to hear this directly from your mouth."

"You've some brass balls on you, Mr. 8 Ballo," Bugsy said.

Lansky looked up from what he was reading. "As you mentioned, we've had some problems with Hartmann straying into our territory with his hooch, heroin, and whores."

"That is none of my concern," 8 said. "I'm merely looking to find Velma Hartmann."

"So you say. Maybe you're here as some sort of recon operation," Lansky said. "Scope out our operation and then report back to that German bastard."

"I'm no stooge. I just want to find the girl and make sure she's okay."

"How do we know that?" Lansky asked.

8 shrugged. "I guess you're going to have to trust me."

"I don't trust anybody," Lansky said.

"We could see what the Kraut has to say," Bugsy said. "See if he knows what these boys are up to."

"Hmm. Either way, we can send a message," Lansky said. "I like it. Levi, go gather the Kraut and bring him back. And a couple of flour sacks."

8 didn't like the sounds of that. He measured the two men across the table. There was still a goon behind him. Even if he got the upper hand, there'd been five or six other fellows in the outer room, and who knew what was outside the door that the man named Levi had just gone through. Plus, one at the door back into the candy shop. He looked sideways at Pearle with a silent message as a gun barrel pressed into the back of his head.

"Sit tight, Mr. Ballo," Lansky said with a smile. "If your intentions are above board, we don't intend to hurt you."

Bugsy pulled a short and ugly pistol from his waistband and pointed it casually at Pearle. The door opened, and the man returned carrying two flour sacks, followed by two more goons dragging a bloodied figure.

"Seat him there, at the head of the table," Bugsy said.

The man's breathing was ragged and broken, indicating that he'd most likely been in the middle of being tortured, and was terrified on top of that. Blood dripped from his nose, mixing with snot to make small bubbles, and when he opened his mouth, jagged teeth were exposed behind split lips.

"Thank you for joining us," Lansky said pleasantly. "My understanding is that you've been very helpful in sharing information. We now have a much better understanding of Fritz Hartmann's operation."

The man's eyes were flat and dull. Lifeless.

"There is one more thing that I require of you," Lansky said. "Could you look at the two gentlemen to your right. Do you know them?"

The man's eyes remained staring at the tabletop.

Bugsy stood up and backhanded the man across the face. "Goddamn it, Kraut. You were asked to do something."

The man's head wobbled, but he was steadied from behind. He looked over at 8 and Pearle. Slowly, he shook his head to the negative.

"You've never seen these men before?" Bugsy asked. "Are you sure?"

"Never." The voice was barely audible.

"Do you know that your boss lost his daughter?" Lansky asked.

The man nodded yes.

"And that he hired a private dick to find her?"

The man nodded yes.

"Do you know what that man's name was?"

"8 Ballo." The name gurgled from the man's bloody mouth.

"Does this 8 Ballo work for your gang?"

"Not that I know of."

Lansky nodded. "I believe you." He nodded at the men behind 8 and Pearle. "Don't worry, gentlemen, this is just so you don't see anything you shouldn't see."

A flour sack settled over 8's head blocking light and sight. This was when they'd be killed, he knew. A simple bullet to the back of the head. But why the flour sacks? He considered throwing himself backward into the man behind him, or maybe flinging himself across the table at Lansky. The goon would hesitate to shoot for fear of hitting the boss.

"Easy, 8," Pearle said. "They're not planning on hurting us."

As if to mock his words, a gunshot rang out, deafening in the confines of the room. 8 heard a body crumple to the floor. A long minute passed, and then the flour sack was pulled from his head.

Pearle still sat next to him. The German was gone. One of the goons was mopping something up, wringing the red water into a bucket.

"See these two out, Levi," Lansky said.

8 and Pearle followed the man Levi to the door.

"Hey, 8 Ballo," Bugsy said.

8 stopped and turned back around.

"Stop looking for the girl. She don't want to be found."

Chapter 17

Wednesday afternoon, 8 sat at his desk with his feet up, pondering the next step. Any sort of leads had dried up regarding Velma, Arkady, or Colleen Brooks. As Bugsy had had his opportunity to murder him and had chosen not to, 8 figured he might as well let Pearle return to running his business empire, at least until 8 had a lead to investigate. Bugsy, had, after all, told him to stop looking for Velma.

It seemed likely that there was a connection between Velma and Bugsy. Coleman Hawkins had suggested that Velma spoke a bit about a fellow named Benji, Siegel's given name. Bugsy was known for being a bit of a ladies' man, especially since gang life had boomed. He wore fancy clothes, smoked expensive cigars, and frequented expensive joints. It wasn't hard to imagine that he'd crossed paths with Velma, and it was just as likely some dive as Delmonico's.

Why would Velma take up with a man who her father was preparing to go to war with? 8 had no doubt that Bugsy and Lansky had killed the man the other night, the German fellow in Hartmann's employ. Retaliation would follow if it hadn't already. He mentally made a note to check in with McGee at the 83rd Precinct to see what the police knew. Probably wouldn't hurt to pay a visit to Marty, as well, because an investigative reporter for the *Brooklyn Eagle* was often ahead of the cops as far as being in the know.

Velma could just be a rebellious daughter acting against the wishes of her father. Going off with the last man who he'd want her to be with, the charismatic enemy threatening his lifestyle and life. Or had Velma, spending time with Bugsy, caused her father to start a war to erase the man who he didn't want her seeing? Of course, 8 had no idea that the Benji who Hawkins referred to even *was* Siegel.

A ringing interrupted his reverie. 8 wasn't a big fan of this telephone thing, but he supposed it served its purpose. He slid his feet to the floor and removed the receiver from the cradle.

"8 Ballo, Private Investigator."

The husky purr of Dottie's voice, already showing the ravages of too many Chesterfields, filled his ear. "Why, yes, Mr. Ballo. I'd like to hire you for the evening."

8 chuckled. "I'm sorry, ma'am, but I don't think you can afford me."

"I quite believe that you are wrong, Mr. Ballo. My payment will be most appreciated."

"That it will," 8 said, blushing slightly. "I'd be happy to take you on as a client."

Dottie snickered. "Don't you want to hear how I plan on paying for your... services?"

"I, yes, um, I would."

"I've made contact with a certain young lady who you've been looking for," Dottie said. "And I believe that I can arrange a meeting between you."

This took 8, expecting a reply of a more carnal nature, a bit by surprise. Even if they'd decided that any sort of physical intimacy was off-limits, this wasn't reflected in their words as they flirtatiously bantered. "Velma?"

"Yes, Mr. Ballo. How'd you think I was going to pay you?"

"I, uh—"

"You do realize that I'm a *married* woman, don't you, Mr. Ballo?"

8 did, indeed, know that. "I wasn't sure what I thought," he said.

"I'm just joshing with you, my dear 8. Eddie and I haven't seen eye to eye in quite some time. He does his thing, and I do mine.

The fact is, we wouldn't be good for each other in bed. I fear it'd ruin our friendship."

"Are we, indeed, friends, Mrs. Parker?"

"I'd love to believe so."

"Well, I will treasure that notion."

"As will I, but back to the matter at hand."

"Where's Velma?"

"Ah, aren't you the impatient one. Not quite yet, Mr. Ballo. I believe that I wanted to hire you for a task."

"Yes, of course. What is it?"

"*Iolanthe* is being presented by the Brooklyn Choristers this evening at the Brooklyn Academy of Music. I just can't find a single soul who'd like to accompany me."

"The Gilbert and Sullivan production?"

"Yes. It's a fundraiser for the St. Vincent Home for Boys."

"Should we do dinner before?"

"If you mean a glass of gin, why, then, yes, that'd be nice."

"Thanks for the pint," McGee said. "I don't imagine this is out of the goodness of your heart."

8 had found the man just getting off his shift at the station and had enticed him down the street to a speakeasy in one of the many pre-Prohibition German breweries.

"What'd you find out about the hit up in Williamsburg the other day?" 8 asked.

"The one where you and Pearle hid under the car?"

"It seemed the prudent decision at the time and still does."

McGee took a healthy belt of the foamy beer. "Don't think he was one of Bugsy and Lansky's gang."

"They're mixed in with some Italians."

"Yeah, but not him. Word on the street is that Tito was a hitter for Nicolò Schirò."

"I forgot all about that fucking Sicilian. He operates out of Williamsburg, doesn't he?"

"You got it. He keeps his nose clean is why you didn't think of him. Deals primarily with other Sicilians."

"Yeah, old guard. What do they call them traditionalists in gangland?"

"Mustache Petes." McGee finished his beer and raised his glass for another. "Only time Schirò has been ever arrested was eighteen years ago for operating a butcher shop on a Sunday. Keeps his head down and deals only with people he trusts."

"No Jews need apply, huh?"

"Not even mainland Italians. Strictly Sicilians."

8 shook his head in consternation. "Why the hell is Hartmann hitting one of Schirò's men? He's starting a war with Bugsy and Lansky down in Brownsville and at the same time taking on the Sicilians in Williamsburg. It doesn't make sense."

"No. Not at all."

"Bugsy killed one of Hartmann's men down at his candy shop the other day," 8 said.

"How ya' know that?" McGee asked with surprise. "I hadn't heard anything about that."

"Me and Pearle were there with bags over our heads." 8 went on to fill in the details of the Sunday escapade.

McGee raised one of his dark eyebrows at him. "And you didn't report it?"

"Like I said, we had bags over our heads, and the body was gone when they pulled 'em off. Fellow was mopping up blood, but what was there to report?"

"Give us coppers a chance to go in and shake them lads up a wee bit, it would."

8 snorted. "Give a couple of fellows in uniform a chance to go in with their hands out and make some vacation money, is what you mean."

"We might look the other way when lads are serving hooch, but we don't take no bribes from murderers," McGee said hotly.

"Is that right?" 8 shook his head no at the offer of another beer. "I saw Hartmann on Sunday as well. Couldn't help but wonder why he wasn't in jail?"

"He had…" McGee trailed off, looked down, and muttered what sounded like an Irish curse word. "Word came down from the top brass to go gently."

"Ah, so the bribe was made at an upper level instead of to a flattie, is that the problem?"

"You come here to insult me, or ya need something more?" McGee asked.

"Yeah, I could use a favor."

"Funny goddamn way to go about asking for a favor."

"Bought you a couple of beers, didn't I?"

McGee laughed. "You know your way to my heart, alright. Go ahead. What do you need?"

"You want to keep your eyes and ears open all things Hartmann? I aim to find his daughter, but I don't want to get caught in the middle of the ring between Jack Dempsey and Tommy Gibbons, if you know what I mean."

"You're in the middle of the ring alright, me lad, but it looks like you got three heavyweights in there with you, not just two. Hartman, Bugsy, and now Schirò? Not much space to dance."

"What do you know about Nicolò Schirò?" 8 asked.

Marty looked back at him over the rim of his pint glass. "Sicilian. Older than a lot of the new blood, which means two things. First, life is changing around him at a pace that is almost incomprehensible to him."

8 waited, but there didn't seem to be any more forthcoming information, not even after Marty polished off half of his beer. It was

becoming an expensive afternoon. "And thing two?" he prompted.

"Thing two is he's still alive and still here after all these years. You don't last long as a gang leader unless you're damn cagey, careful, and savage."

"You know a fellow by the name of Tito Cattaneo? Rumor has it he's a hitter for Schirò."

"I know he got bumped off the other day," Marty said. "Why're you asking?"

"Me, McGee, and Pearle followed some of Hartmann's goons over to Williamsburg. They were the ones who killed him."

"That, I didn't hear," Marty said. "Police kept that quiet. What the hell is Hartmann doing starting a war with Schirò for?"

"That's what I was hoping you'd know."

Marty shook his head. "No idea."

"Can you take a guess?"

"What you don't see with your eyes, don't invent with your mouth." Marty raised his empty pint for a refill.

8 sighed. "Yeah, I know, your grandmother drilled that into your head. I won't hold you to it. What do you hear?"

"Some people say that there's trouble brewing between the old guard of Italian gangsters and the new and upcoming blood. The Mustache Petes don't like working with the Jews and the Irish. The newbies, the modern Italian gangsters, like Salvatore Luciano, don't care what you are, as long as you do your job."

"Interesting. You find out anything more, I'd appreciate it. I think Velma's caught up in all this somehow."

"The best streets in the world go two ways," Marty said.

"Could be a good scoop for you. The story of the year. Put your name all over the country."

"Yeah, you're doing me a favor. Sure." Marty laughed thinly. "You got any more favors you want to bestow upon me?"

"I could tell you that Bugsy bumped off one of Hartmann's men down to Brownsville on Sunday, but I didn't see it with my own eyes, so I won't invent it with my mouth."

"Who'd you hear it from?"

8 chuckled. "Nobody. But this is what I heard and what I saw." He told Marty about Sunday afternoon with Pearle. "I'm betting Bugsy murdered him but can't be sure."

Marty shook his head. "You two saps went to the Candy Store and knocked on the back-room door and asked Bugsy Siegel if he killed young women?"

"Yep, that's pretty much how it went down," 8 said. "Seems that Hartmann is trying to expand outside of Bushwick. Stepping on toes in Williamsburg and Brownsville."

"I'll see what I can find out," Marty said.

8 took the elevated cars down to a gin joint just around the corner from the Brooklyn Academy of Music. He got there early, but Dottie was already at the bar, an admiring crowd of men surrounding her as she expounded caustically on the current mayor of New York City. Her dress was long, brown, and sleeveless with sequins around the low-cut collar. Two longer necklaces drooped low between her cleavage with tiny blue crystals, while a shorter silver necklace with a larger blue crystal clung to her neck.

Dottie allowed herself to be removed from the bar to a table in the corner where she polished off three more drinks while he sipped his single gin. He was not a big fan, preferring brown liquor, or even rum, but when in Rome… She told him that his payment, an arrangement to meet with Velma, would be proffered after he attended *Iolanthe*.

8 was not a huge Gilbert and Sullivan fan. Especially not of comic opera. The flitting relationships between fairies and mortals became boring to him long before the second act, and he had all he could do to keep from falling asleep. Plus, he needed food, and not just gin. At the end, when all the fairies and mortals had found each other, he suggested to Dottie that they get some food.

"Where did you have in mind?" she asked.

"There's a pretty good tavern on the first floor of my building," he said.

"Are you inviting me to come home with you, Mr. Ballo?"

"I'm offering to buy you dinner, Mrs. Parker."

"Do you suppose we could find a smidgen of gin to bring along while… you eat?"

8 chuckled. Dottie had been sipping from a flask in her purse throughout the opera. "There's a speakeasy in the basement underneath the restaurant. They'll bring food down."

Dottie snickered. "My, your building certainly has it all. Hooch in the basement, food on the first floor, a private dick on the second floor, and your bed on the third."

The basement speakeasy had been created out of necessity when Prohibition began. What had once been a hodge-podge of cluttered storage and forgotten items had been cleared out, the windows already only half-exposed to daylight were blacked out, and shelves built to hold alcohol. Now, three years into the teetotaling, a bar had been built, tables added, and the lighting was substantially better, even if still a tad shadowy.

8 started off with a roast beef stew with red cabbage and dumplings, moved onto a Wiener Schnitzel, the breaded cutlet filled with ham and cheese melting in his mouth, and finished with pork knuckle. Dottie ate a canape of anchovies, and for once, didn't speak as she watched him eat with wonder.

"Impressive, my dear 8. I'd ask where it all goes, but you do have quite the chassis, don't you?" Dottie said when he was done.

"Seem to have missed eating today," he said. "And I might need my energy for later."

"Oh, you might, might you? Whatever for?"

8 grinned. "As you seem to be keeping secret my appointment

with the mysterious Velma Hartmann, I suppose I wasn't sure if that might be happening tonight."

"Oh, no, not tonight," Dottie said with what appeared mock horror. "You'll be otherwise preoccupied this evening."

They bantered, flirted, moved upstairs to his dining table with more drinks, but went no further than laughter and playful banter, a few confidences exchanged, youthful—and not so youthful—indiscretions. It seemed that a line in the sand had been drawn, one that was not to be crossed. 8 was fine with that. It wasn't often that one was able to have a woman friend. It'd seem that Dottie Parker might be his first.

Chapter 18

Arkady had managed to withdraw his money from the bank, $942. He'd splurged and taken a room at the Hotel Margaret, on an upper floor, looking out over the Manhattan skyline, the Brooklyn Bridge to his right, and the East River below. Nobody would be looking for him here among the hoity-toity. The concept of hiding in plain sight amused him, and he smiled ironically, the grin quickly vanishing as he thought of his dead beloved, Peter.

He changed his thoughts to the large *chelovek*, the PI, and wondered about contacting him, enlisting his help. The problem was that 8 was busy looking for the girl, hired by Fritz Hartmann, and Arkady was bent upon revenge. Peter had been killed and his own throat cut to stop them from spilling what they knew to a man who might be able to do something about it. The worst part, Arkady thought, was that Peter hadn't wanted to get involved. His lover had suggested that they let sleeping dogs lie, and that it wasn't any of their business.

And now Peter was dead. It was not 8 Ballo's role to find and punish the perpetrator. It was for Arkady to avenge. He slipped his Fedora on and stepped into the hallway and walked down to the elevator. He pushed the button and listened as the pulleys whirred to life and brought the wooden box trundling upward to the fourteenth floor. An older bloke by the name of Henry was the operator today, sliding the metal grating open and greeting him with a friendly smile, calling him Mr. Sokolov, the alias he'd used when checking in.

Arkady had thought it appropriate to use the Russian name meaning bird of prey for the time being. Because that is what he was, a Peregrine Falcon, circling the sky a full kilometer high, looking for his victim. When found, he'd descend at a speed of over 300 kilometers in his hunting stoop to strike his unwitting quarry with a ferocity similar to that which Catherine the Great displayed when she had her husband killed. In that case, Peter had been the victim, and in Arkady's case, Peter would be the avenged.

The lift bumped and groaned itself down to the ground floor. Arkady went around the corner to a shop that sold a variety of items. Only one such item interested him. He bought a Colt revolver and a box of ammunition. He'd have his vengeance and then he'd disappear, maybe down to Miami or out to Chicago. But not until he'd killed, his first, only, and rightful taking of a life.

Colleen Brooks had grown up in the borough of Caldwell, New Jersey. It was time to pay her family a visit, 8 decided, giving Pearle a ring to see if he wanted to venture outside of the city. Pearle said that there was no way he was taking the train, and that he wouldn't be caught dead floating across the Hudson River on a car float, the barges that transported the trains from the city to New Jersey. He did, however, know of somebody with a flatboat that would take them and Pearle's automobile over and back. It seemed the man owed him a favor. Or worked for him. Or something like that.

Caldwell was a small town carved out of the woods next to a swamp. The road in was a rutted mess of bumps, and 8 was scalded by curses from Pearle for most of the sixteen-mile ride. Pearle was not much of a country fellow, a third generation Brooklynite. His grandfather had been freed from slavery during Sherman's march to the sea and had promptly made his way to what was then the village of Bedford in King's County.

They met Dan Brooks at his home above the dry goods store that he owned. His wife, whose name they were never offered, hovered in the doorway, listening and trying not to be seen. Dan told them that Colleen was the third of seven children, and that two of them were still at home, but were currently at school. He said this proudly, boasting that he was well-enough off to allow his children to get an education. The two older ones were currently downstairs. He didn't mention the final two, and 8 surmised they'd struck out on their own or had died, either way, they were dead to Dan Brooks.

"Colly was different," Dan said, his eyes gleaming. "There was something special about her."

"In what way?" 8 asked. "Did she excel in school?"

Dan laughed. He was a thin man with impeccable posture, perhaps to the point of being painful, 8 thought. His eyes seemed to judge the value of every word spoken and had lingered on Pearle a tad too long. 8 had seen the dismissal flicker past, whether of the man or the notion of making a statement, it was hard to tell.

"Colly shone from inside out," Dan said. "She radiated life and made people happy."

8 noted the past tense. "When was the last time you saw your daughter?"

"Two years, three months, and one week ago, tomorrow," Dan said without hesitation.

"Seems you been keeping track," Pearle said.

Dan looked at him with a small wince to the corners of his mouth before turning back to 8. "She was going to be something real special, Colly was. You know she was in a couple of moving pictures, don't you? I never got me a chance to see them, but a gent here in town saw one and said she stole the whole thing, even if she was barely in it at all."

"She was an actress, then?" 8 asked. This he knew, from the assumption by Fritz that she'd gone off to Hollywoodland to become famous, but he figured it'd be helpful to see what Dan Brooks knew of all this.

"Sure. She did some other work as well. She was good girl, Colly was. Worked hard."

"What other work did she do?"

"She sent us a letter once a week, telling us how fabulous Brooklyn was. How many friends she'd made. Said she was working as one of them there telephone operators."

"She give you any names?"

"Not so much. Just said that—"

"She went on and on about a young lady named Velma," Mrs. Brooks said, fluttering slightly inside the door and then bobbing back.

Dan cast a glare at the door. "Yeah, that's right," he said. "Said she was living with her in some fancy mansion. When the letters stopped coming, we went and looked up that Velma. Hartmann was her last name. She lived with her father in a great big house in Bushwick."

8 thought it probably time that he paid a visit to the Hartmann mansion. See what clues might have been left around. "What'd this Velma Hartmann have to tell you?"

"Said that Colly took a train to the West Coast. Was going to Hollywoodland, or some such place. Velma said that Colly was going out there to be in the moving pictures, and that's where they was starting to make them. The new and upcoming moving picture mecca, or some such thing."

8 thought there was a tinge of skepticism to Dan's tone. "But you have your doubts that Colly went to Hollywoodland?"

"She would've told us," Dan said plaintively. "She would've come out to say goodbye first, before she went all the God's way across the whole country."

"Young people these days seem to take off on the slightest whim," 8 said. "You don't suppose a passing fancy put her on a train before she thought it through?"

Dan pursed his thin lips. "It's possible, I suppose. But she would've sent us a letter since, wouldn't she? I mean, we're her family."

"Show 'em the letter," Mrs. Brooks said, again flitting just inside the door. "Show 'em what she sent."

Dan sighed, glared, but stood up and walked over to a rolltop desk, fiddled in a drawer, and came back with an envelope. He carefully pulled a piece of paper out and handed it over to 8. Pearle sidled closer to read it over his shoulder.

It painted a picture of Colleen Brooks that 8 hadn't heard, some made up fairy tale to share with her ma and pa, about a young lady living in Brooklyn who worked hard, went to bed at dark and rose at light. It said nothing about late night speakeasies, dancing in scanty clothes, nor being the kept woman of a man her parents' age.

Of course, 8 thought to himself, *what young flapper would tell her parents the truth?* He didn't blame the girl. Heck, he barely understood, but it was a new age, that was for sure, and women were asserting their rights to experience the pleasures of life same as men, and that certainly seemed fair enough.

But there was one part that stood out like the headlights of an automobile on a dark night.

I've been given by my friend a bunch of dresses. They are very expensive and elegant. But they are a dead woman's and that makes me feel odd about wearing them.

I'm not sure that I have any choice, as it would be rude to refuse a gift such as that. The thing is, it makes me look like her. Ma, you'd love them. When I come see you in May, I will wear one.

"Colly told us in another letter that Velma's mother had died of consumption," Mrs. Brooks said. "I'm thinking it was her dresses that she was talking about."

"She said she was coming over to visit with us," Dan said. "In May. Why'd she write that if she was planning on going out to Hollywoodland?"

"When did she send you this?" 8 asked

"It was the beginning of April. The last one we got," Dan said. His voice sounded a bit choked up.

Chapter 19

8 was again paying the bill. This time it was for Martin Hoffman at Ethan's Delicatessen, underneath the Brooklyn Bridge. The joint was groceries on one side and tables for eating on the other.

If the man was out digging up information for him, it certainly seemed payment enough, but a scoop on the potential story seemed fair enough. Plus, he'd given him the lead on Bugsy and Meyer killing one of Hartmann's minions at the Candy Store. Oh, well. It was not like 8 was actually paying, as he'd be expensing Hartmann for it.

"What'd ya find out about the dead fellow?" 8 asked.

"Tito Cattaneo," Marty said. "Was most certainly in the employ of Nicolò Schirò." He took a bite from his pastrami sandwich, chewing noisily. "Came over from Sicily about five years back and rose up through the ranks."

"Any idea why he got whacked?" 8 looked at the remaining portion of his salami sandwich. He figured he was going to have to get more to eat. It certainly wasn't a portion that he'd recommend for an adult male.

"It could be that Hartmann's trying to get back in the good graces of Rothstein and Luciano. Seems to be a conflict brewing between the modern gangster and the old guard. The purists like Schirò don't think the Italians should be doing business with the Jews and Irish. Luciano seems to be interested in making money, no matter who he's doing it with."

"Even the Germans," 8 said.

"Even the Germans."

"Don't make sense, though, does it?" 8 said. "Hartmann whacks one of Schirò's goons, and then Bugsy turns around and kills one of his. Last time I checked, Lansky and Luciano were bosom buddies, and they keep Bugsy on a tight chain."

"All these gangs are loosely affiliated, in one way or another, but that don't mean they don't act autonomously on most things," Marty said. "Maybe Hartmann's even trying to throw a wedge in between Luciano and the Bugsy and Meyer gang."

"Could be," 8 said doubtfully. "I suppose."

"But I don't actually believe any of that phooey."

"Yeah? Why not?"

"Here's the thing," Marty said, taking another bite. "Tito ran with a bloke named Tomas Lombardo. They shared the apartment that Tito got whacked in."

"Yeah?" 8 rolled that around in his mind. "You thinking if we find Tomas, we might have a better idea of why Hartmann sent some Chicago lightning his way?"

"Nope. Think I might already have a guess."

"Yeah? You thinking about sharing it?"

"I'm thinking about getting a piece of pie," Marty said. "You want some?"

8 was about to reach out and shake his friend into spilling whatever it was that he was building up to, but then caught himself. The pies he'd spied under a glass case when he entered the delicatessen had looked absolutely delicious. "Yeah, that'd be good."

Marty snapped his finger and asked the elderly waiter to bring them two slices of the apple pie. With cream. And coffee.

"Okay, get to it," 8 said. "You're squirming around in your seat like a five-year-old that's got to take a whizz."

"My sources tell me that Tomas Lombardo has been hanging around some broad lately, only she isn't Italian. Quite a scuttlebutt, really, for a Sicilian to be running around with some dame with white skin and German heritage."

"You're not telling me—"

"Haven't got a name yet, but two different sources say she's a flapper, fits the description of Velma Hartmann, and has hooked Tomas by the nose and is leading him around like a prize bull at the fair."

8 whistled. The pie got delivered, and he took the opportunity while eating it to ponder the significance of Velma, if it were she, spending time with some Sicilian gangster. Before he knew it, he was shoveling the last piece into his mouth.

"Sounds like it wasn't a hit," 8 said. "What happened, was, Fritz Hartmann sent these fellows to get his daughter back, only she wasn't there, and the other guy, Tito, made the mistake of answering the door."

"That's how I read it," Marty said.

"Which makes me wonder what Velma is doing with this Tomas fellow, and where they are now."

"*Ken*. That is exactly the question, my gentile friend."

"I just suppose I'll have to ask her, then," 8 said.

"Easier said than done." Marty stood up, indicating he was done. "Isn't the whole point of this to find *where* she is?"

8 chuckled and stood as well. "Velma is supposed to call me this evening to set up a get-together."

"Aha, case closed," Marty said. "You find out where at she wants to meet, you call Hartmann and tell him, and you've found your girl."

"Things have gotten a bit more complicated than that," 8 said, dropping a dollar on the table to cover the lunch.

At 10:00 p.m., the phone in 8's office rang. Right on time.

"This is 8 Ballo."

"Hello, Mr. 8 Ballo. I'm the girl you've been looking for."

"Hello, Velma. Nice to actually speak with you."

"Well, I've been hearing so much about you from Dottie. You've certainly been a busy boy." Her words were only slightly flirtatious, he thought, and not at all girlish or cutesy, either. "I was wondering if you might have a drink with me. We could get to know each other."

"I'd like that. Where do you have in mind?"

"You know a place up in Williamsburg called Bert's? It's a real blind pig, but I know the owner. Figured that'd keep us below the horizon."

"Yeah, I know the joint."

"Half hour." The line went dead.

It was about two miles, so 8 had to step out to make it on time. He packed his pistol, slipped on his bowler, and went on down the stairs. That voice. The voice had been just as he'd imagined, breathy and full of life. 8 wasn't sure what to expect, but his blood raced at finally meeting this mystery woman. He was almost certain that he wouldn't be turning her over to her father, but he could at least pass the message on that Fritz had forgiven her for whatever transgression she'd committed and only wanted her to return home.

Then, 8 would be done with the case. Not that he wanted to be. Sure, the money was good, but it was more than that. He was enthralled with this woman he'd never met, Velma Hartmann, this will-o-wisp dancing through the streets of New York City. There was a vibrancy to the girl he'd come to know from afar—she exuded vim and vinegar, life with a twist of spice and had him absolutely intrigued. No doubt she'd be a disappointment, as he'd raised her star high in the sky. Still, what sort of wealthy young socialite knew of places of such low repute as Bert's?

The speakeasy was in the basement of Bert Johnson's town home, which was more a tenement building than anything. It had started out as drinking establishment for him and those that lived there, expanded to their unsavory friends, and was now open to the public. Getting drunk there usually meant losing your wallet and waking up in the alleyway with bruises you didn't remember getting. 8 went down the alleyway to the basement entrance and was admitted into a darkened room with about twelve drinkers scattered about.

The bar was a piece of plywood over two sawhorses. There were no women in the place. No music played. Conversation was limited to two drunk men arguing about the play of the Superbas that day.

"Looking for a woman," 8 said to the bartender. He thought the man might be Bert, but wasn't quite sure. He was ruffled and his shirt was stained. Three or four days of growth sprouted at odd angles from his chin.

"Aren't we all," the man said. "This ain't that kinda place. What are you drinking?"

"Give me a whiskey. Best you got," 8 said.

The man ruffled around in a box on the floor and came up with a bottle. He poured two fingers in a glass that may've been mostly clean and slid it over. 8 gave him a dollar, and the man put it in his pocket.

"Expensive drink," 8 said, eyeballing the glass.

"You 8 Ballo?"

"That's me."

"There's a car out on the street waiting for you."

8 chuckled. The man had overcharged him for a drink he didn't need before sharing that bit of information. He tossed down the whiskey, figuring if it'd cost him a dollar, he damn well was going to drink it, and went back out. On the street was a black automobile parked on the side of the road with two men in front.

When 8 asked if they were there to give him a ride, neither one answered, but the driver nodded his head for him to get in back. They were both Italians in nice suits. Possibly Sicilian, but 8 couldn't be sure. He pegged them for gangsters, but they didn't respond to any of his inquiries, not even when he asked if they knew

Tomas Lombardo. 8 figured that one of them was probably Tomas. They went over the Williamsburg Bridge and across Manhattan to Greenwich Village.

"Velma will meet you in there," the driver said, pointing into a courtyard.

8 had been to Chumley's a few times before. He knew that the Garden Door was the entrance and how to work his way into this speakeasy that had become a hip joint for socialists, writers, and artists here in the Village. The joint was the exact opposite of Bert's, alive and with a buzz in the air of creativity and excitement rippling just above the edges of the jiving jazz music that vibrated the tables and chairs.

Velma was sitting at a table wearing a black and gold sequined dress, a band around her head from which protruded a feather, and black pearls around her neck. 8 took a moment, standing in the doorway, to appreciate the woman who up until now had existed only in his imagination as a portrait painted by others, and one that was elusive and intoxicating. From this vantage, she was no stunning beauty, but she possessed a confidence, a poise that hinted at much below the surface.

She sat with another woman who was dressed to cut a manly figure, in a flannel shirt, pants, and a beret on her head. 8 noted that her aplomb was no less than that of Velma's, though visually contrasting with everything that Velma was.

As 8 approached the table, Velma waved and called out to him, "8 Ballo, there you are, pull up a chair." It was like they were old friends.

8 looked into her eyes, and he felt the floor sway under his feet. Looking into her eyes, he understood immediately why so many men seemed ready to drop whatever they were doing to be with her on whatever hedonistic adventure was afoot. He sank into the proffered chair without losing contact with the deep sensual smokiness of Velma's soul. "Velma Hartmann. You're one tough cookie to find."

Velma snickered. "I believe I found you. Do you know my friend, Willa?"

This confirmed what 8 had suspected. "Not directly, no, but I, of course know Miss Cather. I've read her novel, *One of Ours*, and thought it smashing." He turned to look at Willa. "You did an astounding job with Claude Wheeler, Miss Cather. Now, when I think back to my days in France in 1918, I can picture him next to me." 8 actually thought nothing of the kind. The Great War had none of the romanticism, nor idealism, that she'd expressed. He was certain that the Claude Wheelers were the first to die. So, if he imagined Claude right next to him at all, it was as a corpse lying broken in the mud. This turned his thoughts to Oliver Harvey and the day that the bullet had turned his face into a blank canvas.

"Why thank you, Mr. 8 Ballo. Velma was just telling me all about you."

"Brilliant," 8 said. "Especially as we've never met."

"She said she thought you were one of the good ones," Willa said and stood up. "Now, if you'll excuse me, an absolutely ravishing young lady has entered the premises, and I must go offer my services."

Velma placed her hand over 8's on the table. "Every person I've spoken with who knows you mentions that you never fail to leave them flabbergasted. Dottie told me you were well read, but," Velma snickered and squeezed his hand, "she didn't tell me you were a liar."

8 raised an eyebrow. He liked the feel of her hand on his. "Liar?"

"You most likely would've killed Claude Wheeler the first time you saw him, now, wouldn't you have?"

8 chuckled. "What else has Dottie told you?"

"She did mention that you know how to handle yourself."

8 wondered in what context that Dottie meant this. "Tell me, Velma, who else have you spoken with about me?" A waiter set a whiskey in front of 8.

"You do prefer whiskey, don't you?" Velma said. "I took the liberty of ordering you a cocktail."

"You do know me well." He took a sip of the brown liquor. It was exponentially better than the best whiskey at Bert's.

"Oh, it wasn't hard to find that you like a fine whiskey, Mr. Ballo. Absolutely everybody knows that. Or at least that you hate gin, especially served in a water glass."

"Please, call me 8, as we seem to know each other intimately already."

Velma snickered. "Strange moniker, but as the eighth child, I suppose it makes sense. I suppose Daddy and Mum could've just called me 1. I can't imagine having one sibling, much less seven more. And look at you? Were you an absolutely humongous baby? You must've done a fair amount of damage entering the world."

"I was just puzzling over the fact that you were an only child," 8 said. "Why was that?"

"There were some complications with my birth." Velma took her hand off his, leaned back, and lit a cigarette. "My Mum wasn't able to have any more babies."

"I imagine your parents spoiled you."

"Rotten. My daddy would do anything I asked of him. Mum?" Velma shrugged. "She put up with me."

"Must've been lonely, growing up an only child."

"Must've been like living in a circus, being one of eight," Velma said. She blew out a cloud of smoke. "I once thought of running off and joining the circus."

"I once thought of running off and joining a monastery," 8 said. There was a moment of silence, and then Velma laughed, an authentic guffaw from the belly.

"Now that you've *found* me, my dear 8, what do you propose to do with me?"

"I'm not quite sure."

"You going to snitch on my whereabouts to Daddy?"

"Is that why you sent me to that wonderful den of illicit liquor called Bert's and had Tomas pick me up and bring me here? Just to make sure that Fritz or his goons weren't following along behind me?"

"Had to be sure that you weren't a skid rogue," Velma said, again blowing smoke out. She hadn't flinched in the slightest at his use of Tomas' name.

"I think you know enough to know I can be trusted. And I'm no bum."

"Girl can never be too careful, is what *I* know."

"Your father asked me to pass on a message when I found you. He said that he didn't believe that you murdered Colleen Brooks and that he'd like it if you came home."

"That's rich." Velma stared him in the eye. "Did he say that I killed that bitch?"

"Nothing quite so direct," 8 said. "He alluded to the fact that you may have thought that he thought you had. Killed her, that is."

"If Colleen is dead, then he's the one who killed her."

8 looked across the room to where the Italian who'd driven him here sat with the man who'd ridden shotgun. "Like he killed Tito?"

Velma winced, just slightly. "Who?"

"Tell me, Velma, does your father want you dead or home?"

"Daddy likes to be in control. Me leaving kind of freaks him out."

"He didn't send his goons to kill you—or someone you were with he didn't like?"

"I don't know what you're talking about."

"I was down the street from a certain wallpaper company in Bushwick the other day and ended up following a carload of guns over to a place in Williamsburg. They went inside and shot a man named Tito Cattaneo full of holes. Tito ran with a fellow by the name of Tomas Lombardo. Tomas has been hanging out with a dame named Velma Hartmann. And what's more, this Tomas picked me up at a blind pig joint in Williamsburg and brought me here." 8 tilted his head to indicate direction. "And... he's now sitting right over there."

The wince was less subtle this time. "Dottie was right. You *are* flabbergasting. So, it was Daddy's men who killed poor Tito?"

8 nodded. "They were sent to retrieve you, it appears, and he got in the way."

Velma waved her glass at a passing waiter, pointed at 8's glass, and held up two fingers. "Me and Tomas went out five minutes before they got there. We were close enough to hear the gunshots."

"What are you going to do?" 8 asked.

"What do you mean?"

"Are you going to keep running around the city, or are you going to go home?"

"I'm not going back to Daddy's house."

"What happened to your mother?"

"She died of consumption."

"Colleen Brooks didn't go out to Hollywoodland, did she?"

The drinks came and Velma took a healthy belt. "She talked about it some after being in those moving pictures. Daddy didn't like that much, the thought of her leaving him, that is."

"You're saying he murdered her?"

Velma shrugged. "One day she was there. The next day she was gone."

The jazz stopped in the middle of a song, and the bartender's voice boomed across the crowded room. "Okay people, eighty-six it."

The patrons erupted in a commotion, and Velma stood up. "Finish your drink. We gotta go. The coppers are coming."

Velma grabbed his hand as the last of the brown liquor slid down his throat and pulled him toward a door different than the one he'd come in. They were crushed among throngs of people crowding to get out. As they squeezed through the exit, 8 saw blue uniforms burst into the speakeasy from the Garden Door.

"This way," Velma said, pulling him behind, her face shining with excitement.

The crowd exploded onto Bedford Street as if from a shotgun, heading in all different directions. Velma and 8 ran to the left, away from the police cars at the opening to the courtyard entrance. Several cops came running out the door hollering for people to stop, but nobody listened. They ran down the street and took a left, and then cut through an alleyway, Velma giggling the whole way, and then slowed to a walk.

"I think we lost 'em," she said in a mock gangster tone.

"What was that whole eighty-six thing?" 8 asked.

"That's the main address on Bedford. The coppers are kind enough to call ahead when they're going to raid the place. They come through the Garden Door. We all leave through the front door. Leland pays a fine in cash, otherwise known as a payoff, and everybody goes on about their business."

8 figured that Leland must be the owner of Chumley's. "I think we lost your babysitter as well," 8 said.

"Good. I told Tomas not to hang around, but he seems to think he's got to watch out for me. Why do you suppose men are so possessive?"

"Guess we're wired that way," 8 said. "Probably goes back to caveman days."

"What now, 8 Ballo?" Velma asked. She was still holding his hand, pulling him to a stop.

8 turned to face her. "It seems I've found you and passed on the message, so I guess I'm done working for your father."

Velma took his other hand and looked up at him, her eyes wide. "I kind of liked having you chase me around."

"You're a fascinating woman, Velma. I sincerely like what I've learned about you. Writer, reader, musician, dancer, and thinker. A true 1920s Renaissance woman."

"Do you think that we might be friends?"

8 felt the heat from her body, scant inches from his own, hunger leaking from her eyes. "What sort of friends?"

Velma leaned into him. He canted his head, and their lips met.

8 was lost for a moment in their deliciousness. When his senses returned, she was tugging at his hand, and he realized they'd stopped in front of a hotel. He wondered if that had been just by chance but didn't really care to dwell upon it.

He forked over three bucks to an overweight man at the desk, and they took the stairs to the second floor, stopping several times to kiss, caress, touch, and nibble. They stumbled and fell through the door, 8 kicking it shut behind them as he pressed her against the wall of their room. Her hands were at his belt, his lips upon hers, his hands grasping her buttocks, her tongue flicking into his mouth.

Then his hands were under the black and gold sequined dress, sliding down to her underdrawers, which were scandalously scant, as his pants slid to the floor. 8 buried his head in the nape of her neck and caught the intoxicating scent of rose, jasmine, and vanilla, a potent brew that made his knees weak. He staggered slightly, and she guided him to the bed, pushing him onto his back as she pulled her dress over her head and shed her undergarments with two fluid movements.

She sank to her knees in front of him, and he groaned and grabbed at her shoulders as she slid her way up his body, tongue trailing small tributaries of pleasure from his knees to his lips. He reveled in the soft wetness of her mouth, and then she began again to flow back down his body, her hair trailing her lips, giving such sensuous pleasure that he felt he couldn't stand it. And then she stopped, and the world aligned itself, and 8 could see again.

Velma stood at the side of the bed, faint light from the streetlamp outside illuminating her nakedness. Her body curved from the breasts inward to her stomach and back out into her bottom, a dark patch of hair between her legs that matched her head and eyes.

Velma straddled him with a wicked grin of desire and settled herself down onto him and the room once again spun in pleasure that he couldn't even begin to grasp.

Chapter 20

8 decided that for his final meeting with Hartmann, he'd pay the man a visit at his house. *More like a mansion*, he thought, as he approached the building, which was not far from his wallpaper factory. A wrought iron fence kept the rabble of Bushwick at bay, and if that didn't work, the two-armed men loitering at the front door would certainly do the trick.

The mansion had terracotta and stone trim with a slate mansard roof, at one corner a tower rising, its incongruity suggesting the architect had attached a lighthouse to the building as an afterthought. 8 encouraged one of the men to rise from his chair and open the gate, suggesting that Fritz Hartmann would most definitely want to see him. He tried to make idle chatter with the man as the other goon went inside to check with Hartmann. 8 thought that the man might not know English, so tried a few Hungarian words out on him, but this was met with an equally impassive response.

Giving up, 8 let his thoughts drift to the seductive temptress, Velma. He now knew what Paris of Troy must've felt, if not thought, when he carried Helen off, well knowing the repercussions that would follow. 8 could envision himself a sailor happily dashing his sailing vessel onto the rocks, lured there by the beautiful voices and erotic allure of the Sirens. With his blood racing in his veins just thinking of Velma, he was just like every man who'd ever thrown away everything for the attention of a woman.

A faint part of 8's rational mind registered this, for him, unusual infatuation. He was just one more man who'd been mesmerized by the enchanting charms of a seductress. *Or*, and 8 thought this with a grin crossing his face like a guilty schoolboy looking out the window and dreaming of stickball, *was it possible that it was indeed something more?* There was no doubt that there'd been a connection. An electricity. A surge of something that 8 had not felt for some time, not since before the Great War. Not since Camila.

There was a strength to Velma, interwoven with an incredible fragility. She was bubbly and innocent and open and dark and reserved all at the same time. Her emotions rippled through and out every pore of her body. Her touch was intoxicating.

But what did he know of her? That she was on the lam from her father, consorted with gangsters and celebrities, many of them men, and was an owl of the night. Even then, she'd been gone from the hotel bed when he awoke this morning at just after seven. 8 was certain that sleep had not claimed them until the very deepest witching hour of the early morning. Had she awakened, gathered herself, and slipped out? Or had Velma not slept, but merely waited for him to nod off, and then went, where? Back to that Tomas fellow?

"Hey, buddy," the stone-faced gatekeeper said, "the boss will see you now."

It was with relief that the second man interrupted 8's tortured thoughts, returning to retrieve him and steering him into the imposing interior of the house, all without a word. The man appeared to have a similar problem with the English language, or perhaps Hartmann only employed the deaf, so 8 gave up and took in the décor as he was led from an entry room, down a hallway with dark portraits adorning the walls, and into a library. One portrait gave him pause, a faint memory tickling his consciousness, but he hurried along to not get left behind. Fritz Hartmann sat behind a desk smoking a cigar, which he waved at 8, seemingly suggesting to him that he sit down.

Bookshelves filled the walls, and the ceiling soared high above with a mural of the world upon it. 8 worried that a fireplace might not be such a great idea in a library, but it wasn't his place to make that suggestion, and thus kept silent. Hartmann's desk was large, made of a dark wood, with no clutter upon it whatsoever. He was busy writing in a ledger, it and a lamp the only two things on the desk, until he lay down the pencil and looked up, making it three items.

"What is it?" Hartmann asked.

"I found your daughter."

"Where is she?"

8 shrugged. She'd been gone from the hotel this morning when he woke up. That was disappointing. He didn't think he should mention that, though. "Met her at Chumley's up in the Village."

"Best place to find that girl is where there's liquor to be had. Speaking of, would you like a scotch?" Hartmann stood up and walked to a mahogany bar trolley atop of which was a decanter of brown liquid and two glasses. Almost like he knew that 8 would be showing up.

"Sure," 8 said. Who was he to pass up free scotch, which he figured was probably pretty damn good? And it was *just* past noon on a Saturday. 8 could see no good reason to say no.

"What'd my dear Velma have to say?" Hartmann asked, handing 8 a glass of scotch and sitting back down.

"She said she wasn't coming back."

Hartmann eyeballed him over the rim of his glass. "Did you tell her I don't blame her for Colleen's… disappearance."

8 took a nip. It was smooth. And good. "She said if anybody killed Colleen, it was you."

Hartmann laughed. "Why would I kill my twenty-something old movie star girlfriend? She was a shining light in my life."

8 thought that calling her a movie star might've been laying it on a bit thick. "Velma suggested that Colleen was talking about

going out to Hollywoodland and that you didn't care for that much. Thought maybe you figured if you couldn't have her, nobody could."

"My daughter has always had an over-active imagination. But I can tell you for a fact that a week before Colleen disappeared, Velma threatened to kill her. I believe her exact words were 'I'm going to slice that bitch up and see if she still floats.'"

8 pondered these harsh words, comparing them with the Velma he'd come to know, first from a distance, and then the previous evening, intimately. "Did you give Colleen your wife's dresses?"

Hartmann choked on his scotch. It appeared touch and go as to whether he'd spit it out, but he finally managed to get control of himself. "Yes. Why not? They're just filling the closet upstairs, and I thought she'd appreciate them."

"Do you have a photograph of your wife?"

"What is this all about?" Hartmann leaned forward over the desk. "I believe our business is concluded, Mr. Ballo. You've found my daughter and passed my message on to her. Thank you for your services, but truth be told, I don't believe I'll be recommending you."

"Did you know that Colleen was sending letters to her parents?"

Hartmann settled back into his chair. "That should come as no real surprise," he said. "A daughter communicating with her parents."

8 wondered if Velma had been communicating with him. There was something missing. "She'd planned on visiting with them right before she disappeared."

Hartmann stood up. "It's time for you to go."

The door opened, and the gunslinger, Mouse, walked in with that insolent sneer on his face. "Come on, big fellow, time for you to vamoose," he said. He kept his hand inside his jacket, the casualness of his twisted mouth not matched by the wary look in his eyes.

8 gave him the dead stare. "You pull that piece out, and I'm gonna shove it up your ass." He turned back to Hartmann. "Good day to you, sir. I'm sorry that things didn't work out better."

As they stepped into the hallway, Mouse stopped, thought better of it, moved further away, and then presented what he must've figured was his best sneer. "I get the word, just a nod of the head, and you're dead," he said.

"How's it feel to be a minion?"

The sneer receded. "What do you mean?"

"Most grown adults do what we want," 8 said. "Not you. I bet you can't take a crap without getting the okay from Fritz. Am I right?"

"Keep it up, big fellow. You're going to find out that a bullet don't care how large you are. You peepers croak just the same as anyone else."

He started walking but paused in the hallway, Mouse a few steps behind. He pointed at a portrait of a lady, painted in dark colors. And then he remembered the photograph of Fritz's wife that he had in his office, a thought that had been tickling the back of his brain since the trip to New Jersey.

"Who's that?" 8 asked, pointing. But he knew. It was Velma's mother. Fritz's dead wife.

"What's it to you?"

"How about you be a stand-up guy for once and just answer the question."

Mouse cleared his throat. "That there's Mrs. Hartmann."

She was about forty in the painting, 8 guessed, thin and angular, with blonde hair and blue eyes. Her face, unlike her body, was plump, with cushioned cheeks that were rosy. Either the artist was terrible at his job, or Mrs. Hartmann didn't look remotely like Colleen Brooks. Or, her daughter, for that matter.

Chapter 21

On Sunday morning, 8 sat at a small outdoor table of a café around the corner from his apartment, enjoying a breakfast of bacon, eggs, and potatoes, with thick pieces of bread. He had coffee, as well as juice, and was reading the *Brooklyn Eagle*. He did like to keep up with what was going on, both in his city and the nation, as well as the world.

He'd meant to make it to the parade on 5th Avenue the previous day, celebrating the 25th Anniversary of the union of all the various towns and cities of New York City into one gigantic metropolis. It sounded like it had been quite a show, with 40,000 participants, wild animals such as tigers, and a production that made Mardi Gras in New Orleans look tame.

The next article was about a rumor that a Klan rally of 20,000 was to have taken place the night before at midnight out on Long Island. 8 couldn't rightly figure out what the hell was wrong with people. He wondered if they were protesting the Blacks, the Irish, or the Italians this time? *Maybe they added Hungarians to their list*, he thought wryly.

8 had fought alongside just about every ethnicity there was during the Great War, and he'd mostly found that backbone and integrity didn't have much to do with the color of skin or who your parents were. While the Black and white units were segregated, that didn't always last when on the Western Front.

He and Pearle had signed up to go immediately upon war being declared. They'd not seen each other until they'd been mustered out, but found they'd often been within ten miles of each other through that hellish time. 8 had found himself fighting alongside many a Black soldier, some valiant and brave, others cowardly and weak. Just like the white men he'd fought with.

He and Pearle both arrived in Europe in January of 1918 as soldiers in the American Expeditionary Front, or the AEF. That was the last they'd see of each other until they were returned home after the armistice in November. 8 was in the 41st Division of the First Corps. It didn't take long to realize that war was not adventure and heroism, but a dirty business of killing and survival. Pearle had been in the 369th Infantry, which served under French command, and he'd nothing but glowing reports of how French officers treated the Blacks, as opposed to those Blacks under U.S. command.

Eight flipped the pages to the sports. The Trolley-Dodgers had won, but so had the Yankees and the Giants. 8 figured it was about time to get out to see a game, especially now that he was no longer working for Hartmann. He'd not heard a word from Velma. His thoughts turned to the young woman with the sparkling wit, quick laugh, and then her brazen audacity in the carnal arts. She reminded him of Camila, not that he'd ever made love with Camila.

He'd met her late in 1916, just before Christmastime, and the first time he looked into her dark eyes he was lost. She was seven years younger than him, attending her final year of college, and he'd just begun his second year as a PI. Their romance was intense, emotionally if not physically, and for the first time, 8 had fallen deeply in love. If he'd had it to do over again, he probably wouldn't have enlisted, but he couldn't be sure.

While the war had been a dark period of his life and led Camila to another man in his absence, enlisting was his civic duty. He didn't reckon that he could turn a blind eye to the German submarines sinking American ships. 8 didn't always agree with everything the government did, but it was a mighty fine country nonetheless, and sometimes you had to fight for the things that were important to you. Obviously, Camila hadn't felt the same way, about fighting for him, that is, because when he got back, she'd gone and married some banker.

A picture in the theater section caught his attention for a split second as it looked like Colleen Brooks. Wouldn't that be the cat's meow if she just showed up as an actress, and not dead after all? But it was somebody named Millicent Hanley at the Schubert Crescent in *Smilin' Through*. Fat chance, 8 thought, of Colleen Brooks still walking around breathing. He could feel it in his bones that she was dead. But why? And who killed her?

8 took the last bite of toast and swig of coffee and stood up to go, leaving a quarter on the table. He left the silver piece eagle down, liberty up, a habit he'd had ever since he'd returned from the Great War. He suddenly felt lonely as he strolled back toward his apartment. Perhaps he should visit with his sister, the oldest, who he was closest to. But that was not what he needed, nor wanted, he knew.

His thoughts turned back to Velma Hartmann. She was such a slender thing, so thin he'd been afraid he would crush her, but there was a strength there. There was nothing delicate about her, nor frail, and he wouldn't again mistake small with weak. 8 thought about the sparkle in her eyes and the infectious laugh. It was as if he'd known her for years, and not just one night.

They'd lain in bed talking about music, books, theater—before resuming touching, exploring, and melding in a way that was all at once delicious, exciting, and intoxicating. Behind that strength of body, will, and emotion, 8 sensed an emotional vulnerability. And when he'd woken in the morning, she was gone, back into the wind, a will-o-wisp that seemed no more than a dream. Gone awry.

Asta was sitting on his front stoop as he approached his building. "Where you been, stranger?" she asked.

8 settled down next to her on the step. "Just now? Breakfast down at Otto's."

Asta elbowed him in the side. "Haven't seen you for a week. Not like you to not give me a ring. Take me out. Take me to your bed."

8 sighed. "Been busy with a case."

"The missing girl?"

"Yeah, only, she's not missing any more. Found her. Well, I'm not quite sure where she is."

Asta turned and stared at him. "Son-of-a-bitch," she said. "You think you've fallen in love."

"What?" 8 chuckled. It was not a convincing laugh. "Nothing of the kind. I'm just a bit mixed up on things, is all."

"Tell me what happened when you found her."

8 squirmed on the step, looked down the street, but it wasn't in him to lie or avoid a question. "She seemed angry with her father. Didn't want to go home. Was scared, even though she didn't let on."

"And you slept with this young, angry, scared, and homeless girl?"

8 turned and stared Asta firmly in the eye. "I think she might be the one."

Asta laughed, a singsong chirp that echoed up and down the quiet street. "You're such a romantic, 8 Ballo. I don't think you'd know what love was if it was right in front of you."

"I'm sorry, Asta. There's just something about her. Her being has burrowed into me and I can't shake her out. She's got *it*."

"First you go all poetic on me and now she just got *it*?"

8 shook his head. "I can't explain. Just it. There's something about her, and for me, she has it."

Asta leaned over and kissed him on the cheek. "I wish you the best, 8," she said wistfully. "But I don't think you know what *it* is." She stood up and walked off down the street.

8 wasn't sure how long he sat there lost in thought, but finally,

he got up, and went up the steps to his office on the second floor. There, he called Pearle. The telephone rang and rang, and he was about to give up, when his friend answered.

"Hey, Pearle, it's 8. You wanna get drunk?"

Pearle had a few things to tie up, giving 8 a chance to go buy a bottle of whiskey and some cigars. Then they met at a speakeasy over in Bedford for a couple of cocktails that might've turned into three or four. They talked of nothing consequential. That time would come. Over the years, the call out for getting drunk had never been ignored by either of them. The reason would reveal itself, good or bad, over the course of the evening.

By the time they were driving out of Brooklyn, late afternoon shadows were starting to streak the road. Just into Queens, on Jamaica Bay, was a tiny beach that somehow had remained pristine since they'd first found it. For about twelve years, maybe a couple of times a year, the two of them had been coming here, starting when the New York Barge Canal Project had started. They'd worried that their little hideaway would be displaced by the creation of this seaport, but the plan had crawled along and now seemed dead in the water.

A bit more than two hundred yards off a dirt road, back in 1911, they'd come upon a small and secluded sandy beach, no more than twenty feet long. The date was etched into 8's mind, because the day before, March 25th, Pearle's mother had been killed in the horrific fire at the Triangle Shirtwaist Company. She was neither an immigrant, nor a teen, like so many of the others, but had been forced to take the job to pay the bills after Pearle's father had been killed in what may or may not have been an accident. Both parents in a six-month span.

This may have been the driving force that would propel Pearle into being such a successful businessman. The loss of his mother and father, both due to financial circumstances, so close to each other, had to have burned deep, 8 figured. They'd found this isolated beach and got drunk, and Pearle had bared his soul and cried. He never again spoke of his parents, nor their deaths. This place was where they talked openly, of the bad, and the good. Of their hopes and desires. The sort of things that they never discussed with each other at any other time, respecting the man code of toughness.

Pearle pulled off the road, where they unloaded a few armloads of wood to supplement what they could scrounge from the surrounding forest, whiskey, glasses, and some steak, corn, and potatoes. Then Pearle drove the car further down the road away from the beach entrance and pulled off while 8 began hauling the items the few hundred yards to the beach. It took them just twenty minutes to bring everything in.

"Should we start a fire?" 8 asked.

"Not until we swim," Pearle said. "I'm not going in that water once the sun goes down."

"Too cold for sharks."

"Too cold for humans. But not for giant squids."

8 laughed, stripping down. "Aye, Captain, the kraken is out there, lurking. But it won't strike in the light of day. No, sir, it will only come out to play at night."

"Actually, I'm thinking another whiskey, and I might not remember how to swim."

"Yeah," 8 said. "I'm seriously concerned about my buoyancy."

The two men looked at each other, and then broke for the water. They weren't as agile as when they had first come, nor as limber, but something about the place brought back their youthful enthusiasm. As they reached the gentle waves, Pearle shoved 8 sideways, and he staggered, and then fell into the water. They wrestled as if they were boys, splashing and crashing through the benign waves of the bay, before clambering back onto the beach.

Within minutes, the first tendrils of flames were licking the darkening sky, and whiskey was again warming their bellies. They dug out sand chairs next to the fire, lit up cigars, and watched the daylight disappear and the night envelop the sky.

"I was thinking about Mrs. Nilsson today," Pearle said. She'd been 8's teacher when he was in the sixth level.

"About the time we saw her walk by and followed her home?" 8 asked.

"What else?"

8 had pointed out the young blonde teacher walking past one day when they were tossing the ball back and forth. He'd suggested they follow her, all the while explaining how cool and good-looking she was.

"She was something," 8 said fondly.

"First time I ever saw boobies."

"Me too," 8 said. *Except for my sisters'*, he thought.

"I think I might still love her," Pearle said. "That sure was something."

They'd followed Mrs. Nilsson to a small home down at the bottom of Bushwick. It wouldn't be for a few days that they'd realized she lived at home with her parents as she wasn't yet married. They saw her moving around behind the curtains of the house, and crept closer, to discover that she'd stripped down to just some underdrawers on her bottom half that hung down to her knees. Her breasts were fully exposed as she stood in front of a mirror.

"Haven't seen anything like that since," 8 said.

"They were perfectly round, and I think they shone with an inner light."

The two men smoked their cigars, lost in thought about Mrs. Nilsson. They'd gone back for the next three days, with less than stellar results, until her father, a hulking brute of a man caught them peeping through the window and had chased them off.

"What was the name of that girl you were head over heels for?" Pearle spilled a bit more whiskey into his glass and then offered the bottle over. "The one you were smitten with before we went off to fight the Krauts?"

"Camila Morales."

"Was she as… sculpted as Mrs. Nilsson?"

8 chuckled. "She had a lot going for her, but Mrs. Nilsson still wins that particular blue ribbon."

"She's probably a bit on the old side now."

"Not for me," 8 said. "She'll always be twenty-three and have milky skin."

"Can you remember what her face looked like?"

8 tossed a pebble off the side of Pearle's head. "Not really," he admitted.

"Ah, to be eleven again."

"Found that girl I was looking for," 8 said.

"Velma?"

"That's the one. Met her at Chumley's for a drink. You know the place, over in the Village?"

"Sure. Heard tell of it. You going to tell Hartmann where she is?"

"Don't know where she is."

Pearle took a few puffs of his cigar. "Sounds to me like you didn't find a girl."

"What's that supposed to mean?"

"Sounds to me like you found a woman."

8 pondered this. "Yeah. She was something. Not the little spoiled rich girl I thought she was going to be."

"You sleep with her?"

"What?" 8 knew there was no sense lying to Pearle. They'd been friends long enough that each usually knew the other's thoughts before he did.

"Okay, don't bother lying to me. Gets kinda complicated when you sleep with one of your clients. Even more so when you make love to the daughter of a client, is all."

"Yeah, that's what I was thinking. I think Hartmann might've killed that other girl, Colleen Brooks. Velma said that Colleen was talking about leaving him, and he didn't much care for that thought."

"And ole Fritz said that Velma killed her," Pearle said. "Sounds like they got some problems between 'em that need to be worked out."

"No love lost there." 8 put his cigar out in the sand. "Seems more likely he killed her."

"Course it does."

"Why's that?"

"Which one you having sex with?"

"Think it might be a bit more than that," 8 said. "Something about her. Can't shake her out of my head."

Pearle laughed. "Okay, partner. Tell me. How's she match up?"

"Match up?"

"To Mrs. Nilsson."

The moon had risen in the sky enough to illuminate them along with the flickering fire, and the two men stared at each other before cracking up in laughter.

They cooked the steak and other food, sipped whiskey, smoked cigars, and talked late into the night. There were no plans to drive. No reason to get home.

As he was starting to nod off, alcohol and lateness having taken their toll, 8 looked over at Pearle. "You awake?"

There was some sort of unintelligible reply, but a reply it was.

"Nobody matches up to Mrs. Nilsson in that department. Nobody. But this Velma is something pretty damn special."

Chapter 22

8 was in his normal position at the office, tilted back in his chair, feet up on the desk. The difference on this particular day was that he was fast asleep, gentle snores rippling from his mouth. Pearle had dropped him home at about nine o'clock that morning, and he'd washed up, eaten a bite, and drank about a gallon of water, none of which had assuaged his hangover.

"Excuse me, Mr. Ballo."

8 couldn't place the voice. It wasn't Velma. Not Dottie. Or Asta. He flicked his eyes open just a tad. He was not in his bedroom. The light was very bright. He was at his desk in his office. He grunted and dropped his feet to the floor and sat upright.

"I was wondering if I might speak with you?"

8 licked his dry lips. "Please have a seat, Mrs. Brooks," he said. He took stock of her, never having gotten much of a glimpse of her when he and Pearle had visited New Jersey. She'd just been a figure flittering in a doorway. She looked much like the pictures of her daughter. Dark hair and eyes. Thin figure. Maybe a few inches over five feet.

"Thank you, Mr. Ballo." She sat down gently on the edge of a seat facing him across the desk.

"What can I do for you?" 8 rubbed the drool from the corner of his mouth.

"I was wondering if I might hire you. To find Colleen."

This seemed to be the month of missing girls, 8 thought wryly.

"You don't believe she went to Hollywoodland?"

"Do you?" Mrs. Brooks showed a bit of mettle, putting an edge to her words.

"What does your husband think?"

"He doesn't know I'm here."

8 pondered that as he waited. She hadn't answered his question.

Mrs. Brooks cleared her throat. "He, um, I think he's afraid of finding out what... where she is."

"He believes she is dead?"

"It's not like her to stop sending letters. And not to visit when she said she would. That's not like our Colleen at all."

"You might not like what I find."

"I understand."

"Yet, you still want to hire me to find her?"

"I need to know."

"I will have to be completely honest with you in what I find," 8 said. "If I work for you."

"Yes."

8 stood up, walked over, shut the door. He spoke from there, to her back. "Your daughter, Mrs. Brooks, was having an affair with Fritz Hartmann. She was living with him."

"Yes."

"You knew?"

Mrs. Brooks turned in her chair, her eyes piercing his. "Of course I knew, Mr. Ballo, if not the specifics, then the general state of things. Mothers always know, don't they?"

"I suppose they do." He certainly hoped that his mother hadn't known everything *he* did before she died. "I suspect that you haven't shared this information with Mr. Brooks."

"It would kill him," she said. "Colleen was the sparkling apple of his eye. He'd be devastated to know that she was fucking a man twice her age, most likely for money, clothes, nice jewelry, whatever. Certainly not love."

Whoa, 8 thought, *Mrs. Brooks had some fire to her.* This was not the flitty woman in the doorway taking a backseat to her husband. "And how about you? Are you devastated?"

"We women do what we have to do. Was her choice better or worse than mine? I don't know and wouldn't pretend to. I only know what I've had to do and what it's gotten me. I don't know what Colleen has had to do or where…" Mrs. Brooks hesitated, sobbed, hiccupped, and wiped her eyes with a handkerchief.

8 tried to read between the lines of that loaded statement. He thought it best to avoid it altogether. "Okay, then. I'll find Colleen for you, or what happened to her, at least." He'd already planned on doing this even before Mrs. Brooks had shown up. It was a loose end, dangling in the breeze, and he could no more ignore it than he could stop breathing. Both would lead to the same result.

"What… how much do you charge for something like this?" Her timidity was back.

8 walked around her and sat down. "How much do you have?"

"I have twenty dollars." She pulled two tens out of her purse and set them on the desk. "But I can get you more."

8 picked up one of the sawbucks. "This should do the trick."

"I'm not looking for charity, Mr. Ballo."

"Truth is, I was planning on finding your daughter, Mrs. Brooks, even before you came in here. Ten dollars is more than fair. That's my price for having to share what I find with you."

"Dan is at work from eight to five most days."

"Let me get your phone connection. If I find anything that you need to know, I'll get in touch with you during the day."

Mrs. Brooks visibly sagged in relief. "Thank you, Mr. Ballo."

"You'll be hearing from me," 8 said.

The logical place to start the search for Colleen Brooks was with the found girl, Velma Hartmann, 8 reasoned after Mrs. Brooks left. Or perhaps he was rationalizing? 8 didn't much care for people who lied, and he thought it was particularly bad form to lie to oneself. Before he knew it, his feet were back up on the desk and he was tilted back, doing his job. Thinking. Most people didn't spend enough time probing the inner recesses of their own mind for answers.

8 contemplated on why Dan Brooks didn't want to find out what happened to his daughter. Maybe people didn't want answers to questions that were uncomfortable. Before 8 knew it, his deliberation had grown to encompass all the potentially awkward realities that people faced every day. Like whether or not they liked their spouses, jobs, lives, heck, themselves. And so figured that by avoiding asking the question, the answer could be ignored.

Perhaps this was what Mrs. Brooks had been touching on when she said that 'we women do what we have to'. If Colleen chose to have sex with a man because he lavished her with gifts, was it truly any different than the life of many women within the institution of marriage? That seemed to leave out the concept of love, an idea that 8 already was skeptical of, even though that particular beast had been tickling his heart the last few days.

8 shook his head, banishing that emotion from his thoughts, and tried to concentrate on what the first step should be to find Colleen Brooks. He understood that his heart was arguing that the best place to start would be with Velma. But the fact was that the only leads he had in conjunction to Colleen were Fritz and Velma Hartmann. Fritz seemed to be fairly angry with him and would most likely be unhelpful. That left Velma.

There was the slight problem of Velma's whereabouts. Where she was staying hadn't come up in conversation the one night they'd spent together. He'd an inkling, though, that she was most likely still with that fellow Tomas. It seemed likely that Fritz had sent his goons out to get Velma because he'd found out she was shacked up with an Italian in Williamsburg. 8 wondered why he hadn't heard back from Velma. He thought that it'd been a perfectly pleasurable night and hoped that he hadn't disappointed on his end.

It would probably be easier to find an Italian gangster than the elusive will-o-wisp known as Velma. 8 avoided lingering on the details of Velma shacking up with Tomas. He knew that he'd no claim to the loyalty of a woman he'd met just the once. But there it was, the tug of jealousy that he hadn't experienced in over five years, ever since Camila. That was another one of those real questions that people liked to avoid, and to this end, 8 realized why. He wasn't sure he wanted to delve too deeply into his own feelings—and motivations—when it came to the elusive Velma Hartmann.

"Knock, knock," Bugsy said as he walked through the door.

Sitting on one's ass, 8 thought, *was sometimes the best way to make things happen.* "Come right in, Benji," he said.

Bugsy glared at him. "Dames call me Benji."

"I'll go back to calling you Bugsy, then."

"You got a pretty good mouth for somebody I thought about popping just a week ago."

"Why don't you have a seat and tell me what brings you in here today." 8 had not forgotten about the sack over his head and the threat of murder. He contemplated knocking the smug arrogance off the man's pretty face.

Bugsy looked like he was caught between sitting and pulling his pistol out and shooting 8, but in the end, sat down. "You have any luck finding that dame?"

"Who would that dame be?"

"Ya know who I'm talking about. Velma."

"You told me to stop looking for her."

"You strike me as a gent who don't always listen real well," Bugsy said.

"Not to threats, no, they tend to irritate me."

"Did you find Hartmann's daughter or not?"

"My business has been concluded with Fritz Hartmann."

"That mean you found her?"

8 shrugged.

"She didn't go back to that dirty German bastard, did she?"

"I don't know where she is."

Bugsy stared at him, his bulging eyes slowly receding back into his head. "I believe you," he said softly. "How about I hire you to find her for me?"

8 grinned wryly. If this wasn't one more confirmation, as if he needed it, of the obsessive power that Velma sparked in men... "I'd say you're fickle, Mr. Siegel. You want me to tell you what I find, then you want me to stop looking, and now you want to pay me to find her."

"How much you want?"

"I charge twenty a day plus expenses." He'd no thought that he'd be telling Bugsy where Velma was, but he'd take the man's money, and maybe garner some information.

Bugsy pulled a billfold out and counted five twenties out. "This enough to get you started?"

8 took the money. "You know a fellow by the name of Tomas Lombardo?"

"Sure. He's a hired gun for Schirò up to Williamsburg."

"Know where he lives?"

Bugsy grinned, the smile illuminating his entire face, making him look like a movie star. "Nah. Somebody whacked his buddy at their place last week, and he went on the lam. Why? He know something about Velma?"

"Nope. Looking for him about something else. Thought if I helped you, you could help me." 8 didn't really consider this a lie, but was that him just lying to himself? *This introspection thing wasn't always a garden of roses*, he thought.

"That work for you?" Bugsy asked.

"What? Sorry. Does what work for me?"

"I'll ask around. Things aren't real friendly between us and his gang right now. Might be a little dicey."

"That'd be appreciated."

"And you'll find that girl for me?"

"I'll let her know you're looking for her," 8 said.

"I got that word on the street already. I want her found. And given to me."

"I don't do that."

Bugsy' eyes started to bulge. "You're just dying to get capped, aren't you?"

8 wasn't sure if that referred to being shot or having his knees broken. Neither one sounded very good. "How about I set up a meeting between you and her in a public place?"

"That'd be okay."

8 could see the wheels turning in the man's brain. If the meeting weren't to his taste, he could always haul her away to a place more to his liking. "And you gotta stop threatening to kill me," he said. "That hurts my feelings."

Chapter 23

"I've always wanted to be invited to a lunch engagement," Pearle said. They were once again bouncing down the road to the Fitzgerald home in Great Neck on the north shore of Long Island. "I hope I wore the right shoes."

8 looked over at him, not sure if he was being sarcastic or not. Pearle was known for being a snappy dresser and might have actually been concerned about his shoes. "Isn't there some rule about not wearing white before Decoration Day?"

"For your information, this baby is cream-colored, and not white," Pearle said. He had a light-colored two-button jacket with a brown waistcoat underneath. "After tomorrow I can break out the straight-up white. I'm just easing into it."

8 considered pointing out that cream was white but didn't think it was worth it. "Dottie said it's just a small and informal get-together."

"Not sure if you read the newspapers, my friend, but the Fitzgeralds don't throw small and informal get-togethers. This is going to be a soiree."

"Well, if you're right, I'm not so sure how well we'll fit in. I'm starting to feel old."

"The details are a bit hazy, my friend, but weren't you expressing your love of some young flapper to me just the other night at the beach?"

"It might've been the hooch talking," 8 said.

"So, you haven't become absolutely enamored by those smoky eyes of Velma Hartmann?"

8 dimly remembered referencing her eyes in that fashion. Pearle's memory was far too good, even that far into a bottle of whiskey. "They are somewhat bewitching."

Pearle laughed a deep rumble. "Yet, here we are on our way to a lunch date with another woman?"

"It is a social engagement," 8 said. "I accepted because I think they might be able to help me find Velma."

"They?"

"Dottie, Zelda, and whoever else might be out there."

"I thought you found her, passed on the message from her father, and are now done looking for her."

"I've been hired by the mother of Colleen Brooks to find her daughter. It seems that Velma would be able to help me with that."

Pearle slammed on the brakes, the car coming to a shuddering halt in the middle of the road. "Is that the broad who was having the affair with Fritz Hartmann?"

"That'd be the one."

"Son-of-a-gun," Pearle said, starting the automobile back down the road. "You been advertising yourself as the guru of finding lost girls?"

"Guess so. And besides, I got hired again to find Velma."

"By Fritz?"

"Bugsy."

This time Pearle almost swerved off the road. "Siegel?"

"That'd be the one."

"You turned him down, of course."

"Took his money."

"You're going to find Velma for Bugsy Siegel?" The disbelief in Pearle dripped from every word.

"Of course not."

"I thought you hated dishonesty?"

"Is it wrong to cheat a murdering gangster punk out of his money?" 8 asked.

"Guess you got a point there. What's he want with Velma?"

"Same thing I do, I imagine."

"Taking his money and not delivering is the same thing as stealing, at least in the eyes of Bugsy Siegel," Pearle said. "At some point he's going to figure out you played him, and then he's going to come after you."

They passed a field filled with automobiles. Pearle looked at 8. The next house was the Fitzgerald place. There were a line of cars and a slew of young men driving them to the field to be parked. "This certainly looks to be a small and informal soiree," Pearle said.

Guests milled across the front yard and music came wafting from behind the house. 8 and Pearle left the car with the valets and wandered around to the backyard. A band was playing, and there were tables with seating for at least a couple of hundred people.

"You know who that is singing?" Pearle asked.

"Looks to be Al Jolson."

> *Swanee!*
> *How I love you, how I love!*
> *My dear ol' Swanee*
> *I'd give the world to be*
> *Among the folks in*
> *D-I-X-I-E-ven no[w]*
>
> *My mammy's*
> *Waiting for me*
> *Praying for me*
> *Down by the Swanee*
> *The folks up north will see me no more*
> *When I go to the Swanee Shore!*

A waiter came by, and they plucked glasses of champagne from his tray. 8 was not much of a bubbly drinker, but he figured, when in Rome, do as the Romans do. "See who's on the piano?" he asked.

"Is that Gershwin?"

"George himself," 8 said. "And Clarissa's friend playing the saxophone."

"Son-of-gun," Pearle said. "Coleman Hawkins. I been meaning to punch that feller in the face."

8 chuckled. The song ended, and the crowd clapped enthusiastically. To have the composer of the music and the man who made the song famous at a "small social engagement" in Great Neck perform together was nothing short of amazing. The audience showed their appreciation, recognizing the specialness of the moment.

As the clapping died down, Jolson raised one hand over his head, a broad smile under his carefully combed hair. "Folks, you ain't heard nothing yet," he said.

The crowd hooted and cheered as the band swung into their next number.

"8 Ballo. I'm glad you were able to make it," Scott Fitzgerald said, approaching them. He looked as if he might have passed the champagne and started right in on the gin.

"Hello, Scott. This is my friend and associate, Pearle Hill. Pearle, Scott Fitzgerald." 8 shook the man's hand, thinking that he was really quite odd-looking with his hair parted in the middle and puffed up on either side, perhaps to distract from the odd shape of his face and the gaps between his teeth. *But the man sure knows how to write*, 8 thought.

"Good to meet you, Pearle." Scott shook his hand as well. "I thought that you might be with the catering company."

"How'd you ever get Gershwin, Jolson, and Hawkins together?" Pearle asked.

Scott smiled. His eyes were slightly glassy. "The old-fashioned way, my boy. Money." He rubbed his fingers together.

"I take it book sales have been good." 8 waved his arm to encompass the elaborate buffet, the musicians, and the attendees with servants filtering throughout.

"Actually, I'm quite broke." Scott smiled thinly.

"How are you able to afford this?" 8 asked.

"I'm not. I quite imagine we'll be out on the street within the week."

"Well, you'll go out in style," Pearle said. "Damn fine style."

They stood in an awkward silence for a few moments. "What are you working on now?" 8 finally asked.

"I've a play coming out in November. *The Vegetable*."

8 thought this was an atrocious name. He was saved a reply by the arrival of a garrulous man smoking a fat cigar. "Scott, absolutely stunning party, old sport." He went on about some story or another that didn't make a whole lot of sense and then walked off mid-sentence.

"Does anybody have any idea what the hell he was talking about?" Pearle asked.

"That was Max. He supplied all the hooch for today, so I suppose we should let him ramble," Scott said.

"Max who?" 8 asked.

"Gatsby. The Great Gatsby," Scott mumbled. "Excuse me, old chaps, but I must check with the cooks."

"Well, thank you for having us," Pearle said.

"I'm not sure it was I who invited you," Scott said. "But perhaps you might be able to amuse the guests a bit?" He raised his glass and walked off.

"Amuse the guests?" Pearle said to 8. "Thought I might be part of the catering staff?"

8 grinned. "Can't say that I see many guests here with skin as dark as yours."

Pearle glared at him. "Looks like I got three choices," he said. "I can be here serving people drinks and food, or I can go up on stage and make a fool of myself for everybody's amusement."

8 wondered if serving drinks and food counted as two choices. "Was there a third option?" he asked.

"I could shoot somebody in the head."

"That might be a bit on the drastic side. They just don't know any better. These people live in their own world."

"This is how the other half lives, huh?" Pearle said. "Seems a bit pretentious."

"I like the music, and I have a feeling the food is going to be exquisite."

"You have a point there," Pearle agreed. "How about we have ourselves a feed and I'll hold off on shooting anybody until after we eat."

They heaped their plates with prime rib, creamed spinach, and scalloped potatoes, and grilled corn on the cob, among other dishes as well as a few things they couldn't exactly identify, and then found their way to their assigned table. Dorothy Parker and Zelda Fitzgerald were already sitting there. 8 ordered a whiskey from a waiter and took a moment to appreciate the lushness of the moment. It was a corker of a day, with just a light breeze coming in off Little Neck Bay. The food smelled amazing. The music was scintillating. And he was seated with his best friend and two brilliant women for lunch.

"I imagine this is what you looked like on Christmas morning as a boy." Dottie interrupted his reverie.

"Just stopping to smell the roses," 8 said. "I thought you were Jewish?"

Dottie snickered. "My father was Jewish. My stepmother was Protestant. So, as a compromise, they sent me to Catholic school."

"The perfect religious trifecta," 8 said.

"I do check all the boxes, my dear 8."

"Well, Zelda, I'd have to say, this is one heckuva party," 8 said. "Thank you for the invite."

"You've Dottie to thank for that," Zelda said. "We were trying to keep the numbers down, but she absolutely insisted."

8 looked around at the hundreds of people eating and drinking. "I hope we're not the reason for your financial ruin."

Zelda tittered. "As I said in my high school yearbook, why should all life be work, when we all can borrow? Let's think only of today, and not worry about tomorrow."

"Not all of us have a public waiting anxiously for our next book release," 8 said. "I understand that a fair amount of Scott's work is inspired by you, and that he may've even lifted one of your diaries as material."

"You read my review in the *Tribune*? Well, it's good to know somebody did. I suppose what is mine, is his, and what is his, is his."

"I understand that you found our lovely Velma," Dottie said. "Is your business there concluded?"

"Thanks to you, I did indeed get a chance to meet with her and pass on the message from her father. Thank you for that." Luckily, the whiskey arrived, and he took a nip.

"All the boys seem to be quite mesmerized by her," Zelda said. "How did you find her?"

"She seemed to be a remarkable young lady," 8 said. "As a matter of fact, I was hoping to have another chat with her. About another young lady who's missing."

"Very few men seem satisfied with having only one *chat* with our lovely Velma," Dottie said. "I hear that she's taken up with a Sicilian gangster."

"I believe that might be correct," 8 said. "Do you know where they might be making their love nest?"

"Somewhere in Williamsburg," Dottie said, waving her hand impatiently.

"Maybe Arnie can help out," Zelda said. "Arnie, come join us for a moment, would you?"

A well-dressed man with a seemingly permanent sneer on his face switched directions and came over, kissing Zelda on either cheek and nodding to the others. "What can I do for you, my beautiful Zelda?"

"8 Ballo, this is Arnold Rothstein. I believe he may know the man you're looking for."

8 stared into the eyes of the rogue who'd fixed the 1919 World Series, one of the most influential and certainly richest gangsters in the world. "Hello, Mr. Rothstein," 8 said. "I been looking for a young lady named Velma Hartmann. I believe you might know of the man she's staying with."

Rothstein's eyes flashed in anger. "Is she Fritz Hartmann's brat?"

"That's her," 8 said. "If it helps, they are estranged." He knew that there was bad blood developing between Hartmann and the Bugsy Meyer gang, but it appeared that this ill will had climbed up the ladder to the very top rung. 8 sensed an opportunity to perhaps counterbalance the ill-will he'd seemingly inspired in Fritz Hartmann, especially if he were to continue to pursue finding Velma and discover the true circumstances of Colleen's disappearance.

Rothstein laughed. "Even his daughter doesn't like the prick. So, she's shacking up with some fellow I might know?"

8 winced. "I believe she may be staying with Tomas Lombardo who works for Nicolò Schirò."

"I know of Tomas."

"Do you know where he's living?"

Rothstein shook his head. "He hasn't been home since that bastard Hartmann killed... wait, did that shooting have something to do with this Velma?"

"I don't know for sure," 8 said, "but it's quite possible that Tito was murdered because Hartmann's men were searching for Velma."

"If that's the case, you might want to find her before Nicolò realizes the connection. He's none too happy with Fritz Hartmann right now."

8 figured this was a polite way of saying at a ritzy social luncheon that Schirò planned on killing Hartmann. And then maybe Velma.

"How about you, Mr. Rothstein? Are you also unhappy with Fritz?"

"He's been interfering with some of my business interests. That, I do not like."

The others at the table had given up the pretense of not listening, and 8 figured he might get more from the man in private, so he stood up. "Excuse us for a moment," he said to the others. "A word in private, Mr. Rothstein?" Two men loitering a few feet away suddenly straightened and put their hands inside their jackets.

"Meyer said you were a giant of a man," Rothstein said, stepping away from the table. "I was on my way to my automobile. Walk with me."

"I'd say that to Meyer Lansky, just about everybody is a giant of a man," 8 said.

Rothstein looked at him with a piercing gaze, that suddenly softened, and he guffawed. "I suppose you're right, there."

"Did you know that Bugsy hired me to find the girl?" 8 asked.

"Find the girl? You mean Velma?"

"That'd be her."

"No," Rothstein said.

8 figured that the man's eyes said yes, though. He didn't suppose Rothstein missed much. "I suppose if you can give me any help, it'd be doing Bugsy a favor."

"I don't need to be doing favors for anybody, especially Bugsy Siegel."

"I imagine in your line of work Bugsy would be a good fellow to have around."

"What is my line of work, Mr. Ballo?"

"You are a businessman."

"Ah, yes. And as a businessman, I'd be neglectful if I didn't get something for finding your Velma."

"What do you want?"

"I want dirt on her father. The type of thing she might share with a private investigator who she's fucking."

8 paused and put his hand on Rothstein's elbow and squeezed. Not so hard as to cause his bodyguards to fill 8 full of holes, but hard enough. "Don't make me kick your ass. Because I will if you don't watch how you talk about women, particularly that woman."

"Take your hand off me," Rothstein said in a low voice.

"Do we have an understanding?" 8 squeezed harder. He'd once broken a man's elbow in a like fashion.

"I'll not speak poorly of women in your presence. But if you ever lay your hands on me again, you'll be dead. Do *we* have an understanding?"

8 let go and smiled. "I'm sure we'll both do our best."

"I'm sure when you see Velma, you will, should anything come of it, inform me." Rothstein finished drily.

"As it happens, I'm currently investigating a matter that I believe will be very unfavorable to Fritz Hartmann. If, and when I find the proof, I will share that with you."

Rothstein stared him in the eye as if trying to read his mind, his eyebrows creasing

"I don't like sharing theories, hunches, gossip, or rumors," 8 said, shaking his head. "But if I uncover what I think I'm going to uncover, I'll give you enough evidence to destroy Fritz Hartmann. Take my card. It has my telephone connection on it."

"Alright, Mr. Ballo. I'll find out where Tomas has been hanging his hat and have my man ring." Rothstein stepped up to his car, a white Rolls Royce, where a man held the door for him. Another man sat in the shotgun seat. The two goons who'd been following them went and stood by a second car.

"Mr. Rothstein," 8 said. The man paused and turned. "And you'll promise not to harm Velma."

"I'm not in the habit of hurting women." Rothstein got into the automobile. "But you best present me with the information you have promised. I don't like unpaid accounts."

8 decided it'd be a good time to take a gander at the inside of the

Fitzgerald house. People were wandering into the house from the grounds, and he followed, finding his way to the bathroom. There seemed to be nothing personal about the house. No photographs. The paintings of landscapes on the wall looked as if they'd come with the place. There was a bookcase that looked like it might be owned by the Fitzgeralds. *Ulysses* by James Joyce. *Babbitt* by Sinclair Lewis. *Affair at Styles* by Agatha Christie. 8 had been quite taken with this last one and thoroughly enjoyed this British lady's writing style. He especially liked the Belgian character, Hercule Poirot. All in all, it was a nice collection of books.

As 8 stepped back out through the door, a commotion arose, unfortunately in the direction of his table. A high voice with an unmistakable southern twang pierced the air.

"*Ahh* don't care who invited him, *ahh'll* not be seated next to a—"

The voice was cut off with a wet gurgling sound. 8 pushed his way through the crowd. A rotund man in a white tuxedo with a straw hat was grasping weakly at a hand belonging to Pearle, a hand which was wrapped around the man's throat.

"Figure I'm doing you a favor," Pearle said. "Stopping you from saying something that might get you killed."

"There you are," Dottie said, looking at 8. "Do something, would you?"

8 shrugged as he walked closer. "Sounds to me like it's being handled," he said.

Pearle lifted the man up to his tiptoes, and then pushed him over backward. Four or five men caught him before he could tumble to the ground. Their faces were angry, and they shot dark looks toward the Black man. 8 looked around to see a mixture of intolerance, sympathy, and apathy. There was not another Black face in sight.

The man in the white tuxedo rubbed his throat with his hand. "Goddamn you," he said. "*Ahh'll* teach you a lesson, you—" he cut off his sentence as Pearle again stepped toward him.

One of the others reached his hand into his jacket, and 8 pulled out his .38. "Let's all keep our hands out in plain sight," he said.

"Don't be saying what I'm thinking you're about to say," Pearle said. "You bring that shit out in the open, and you're going to get your ass kicked."

"Somebody do something," White Tux said. "This man assaulted me."

8 looked around. Most people were here for a good time and could care less that this obnoxious white fellow had gotten pushed around a bit by a Black man. There were five or six sneering faces looking for an opportunity to turn the tables, but that was it.

"How about we get out of here, Pearle," 8 said. "I think we've worn out our welcome."

They backed to the corner of the house, 8 pointing the .38 at White Tux, and made their way to the automobile. It seems that none of the offended men wanted to be the first to peek around the house, and they were in the motorcar and on their way before the first shout was heard.

Chapter 24

The following day found 8 sitting in the cemetery along with Pearle, McGee, and Marty. It was Decoration Day, and a reverend was giving an invocation to a crowd of several thousand. The day was a bit overcast, as if in honor of the dismal memories of the living present here, veterans and their families, remembering those heroes who had served and paid the highest price in their quest to make America a great and wonderful country, as well as a safe land for all. It was interesting to compare the veterans of the Civil War with those of the more recent Great War.

Those who had fought in the Civil War were now in their eighties, stooped and grown old, faces lined, but eyes still fierce and proud, gratified to be honored thus. And then there were the more recent veterans, many still in their early twenties, some just recently having begun to shave. 8 was older than many of these new soldiers who'd fought for life and liberty in a war whose flames had been fanned by the sinking of the *Lusitania*, barbarities in Belgium, and the Zimmerman telegraph where the Germans proposed divvying up the United States at the conclusion of the war.

The Beck Veterans Band broke into an overture of *American Airs* by Catlin. 8 mused that it was ironic having a German conductor and his band celebrating the Allied victory over the Central Powers led by the Germans, joined by 8's own homeland of Austria-Hungary. 8 personally knew five Hungarians and seven Germans who had died fighting for Lady Liberty, six of them buried right here in Evergreen

Cemetery. Several more had been killed by the Spanish Flu that had so devastated the population in the war's final year.

As if reading his mind, Pearle leaned closer and whispered. "You think that if Africa had tried to conquer the world that we'd have a Black band playing here today?"

"It'd probably jazz things up if they did," 8 said. He nudged McGee's shoulder. "You find out anything on Hartmann for me?"

"He's clean. Too clean."

"So clean he must be dirty, huh?"

"You got that right."

"Would it help if I told you that he admitted to running hooch and several other endeavors?" 8 looked at the makeshift stage where an octogenarian was mumbling something about turning the Rebels back at Gettysburg. "And Pearle has suggested that those endeavors might involve brothels and possibly heroin."

"Yeah, that's the rumor on the street," McGee said. "But officially? Nothing. Hartmann isn't to be touched or investigated."

"Sticky fingers out there," 8 said.

"That's about it. He must've some of the top brass in his pocket. I don't know why a wallpaper manufacturer needs to keep guns and muscle on the payroll. But when I asked, I was called into the Chief's office and told that any more inquiries of that nature, and I'd be out on my ass."

Up on stage they introduced a gentleman from the local chapter of the Grand Army of the Republic who was the oldest living veteran in Brooklyn. He made the previous fellow look like a young sprite. 8 thought that it was possible that he'd fought in the Mexican-American War. He began reading the Gettysburg Address.

"You're telling me that even if we dig up something on the man, the police aren't going to do anything about it?"

"I'm telling you that if I don't lie low and keep my nose clean of this whole *shite*, well then, I'll be applying for a job as one of Hartmann's goons."

"I don't think he'd hire an Irishman," Pearle said across 8's body. "Just saying."

"He'd probably hire you on as a manservant or to muck out his stables," Marty said.

"Heard they're planning on building a bridge over the Hudson," 8 said. "Maybe you could get in on the ground floor."

"The hell with you lads," McGee said. "I'm not working for Hartmann and I ain't building no damn bridge."

"Sounds like you got to either give up your morals and principles, or you got to nail Hartmann's ass to a cross so securely that none of those suits pretending to be coppers can cast a shadow on you," Pearle said.

"C'mon," 8 said. "Are you saying the police in Bushwick won't do anything about a guy bootlegging, selling sex, and dealing heroin?"

McGee sighed. "Probably not officially."

"So, you got nothing for me?" 8 asked. "I mean, let me do the dirty work and you keep your hands clean, if not your nose. Give me something to work with."

McGee looked left and right, and then over his shoulder. The band broke into another patriotic song, giving him some cover. He leaned over to 8 and whispered in his ear. "Talked to a housekeeper, former housekeeper, of Hartmann's yesterday. She got let go the day after Colleen Brooks supposedly left for Hollywoodland."

"That's a coincidence," 8 said. "One have anything to do with the other?"

"The maid said that Colleen Brooks was real nice to her. She told Mr. Hartmann that she was surprised that Colleen hadn't said goodbye and that it was strange that she hadn't taken any of her belongings with her. The next thing you know, she was packing her own bag, no pun intended."

Marty, from the far side of McGee, leaned closer. "You don't even know what a pun is, so I'm sure it wasn't intended."

McGee elbowed him. "I forget, what unit did you fight in?"

"Somebody had to stay home and inform the American public what a fine job you were all doing," Marty said. "We couldn't all desert our jobs as public servants."

"The maid have anything else to say?" 8 asked. The band struck up *The Battle Song of Liberty*.

"Said that she saw something that looked like a bloodstain on the floor. Then she was hustled out the door and told to keep her mouth shut."

"Sounds like Colleen didn't go to Hollywoodland," 8 said. "It sounds like the vamp's final role played out in a mansion in Bushwick instead. It'd be nice if her final audience had more than one person, somebody willing to review this concluding performance."

"I doubt Hartmann disposed of the body himself," McGee said.

"You know his muscle? Fellow by the name of Bull? And his gunslinger, goes by the moniker Mouse?"

"Yeah, I know them," McGee said.

"I'd bet dollars to donuts that those two know what happened," 8 said. "Or, at least, where Colleen is."

"I'll have a go at them, see what I can find." McGee looked nervously over his shoulder. "But I gotta keep this quiet."

"Be careful. Even a Mouse can pull a trigger, and he's itching for a kill."

The band broke into *The Star-Spangled Banner*, and everybody came to their feet and added their voices to the lyrics.

Velma woke up to find Tomas sitting in a chair watching her. She yawned, stretched, allowing the falling sheet to expose her nakedness. He was such a pretty man, she thought, his features fine and delicate. He was almost as thin as she, and that was saying something. Not at all like the burly 8 Ballo, whose memory crooked a smile at the corner of her mouth.

"What are you smiling at?" Tomas asked.

"I was thinking about you."

"We gotta talk."

"Sure thing, sugar." Velma sat up, her back against the headboard, sheet at her waist. His eyes greedily drank her in. "What shall we converse about?"

"I just been told that it was your father who whacked Tito."

"That's not much of a surprise."

Tomas shifted his feet. "I know he's your father and all, but he can't get away with that. He's gotta pay."

"Oh, my daddy's going to pay. That's not in doubt."

"You okay with me taking a few *gents* down to Bushwick and whacking him?"

Velma yawned, and stretched lazily again, the sheet sliding further down onto her thighs. Tomas was such a delightfully simple man, she thought. "He's pretty heavily fortified. You wouldn't get close to him."

"I'm not going to sit on my *culo* and do nothing. He killed my partner. I will be avenged."

"Oh, you will be, sugar. We just have to be smart about it."

"What's that mean?" Tomas stood up angrily. "You saying I'm not smart?"

"Not at all, sugar. That's not what I'm saying at all. I just had an idea that might help you out, is all."

"Yeah? What is it?"

Velma nibbled on the end of her finger and then let it trail down her chin, slightly grazing over her right breast, and onto her belly. "I thought I might help you kill two birds with one stone, sugar."

Tomas' eyes were pinned to her naked body. When he spoke again, his angry tone had largely dissipated, and his voice was husky. "You are one amazing looking bird," he said.

"How about you slide out of your clothes and come join me," Velma said. "And I'll tell you exactly what I'm thinking." She pushed a lock of hair back with her other hand, her fingers sliding down her cheek, brushing past her breast, trailing down past the hand on her belly, and finally coming to rest down there. "I'm feeling lonely."

Tomas went down the stairs, his mind lost in the ravishing late morning coupling with Velma. His body still tingled in pleasant memory, and in his mind, he was an invincible warrior. An automobile was at the curb, the motor running, three men in it with long jackets and fedoras pulled low. He climbed into the shotgun seat. A Tommy gun awaited him there, and he checked the rounds as they pulled out on the street.

"Who we gonna hit?" the driver asked.

"A fellow by the name of Spoons Goldman."

"Ain't Spoons a good buddy with Bugsy Siegel?" This from the backseat.

"That he is."

"You saying we're digging our own grave whacking one of Bugsy's friends?" the driver asked.

"This is on the orders of Mr. Schirò?" Another asked.

"He knows nothing of this."

"We're whacking one of Bugsy's men without the boss's knowledge?"

"I got a plan," Tomas said. He thought about what Velma had told him. "To avenge Tito."

"This guy is the one who killed Tito?" the driver asked. "I thought it was that Kraut bastard, Hartmann."

"Trust me," Tomas said. His mind played back to Velma pushing him to his back and climbing atop of him, her lips at his neck, her body writhing. "Bugsy's gonna think it was somebody else did the killing."

"Yeah? Who's he gonna think did it?"

"Fritz Hartmann."

"*Santa merda*," the driver said.

"Nothing holy about that piece of crap Hartmann," Tomas said. "He's gonna get his for gunning down Tito. And we're gonna let Bugsy Siegel do it for us."

"Where we find this Spoons Goldman?" the driver asked.

"I been told that he throws dice for about an hour every single day just around the corner from the Candy Store down to Brownsville," Tomas said. "At three o'clock he walks east three blocks to a joint to pick up the daily take. We hit him between those two places."

"How about we hit him after he picks up the daily take?" the driver asked.

"Not a bad idea," Tomas said. "A little spending money and Hartmann gets blamed. He laughed, the sound brittle in the car. "Let's take a drive and scope out the best place to do it."

A couple hours later, when Spoons Goldman came walking down the sidewalk whistling, they were parked across the street in the shade of a tree. They pulled out, driving past him and the speakeasy that was his pickup, pulling a U-turn further down the street, and again parking about a hundred yards away. They watched as Spoons went inside without a care in the world, like he was going for a drink, and not to pick up a pile of cash.

He was inside for no more than ten minutes before he came back out holding a bag. He turned left and began walking back toward the Candy Store. The driver pulled them alongside Spoons as he was walking past an empty lot, and Tomas and the two men from the back shot him full of holes, his body jerking, the barrage of bullets not allowing him to fall, somehow holding him up like invisible wires, before he finally crumpled to the ground, blood seeping from numerous bullet wounds.

Tomas got out of the car, looking left and right, knowing that if he were spotted, that it could blow the whole plan, and most likely get him killed. Spoons was gasping on the ground, blood gurgling from his mouth, but he did manage to ask Tomas if he had a death wish before a wracking spasm overtook his body. While he was still twitching, Tomas collected the bag of cash then leaned down and put a piece of paper on the man's lapel and pinned it there with a Damascus pocketknife, driving the blade to the hilt right below the ribcage. Engraved on the ivory handle was a name, Fritz Hartmann.

The note said: *Kill one of ours, we kill one of yours.*

Chapter 25

8 met McGee for a cup of coffee at a drugstore on Gates Avenue, just down from the police station. They brushed the rain from their jackets before sitting down on round stools at the gleaming bar. It was that kind of day.

"What you got?" 8 asked. He took off his bowler, letting the water run in rivulets from the top. "Something more on the missing woman?"

"Yeah, but not what you think," McGee said. "Looks like Hartmann whacked one of Bugsy Siegel's guys. Not just anyone, but Spoons Goldman."

"Spoons Goldman?"

"Grew up with Bugsy. Been one of his top lieutenants all the way in his rise to Mayor of Brownsville, or whatever the *feck* that bug-eyed bastard is."

"What the heck is Hartmann doing? One day he's hitting one of Schirò's men, the next he's whacking one of Bugsy's top lieutenants. Something don't smell right."

"No, it don't."

The soda jerk handed them coffee and asked if they wanted menus, which they declined. He was a balding and bespectacled elderly man. At this time of day, there were only a few people sipping coffee or eating a light breakfast. Later on, young people would fill the counter getting ice cream, soda pop, and a mixture of the two.

"How ya know it was Hartmann's goons?" 8 asked.

"They left a note. Said 'kill one of ours, we kill one of yours'."

8 contemplated that. "You figuring this was in retaliation for Hartmann's fellow that Bugsy clipped in front of me and Pearle while we had bags over our heads?"

"You mean the lad you *didn't* see killed and there is *no* body for?"

"Yeah, that'd be the one."

McGee chuckled. "Yeah, more than likely."

"It could've been anybody. Probably lots of people out there with a grudge. Heck, Bugsy has killed more fellows than most people have seen moving pictures."

"There's one more thing. The note was pinned to Spoons with a pocketknife with the name Fritz Hartmann engraved on it."

"Son of a gun," 8 said.

"Seems like he wanted Bugsy to know who did it. Send a message."

"Or somebody wanted it to look like it was Hartmann." 8 looked at the mirror behind the bar blocked by shelves of glasses, spigots for the soda and coffee, and a variety of lights. "What now?"

"Now?" McGee asked. "Now we get ready for war. Bugsy ain't gonna wait. He'll be coming up the street real quick and hard. I think Lansky's been reining him in this long, but there'll be no stopping him now. My bet is the streets are gonna run red with blood. I'm just hoping no civilians get caught in the crossfire."

"Aren't you all doom and despondence."

"Us Irish know when a blight is upon us."

"Maybe I can have a chat with Bugsy. Get him to give it a couple of days. See if I can find something out."

McGee guffawed. "Didn't you end up with a bag on your head and almost dead last time you tried to have a chat with that twisted child?"

"Actually, I've seen him since. He hired me to find Velma."

McGee guffawed louder and harder. "That's rich is what that is. Seems like a lot of lads are looking for that one."

"She's quite a woman."

McGee gave him a sideways look. "You said you passed on Fritz's message to his daughter. Is that all you did?"

"You got the address for that maid that got fired?"

"Take you over there if you want."

"No offense, but I think she might be more willing to speak if there isn't a flattie standing there."

"You might be right there. Plus, if anybody at the precinct gets wind of what I'm doing, I'll be down in a caisson pouring pylons in the Hudson River right soon afterward."

"Women have been known to open up to me," 8 said. "Especially if I'm offering money."

"That's called going to a brothel." McGee laughed. "And they're most likely lying to you."

8 colored and then chuckled. "You know what I mean."

McGee nodded. "She'd probably welcome a few extra dollars to the coffers. Last I knew, she hadn't gotten herself a new position yet."

Millicent Winter was a thin woman with dark hair and eyes. She reminded 8 of Velma in appearance, if not sex appeal, and certainly not smokiness to her eyes, a warmth flushing his skin with just the thought. Millicent lived in a tenement building behind the factories that dotted the neighborhood around the intersection of Wykoff and Flushing Avenues. She opened the door with a tremulous hand and fluttering eyes.

"What do you want?" She had a faint German accent.

"I'm looking for Millicent Winter."

The tremors stretched from her hand, down her arm, and shook her entire body. "That is me."

"Millicent, my name is 8 Ballo. I'm a private investigator. Can I come in for a moment?"

"My roommates are all at work. It wouldn't be proper."

8 guessed that she'd only been in America for a few years at most.

"I'm investigating the disappearance of Colleen Brooks. I think our conversation would be best in private."

Millicent wavered, her dark eyes pleading with him to go away, but either her manners, subservience, or fear got the better of her, and she opened the door wide, waving him into an apartment that was the size of 8's living room, yet he counted five sleeping rolls on the floor. One corner had a table with just two chairs. She offered water. He declined. They sat down.

"I'm told that you, until recently, worked for Fritz Hartmann."

Millicent nodded yes.

"Why were you let go?"

"They told me that a necklace was missing. They accused me of stealing."

"Did you?"

"No!" Her eyes flashed, anger driving back the fear. "I do not steal."

"But they thought you did?"

"I do not think so. I think they did not like me asking questions about what happened to Missus Brooks."

"Tell me about that."

"Mr. Hartmann told me to never talk about Missus Brooks. Never again."

8 leaned forward, trying to be as gentle as his robust build would allow. He laid a ten-dollar bill on the table. "I'll never mention your name."

"He can never find out." Millicent's eyes flickered to the sawbuck. "Or he will kill me like he killed her."

8 doubled the sawbuck on the tabletop. What the heck, he figured, it was either Hartmann's money he was spending or Bugsy Siegel's. And he was sure that Millicent Winter could most likely use it. There weren't many choices for unmarried women once they'd been fired. Maid, governess, store clerk. People would be reluctant to hire her with the stigma of being a thief hanging around her neck. This would most likely force her into a brothel to ply the

only marketable wares left to her, unless, of course, she found a man willing to marry a thief.

Millicent looked at the money. Tears filled her eyes. "The little one who they call Mouse, you know him?"

8 nodded yes.

"He took me up to Missus Brooks' room and told me to pack her things. Said that she'd moved out. To pack her things… not in suitcases. But in pillowcases. I asked why she didn't take her clothes and whatnots with her. He slapped me. Hard. Twice. So I did what I was told."

"What happened to her things?" 8 asked.

"They had me bring them downstairs and put them in the front hall."

"Is that all?"

"When I went in to make Master Hartmann's bed, there was a spot on the floor, dark, like it may've been blood, but I didn't say nothing more." Millicent began crying softly at the memory.

"Officer McGee told me about all that," 8 said. He thought about breaking the little gunslinger into pieces over his knee. "Minus the part about Mouse hitting you."

"There's something I didn't tell the police," Millicent said.

"Yes. What's that?"

"You won't tell him? You won't tell Master Hartmann?"

"I promise."

Millicent sobbed. "When I was done, that Mouse, he went and got that big man, the one they call Bull, to help carry everything out of the house. I heard Bull tell Mouse that it'd all been taken care of, and then he laughed, that tiny squeal of his, coming from such a big man, sounds so odd."

"What had all been taken care of?"

"He didn't say, but he did say that the sunflowers were going to be particularly beautiful this year. And he laughed again, like a swine squealing, and it made me sick to my stomach."

8 reflected on what this could mean and came up with one ready solution. "Where are the sunflowers planted?" he asked.

"In the corner of the backyard, right near the wooden trellis."

"I take it Bull is not usually in charge of the landscaping?"

Millicent snorted. "No. Not unless he was growing hot dogs."

"I'm sorry you lost your job, Millicent." 8 stood up.

"I'm not. I would've quit if I hadn't been fired."

"You didn't like it there?"

"It's just… just…" Millicent sobbed. "Now, with Missus Brooks gone… I was afraid."

"Afraid of what?"

"That Master Hartmann was going to make me do things with him again. Sinful things."

8 curled his hands into fists. "Fritz will get what he has coming to him," he said. "And Millicent? Give me a few days and then stop by, and we'll see if we can find you a job. I know a few people. Decent people." He handed her a card. "That's my office address on Bushwick Avenue."

"If Master Hartmann hears that I went to the office of a private investigator, I'm as good as dead."

"Wait until it's safe to come," 8 said. "And then swing on by."

"Safe? When will it ever be safe? How will I know?"

8 smiled. "You'll know."

Fritz Hartmann was angry. Anger was part of his everyday life, but this was something new. The fury surged through his mind like a branding iron. He didn't dislike it. It made him feel alive. Much like killing a man or taking a woman caused his adrenalin to run hot, his rage stoked the coals that told him he was alive, not just existing.

"Tell me again," Hartmann said. He was in his study at home. It seemed the safest place to be at this time. Across from him sat

Mouse and Bull.

"Somebody strung Lefty up a flagpole down towards the cemetery, round the corner from where he lives," Mouse said. His head jerked as he spoke, and he kept licking his lips. "I'm betting it was that maniac Bugsy."

"In retaliation for what happened to Spoons," Bull said, his high-pitched voice at odds with his enormous size.

"Something we had nothing to do with," Hartmann said. His words were short and clipped.

"Rumor has it that there was a pocketknife sticking out of Spoons' chest with your name on it," Mouse said.

Hartmann had already gone and looked in the box on top of his dresser. The pocketknife that had been a Christmas gift from Velma a few years back was indeed gone. "Somebody's setting me up. The question is, how did that somebody get my goddamn knife?"

Mouse and Bull said nothing.

"How'd they kill Lefty?" Hartmann's voice was barely a whisper.

Mouse's tongue flickered in and out of his mouth. "Somebody broke most of the bones in his body. Sir."

"Bugsy Siegel likes to work people over with a baseball bat, doesn't he?" Hartmann asked.

"Sure does," Bull said. "Sir."

"I want to know who's fucking me over, and I want to know yesterday," Hartmann said. "Do you fucking morons understand?"

"Yessir," two voices said, and two heads bobbed.

"We need to beef up protection at all our businesses," Hartmann said. "I don't want anything getting burnt down."

"We're already stretched thin," Bull said.

Hartmann grasped and threw a paperweight from his desk and hit Bull square in the forehead. He didn't react in any way, but there was a red imprint planted there. "Stop running the booze. Put the bootleggers to work with Tommy guns. And stop making fucking excuses."

"Yessir," Bull said.

"What the fuck are you waiting for?" Hartmann said. "Go."

The two men stood up.

"Not you, Mouse. Stay for a moment."

Bull left the room.

"Where's my daughter?" Hartmann asked. "I want her home."

"I think she's somewhere in Williamsburg with a man named Tomas Lombardo." Mouse's eyes and tongue darted this way and that as he spoke.

"Did you hear me?" Hartmann asked. "I want her home."

"I'll put the word out."

"You will go get her and bring her to me."

"Me?"

"I cannot abide failure on this. She's all that I have left, and I want her here, with me, because I believe a war is brewing. Don't let me down, Mouse." His eyes narrowed, and Mouse licked his lips and swallowed against the fear. "Bring me my daughter."

Chapter 26

Marty had an idea. And his instincts were usually good. So he followed the idea, the instincts, and the man. The notion was that Arkady had been staying with Nikos, meaning they were pretty tight, and if he was going to reach out to anybody, it would be the Greek. He'd checked the speakeasy, and Nikos was due to work at six. Marty doubted the man got up before noontime, not with his late hours.

Thus, a few minutes before twelve, Marty was parked on a stoop down and across the street with a cup of joe. He grinned, thinking about this slang term for coffee. That'd been one of his first stories he'd written for the *Eagle*, how back in 1914 Secretary of the Navy Joe Daniels banned alcohol from all U.S. Navy ships. From that point onward, the strongest drink available was coffee, or a *cup of joe*, as the young men started to call it. Marty had never been sure if it was due to disdain or respect. He suspected the former.

A little after one, Nikos emerged from his building, but only went as far as the corner grocery, before returning home, presumably to make something to eat. Marty had written some big stories over the past nine years, but this one had the potential to be his white whale, if he could only catch it. Why was Velma on the lam from her father, he wondered? Had Hartmann indeed killed Colleen Brooks? Marty knew that if he could write an exposé on the man as not just a common criminal but the cold-blooded murderer of an innocent Irish girl, all while tying in known gangsters Bugsy and

Meyer, as well as Schirò, why then he'd be well on his way to an award-winning piece.

The lynchpin would have to be the pretty little flapper lady, Velma. She had something to share. But so did this Arkady fellow. What information had he been bringing to share with 8, and why was *he* now on the lam? Of course, what Marty risked was that what Velma knew was so inflammatory, causing not just her to flee but also ending at least one life, so damning that he himself would be in jeopardy. Marty was not himself a very tough man, that he knew, but his friends 8, Pearle, and McGee were, and they'd have his back.

At three o'clock, Nikos came out of his apartment carrying a bag, and this time, there was more purpose to his walk. Marty followed him to the trolley stop and hopped on the back, as they trundled along. Nikos got off in Brooklyn Heights, and Marty followed him to the corner of Columbia Heights and Orange Street. The Greek looked both ways, and over his shoulder, before darting into the Hotel Margaret, which towered high over everything nearby. *Hmm, interesting*, Marty thought. *Who would Nikos know staying at such a swanky place as this?*

Marty followed him inside, watching as Nikos went to the front desk and then over to the lift. The hair bristling on the back of Marty's neck told him that this was where the Russian, Arkady, was hiding out. Right in plain sight in one of the nicest hotels in all of Brooklyn. He went over to the desk and asked whose room that man had been inquiring about. The desk worker refused that information, but Marty flashed his media badge, the manager was called over, and he got what he wanted.

Only it wasn't what he expected. Nikos was on his way to Peter Sokolov's room. Not Arkady Bortnik's. Of course, Marty realized, the man was hiding out from a murderer. He wouldn't give out his real name. And his partner, who'd been killed, had been named Peter. Perhaps a reminder.

Marty asked to use the phone and called 8. Luckily, 8 was in his office, and said he'd be there as fast as he could. That type of fast turned out to be forty-nine minutes.

8 and Marty simply went up to the door and knocked. Sometimes the easy way was the best way. Not usually, but on occasion.

"Who is it?" the muffled voice came through the door.

"Package for Peter Sokolov."

The door opened a crack, and 8 put one massive forearm against the door and pushed his way into the room. "Hello, Arkady," he said. "You're going to have to be more careful than that if you want to stay alive."

8 pushed Arkady into the center of the room. Marty followed them in, shutting the door behind him. 8 had to duck underneath the simple chandelier lighting the interior. There were three mustard-colored, Federal-style armchairs, a bed, and a desk in the opulent hotel room. Nikos was sitting in one of the chairs. 8 sat down next to him, gesturing for Arkady to have a seat in the third one, leaving Marty standing awkwardly by the door.

"I suppose I'm glad you found me and not Hartmann," Arkady said.

"It seems that I'd have to agree," 8 said. "I'm here to help."

"Or get me killed." The Russian spoke in flat-clipped tones. He appeared more angry than scared.

"I'm sorry about Peter," 8 said.

"So am I," Arkady said. "And somebody will have to answer for killing him."

"What did you want to tell me that night?" 8 asked gently. "Something to do with Hartmann killing Colleen Brooks?"

"Yes. She told us she did it, but it was in confidence, so we didn't share it with you that first time you came to us," Arkady said. "Peter didn't want to share with you at all, but I insisted. And now he's dead."

"She?"

"Velma. Velma Hartmann. Who'd you think I was talking about?"

8 sat in stunned silence for a bit. "So… you… just now, were afraid that it was Velma Hartmann come to kill you?"

Arkady bowed his head. "The thought had crossed my mind."

"Do you want to tell me now?"

There was no answer at first, and 8 realized that Arkady was trying to get control of his emotions, fighting back tears at being reminded so harshly of his dead partner and lover.

"You followed me, didn't you?" Nikos was staring at Marty. "I thought I saw you skulking along behind me, but figured I was just paranoid."

Marty nodded yes. "But if I thought of tailing you, you can bet that somebody else will soon have the same idea, if he hasn't already."

They all looked at the door. Arkady cleared his throat. "We were out listening to music and drinking one night with Velma, and from out of nowhere, she blurted out that she did it, that she killed Colleen."

"What?" 8 said. Velma? Beautiful and sexy Velma had killed Colleen Brooks. "Just to be clear, you mean, when you say that it was Hartmann, you were talking about Velma Hartmann, and not Fritz Hartmann?"

"Ah, yes," Arkady said. "I see how you could jump to that conclusion, but no, Peter and I often called our dear little Velma by her last name. Just Hartmann. I'm not sure why. It just seemed to fit."

"But why would she kill Colleen?" 8 asked.

Arkady shook his head. "She wouldn't talk any more about it, not after she blurted it out, that she'd killed her. That was it. And she made us promise to keep our mouths shut. We didn't know this Colleen, really by name only, maybe we crossed paths once or twice, but that was it."

"And you think that she killed Peter?" 8 asked. "Or had him killed?"

"I don't know." Arkady put his head down into his hands. "But it goes to figure, doesn't it? I mean, we were coming to tell you that she was the killer, and then two men slash our throats. Someone seemed to be intent on stopping us from speaking what we knew."

"How'd she know where to find you?" 8 asked.

"Maybe she was having us watched?"

"You make it sound like she's running a criminal syndicate with minions following her orders," 8 said. "I don't see that. I see a scared and lonely young lady hiding out from her father."

"Hartmann... Velma, could always get men to do her bidding." Arkady chuckled softly. "She was gifted in that way. She just had *something*. What every man seemed to want. Men were willing to bend over backwards, steal, cheat, and yes, maybe even murder for her."

8 started to retort and checked himself. Wasn't he, after all, doing Velma's bidding? "What do you plan on doing?" he asked Arkady instead.

"I thought I might ask her if she killed Peter," Arkady said. "And if she did, the thought had crossed my mind that I might shoot her right between her pretty little eyes."

When 8 got back to his office, Bugsy Siegel was waiting for him out front of the building. He was surrounded by five or six other fellows who all had narrow faces and looked like they'd woken up on the wrong side of the bed. Next to the *other* four men loitering by several cars smoking cigarettes and carrying Tommy guns, they looked downright cheerful. 8 figured that this was more than just a casual visit to get an update, but was also a message to Fritz Hartmann that he wasn't afraid of the German and would waltz into his territory whenever he wanted.

"8, where the hell you been?" Bugsy flashed a wide smile to show that he was just having fun. "We been here about a half-hour waiting for you. You know what you need? You need a receptionist. Some pretty lady who answers your phone and can tell blokes like me when you'll be back."

8 had had a thought that this might be true and had wondered if Millicent, Hartmann's fired maid, would be good at the job. "You seem to have brought a few friends," he said. "Are we celebrating something?"

"Every day we wake up on this side of the ground is a cause for celebration, don't you think?" Bugsy said with a smile, but his eyes spoke the truth of his statement. He wasn't a man who took living for granted.

"Don't have anything on the girl, yet, if that's what you're doing here," 8 said.

"I got a message from Arnie for you," Bugsy said. "Maybe we could go up to your office?"

"Sure," 8 said. "It's not that big, you might need to leave a few of your friends behind."

"This conversation is between you and me. Let's go." Bugsy snapped his fingers.

8 read the easy command that Bugsy had over the others. Which was amazing, as he really wasn't much more than a boy. But 8 knew a lot of boys who had grown up quick during the Great War. And became stone cold killers. He imagined that the streets of New York had been Bugsy's Great War, and that from a fairly young age. The gangsters fanned out behind them as they went up the stairs and into the building.

"If you had a pretty little receptionist, then she could offer me a cup of joe," Bugsy said as they entered the office and sat down.

"I got an office out back, but no door," 8 said. "It'd be hard to have any privacy."

"You can talk in front of a dame. They don't understand much of what you say, anyway. Or you could just put a damn door on."

8 looked at him, wondering what women he'd been around in his

young life. He thought of Marie Laveau, the Voodoo Queen back in the 19th century, who'd opened a hair salon just to learn the intimate secrets of women and a brothel to gain the confidences of men.

"Let me give you a piece of advice," 8 said. "Women are smarter than men. And if you talk openly about your business in front of them, I sure hope you trust them and don't treat them like a house plant."

"Ha. That's a lark. Women smarter than men." Bugsy sat down. "Maybe in raising children and the like."

"Hey, take it or leave it. The advice is free," 8 said.

"You sure have some strange ideas." Bugsy shook his head, an incredulous look upon his face. "What'cha got for me on my Velma?"

"What's with all the firepower outside?" 8 asked.

"Velma's old man messed with the wrong people."

"That was a shame what happened to Spoons. You sure it was Hartmann?"

"It was Hartmann's goddamn knife pinning a note to his chest, so yeah, I'm pretty sure he's the rotten coward that sent some of his boys out to cause us some damage. Spoons, he was like a brother to me."

"Why would he leave a knife with his name on it in the victim?"

"I already told you, to send a goddamn message. We kill one of his, he kills one of ours." Bugsy was leaning over the desk, face red, eyes bulging—then he suddenly flipped a page and took a breath and sat back. "But that ain't none of your business. You best be finding me Velma real soon, or I'm going to get angry with you."

8 also leaned back in his chair. "I told you that it hurts my feelings when you threaten me," he said.

"You're a cool cucumber, alright. Don't make me find out if you got anything to back it up with."

"What if it wasn't Hartmann who killed Spoons?" 8 asked.

"What the hell you mean?"

"Supposing," 8 said cautiously, "someone was wanting it to look like Hartmann. Pretty good way to do that would be to leave his pocketknife in the chest of the dead man, don't you think?"

Bugsy took a deep breath. "Nobody else is stupid enough to start a war with us," he said.

"Just consider the possibility, is all I'm asking. If I find out more, I'll pass the information onto you. Gratis."

"What?"

"Free of charge."

"You're one odd duck, Mr. 8 Ballo." Bugsy shook his head.

"You said you got a message for me?"

Bugsy reached in his pocket, pulled out an envelope, and dropped it on the desk. 8 turned it over and saw that it'd been opened, and poorly resealed. He pulled a pocketknife from his desk, noting that it did not have *his* name on the handle, and ripped it open. The note was simple:

> He'll be at 44 Roebling Street. 3B.
> Williamsburg. Tomorrow night.

"What business you got with Arnie?" Bugsy asked.

"Was looking for a fellow who dodged out on his wife, is all. Ran into Rothstein at a luncheon the other day, and we were talking about this and that and it came up. He thought he might know the fellow I was talking about and would see about getting me an address." 8 shrugged. "Guess we'll see if it's the right one, sure enough."

Bugsy nodded, seemingly accepting the explanation. "Don't be wasting time on that stuff when you should be finding my gal."

"Finding Velma is my first priority," 8 said.

"You know, she sure hates her father. I'm thinking if I kill the Kraut, she might just come find me for a proper thank you."

"Yeah? Why you think that?"

"She told me so," Bugsy said. "Last time I saw her, she said she'd like to spit on his grave and kiss the man who killed him."

Chapter 27

"So, Rothstein came through with an address, did he?" Pearle asked by way of greeting when he answered the door. The sun had left a faint glow to the night sky.

"He gave me an address," 8 said. "Could be anything."

"What means you?" Pearle asked with a quirky smile.

"It means for one that the old Italian guard, such as Tomas Lombardo, who are strictly Sicilians, are having a hard time with the emergence of newcomer Italians fraternizing with the Jews and others."

"You're thinking Rothstein might be making a power play against Schirò by using you to open the door?"

"The thought has crossed my mind. Bugsy hires me to find Velma. Who happens to be staying with Tomas. Then Bugsy shows up with an address for Tomas. Who has Velma staying with him. It's all a bit too pat for me."

"Whoa, hold on," Pearle said. "You think they're using you to find Tomas and then they're going to take him out?"

"They seem to know where Tomas is," 8 said. "Which means maybe they want me to open the door for them and then make it look like I was the one who killed him."

"Pretty complicated. What makes you think that?"

"I don't know. All I know is everything is a little too organized for my taste. Something fishy is going on."

"Then you got the strife between Bugsy and Hartmann going,"

Pearle said. "They could be killing two birds with one stone, much like Daedalus did."

8 and Pearle both had a love for Greek mythology. "And then use their wings to fly first to freedom and then to fall to their deaths from their own hubris," 8 said wryly.

"Kill Schirò's top hitter and Hartmann's daughter all in one fell swoop," Pearle said. "Holy Christ."

"Only, I don't think they plan on killing Velma. If Hartmann really wants his daughter back safely, it will behoove Bugsy to have her as a captive. And I truly believe he'd like her company, should she be willing or not."

"What you're saying is, is we'd be stupid to walk into the middle of that hornet's nest."

"Don't see any other option," 8 said.

"No other option?"

"I'm looking for Velma. I know where she is. She's most likely in danger. No other option, for me at least."

"Wait up, then," Pearle said. He went back into the house only to reappear less than a minute later with a Tommy gun. "No sense bringing a lousy pea shooter to a gangster war."

"Why the heck does everybody have those?" 8 asked. "And where do you get one?"

"You saw it the other day when I pulled it out for McGee to play with," Pearle said.

"Yeah, I've been meaning to ask ever since. Lot going on."

"Easy enough if you got two-hundred bucks," Pearle said. "It seems that the only people who can afford them are gangsters, though."

"And legitimate businessmen such as yourself," 8 said drily.

"You make a lot of money, people want to take it from you," Pearle said. "Especially if you're Black. Let's go save the girl."

They clambered into Pearle's car, the Tommy gun on the seat between them. "One thing I didn't tell you yet," 8 said. "I found that Arkady fellow, or rather, Marty did. He said that Velma told him and Peter that she was the one who killed Colleen Brooks, and Arkady believes that it was most likely her that killed Peter, to keep the two of them from talking to me."

Pearle whistled. "And the plot thickens. We're going to save a murderer—*if* she is a murderer—from three different New York gangs and one Russian bent on vengeance. Why is that again?"

"I don't believe—"

"Oh, that's right," Pearle interrupted him. "Because she's a real doll with gams that stretch forever in a shapely manner."

"And outstanding eyes," 8 said sheepishly. "And I don't believe that she killed Colleen or Peter."

"Based on her eyes?" Pearle asked.

"Well, yeah, that amongst other things."

Pearle laughed a deep booming rumble. "Well, I suppose that's good enough reason for me to go into the hornet's nest. You say they're on Roebling?"

They parked on the corner, facing away from 44 Roebling, just in front of a horse-drawn wagon with the last crates of unsold farm produce being packed up for the day. The farmer was giving out carrots to the street urchins who were taking them and dashing off. And then it was full on dark, and the farmer climbed onto the wagon and went off.

"Long day," Pearle said.

"He'll be back before dawn," 8 said.

"Glad I'm not a farmer."

"Was kind of thinking it must be nice to not get shot at."

"Yeah, well farmers have locusts and dust storms and things like that. And they gotta bust their ass all day."

8 chuckled. "Okay, then. I'm going to go get Velma, and we'll be back in a jiffy." He opened the automobile door.

"You know, according to the scientist Gilbert Newton Lewis, a jiffy is the amount of time it takes light to travel one centimeter in a vacuum, which is about one trillionth of a second."

8 chuckled. "You read too much, my friend. But, I believe that is faster than a bullet, so I'll try to keep it to a jiffy. Safer that way."

"Sure you don't want me to come with you?"

"This is my folly. Wouldn't feel right putting you into an almost certain trap."

"Women." Pearle shook his head.

"You keep an eye out. Give a warning if the bad guys show up. Be ready to go when I come back."

As 8 walked off, he heard Pearle get out of the car. He knew that his friend would light a cigar and watch his back as he went into the lion's den. He realized that he'd not get a warm reception from Tomas Lombardo and his friends. Then there was Bugsy who might be showing up to double-cross and kill him, taking Velma for himself. Yet, he walked on, not because of Velma's sexy eyes and delicious lips and pleasurable bedroom antics, but because he felt she needed to be protected from all these forces clawing at her. His rational self, of course, wondered just how much he might be rationalizing, but he'd made up his mind.

There was no one out front. That was pretty lax what with Tito having just been whacked and the increasing rumble of trouble brewing. This was not the case for the third floor. A man sat out front of 3B, and when 8 approached, he stood up and pushed his jacket back to reveal a pistol at his side. The man had a scowl that wrapped its way around the scar on his cheek.

"What'cha want?" he asked.

8 punched him in the chin, driving him back into the wall with a shudder. His knees buckled, and he slid to the floor. 8 reached down and pulled the gat from his waistband, hit him in the side of the head with it, stepped back, and then forward, putting his shoulder to the wooden door that burst open was as if it were made from matchwood.

There were two men sitting at a table off to the right and another on an armchair on the left. 8 pulled his own pistol and leveled one gun in either direction. It seemed that Tomas had holed up with a few of Schirò's gang to back him up.

"I'm looking for Velma Hartmann."

"Who the hell are you?" the man in the armchair asked.

"Name's 8 Ballo. Who are you?"

The driver who'd taken him to Velma the other night stepped through a doorway from across the room. He held a pistol leveled at 8. "What do you want here?" he asked.

8 shifted his left hand to aim the pistol back at the man. "Hello, Tomas. I believe that you have some unwanted visitors coming."

"I think he's already here." Tomas was a handsome man with high cheekbones and a smooth face with a faint mustache under a well-formed nose. "And I'm about to shoot him in the head."

"Any reason why Bugsy Siegel would want you dead?" 8 asked.

Tomas shifted his feet. "None that I can think of off the top of my head."

Outside, a gunshot rang out on the street. "Well, I think he's here now, and you best be ready for him or ready to be dead," 8 said. The pistol fire had been a warning from Pearle that they had company.

"I think you're lying," Tomas said.

Velma stepped up behind him. "He's here to help, darling. Put down the weapon. We got troubles."

Tomas let his arm be pushed toward the floor.

"Is there a back way out of here?" 8 asked.

"Down the end of the hallway there's backstairs," Tomas said. He motioned to the three men. "Let's go. We gotta clear out of here."

A burst of automatic weapon fire erupted from outside and then was drowned out by an overwhelming crescendo.

The two men from the table led the way, but were no more than two steps through the front door of the apartment when bullets ripped into them from the stairway. Tomas snapped a shot from his pistol through the opening. "What've you done?" he yelled. "There must be a dozen men coming at us."

8 caught Velma under one arm and carried her through the inner entrance to the hallway and then into the second door on the left. It was a bedroom.

"My, my, dear 8, do you really think we have time for this now?" she asked.

8 peered around the corner to see Tomas at the end of the hallway with his pistol leveled, pulling the trigger, and then his body slumped to the ground, half of his skull missing and brain matter coating the wallpaper. 8 looked around. He handed the pistol he'd taken from the guard out front to Velma, told her to point at the doorway and pull the trigger to buy him some time. There was no window. He took three steps low and hard and crashed his shoulder into the wall and it splintered.

Behind him, Velma fired the gun, *crack, crack, crack*. 8 backed up and drove at the wall again. This time, a hole appeared, and he pulled at the new-fangled plasterboard that had replaced the labor-intensive horsehair plastering and kicked at the pine studs to create an opening large enough for a person to fit through. From behind him, he heard Velma firing. Crack-crack-click.

"C'mon," he yelled. "Through here." He stepped back past her to the door and took two shots of his own before turning and diving through the opening behind Velma. There was a very surprised man and woman huddled against the far wall. "Where's the fire escape?" he asked.

The man pointed at the door. "Down to the left," he said in a shaking voice.

8 followed Velma, turning just as a man poked a Tommy gun through the opening. 8 shot the fellow in the face. They went down to another door and through it, pushing open a window, and

clambering out onto the fire escape. Velma proved quite nimble down the ladder, jumping the last few feet to the alleyway with 8 landing next to her.

"This way," 8 said, grabbing her hand and pulling her toward Roebling Street. His sense of direction was good, and they came out right next to Pearle's automobile, the man himself crouched down by the rear tire. "Hey, Pearle, how about we skedaddle?"

Pearle turned with the weapon leveled at them. "Shouldn't be sneaking up on a guy like that," he said.

"I thought the gunfire might've announced our arrival," 8 said.

"Well, let's git, then," Pearle said. He stepped to the driver's door and got in as 8 and Velma tumbled into the back.

"Nobody shooting back at you?" 8 asked as they pulled onto the street and took a turn immediately.

"None of the ones left outside are still alive," Pearle said. "Was only three of 'em."

"Who was it?" 8 asked.

"You didn't catch a glimpse of any of 'em?" Pearle asked.

"Just one guy, but his face was a bit unrecognizable." *More so after I shot the fellow in his craggy visage*, 8 thought.

"It was Bugsy, alright. Could see him plain as day when he got out of the automobile. Went through the door first, he did. That guy don't mind putting himself in harm's way, not at all."

"Well, that's not the fellow I shot in the noggin. Too bad. The world would be a better place without that bug-eyed bastard."

Velma didn't begin shaking until they got back to Pearle's house. 8 figured Bugsy would be looking for him at his own place, so it was best to lay low. Perhaps the man had been appeased after killing Tomas and his friends. Perhaps not.

Pearle brought a bottle of whiskey and three glasses into the living room. He set the glasses on a table, sloshed each halfway full of brown liquor, and delivered two of them to 8 and Velma where they sat on the couch. He grasped his own drink and settled into an armchair across from them.

"He's dead, isn't he?" Velma said. "I saw him lying there in the hallway. So much blood."

"Yes. Tomas is dead," 8 said.

"What's it all for?" Velma sobbed.

"I was hoping you could tell me," 8 said.

"It's my fault. All my fault. I killed him."

"No, no you didn't. Tomas knew what game he was playing. He knew the stakes. Bugsy and his men, they're the ones who killed him." 8 put his arm around her. He'd meant to refrain from physical contact until he got to the bottom of who killed Colleen and Peter, but she seemed suddenly so fragile, so in need of protection. "But why was Bugsy there?"

"They were looking for me, weren't they?" Velma laid her head into the crook of 8's neck and sobbed. "So, in a way, I did kill him."

"I guess in a way, you're responsible. But so am I. So is Pearle."

"Me?" Pearle asked, his hands up at his shoulders.

8 shot him a look. He took the hint, stood, gave a small wave, and left the room.

"Tomas was a nice man."

"He was a hitman for a Sicilian gangster. He knew the stakes."

Velma pulled herself back from 8, visibly composing her face. "Thank you for saving me," she said.

"I don't know if Bugsy and his gang would have been there if I wasn't," he said. "But they might've gone anyway."

"And they would've killed me, too," Velma said.

8 thought of the man who he'd busted in the head and then how he broke down the door, erasing two obstacles that would have otherwise prevented Bugsy and his goons from getting into the apartment. "I gotta ask you something. Did you tell Arkady Bortnik that you killed Colleen Brooks?"

Velma reached for her whiskey and took a healthy slug, giving a slight gasp after she swallowed. "No, I never said I killed Colleen. Why?"

"He tells me you did."

"That's not true, I never..." Velma trailed off, a faraway look in her eyes, and took another drink.

"Yes?" 8 asked.

"Right after, I was upset, the very next night, and I was drinking with Arkady and Peter, and I blurted out that I'd killed her." Velma turned her eyes from inward to imploring 8. "But I didn't mean I actually killed her. I meant it was my fault. Like tonight."

"Right after what?"

"Right after Daddy killed her."

"If Fritz did the deed, why was it your fault?"

"I came home and heard the most awful ruckus taking place. The yelling wasn't abnormal, but this time there was a physical altercation. Oh, sure, Daddy had hit her a few times, but this was more. He was yelling that he wouldn't let her leave, calling her the most vile things, and you could hear him punching her and throwing her into the wall, and she was screaming and screaming and screaming. I went to Daddy's bedroom and opened the door. I didn't know what I was going to do, but I had to do something. And it was quiet. Just like that. The most awful noise to just nothing. Colleen was on the floor like an injured bird, her dress torn, her face bloody, her leg crooked wrong, and her neck, oh god, her neck was at an impossible angle." Velma put her head in her hands, but she didn't sob or make a noise. "Daddy had beaten her to death."

"What happened next?"

"Bull came in and... he grabbed me from behind and carried me to my room and flung me on my bed and closed the door. After a bit, I tried to leave, and there was another man there, I don't know his name. He just put his hand against my forehead and pushed me back and shut the door, and then I just gave it up, and lay down. Next thing you know, it was the next day. About noontime. I opened the door, and there was nobody there. I went downstairs, and Daddy was there, but he didn't say a word about what happened. Just like it hadn't, and God, I don't know, I just went about life like I was sleepwalking, but I wasn't, was I?"

"Why did you say that you killed Colleen?"

Velma sniffled, shook her head, and looked 8 in the eye. "I brought her home to him. I knew that he'd like her and that *she'd* like to be taken care of."

"And you were right?"

"Yes. Until I wasn't. She got tired of how he told her what she could do, who she could talk to, what she could wear, who she could go out with and where. So, she told him she was going to leave. Talked about going out to Hollywoodland. That drove him crazy. At first, he bought her more things. Gave her all my mother's dresses and jewelry. Lavished her with gifts. Took her to the theater. But what she wanted, he could never giver her. He wanted more than she could give, probably more than any woman could possibly give. So, he killed her. Just like that."

8 thought of Millicent telling him that she believed Colleen to be buried under the bed of sunflowers in the backyard. "Do you know what happened to Colleen, her body?"

"No. Like I said, when I got up the next day, she was just gone. Like it never happened."

"And that's why you left your father's house?"

"It was the final straw. It took me a few weeks to get my courage up. Then, a Forty-Niner came along, so I packed a bag and moved into the Hotel Albert with him. It was my way out."

"A Forty-Niner?"

Velma snickered. It lightened her distraught features to a blend of sad and sexy. "Yeah, you know, he was a Father Time, had to be at least forty, and was prospecting for a rich wife. Thought if he put the handcuffs on me, then he'd be privy to Daddy's fortune."

8 dimly remembered that handcuffs referred to a wedding ring in the new lingo. "How'd you end up with Tomas?"

Velma's face fell, and then became defiant. "Met him in a juice joint. He was a real sheik, don't you think?"

"Bugsy hired me to find you," 8 said. "I took his money. I wasn't planning on telling him where you were when I found you, but I think he must've followed me." That wasn't the whole truth, 8 thought, but pretty much summed it up.

"And here I thought you just wanted to find me for yourself, Mr. 8 Ballo."

"You are quite mysterious, Miss Velma Hartmann."

"What now?"

"I say we sleep on it and come back with fresh perspectives in the morning."

"Ugh, I don't really do mornings. Unless you're just trying to get me into bed?"

8 chuckled. "Pearle has a guest room. We'll put you in there, and I'll bunk down out here on the couch."

Velma looked at him, and then at the couch they were crowded onto. "I don't believe you'll fit very well."

"I'll be fine." 8 stood up and offered his hand and led Velma to the spare bedroom.

At the doorway, Velma clutched onto him. "Lie with me for a moment. I don't want to be alone."

8 put up nominal resistance, but in the end, lay down next to her, spooning her tiny body in his embrace. He could feel the flutter of her heart, the coolness of her skin, and smell the essence of her body. He dozed off, slipping into dreams of guns and gangsters. When he woke, Velma was astride him, an animal ferocity on her face. 8 realized his pants had been pulled off and that he was erect, and then he was inside of her and she began to ride him frenziedly, not an act of love, but a means of forgetting. It was a temporary alleviation of the blood and pain and terror of the evening, and

the two of them bumped and grunted and groaned until finally falling together in a sweaty embrace and falling back to sleep.

When 8 woke in the morning before dawn, she was gone.

Chapter 28

Pearle was in the kitchen cooking pancakes and bacon when 8 walked in. "I could get used to staying here. Hope you got coffee on."

Pearle handed him a cup of coffee. "What's not to like? The pleasures of a beautiful woman at night, then in the morning, coffee to hand, and breakfast almost served."

"Nothing happened," 8 said. "I was just comforting her after a difficult night."

"Man, you're a liar. I could hear the two of you. Had to put a pillow over my head. Eight ball in the corner pocket, off the headboard." Pearle guffawed loudly, clearly thinking he was tremendously funny.

"Okay, maybe we were intimate, well, not really. There was nothing intimate about it. There was something mighty odd about our lovemaking last night." 8 took a sip of coffee. "She's not quite the woman I thought she was."

"Yeah? Who is she, then?"

"She's a sweet and confused young lady."

"Yeah? Did she tell you why she killed Colleen Brooks?"

"Velma didn't kill her. She just felt responsible because she brought Colleen into the bear's den. Fritz beat her to death."

"So she says," Pearle said. "How about that other guy, Peter, you know, the partner of Arkady? Who slashed their throats?"

"I didn't ask." 8 sat down at the table. "Think that might've been my fault."

"Oh, yeah? Do tell."

"I saw Hartmann earlier that day before I was supposed to meet Arkady and Peter. I let on that I had a lead, that I was going to be talking to two fellows later that night—and mentioned they were from Coney Island. Fritz guessed or found out about them. He had a picture of them after all, from Velma's bedroom."

Pearle set a plate down in front of 8 and sat across from him with his own. "So, the thinking is that Fritz was afraid that those fellers were going to point a finger at him being the killer?"

"He didn't know that they were going to finger Velma as the killer. He just knew that they had information to share. He probably figured that Velma told them the truth. That it was Fritz who killed Colleen. How could he know that she'd confessed to being responsible, and hadn't mentioned what she witnessed, that it was actually her father who killed the girl?"

"Pretty thin, if you ask me," Pearle said.

"Velma doesn't strike me as a killer."

"You know what they say about the quiet ones, don't you?"

8 chuckled. "Velma is far from a quiet one. She just doesn't have that look, you know, in the eyes, of somebody who has actually killed another person."

Pearle nodded somberly. "Lot of boys got that look by the end of the war," he said.

"Sure enough," 8 said. "All the same, I might be wrong about Velma being the one."

"Could've told you that."

"Why didn't you?"

"Some things you gotta figure out for yourself."

They ate the rest of their breakfast in silence as the rising sun filled the room.

"What time your girl leave this morning?" Pearle asked.

8 shrugged. "Don't know. Before I woke."

"She's an unusually early riser for a flapper, ain't she?"

"Might've left in the middle of the night."

"Love 'em and leave 'em, huh?"

"And quiet about it, too."

Pearle finished the last of the coffee in his cup. "What now?"

"I believe that Fritz is a Sunday morning, church-going kind of fellow," 8 said.

"What's that mean for us?"

"Seems like it might be a good time to go dig up a sunflower bed."

8 and Pearle were sitting down the street when the wide gates of the Hartmann mansion swung open and two cars pulled out, right on time for Sunday morning services.

The gate remained open after the cars pulled out. Pearle looked at 8, who shrugged. They got out, grabbed a shovel, and walked through the unlocked gate.

"Pretty careless, if you ask me," Pearle said. "Leaving this open in the middle of a gang war."

"I think that on the precipice of a gang war would be more accurate," 8 said. "So far, it's more like foreplay."

"Kinda stroking each other before they bump uglies, huh?" Pearle asked.

"Still time to change their minds," 8 agreed. "And you're just mad you didn't get to use your bolt cutter."

"Seemed like the perfect opportunity to use those damn things."

The two of them traversed the short driveway to where two men stood by the front door.

"What'cha want?" the shorter and wider man asked.

"You're that private dick that was out to here the other day," the middle-sized man said.

"Is Mr. Hartmann in?" 8 asked.

"Nope. He went off to church."

"What'cha doing with that thing?" Short and Wide asked, looking at 8.

"It's a shovel," 8 said.

"What's it for?" Middle Sized asked.

"Digging," 8 said.

"Anybody else home?" Pearle asked.

Short and Wide stared at him with a toothpick rolling back and forth in his mouth. "Who the hell is you?"

"Mr. Hartmann wanted us to drop something off," 8 said. "Is Mouse or Bull around?"

"Ain't nobody around 'cept us two," Middle Sized said.

"You got a key to the door?" Pearle asked.

"Why you wanna know?"

8 and Pearle pulled their pistols and pressed them against the foreheads of the two men.

"Cause I'd hate to have to break a window," Pearle said.

Turns out one of them did have a key. 8 and Pearle tied and gagged them in a corner of the dining room, tying them to the legs of a massive coal stove.

"You want to dig the hole or root through the house?"

"You can dig," Pearle said, then paused. "You know you're making a pretty serious enemy in Hartmann right now, don't you?"

"Sorry, my friend. *We're* making an enemy of the man."

"Why didn't you… we… let the police handle it?"

"McGee said that I needed more proof before the flatfoots came in and mussed around with things. Said that the powers that be believed Fritz is a solid and wealthy citizen. Something about him providing jobs and giving to charities. Then there was the cash…"

"Do you suppose if you find a body in the sunflower bed that will suffice?" Pearle asked.

"Should do the trick. Just in case, why don't you see what you can dig up in here."

"Ha," Pearle said. "I get what you did with that whole *dig* thing. I dig in here, you dig out there."

8 waved his hand and went toward the back of the house, found

a door, and walked toward the corner of the backyard where a host of yellow sunflowers were greedily drinking in the sunlight. They were about seven feet high and seemed to be flourishing.

It was a shame, but 8 dug into them with a vengeance, pulling them free as he shoveled into the earth in search of the missing Colleen Brooks. It was a hot morning, and he paused to take his jacket off and lay it off to the side.

To properly bury a person so that they didn't come floating back to the surface usually took a hole about six feet. 8 was hoping that Bull and the henchmen had been lazy. Not knowing exactly where to dig was a problem, as the bed was about twelve feet long by four feet wide. 8 figured it was best to be methodical, removing the dirt a layer at a time. At two feet, there was still no sign of a body. At three feet, he found her. That's when the shadow cast itself over 8. He looked up at the extremely enormous man. Bull.

"How about you take that there gat off your side and throw it over there," Bull said, jerking his head to the side. He was holding a pistol in his hand that looked like a toy in his enormous paw.

8 paused his digging and stood up. He snuck a glance at the house, figuring if he bought some time, Pearle would come out and get the advantage. Instead, he saw his friend coming out the back door with his hands up, Mouse behind him with a gun stuck into his back.

"You got a pretty big mouth, don't you?" Bull said. "But I don't hear you yapping about nothing now."

"Never figured you for the sort of gent who'd hide behind a weapon," 8 said.

"Should we shoot 'em here and bury them with the girl?" Mouse asked.

"Close your mouth, Mouse," Bull said.

"Don't tell me to shut up, else I'll bury you right here along with 'em."

8 noticed a nervous tightening to Bull's eyes. "Nobody needs to shoot anybody," he said.

"You shoot us, the coppers are going to descend upon you like locusts on a wheatfield," Pearle said.

"Mr. Hartmann wouldn't be too happy with that, now, would he?" 8 asked.

"Maybe I'll just kill you with my fists," Bull said. "Quiet but deadly, these are." He held up his left fist, as big as an entire ham shank.

8 weighed his options. Pearle looked to be disarmed. Two guns were on him. "You don't have the guts to fight me man to man."

A wide smile rippled across the broad face of Bull. "Usually, I gots to fight three men to have any fun at all."

8 stepped up out of the hole. He considered hitting Bull in the face with the shovel, but Mouse stood at Pearle's back with a gun. He threw it aside.

"Now the gat," Bull said.

"Let's just kill 'em and get it over with," Mouse said.

8 carefully eased the pistol out of the holster at his waist and tossed it to the side.

Bull stepped back next to Mouse. "Hold my gat," he said. He took off his jacket, and then stripped his shirt off.

8 thought that he looked like a large Hercules. Or a giant Samson.

"You ready to be beaten to death?" Bull asked.

8 took a few steps to his left, circling, judging the agility of the man.

Bull followed him, his steps light like a ballerina, his hands up in a boxer's pose. "No single man has ever lasted more than ten minutes with me," he said.

8 figured the man had some training in boxing, by the look of him, and he moved with the grace of a cat.

"I'm gonna batter you faceless," Bull said, stepping forward, closing ground.

8 stepped forward and snapped a left jab into the man's chin. It was like hitting a concrete block. He danced back, watching.

Bull smiled. He moved closer. "Come on out and play, Mr. 8 Ballo."

8 circled back to the right. When Bull moved closer, he snapped another left jab into the man's nose, and then followed with a hard right to the solar plexus. Bull's nose sprouted red, and he gasped, but that didn't stop him from rushing forward, trying to grab 8 in a bear hug. 8 avoided the encircling arms but fell backward.

Bull kicked him in the side as he was rolling away. As 8 came to his feet, Bull swept a roundhouse into the side of his head, and it was like the Fourth of July come early. 8 managed to stagger to his feet in time to be hit with a blow that glanced off his shoulder.

Enough dancing, 8 thought, the pain and anger overtaking the rationale. A blackness of rage was descending, and he stepped in to meet the rushing Bull, slamming the top of his forehead into the man's nose. 8 felt the bone and gristle break and rip all the way down through his body to the tips of his toes. It felt good. He hooked his foot behind Bull's ankle and shoved, sending the wailing behemoth toppling to the ground.

Even with the madness grasping at him, 8 knew enough not to get into a wrestling match with the man and moved back out of reach, looking for an opening as Bull stood back up.

"You busted my nose," Bull said, putting a hand to his face, a look of wonder creasing his features. He stepped toward 8, more wary this time.

8 stepped in and hit him in the cheekbone with a left, but the man deflected his right cross. Bull struck 8 in the chin with the palm of his hand and then followed with a punch to his forehead. They stood toe to toe slugging it out for twenty seconds, before Bull landed a haymaker to 8's chin that swept him from his feet with all the ferocity of a hurricane hitting shore.

This time, 8 couldn't gather his addled wits before Bull was on him, some three hundred pounds pinning him to the ground, the man's forearm across his throat. 8 tried to twist free, but Bull had a leg pinned between his. The blackness of anger started to be overcome by the dark of unconsciousness. No, he wouldn't give in, 8 thought, his mind and heart screaming at him to fight back. A fresh course of adrenaline shot through his veins, enough to clear his head, and he grabbed the wrist of the arm across his throat and started to force it up and off his neck.

Bull's eyes widened incredulously as his arm was detached from 8's neck, a moment of wonder, and then he was thrown to the side, and 8 was straddling him, raining blows into the man's face, his neck, his chest, battering him like Vikings pounding at the castle doors.

"I think he's had enough." Pearle's voice came from far away.

8 slowed his smashing blows, looking at his bloodied and broken handiwork below. He stood and turned. Pearle was standing there holding his pistol, Mouse inert at his feet.

"What happened to him?" 8 asked.

"He got more interested in the fight than paying attention to me," Pearle said.

"When'd that happen?"

"A little bit back."

"You didn't want to step in?"

"You seemed to be doing okay on your own. I didn't want to interfere. Plus, I enjoyed the show."

8 walked over and picked up his pistol. The holster had been torn from his waist. He stuck it in his waistband. "Did you have the upper hand when that bastard was lying on top of me strangling me to death?"

The sound of engines racing came roaring up the street and then squealing tires.

"Sounds like the alert is out," Pearle said. "What say we skedaddle?"

Chapter 29

Fritz Hartmann steepled his fingers under his chin. Across from him were Mouse and Bull. Mouse had a knot on his head, but that was the extent of his injuries. Bull looked like a side of beef that'd been dragged behind a truck through jagged glass.

"Mind telling me what happened?" Hartmann asked. His voice was gentle. Soft.

"I, uh, got word that your daughter ran off with that 8 Ballo, right after Bugsy's men hit the place where she and Tomas Lombardo were staying," Mouse said. "I went and watched his apartment to see if he showed up there, but no go. Then I got word they drove off with some Black son-of-a-bitch, so I got asking around who that might be, but by this time, it was well past midnight. Then Barry Blue Eyes—"

"Get to the fucking point." Hartmann's voice was barely audible. Barely.

"Barry Blue Eyes directed me to this house in Bedford. Black neighborhood. Pearle Hill is his name. I pulled up as that private dick and the Black guy came waltzing out the front door. We decided to check if Velma was inside—"

"Who is we?"

Mouse's eyes flickered warily. "Bull was with me. We busted in, but no Velma. We decided to come back by here and see if there was any more word. We got suspicious when there was nobody guarding the front of the house and came on in with guns drawn. That Black bastard was rifling through your desk when I put the gun up to the back of his head. The private dick was out at the sunflowers shoveling, so we sat inside while Bull went out and braced him."

Hartmann turned to look at Bull. "How'd your face get like that?"

Bull's eyes were mere slits, the swollen skin starting to mottle and change colors. His lips were shreds dangling over his chin. "Thut I'd knuck him 'round a bit."

"You put down your gun and fought him?" Hartmann asked. His voice rose a notch.

"Wunted to teach 'im a lesson."

"I told him not to do it," Mouse said.

"The beauty of a gun is, it is simple," Hartmann said. He pulled a blocky pistol out from his desk. He pointed it at Bull and shot him three times in the head. "One problem solved." He turned to look at Mouse as Bull fell over backward, his chest and throat rattling and gasping into sudden silence. "And why do you have a knot on your head instead of this Pearle Hill and 8 Ballo lying in a bed of sunflowers with a dead girl?"

The door opened and two men rushed into the room, their eyes going to the dead Bull on the floor. Hartmann impatiently waved them away. He then looked back at Mouse for his reply.

"I got distracted by the fight," Mouse said sullenly. "Bull was beating the crap out of him, next thing I know, I'm coming to with Nibbles shaking my arm."

Hartmann absently tapped his desk with the barrel of the pistol, which was still pointed at Mouse. On the one hand, he thought, Mouse was like an adolescent child who needed to be constantly disciplined so the little fucker knew his boundaries. On the other hand, Mouse was a stone-cold killer who'd ice his grandmother and have a bowl of ice cream while she lay twitching on the floor.

"We got ourselves a dilemma," Hartmann said.

"Dilemma?" Mouse asked.

"We got a problem. Bugsy Siegel is nipping at our heels like a Jack Russell terrier. Now, it's not the dog that the fox is really scared of, but the people coming along behind that is the problem."

"Sir?"

"I'm not afraid of some snot-faced kid walking around playing gangster," Hartmann said. "But the organization behind him, Rothstein and Luciano, that's slightly more disconcerting. I need to strike before they get involved. But I have this nagging problem."

"What's that, sir?"

"My daughter is floating around the city with potentially damaging information that could hurt me. And this 8 Ballo keeps sticking his ugly mug in where it doesn't belong."

"But you hired him, sir."

Hartmann tipped the pistol up so it was now aimed at Mouse. It took all his will not to pull the trigger. He'd never had a young boy, but he imagined that they weren't that much different than young girls. They didn't know when to shut up. But he couldn't afford to lose the boy now. As they were speaking, Colleen Brooks was being transported to the East River, where she should've ended up in the first place. It was time to tie up loose ends.

"I could kill him, sir," Mouse said desperately.

"I believe that I gave you the job of finding my daughter. A duty that you have fucked up terribly."

"I will get her and bring her home," Mouse said. "I swear on my mother's grave."

"Bring Nibbles with you. I want it done. No more screw-ups, Mouse. You bring Velma home. I'll take care of 8 Ballo and then we go deal with Bugsy fucking Siegel. Tell Barry Blue Eyes I want to see him on your way out."

Mouse left almost immediately. Barry Blue Eyes came through the door. He stood in front of the desk nervously, his hat twisting in his hands. "What'cha want, Boss?"

"I want you to gather a team of our six best shooters, and I want you to go kill 8 Ballo. I want you to send four others to that house in Bedford and take out Pearle Hill. Just to make sure, I want you to put the word on the street that it's worth a thousand bucks to anybody who kills this 8 Ballo. Do you understand?"

-◦≻═◑ ◐═≺◦-

"Hartmann's gonna be mad as a hornet," Pearle said. He and 8 were in a deli having coffee.

"Yeah," 8 agreed. "That might've been a bit rash."

"Ya think?" Pearle asked. He smiled. "But damn that was fun watching you put a beat down on that big lug."

"Glad you enjoyed yourself." 8 ran his tongue over his split lip. "For the record, next time, feel free to intervene if you're standing around holding a gun with nothing else to do."

"People pay good money for a fight like that. You know how much I spent to go see Dempsey knock out Georges Carpentier last year in Jersey City?"

"Yeah, well, if I ever get in a fight with Dempsey, just shoot me before I get churned into hamburger."

"He's gonna come after us, ya know."

"Me for sure. Don't know if he knows who you are."

"Hartmann ain't no dummy. He'll figure it out and send his chopper squad to pay me a visit. They're probably already at your place." Pearle laughed hoarsely. "Oh, and yeah, that's right, we provoked that bug-eyed bastard Siegel last night too. Maybe the two hit squads will kill each other when they show up at your place."

Hmm, 8 thought. *That was an interesting proposition.* "We do seem to be up a tree with a pack of wolves trying to get us."

"I'm not sure there are any more bad guys in all of Brooklyn for you to anger."

"Sorry to pull you into this."

"Sorry? Heck, I'm having the time of my life. What'd McGee have to say?"

8 had used the deli telephone before joining Pearle at a table.

"Said he'd go have a look with a couple of men."

"I'm thinking that your dead girl was being trundled away to never be seen again before we got around the corner."

"Yeah. Can't hurt to give Hartmann a little official jostle, though."

"Damn straight," Pearle said.

"What're you going to do?"

"I think it best if we lie low," Pearle said. "I've got a friend in the heart of Black Bedford. Probably go stay with him. I'd invite you along, but you'd stick out like a dog's balls."

8 was still contemplating that as Pearle stood up. "Keep your head low," he said.

"Escaping Bushwick," Pearle said. "That'd make a good moving picture. You got somewhere to go?"

"Yeah, I'm good." 8 stood up and walked out the door.

"You need a ride?"

"Nope." 8 wasn't sure where he'd go, but he didn't want to tell Pearle that.

Pearle handed him a piece of paper. There was a telephone number on it. "This is where I'll be. Guy's name is Elijah. Give me a ring when you're ready to go get those motherfuckers."

8 watched Pearle drive off and then walked in the other direction. He couldn't go to any of his friends' homes. He wasn't going to risk their lives. He thought about McGee, being a policeman and all, but the man had a wife and children. And Hartmann and Bugsy probably were not afraid of killing a copper. It had to be somebody that nobody knew about.

He didn't realize where he was going until he was almost there. Asta Holm lived on Ellery Street, in the very tip of the northwest corner of Bushwick. Very few people knew about their relationship. The outer door to the tenement building was open, and 8 made his way to the third floor and knocked on her door. Asta swung the door open. Her ample cheeks were rosy, and her hair tied back in a bun. She was also barefoot.

"My, if it isn't 8. What happened? Did your new love dump you?"

"Hi, Asta. Is your roommate here?"

"No. She's visiting her brother in Connecticut. But don't you be getting no ideas. I'm not some dame to be treated like a yo-yo." Her blue eyes flashed dangerously.

"I, uh, need a favor. Can I come in."

"You got some nerve." She didn't move.

"I have some people after me. Some very bad people. And they want to kill me."

Asta snickered. "And you think you'd be safer with me?"

"Please."

"I think I might make you beg." Asta snickered again. "But that would be too disappointing." She turned around and went back into the apartment. "I'm baking bread. Have a seat at the table, and I'll be right with you."

8 had been here once before. Asta lived with another woman to share expenses. Telephone operators didn't make a very good salary. Even with the joint incomes, the apartment was threadbare and worn-looking.

"Something to drink?" Asta called as 8 sat down.

"I'm fine."

Asta peeked around the corner. She disappeared back into the kitchen and returned with a bottle of whiskey half full and two glasses. "You don't look fine. You look like you could use a good stiff one."

"That I could," 8 said. "You're an angel."

Asta poured a couple fingers into one glass and pushed it over to him. She put just a tad in her own glass. "Who's been beating up on my handsome 8?" she asked.

8 told her about finding the body of Colleen Brooks in Hartmann's sunflower bed and the subsequent fight with Bull.

"Fritz Hartmann is a very bad man," Asta said.

"Do you know him?"

"*Ja.* He owns this building."

8 stared at her and then chuckled. "Now that's funny. I'm hiding out from him in his own place."

Asta laughed and raised her glass. "Fuck him," she said.

8 clinked his glass to hers. "Yes. Fuck him."

"And you're in love with the man's daughter."

"I'm not in love," 8 said. "There's just something about her that I can't quite clean out of my mind."

Asta nodded. "Could be love. Could be a disease. It could be lots of things."

"*Ja*," 8 said.

"Are you making fun of my Dutch?" Asta asked. "Because I could call my landlord and tell him where you are, if that's the case."

8 smiled. The brown liquor was calming his nerves. "No, I'm relishing in your Dutch. You are good for me."

"Good for you, eh?" Asta poured a bit more whiskey into each of their glasses. "Kind of like a warm pair of *sokken*?" At his perplexed look, she added, "Socks."

"Don't underestimate a warm pair of socks," 8 said.

"*Ja*. This is true. But there is a time and place for them. And there is a time and place to be barefoot."

"Do you mind if I lay low here while I figure out what to do about all this mess?"

"Are you talking overnight?"

"Probably. I don't have anywhere else to go."

"*Ja*. You can stay. But you sleep in Liesbeth's bed."

They chatted the afternoon away. Asta made a stew to go with the fresh bread. While she was in the kitchen, 8 called Pearle to come pick him up at sunrise. Pearle laughed to hear that he was staying with Asta but agreed to come get him there.

8 was beginning to formulate a plan. It really wasn't much more than an idea, but at least it was something.

After a few drinks and conversation, 8 went to bed in Liesbeth's bed. At some point in the night, Asta joined him.

Chapter 30

Pearle picked 8 up just after the sun rose in the east. Asta was still fast asleep as 8 eased his way out of her home, leaving a note on the table that he'd be back later. There was a ticklish thought in the back of his mind. Velma seemed almost like a fever, coming on afire and burning brightly, but then fading just as quickly. Asta was a more constant flame, if one whose intensity was always genuine, however sporadic. He really quite liked her.

"Kinda early," Pearle said. "You best be having a good reason for getting me out of my pajamas this morning. Like, say, we're going to go kill some motherfuckers."

8 grinned. Pearle looked like he'd been up for hours. He was smoothly shaven and had on a straw boater hat with a silk band that matched his suit jacket and kerchief in the pocket.

"Not yet," 8 said. "Patience, my friend."

"Where should I navigate this chariot to, if not down to Bushwick and the Hartmann estate?"

"The Hotel Margaret."

"That the place up to Brooklyn Heights where the Russian gent's been hiding out?"

"Yep."

Pearle put the car in gear. "Why we going to see him?"

"First, to let him know that Velma didn't kill his partner, Peter, so he shouldn't be rushing off to shoot her in vengeance."

"Speaking of that dainty young lady who may or may not be

bamboozling you by way of her charms, bedroom and otherwise, what in heck am I doing picking you up outside of Asta Holm's humble abode at the crack of dawn?"

"Figured her apartment was the safest place to hole up for the night, seeing as you're the only one who knows about our... sleeping together."

"Interesting choice of words." Pearle laughed. "But I gotta be honest with you, Asta suits you better than that flapper chick."

"Asta is good people."

Arkady opened the door in his two-piece pajamas with vertical stripes underneath an untied robe with a colorful Asian print. His eyes were bleary, suggesting that he didn't often see this time of the day.

"You must be bearing bad news. Nothing good happens before noontime," Arkady said, ushering them in.

"Just want to check in with some new information we learned," 8 said, sitting down in the same chair as last time.

"You want coffee?" Arkady asked. When Pearle and 8 assented, he called downstairs to get a pot sent up.

"Pretty posh, here," 8 said. "Who ever heard of calling the front desk for coffee?"

"You find Velma?" Arkady asked.

"Yes. She was in Williamsburg with a fellow named Tomas Lombardo," 8 said. "She told me that she most definitely did not kill Colleen, nor Peter. She said she walked in on her father right after he beat the poor girl to death. She felt responsible, seeing as she introduced Colleen to her father."

"She felt responsible?" Arkady asked. "How so?"

"I think she knew what she was doing when she brought Colleen home," 8 said. "That her father would take a shine to her young friend, and that Colleen would be bowled over by lavish gifts and lifestyle, if not carried away by love and passion."

Arkady seemed to ponder this latest information. "This Tomas bloke look like somebody who might slit somebody's throat?"

"He was a hitter for Nicolò Schirò, so yes, I suppose he could've."

"Was?"

There was a knock at the door, and a bellboy brought in the coffee and cups and set it down on the table. Arkady shooed him out the door with a dollar and poured three mugs full.

"Tomas is dead along with his crew."

"That pretty little Velma is sure an angel of destruction," Arkady said. "She kill him?"

"It was Bugsy Siegel and a chopper squad."

"Everywhere she goes, somebody dies. She doesn't sound all that innocent to me."

"Probably not," 8 said. "But I don't believe that she killed Colleen or Peter. I think that Fritz Hartmann thought that Velma had told you that he'd killed Colleen, so he took steps to stop you from sharing that with me."

"How'd he know we were even meeting with you?"

"That might be my fault," 8 said. "I told him I was meeting somebody coming over from Coney Island. Told him that this person had information about Velma. From that, he surmised that it was you. Turns out Velma has a photograph of you and Peter in her bedroom. She liked to talk about the two of as a couple as the gay angle made Fritz very uncomfortable."

"So, Fritz is the one who had Peter killed?" Arkady stood up and walked to the window, the untied belt of his robe trailing behind. "What's your part in all this?"

Pearle laughed. "He has no idea, but he thinks your Velma is prettier than a speckled puppy."

"She does seem to have that effect on men. Most men. Heck, I think I might even have a crush on her." Arkady grabbed a cigarette from a shelf and lit it, his back still facing them.

"Right now, I'd settle for just staying alive," 8 said.

"And I'd like to see Hartmann dead," Arkady said, turning around and facing them.

"I think that our two goals might be intertwined," 8 said.

"What do you want from me?" Arkady asked.

"I'm setting a few things in motion," 8 said. He took a small notebook from his pocket and scribbled on a page then ripped it out. It was pink and had a ribbon on it. He'd taken it from Asta's apartment. "Come here tomorrow night at eight." He handed Arkady the paper, on it Asta's address.

The next stop was the ritzy apartment of Dorothy Parker. Luckily, her husband, Edwin, was not home. He was off golfing. 8 thought this rather amusing, grown men and women striking a ball again and again until it went in a hole. Nothing like the purity of the game of baseball. At least there, you just whacked the thing once and lived with the results.

Dorothy was also in a robe, even if it was now noontime. She was smoking a cigarette in a long holder. "Excuse my appearance, loves, but I believe I might've drunk myself right underneath the host last night."

8 grinned. "You look fantastic," he said.

"You, my dear 8, are full of shit," she said. "Would either of you like a cocktail?"

Pearle looked at his pocket watch. "You got any gin?" he asked.

"I think I like you," Dottie said. "How about a Bees Knees. A great way to start the day. Gin for the kick, honey and lemon juice for the obvious health benefits."

"You heard from Velma?" 8 asked once they were settled with drinks in hand.

"Shouldn't you be more subtle when inquiring about a woman with another woman that you've spent the night with?" Dottie asked with a malicious gleam to her eyes.

Pearle made a choking sound but managed to control himself.

8 wasn't sure that a married woman had the right to be calling him out, but then realized she was only having fun with him. They'd spent the night together on two occasions, even if it was only having great conversation. "She is quite the intoxicating drink, that Velma Hartmann," he said. "Right now, I'm concerned about her safety. I fear that her father means her harm."

"That girl is straight whiskey with no ice," Dottie said.

8 chuckled. "To be honest, she might have a bit too much kick for my taste."

"Somebody might've mentioned last night that she's staying with Zelda and Scott," Dottie said. "Something about problems with her father. Tell me, my love, does she call you Daddy when you're together?"

Pearle again choked on his cocktail. "I think I like you," he said.

"Do you ever have an opportunity to converse with Arnold Rothstein?" 8 asked.

"Arnie? Not so much. I'm more about the theater, and he's more of a bribery and blackmail aficionado."

"Do you think you could make it a point to run into him and pass on a message?"

"Am I now your errand girl, Mr. Ballo?"

"I'd be forever in your debt."

"You'll have to take me to the opera and pretend to enjoy it. Edwin does so hate going and is just a beast if I make him."

"Done." 8 inwardly flinched.

"What is this message?"

"Well, here's the thing. It's not really a message. I just want you to drop into the conversation that Hartmann has been boasting around about killing Spoons Goldman. Maybe he even said that the only good Jew is a dead Jew."

"You know there's a thousand-dollar bounty out on your head," Marty Hoffman said to 8. "Every person in New York City who owns a gun is currently out on the streets looking for you. To shoot you. Dead."

"A thousand?" Pearle asked. "Shit, man, I might shoot him myself."

They were eating a sandwich around the corner from the *Eagle*. The one gin drink with Dottie had probably been just the start to her day, but they were back on water.

"I feel like a celebrity," 8 said drily.

"Just sitting next to you makes me nervous," Marty said. "How about we cut to the chase. What do you want?"

"I need you to write a story about how Spoons Goldman was killed and a pocketknife with Fritz Hartmann's name was found stabbed into his chest," 8 said. "And it needs to be in tomorrow's newspaper."

"We're a reputable newspaper," Marty said. "But I did hear that. Was it true?"

8 nodded. "As I understand it, those are the facts."

"Did Hartmann really have Spoons Goldman killed?'

8 breathed deeply. He liked to be honest. He especially didn't believe in lying to friends. "No. I think that Tomas Lombardo killed him."

Pearle swore under his breath. "You think Velma was behind it?"

"I don't think that Fritz Hartmann is so stupid as to openly antagonize a psychopath like Bugsy Siegel by killing a close friend and top lieutenant. So, in my mind, who does that leave? Somebody with access to his pocketknife. Somebody who has animosity towards Fritz and would like to see the wrath of the Bugsy and Meyer gang come down on him."

"So, let me get this straight," Marty said. "You believe that Velma Hartmann is responsible for the death of Spoons Goldman, but you want me to lie, in print, and say that it was her father, Fritz Hartmann, who was actually responsible. Why would I do this?"

"Well, first of all, we're friends, and that's what friends do," 8 said.

Marty merely stared at him.

"If that's not enough," 8 said, "I could possibly offer up an exclusive, ready for print the day after tomorrow, that will scoop every other newspaper in the city. In the nation. And it'll be big news."

"I might be interested." Marty tossed the second half of his sandwich down.

8 wrote down an address in the pink notebook with a bow. "Come here tomorrow night at eight. You'll get a front row seat."

"Might want to bring a gun," Pearle said.

"Hartmann has your top brass right in his pocket," 8 said. "You know it, I know it, everybody knows it. So, let's quit pretending."

McGee sighed, leaned back, and closed his eyes. They were sitting at a juice joint just down the street from the 83rd Precinct. Pearle was keeping a careful eye on the door in case any of Hartmann's men happened to pop in by chance. His house, after all, was just a few blocks away.

"I'm afraid you might be right," McGee said.

"What'd you find yesterday at Hartmann's place?" 8 asked. "After I called you."

"Not a thing."

"What about the sunflower bed?"

"Nothing there. I asked why it was such a mess. Hartmann said you broke into his house, dug it all up, beat up one of his men, bloke by the name of Bull, and then shot him in the face. The top brass wants you in jail real bad."

"Huh," Pearle grunted.

"Three out of four ain't bad," 8 said. "I didn't shoot Bull, though. He looked like raw hamburger when we left, but he was most definitely still breathing."

"How quick you get out there?" Pearle asked.

"Two hours after you called," McGee said with a sheepish look to his face. "Got held up by a lieutenant."

"Plenty of time to cover up the mess," Pearle said.

"And shoot Bull," 8 said.

"Why shoot his own man?" McGee asked.

"For getting his ass kicked," Pearle said.

"I noticed a few scrapes and bruises on your mug," McGee said to 8. "That must've been some fierce bare knuckles. Wish'd I'd seen it."

"It was a sight to behold," Pearle said.

"You going to help us out?" 8 asked.

"I could lose my job by not arresting you," McGee said.

"If you don't tell, I won't tell."

"What do you want from me?"

"The way I see it is that both Bugsy and Hartmann want me dead. They also want each other dead. Seems to me it'd be best if they killed each other before they got around to me."

"And me! Why do you white people always forget us Black people?" Pearle asked mockingly. "Don't forget you got me in their cross hairs now as well."

"You want me to help you ignite a gang war in Bushwick? What kind of *gobshite* do you think I am?"

"The kind that is loyal to his friends," 8 said. "Hartmann has a thousand bucks on my head. Every criminal in the city is looking for me, and now you tell me every copper is, too."

"Bollocks," McGee said. "You know I'm in. What do you want from me?"

"She was here last night," Zelda said. "She was scared to death." They were seated in the kitchen of the large house in Great Neck.

"I'm trying to help her," 8 said. "Anything you know about where she is, that would be kind."

"She spoke well of you." Zelda lit a cigarette to go with the gin drink in hand. 8 and Pearle had accepted the offer of a cocktail but hadn't yet touched theirs. "But she doesn't think you can protect her."

"I got a plan," 8 said.

"She's brittle, I'd say," Zelda said. "About to break."

"I can help."

"Why do you want to find her?"

Why indeed, 8 wondered. What was his real obsession with tracking down Velma, who kept disappearing on him? "I believe she's gotten herself in trouble and is in over her head."

"Her? Or you?" Zelda gave him a penetrating look.

"I just want to find the truth," 8 said, the words sounding lame even to his ears. And then there was always his own self-preservation.

"The truth?" Zelda sked, "You don't want that. You want everything tied up in some neat tidy package that works for the general public."

Pearle cleared his throat. "If there's one thing my friend wants, I can assure you that tidy is not something he's looking for."

Zelda appeared to weigh that statement. "Velma did say you were one of the good ones."

"I believe that her father means her harm because she witnessed something that he doesn't want exposed," 8 said. "Furthermore, the gangster Bugsy Siegel seems to be interested in her, whether because she's charmed him or he wants an angle to use against her father, I don't know. But getting tangled up with that fellow doesn't end real well for most people. She's in deep, real deep, Zelda, and anything you can share would be one step to finding her."

"She does seem to hate her dapper," Zelda said. "Her face goes dark any time that Fritz Hartmann is mentioned."

"She shared one potential reason with me," 8 said.

"Did Arnie help you in finding her the other day?" Zelda asked.

"Yes, but I think we led Bugsy right to her. We barely escaped, which is more than I can say for the men she was with. She's become a pawn in a chess game between two heavyweights."

Zelda laughed, a high pealing chirp. "Velma might be many things, my dear, but a pawn she is not."

"You might be right, but she is most certainly playing a dangerous game."

"It's like sex, isn't it?" Zelda asked.

"What?"

"Danger. At first it is a tantalizingly tease, sliding up and around you, and then it begins to build and build, and you can't turn away from it even if you want to and then you climax and lay back and wonder what all the fuss was."

8 supposed that is why he did what he did. Danger was addictive. Much like brown liquor. And sex. The three things that gave a thrill to the humdrum existence of life. He kept hoping there was something more, but he'd not seen it since before going off to the Great War. That'd been a life altering experience, and then to return, and discover his girl married to another had dulled the edges and darkened the corners of his existence.

"Oh, what the hell," Zelda said. "I think you mean her well. Velma did mention that there was a big whangdoodle taking place tonight where she's staying. Said her friend Coleman Hawkins was playing with Ethel Waters and Smack Henderson and it was going to be the bee's knees."

"Where's she staying?" 8 asked.

"At the Hotel Bossert," Pearle said. "That'd be where that group is entertaining. Saw that in the newspaper."

"That'd be the place," Zelda said.

Chapter 31

8 and Pearle found themselves on their way back to Brooklyn Heights, the same neighborhood in which they'd started their day. 8 found it amusing that Velma was staying just down the street from Arkady, who'd been searching for her, and both in equally posh hotels.

"Not sure what the plan is here, Bo," Pearle said.

"Neither am I," 8 said.

"That's comforting."

"I was kinda thinking I'd like to help Velma be safe from her father."

"You got a thousand bucks on your head, and you think that attaching yourself to the girl is going to make her safer?" Pearle laughed.

"I got a bounty on my head, alright, but it's not Fritz Hartmann coming after me. It's his goon squad and every lowlife in the city."

"You're thinking that if Velma is with us, it might lure Fritz out of his fortress in Bushwick? Hmm. Interesting. Then what?"

"McGee leaks to the right people in the department where we're at. The crooks on the payroll will in turn share that with Fritz. He'll gather an army and come for Velma."

"You're saying we're going to poke the bear until it kills us?"

8 chuckled. "If you know the bear is coming, it shouldn't be a problem. When you surprise each other in the woods, *that's* a problem."

"Yeah? How we going to prepare?"

"At the same time, we let Bugsy know where Hartmann will be and when."

"After Rothstein shares what Dottie tells him with Bugsy, and he sees it in the *Eagle* in Marty's story, Bugsy will be hopping mad to avenge Spoons. Hopefully his eyes don't pop right out of his skull. He'll put together his own army and come down to waylay Hartmann."

"In a perfect world they'll kill each other off," 8 said.

"And we just climb into a hole and cover our heads while they do that?"

"Something like that."

"Lot of moving pieces," Pearle said.

"Lots of moving pieces," 8 agreed.

"Think Velma will go for it?" Pearle pulled up to the side of Hotel Bossert. "Being used for bait?"

"I don't know," 8 said. "I know she hates her father, but that's a long way from wanting him dead."

"If you're right about her being the one behind sticking a pocketknife with her daddy's name on it into Spoons, I reckon she might just be wanting him dead."

"Sometimes things look good on paper, but when it's time to actually do the deed, it's a bit harder."

"Ain't that the truth," Pearle said.

"We might just have to nudge her along," 8 said. "But I wouldn't be surprised if she went back to her father."

"I suppose if Velma reconciles with Fritz, she could put in a good word for us."

There was nobody staying at the hotel under the name Velma Hartmann. The old duffer at the desk couldn't recall anybody matching her description, even when offered a sawbuck.

"Took your tenner and didn't tell you anything," Pearle said, shaking his head. "What's the world coming to. Everybody wants a free ride."

"I told him we'd be up in the restaurant if he happened to see any young ladies matching the description I gave him."

"Short, thin, dark hair cut in a bob, with inky eyes. That fits the appearance of half the young women in Brooklyn."

"*Smoldering* inky eyes," 8 said. They stood side by side behind the elevator operator as they ascended to the fourteenth floor and the Marine Restaurant, a two-story rooftop establishment overlooking the Manhattan skyline.

The elevator operator turned around. "You must be talking about Miss Brooks. She's a real doll. Has a dimple on her left cheek and a brown mark just to the right of her nose." The boy had obviously been paying close attention. Velma had that effect on males.

"That'd be her." 8 pulled a second sawbuck out and gave it to the young man. "What room's she in?"

"I'm not sure but she's on the eighth floor," the young man said.

"How about we stop there on our way up," 8 said.

"She's not there. Took her down to the Grand Foyer 'bout an hour ago."

"She down there now?"

"Not that I was looking, mind you, but I did take a peek around while I had some time, you know, to see if I might say hello, but she wasn't down there. Must've gone out."

The lift stopped at the top floor. "Me and my friend are going to be having a bite to eat and listen to some jazz music. If… Miss Brooks comes back, you come let us know. And find out what room she's in. That'll be worth a double sawbuck."

They stepped out onto the rooftop. "You made of money?" Pearle asked. "Heck, you're throwing it around like it's fool's gold."

"Still spending Bugsy's money. Kinda feel guilty having taken it, so I'm trying to share the wealth. Makes me feel better."

8 told the host they wanted a table, and they were seated at the

railing on the edge of the building. The theme was nautical, and life preservers, sails, ropes, and navigational equipment dotted the restaurant.

"That's a long way down," Pearle said, looking over the edge.

8 took a peek and quickly thought better of it. He moved his chair away from the roof edge far enough that he was blocking the aisle. "Why anybody would construct a building this high is beyond me. Seems that a stiff breeze could knock this thing right over."

"And then put a restaurant on top with no walls or roof?" Pearle shook his head. "People be crazy, sometimes."

The waiter came by, and Pearle got a Gin Rickey and 8 an Old Fashioned. Short steps led up to a higher level, with more tables, and a small stage where Coleman Hawkins, Smack Henderson, and Ethel Waters were setting up some equipment.

"I'm going to go up and see if Hawk has heard from Velma," 8 said.

"Oh, Hawk is it now, like the two of you are best friends. You can't be friends with a guy who tried to make time with my girl, Bo. That's buddies rule number one."

8 chuckled. "Okay, I won't be nice to him." He went up the seven stairs to the upper level of the rooftop joint and over to the stage.

"You keep popping up all over the place," Hawkins said as 8 walked up. "Mr. 8 Ballo. I almost believe you might be following me."

"It's me who he's following," Ethel said. "Somebody tell him I'm spoken for."

"You bring that fine-looking blonde woman along with you?" Smack asked.

"I was actually wondering if any of you've seen Velma," 8 said.

"She was walking out the front door when we arrived," Smack said. "Said she'd be back."

"Hawk, he was all excited, and then *he* got here," Ethel said, nodding her chin over to the corner of the outdoor level.

8 looked in that direction. "Is that Babe Ruth?" he asked.

"Sure is," Ethel said. "Rumor is that Velma and he had a thing."

Ruth had a cigar the size of soda can jutting out of his hangdog face, which somehow still managed to be creased in a broad smile. He was dressed in pin-striped jacket and slacks, a white shirt underneath, a gold chain around his neck. In his hand was a drink, on his lap was a brunette, and around his table were two other women and a man.

8 walked over as the Babe regaled everybody within earshot about the time in Detroit a man came to his hotel room and found the Babe with his wife and chased him naked onto the streets of that city with a gun. "So, once I get away from this poor sap, I notice I'm right in front of a whore house, and I figure, what the hell, I'm already naked, and I still haven't finished what I started, so I went on in and spent the night. Had to call my manager to bring me some clothes in the morning so I could make it to the ballpark."

8 didn't particularly like Babe Ruth. He played for the hated Yankees and always seemed a bit too bombastic for 8's taste. "He have to bring you some money to pay for your fancy lady as well?" he asked. He knew he was being petty but couldn't help himself. There was something about the man that just plain irked him.

Babe took the cigar from his mouth and held it out to the woman on his lap. "Honey, hold my cigar for a moment, will you?" He swigged back the last of his drink and looked up. "Ladies, my good man, ladies, and no, I did not have to pay. It was on the house, on account of my incredible prowess in that department."

8 thought that he might pull his own gun out and shoot the man in his smug face. "Was wondering if you could answer a question for me," he said instead.

"And who the hell are you?" Babe asked.

"Just a guy with a question."

"I'd be happy to give you an autograph if you buy me a drink," Babe said.

"Actually, I was wondering if you knew a woman named Velma Hartmann?"

Babe waved a swirling hand at the waiter suggesting another round of drinks for the table. "Sure, I know Vel. She's supposed to be meeting me here, but she doesn't always follow through on appearing, so I got myself a few substitutes in case she's a no-show." He reached up and cupped the brunette's breast and gave a little squeeze. She squealed and slapped his hand away but didn't seem to be offended.

8 could think of no reply and was turning to go when Babe pointed over his shoulder. "There's Vel now. Hot damn, she made it."

8 continued to turn and saw Velma just at the top of the stairs. She'd paused and was looking around, probably for the gregarious Babe. And then, two men walked up and grabbed her by either arm and propelled her backward. A third man surveyed the crowd. 8 recognized Hartmann's gunslinger, Mouse.

8 yelled and took two steps in that direction. Out of the corner of his eye, he could see Pearle coming up out of his seat, and then Mouse was swinging a Tommy gun up from under his overcoat. "Gun," 8 yelled, a split second before the chatter of automatic weapon fire began beating a steady rhythm into the night air.

8 went flat on his stomach, his pistol in his hand, but had no shot as fleeing bodies obstructed his target. Mouse smiled insolently and turned to go. A single shot rang out, seemingly creasing Mouse's ear as he slapped a hand to the side of his head. Mouse sent another burst of lead in Pearle's direction, or at the table he'd pulled over and ducked behind.

Mouse turned and went down the stairs after his two henchmen and Velma. 8 came to his feet and battered his way through the frenzied crowd, all of whom were trying to flee the scene while he was trying to get to the stairs. 8 and Pearle reached the stairs down to the lift at the same time and went down them in several long bounds, pistols leading the way. The elevator was already on its downward descent, ticking its way toward the ground floor.

"Stairs!" Pearle yelled, leading the way down the hall to the stairwell. Fourteen floors proved to be daunting, and they were both gasping by the time they reached the Grand Foyer. There was no sight of Mouse or his fellow thugs. Velma was gone. Gone awry.

Chapter 32

"Telephone's for you," Asta said, shaking his arm.

8 looked around, the events of the previous day coming back. He'd been so close to finding Velma and putting the pieces of his plan into place. After rushing through the Grand Foyer and into the street to find Velma and Mouse gone, 8 and Pearle had thought it best to vamoose themselves. The coppers were already looking for them in connection with the shooting of Bull. If they got pulled in at this stage, they'd find themselves in a jail cell pretty quick.

He was in Asta's bed. Velma was gone.

"I think it's that girl you're in love with," Asta said.

8 slid from bed and walked naked to the table just outside the kitchen where the telephone was located. He didn't know how to reply to Asta. He always figured it best to keep your mouth shut when you didn't know what to say.

"I'm off to work. I'll be back about seven o'clock. Will you be here?" Asta asked.

"Might be a few people coming over at eight. But then we'll be out of your hair."

"Not sure I want you out of my hair," Asta said.

8 paused, looked at her. "And I'm not in love with her. I was bewitched by her but am regaining myself. I know that doesn't help, but that's all I got right now."

"Be careful," Asta said. "I kinda like you even if you don't know what the hell you want." She turned and walked out the front door.

8 stared at her back for just a moment and then banished those thoughts for the more pressing matter at hand. He picked up the telephone receiver. "Hello. 8 Ballo."

"8, this is Velma. I'm in trouble." The voice was barely a whisper. "I think my Daddy's gonna kill me."

"How'd you get this connection?"

"I called Dottie, and she gave it to me."

"Where are you?"

"Home, in Bushwick. Mouse came to get me. Two of his goons took me from my hotel and brought me back to Daddy."

"I was there," 8 said. "I tried to stop them."

"Is that what the shooting was all about? Are you okay?"

"I'm fine. What about you. Tell me."

"I think my Daddy's going to do terrible things to me and then kill me and get rid of me like he did Colleen." A low sob rippled across the phone line into 8's ear. "Can you help me?"

"I'm working on it," 8 said grimly.

"I overheard Daddy and Mouse talking. They're planning on sending a chopper squad to hit one of Bugsy's hooch shipments. They said it was a big one, and they couldn't pass it up. Said it'd send a message to that Jew bastard to stay out of their territory."

"That's real interesting. When?"

"Ten o'clock tonight. I didn't hear where they're going to hit it, but it's gonna be at ten. There won't be hardly any of Daddy's men here at that time. They said the risk was worth it, and it wouldn't take long. Can you come get me?"

"I'll come get you," 8 promised.

"Mouse has been watching me, everywhere I go, even to the goddamn bathroom. I got to keep the door open while he stands outside. I just opened my bedroom door, and he was sleeping in a chair outside, so I tiptoed past to the telephone."

"Can you leave?"

"No. There's men at the front and back door. They're prepared for war over here."

"I gotta ask you something, Velma. Has your father been molesting you?"

8 heard an intake of breath that initially, he thought, was in reaction to his question, but then Velma cried out, first in anger, and then in pain.

"Who is this?" the weaselly voice of Mouse came trickling over the phone. "Who the hell is this?"

"This is 8 Ballo, Mouse. I'm gonna give you twenty-four hours to let the girl go. If you haven't done so by noon tomorrow, I'm gonna come get her. And I'm gonna kill you. You hear me? You got until tomorrow at noon."

"I'll be looking for you," Mouse said and slammed down the phone.

8 continued into the kitchen and got a glass of water. A piece of bread and butter took the edge off his hunger. He was barely aware of what he was doing, so lost in thought was he. He'd purposely given Mouse a twenty-four window, hoping to make him lax, unready for what was going to happen tonight at ten. 8 had no doubt that he'd be making some attempt at rescuing Velma this evening, he just wasn't sure of the parameters.

Plans were always changing. Yesterday's plan of baiting Hartmann into coming out of his lair to retrieve Velma had become obsolete the moment Mouse had snatched the girl. Now, he had to come up with a new plan. One based around quietly extracting Velma from the Hartmann mansion while the bulk of the goons were off stealing a shipment of bootlegged booze belonging to Bugsy Siegel.

Asta had left a half-pot of hot coffee, and he poured himself a mug. She was one of the good ones. She'd stood by him when he needed her, and had not held it against him—well, not for too long, anyway—that he'd taken a turn with the young flapper. A fling that 8 was starting to believe was a craving for something different and fresh, not necessarily something that would last. When he examined the situation outside of the sexual, 8 had little idea of where a relationship with Velma might go. What would they talk about? How could they possibly reconcile their two vastly different lifestyles?

Velma had just supplied him with the key to saving her life. But saving her from the house would not protect her or 8, or for that matter, Pearle from the wrath of Hartmann. And then there was Bugsy to deal with. If Hartmann were eliminated, perhaps Bugsy would leave Velma alone, but he'd most certainly seek vengeance against 8 for having killed one of his men the other night.

8 picked up the phone and called Dottie. Surprisingly, she was awake and answered the telephone. She hadn't yet spoken with Arnold Rothstein but had a lunch date with him at one o'clock. That was good. Very good. A plan began to formulate in 8's mind.

After he hung up with Dottie, 8 got himself put through to the Candy Store down in Brownsville. It took some haggling with the lady who ran the front of the establishment, but he finally got put through to Bugsy.

"You got some balls, calling me like this," Bugsy said by way of a greeting.

"Think we need to talk," 8 said.

"Why don't you come on down here, and we'll have a few drinks and share some stories of our happy childhoods."

"Seems to me you might kill me before you heard what I have to tell you."

"Right there, Mr. Ballo, you showcase the fact that you're not just some dumb private dick, but rather, a quite intelligent gumshoe. Now, what I got to be asking myself, is why did you do something so dumb as to shoot John Double Chin in the face?"

"I didn't know he was your man," 8 said. It wasn't quite a lie, he rationalized, as he hadn't actually been certain that it was Bugsy and his men ambushing the Sicilians and Velma. "I found the girl, like you wanted, and some men came up the stairs shooting. I thought it best to get her the hell out of there. Your guy stuck his face through a hole in the wall and was making to shoot me full of lead when I shot him."

"Yeah, is that so? Why didn't you turn her over to me when you found out it was me?"

"Because she took off on me. Disappeared. I tracked her up to the Hotel Bossert, but before I could get to her, that gunslinger for Hartmann, the one they call Mouse, he and a couple of goons snatched her and shot up the place."

"Well, how about you go find her, bring her to me, and maybe we won't kill you and that Black gent who was with you."

"How about I do you one better, Mr. Siegel?"

"Yeah, what's that?"

8 paused, collecting his words. "What'd it be worth if I saved you a bit of money and served up Fritz Hartmann on a silver platter?"

"I'm listening."

At 2:00 p.m., 8 walked into the Candy Store in Brownsville. He wasn't sure if this was the wisest idea he'd ever had, but he hadn't been able to come up with an alternative. Last time he'd come here, a bag had been put over his head, and he'd been a few wrong words from death. And that was before he'd shot one of Bugsy's thugs.

The fact was, he either had to make things right with Bugsy, kill him, or leave the country. Maybe California would be an option. But, no, it really wasn't. Brooklyn was his home. He had family here. He had friends here, if he didn't get them all killed. No, things had to be resolved with both Bugsy and Hartmann.

He was again escorted into the back of the building and seated at the same table he and Pearle had almost died at not so long ago. At least this time he hadn't brought his best friend into the lion's den for possible execution.

"Welcome, Mr. 8 Ballo, to my humble bode of iniquity," Bugsy said. Two other men sat at the table. Neither one was Meyer Lansky.

"Hello, Mr. Siegel."

"Tell me about Velma being snatched from the Hotel Bossert," Bugsy said.

8 told him about tracking her there, leaving out that she was using the alias of Brooks. When he mentioned speaking with Babe Ruth, Bugsy whistled and said something about the Bambino and the Sultan of Swat, but was otherwise quiet as 8 filled him in on the details of what had happened.

"The *Eagle* mentioned the shooting over there," Bugsy said. "It said nobody got shot, and the only injuries were caused from crowd panic."

8 nodded. "Didn't realize it at the time, but I think Mouse must've just sent a burst overhead to scare people."

"Saw in the *Eagle* that it was Hartmann who whacked Spoons the other day. Kind of knew that already, but you see it in the newspaper, well then, it becomes real, doesn't it?"

"You got some real problems with Hartmann," 8 agreed. "That's what I'm here to help you out with."

"So, how does any of this help me?"

"Velma called me this morning," 8 said.

"And?"

8 took a deep breath. "I make you a bundle of money and deliver Hartmann and we're even. You don't harm me, my friends, or Velma."

"I never meant harm to that girl. She's a real peach," Bugsy said.

"No harm to any of us, and you leave the girl alone."

Bugsy laughed. Then he pushed his chair back and laughed harder. He laughed until his face grew red. And then he stopped. His eyes began to bulge and he stood up. One of the men handed him a baseball bat. He began to circle the table, tapping it into his hand.

"You shoot one of my men," Bugsy said. "And then you got the balls to come to my place and dictate terms. I'm not only going to kill you, you fuck. First, I'm going to kill everyone you know, and then I'm going to take my pleasures with Velma, before I slit her throat. And *then* I'm going to kill you."

8 looked at the door. The other two men in the room were pointing pistols at him. Bugsy stopped behind him, the bat going *thwack-thwack-thwack* in his hand. 8 figured his best bet was to dodge the imminent blow, grab the bat, swing himself behind Bugsy, relieve him of his gun, and either back his way out using the man as a shield or shoot his way out, depending on what the goons did. Either way, he figured his chances of survival to be minimal.

The telephone rang.

The thwacking of the bat was replaced by *ring... ring... ring*.

One of the men stood up and stepped to a desk in the corner. He picked up the receiver and said hello as time seemed to stand still.

"Bugsy, it's for you," the man said.

"Tell 'em I'm busy."

"It's Mr. Rothstein."

There was a terrible pause, and then Bugsy went and spoke into the phone. His answers were terse replies. "Yes. No. I see. I understand."

Bugsy hung up the receiver, leaned the bat in a corner, and came back to sit down. His eyes were about popping out of his skull, stretching the skin so tight that his visage was ghostly white. "Mr. Rothstein has suggested that I hear you out."

8 breathed. *Thank you, Dorothy Parker*, he thought. It looked like the opera was in his future. At least he had a future, even if it held large people in flowing robes singing in Italian.

"You're running a shipment of hooch tonight," 8 said. "A big one."

"How do you know that?"

"Told you. I had a telephone call from Velma. She overheard Fritz Hartmann making plans to hit it. They plan on taking your booze and killing all your men." 8 embellished this last part, but hey, it could be true.

Bugsy twitched, his shoulders jerking, his eyes flickering. "So, we don't do the run. I appreciate the information, but that don't make us even. Not even close."

"On the contrary, Mr. Siegel, I'm suggesting that you do the run. Only, when they ambush you, you ambush them back. You take out the bulk of Hartmann's most trusted men, crippling his operation."

Bugsy started to speak, stopped, settled back in his chair. "That idea has merit. I'll give you that."

"While you're busy with that, I'll be taking care of the rest. After tonight, you won't have to worry about Fritz Hartmann ever again."

"Yeah? What's going to happen to him?"

"Either he'll be dead, or he'll be in Sing Sing for the rest of his life."

Bugsy smiled. "I'm not sure which would be better. Death or life in that hellhole. Maybe we can make a deal after all." He smiled broadly.

Chapter 33

Velma dipped her blood-red lipstick in some soot she'd gathered from the fireplace. It made the dark red look almost black, matching her eyelashes. She pursed her lips, looking left, then right, in the large round mirror over her three-level vanity. Lightbulbs ringed the reflecting glass, illuminating her dark features, accented by dusky made-up cheeks, under her inky eyes.

Her black dress descended into tassels at the mid-thigh area. The lacy material poofed slightly from the shoulder, and the neckline plunged down toward her navel. Three strands of black pearls were layered from her neck to her breasts. She picked up the brain binder band and pulled it snugly onto her head to hold her hair in place, a solitary black feather sprouting into the air behind her left ear.

Perfect, she thought. It'd taken a few hours, but this was the perfect look for killing your daddy. It'd taken eleven years, but she now knew that was the only way to be free.

It wasn't until she was sixteen that Velma had realized it was wrong. At eighteen, she never wanted to see him again. It wasn't for another four years that she began to do what she could to stop him. She found that by bringing other young women home who looked like her, she could deflect Daddy's desires, his lust, and his perversions.

But the desire to kill him and watch him bleed out at her feet was only a few months old.

Velma walked over to her bureau and pulled open the drawer in which she kept her nightwear. She took the Borchardt C93 semi-automatic pistol out and turned it wonderingly in her hand. *What an ugly instrument for inflicting death*, she thought. And yet somehow, that was apropos, because was not death grotesque? No, she decided, not always. This grisly tool would soon inflict a glorious renewal of life as it in turn ended the life of a hideous creation that could only have been spawned by Satan.

A few hours earlier, she'd slipped this beastly weapon from the display case in the study when she was pretending to be looking for a book to read. It'd been hard to manage, as Mouse's eyes clung to her body with a magnetism that revolted her. The man had never once looked at her face and most likely couldn't tell you what color her eyes were, but at the same time, never stopped staring at her. It was creepy.

Finally, he'd been distracted by the bar trolley, pouring himself a drink, while Velma deftly opened the top of the case and plucked the pistol from within. Earlier, she'd come across the 8-round detachable magazine in the bottom drawer of the desk, which had given her the idea. She'd tucked the pistol into her undergarments, hoping they were tight enough to keep it from sliding to the floor.

With a twirl, Velma had grabbed *Jacob's Room* by the haunting writer, Virginia Woolf. It'd been the first book to hand, one she'd read several times before, but it seemed like fate, as she'd often wondered if she actually existed as anything other than an object formed of the perception of others. Was life really anything more than a collection of memories and senses, Velma wondered, and would death really be all that different than life?

Daddy had sent word that dinner would be at nine o'clock and that her presence was demanded. He didn't bother with the subtlety of pretending to request her to appear. She sensed a death knell in that insistence, one that she was ready to embrace, only if it didn't come with the foreplay.

Tonight, one way or another, it would be over.

-◦❯═◉═❮◦-

Arkady stepped out the front door of the Hotel Margaret. He'd a lot to think about and was going to walk to the address that the PI, 8 Ballo, had given him while he tried to sort out the swirling thoughts in his head. Of course, option two was to not go there at all. It sounded like it was a planning session. He was through with strategizing his vengeance. It was time to act. It might be worthwhile to hear what was said, but it seemed immensely easier to continue on past the northeast corner of Bushwick to Fritz Hartmann's mansion and just shoot him in the head.

The only downside to that was that he'd almost certainly be killed. His musings as he walked were about whether that mattered. Peter was dead. The love of his life. His soulmate. The very meaning of his existence. Gone. The world had become a gloomy and dismal place without Peter. It'd be like killing two birds with one stone. Arkady laughed as he walked, drawing stares from other pedestrians.

There was a certain poetic justice, he figured, in killing the man who'd ordered Peter's murder and then dying in a hail of gunfire. *But what of the men who'd done the actual slashing?* he thought, his feet slowing to a halt. *Shouldn't they pay for what they'd done?* Arkady's hand went tentatively to his throat, feeling the still-angry scar on his neck.

These were his thoughts as he passed by the address given to him by 8 Ballo, not bothering to pull the scrap of paper out of his pocket. Night was descending on the city, casting shadows onto the streets, as he mulled over what form his vengeance would take. His death, he knew, was a foregone conclusion. But who would he take with him?

A few blocks from the Hartmann mansion, noise spilled from a second-floor window, and Arkady realized there must be a speakeasy up there. Without thinking, his feet altered their path, going through the door, up the stairs, and into the juice joint. He realized where he was only after the gin was set down in front of him and he'd taken the first sip. One drink, he thought, just to get his intentions in order. And then he'd go kill a person or three and likely die himself.

Chapter 34

It'd taken Arkady three drinks to work up the nerve, if not the good sense, to follow through on his plan to kill Hartmann. It was just about nine-thirty when he approached the front of the mansion. He told the two men out front that he'd important information for Fritz Hartmann about Bugsy Siegel. The heavier man led him through the gate and down the drive to where a man was sitting on the front porch. This man patted him down, took his pistol, and told the heavier man to bring him on inside.

"You're that fancy man that got away, aren't you?" Fritz Hartmann asked, looking up from his plate as Arkady entered the dining room.

Fritz, Mouse, and Velma were sitting at one end of the long dark table that was built for sixteen.

"He had a gun on him, Boss," the heavier man said. He stepped forward and placed the pistol at the far end of the table.

Arkady hadn't planned to be frisked and his gun taken away. *Perhaps those three gin drinks clouded my mind,* he thought, *but what the hell, I'm still going to find a way to kill the bastard.*

Mouse stood up and in one fluid motion brought a pistol from his waist and placed the barrel against Arkady's head. "Get back to your post," Mouse said to the heavier man.

"Arkan, or something like that," Fritz said. "Velma, dear, what is your fairy friend's name?"

Arkady looked at Velma. Her mouth made the most perfect

circle. She was dressed all in black. Dress, pearls, and makeup. "Arkady Bortnik," he said. "And I came here to kill you."

Fritz laughed uproariously. "Now, you *are* a funny fellow," he said. "Sit down." He rang a bell and a man in a tuxedo stepped through another door into the room. "Hans, do bring another setting out for Mr. Bortnik, and do pour him a glass of wine."

"Sit," Fritz said as Hans went off to retrieve another place setting.

Arkady felt foolish, but with little choice, sat across from Velma in the indicated chair. Mouse remained standing, the pistol still in his hand.

"Don't be foolish, Mouse, put your gun away and sit back down. This funny fellow poses us no real danger."

Mouse looked hesitant, but put his pistol in his waistband and sat down between Fritz and Arkady.

"I'm so sorry about Peter," Velma said.

"Ah, that's right," Fritz said. "Somebody slit your bedfellow's throat, didn't they?" He snapped his fingers suddenly with a triumphant look on his face. "I do believe that it was Nibbles who killed him. And the good news for you is, he's right out the back door. Mouse, be a good fellow and go stand guard out back and send Nibbles in."

Mouse stood up slowly. His face indicated his displeasure.

"Don't worry about me." Fritz lay a pistol on the table in front of him. "If the fancy fellow gets any ideas, I'll kill him."

"Why don't we just shoot him and be done with it?" Mouse asked.

"I'd like him to meet Nibbles, is why. It'll be fun to have him meet the man who slit the throat of his perverse lover."

"Daddy, don't do this," Velma said.

"I'll have Hans bring you a plate," Fritz said to Mouse as he went out the door.

"Thank you, Mr. Hartmann, for sending for Nibbles," Arkady said. "For I'd like to kill him as well."

Fritz laughed. "Damn, you're a funny fellow."

Velma pushed her chair back.

"Sit your ass down," Fritz said, his voice going hard and dark. He picked up the pistol and pointed it at her.

Nibbles came through the door. "Boss?"

"Ah, Nibbles," Fritz said. "Do you have your blade with you?"

"Uh, yeah, I got it."

"Do you remember this man?" Fritz asked.

Nibbles stepped to the side to get a look at Arkady's profile. "Don't think so."

"Look at his neck," Fritz said.

"Ah, this is the guy that Lefty didn't cut deep enough," Nibbles said. "You want me to finish the job?"

"Not just yet," Fritz said. "Why don't you join us for dinner. Sit next to Velma, so that our friend Arkady can see the man who slit the throat of his lover and will soon do the same to him. That should give him an appetite for his last meal."

Nibbles sat in the assigned seat on the far side of Velma as Hans began serving the food, pushing Mouse's place setting across the table, even including the half-finished glass of wine.

"So, tell me, my friend, how are you planning on killing me?" Fritz asked.

That's when the shot rang out.

⊷⟫⊙⊜⟪⊷

"Four cars just left the Hartmann mansion," Asta said. "Looks like they were loaded for bear."

"Thanks. Go home now. I'll let you know when it's over," 8 said. They were at a phone booth, attached to a streetlamp, just around the corner from Hartmann's. Pearle and Marty were also there.

"About twenty minutes ago, just before the cars left, a man showed up. He talked to the two bozos out front and then one of them walked him through the gate."

"Hmm." 8 thought on that one. "Probably just a late arriving assassin. Maybe they were waiting for him to get there before they left."

"I can stay and help," Asta said.

"No, I'd feel better knowing you're safe."

"I wasn't really asking," Asta said.

8 had realized long ago that arguing with a woman was a bad idea. Especially Asta. "Okay, but stay here with Marty, would you?"

Asta nodded.

"If you hear shots fired, call McGee at the station," 8 said to Marty.

"And if I don't hear shots?"

"We'll come get you," Pearle said. "And give you first dibs before the police get here."

"What if they subdue you or kill you?"

"Hadn't really thought of that scenario." 8 chuckled. "Guess if you haven't heard anything, in say, an hour, you should call McGee and tell him we're dead."

"That man ain't about to take any prisoners," Pearle said.

"Well, try to stay alive," Marty said. "I don't want my story ruined."

Pearle laughed loudly, and then stopped, looking down the street. "If you don't hear shots and a car leaves, you may want to follow it to see where we're being buried."

"The East River Cemetery, I'd think," 8 said.

"I'll stand watch at the corner," Asta said. "If a car leaves, I'll follow it in Pearle's car, and Marty can call in the troops."

"You two look like you're going to a dinner party," Marty said. "Not like you're crashing the house of one of the most powerful gangsters in Brooklyn with intent to harm."

"Dress for success," Pearle said.

8 took his timepiece out. "Fifteen minutes before ten o'clock.

You haven't heard anything by eleven o'clock, call McGee." He set off down the sidewalk, and Pearle went the other way, circling the block to come up from around the back.

8 felt the ball of the weapon Pearle had given him. He'd called it a blackjack and ensured him that it'd crack a skull and render a man unconscious if used properly and with the right amount of force. It was a solid cylinder of wood with a lead ball covered in leather attached to the end.

When 8 reached the corner, he slid the blackjack sap up the sleeve of his jacket. He'd practiced for twenty minutes letting it slide out, grasping the end, and swinging it before being comfortable that he wouldn't just drop it. Guns were for once they were inside the mansion. Outside, quiet was their friend.

They'd driven past the house to get the lay of the land. At the gate, skulking in the shadows, were two men in long jackets with fedoras pulled low. Asta had watched the house from across the way, in an empty lot grown over with trees, waiting for Hartmann's crew to go out and hit Bugsy's hooch shipment. 8's plan had been to have Arkady fill that position of spotter, but the man hadn't shown up. *That was surprising, but plans rarely go without a hitch*, 8 thought, and Asta had stepped in as spotter.

8 pulled the black bowler low over his eyes and shuffled his way up to the two men, passing himself off as drunk, on his way home from a juice joint. Luckily, the two guards were in the shadows, so hopefully he'd have a moment before they recognized him. He didn't imagine that Hartmann had thought 8 would be so bold as to come to his house.

8 stumbled, righted himself, and took the last couple of steps to the men who were watching him with interest.

"You got a light?" 8 asked. He pulled one of Asta's cigarettes out of the pack, a Capstan, and broke it in half, dropping it to the ground. This kept his face turned down, avoiding possible recognition.

"Ha," the heavier man said. "You want me to light it on the ground."

"Move it along, you drunk," the other fellow said.

"I gots another one, hold on a moment," 8 said, shaking the pack so that the rest fell to the ground. "Dammit."

The heavier man stepped forward and put his foot on the cigarettes and ground them down.

"Hey," the other fellow said, "I could've used those after we get rid—" And then there was an ominous thunk and he fell to the ground as if poleaxed.

"What?" the heavier man said, turning to face the unseen enemy.

8 let the blackjack sap slide from his coat sleeve. He swung it in a high arcing motion and brought it down upon the man's head with ferocity. He didn't want to kill him, but he didn't want him sounding the alarm, or coming to in the next few minutes. As was, the man barely grunted, crumbling to the ground.

"You were pretty darn convincing," Pearle said. "You almost had me believing you were drunk."

8 chuckled. "I don't often remember my actions when I'm that drunk, so that was all conjecture."

"What do you want to do with them?" Pearle nodded at the unconscious men.

"Leave 'em. They'll still be here when McGee gets here."

The gate was locked, but the fence was low. The two of them walked side by side up to the man sitting at a chair on the front porch.

"Hey," the man said. "What're you two doing leaving the street?"

The hope was, that in the black moonless night, they'd be upon him before he recognized that they weren't the guards out front. It wasn't to be.

The man pulled a pistol from his waistband. "You're that 8 Ballo fellow, aren't—?"

Pearle shot him in the mouth.

⊷⫘⊷⫘⊷

Two cars blocked a quiet stretch of empty road between Brownsville and Gravesend. Hartmann's men made quiet jokes belying their anxiety. These minutes right before the action and the killing were the hardest. Then headlights illuminated the trees down the road, and the men readied themselves.

There were three trucks, signifying what a large shipment of bootleg liquor this was. In the face of the automobiles blocking the roadway, the first truck came to a halt, the driver looking over his shoulder. He couldn't see the road behind him, as it was blocked out by the other two trucks.

It was only the driver of the third truck who was able to see the two automobiles that blocked their escape route. Men piled out of the cars carrying Tommy guns leveled at the drivers and the men riding shotgun. There were eight armed men in front and the same number in back.

In lieu of this firepower, the men in the trucks raised their hands compliantly.

"Get out and take your clothes off."

The men climbed out of the trucks, ready to throw themselves to the ground.

"I said take your goddamn clothes off."

"What for?" one of the drivers asked, buying time.

A man stepped up to him and smashed him in the face with the butt of his rifle. The others began to disrobe.

Nobody noticed the men dropping down from the secret compartments in the back of the trucks to the road below. They lay on their bellies, orienting themselves. When the men rolled out from underneath the front truck and started shooting, that was the cue for the rest to follow suit. Some remained prone, sending bursts of bullets into Fritz Hartmann's soldiers, while others rose to their feet and circled to create a deadly crossfire.

A few men survived the initial onslaught and managed to get behind their automobiles for protection, but those circling soon had them within their sights. Two men dropped their weapons and raised their hands. They were shot anyway. Bugsy Siegel walked around the fallen men and fired a bullet into each head to make sure they were dead.

It was over in just a few minutes, sixteen dead Germans on a desolate road in deepest, darkest Brooklyn.

Chapter 35

After Pearle shot the man in the mouth, he and 8 walked through the front door and down the hallway to the back of the house. 8 pointed at the door that led to the dining room, held up two fingers to Pearle, and then went through the door to the kitchen where he found a chef and a butler cowering in the corner. He suggested that they should leave the premises and not come back. They seemed quite agreeable to that idea. 8 took a deep breath and slammed open the door to the dining room at the same time that Pearle came in from the living room.

"Welcome to my humble abode, gentlemen," Fritz said. "You *are* one persistent *mutterficker.*"

8 didn't speak German but he got the gist of the insult. "Are we late for dinner?" he asked.

The large man they'd tied up the other day stood next to a seated Velma with a pistol drawn and pointed at 8. Hartman was sitting at the head of the table with a gun pointed at Pearle. And Arkady Bortnik sat with both hands on the table.

"I'll have Hans set you a plate," Fritz said.

"I believe that Hans has left the building," 8 said.

"What is it that you think you're doing here?" Fritz asked. "Saving the girl?" He raised his eyebrow. "The poor, innocent girl?"

"No, I'm saving the girl who you robbed of her innocence," 8 said.

"Ah, so I'm the monster in this fable," Fritz said. "Do tell."

8 was hoping to buy some time so that Marty could call McGee

and get the cavalry here to save the day. "I first began to have questions when Velma would refer to you as Daddy in a childish, and at the same time, sultry voice. There was just something about it that rang wrong in my head. And then Mrs. Brooks shared a letter that Collen had sent her. She referred to dresses that she'd been given that made Colleen look like *her.* I took that to mean your dead wife, Fritz, that is, until I saw her portrait in the hallway. She looked nothing like Colleen. The other day I tracked Velma to the Hotel Bossert, only they didn't have her registered at the desk. So I described her to the man at the desk, and Pearle pointed out that the description could fit half the young women in Brooklyn, or of the flappers, anyway. And then the elevator operator told us that it sounded much like Miss Brooks."

"Stop," Velma said.

"Go on," Fritz said.

"You picked a mistress that looked like, and then dressed her like your daughter." 8 tilted his pistol to point at Hartmann's head. "You've been molesting your only child, Fritz, haven't you, and then in an effort to stop, you replaced her with one of her friends. And then you killed that friend, and you again began molesting your daughter. You're a sick man, Fritz Hartmann."

"You may be right about some of this, my dear 8, but it was Velma who brought me Colleen. As a present." Fritz smiled lazily.

"I told him that it had to stop," Velma said. "It started when I was thirteen years old. My mother was sick with consumption, and Daddy told me that I had to take over her chores. I had to become the woman of the house. One of those *chores* was doing things like that with Daddy."

"And you enjoyed it," Fritz said.

"It was the first time he'd ever paid me attention," Velma said in a wooden voice. "I felt important. I felt loved. I'd become the lady of the house. But I didn't enjoy it. It wasn't until I was almost sixteen that I realized how wrong it was. How sick it was. But I couldn't make it stop. I didn't know how to say no." Tears were streaming down her face, tiny rivers of black.

8 felt sick to his stomach. "You're a bastard," he said to Fritz.

Fritz smiled. "Ask Velma what happened to her mother."

"I killed her." Velma's voice was cracked and jagged. "He told me that she wanted to die. That she wanted it all to end. And that she'd told Daddy that as long as she was alive, I'd not be the woman of the house. That Daddy's attentions to me would have to end. That I'd have to go back to just being a silly little girl. So, one day, I walked into the bedroom when she was sleeping and put a pillow over her face and held it there until she stopped struggling. And then I was the lady of the house again."

8 thought of the young girl who had been Velma. Abused. Physically and mentally. Goaded into killing her own mother. He looked at Fritz. "You're going to Sing Sing," he said. "And I'm going to attend your execution in the electric chair."

"Me? Or Velma?" Fritz laughed. "She's the one, after all, who killed my beloved wife, and now she's confessed it to you."

"It will be you locked away in Sing Sing until they fry your rotten soul," 8 said. "For killing Colleen Brooks and raping your own daughter."

"I knew what he was like," Velma said. "Still, I brought Colleen to him. Offered her up as a sacrificial lamb. He told me that it was the only way that he'd stop. I knew she'd be blinded by the money and gifts. She was always so envious of everything I had. And one day, she was over to the house, and we were in my room, and she said that my dapper was dandy. That she thought Daddy was good looking for an older man. So, I arranged for them to get to know each other."

"Why didn't you just leave?" Arkady asked. "I mean, before?"

Velma looked across the table at him. "He said that if I left, if I tried to stop, that he'd turn me over to the coppers for killing my mother. That I'd go to jail. That the newspapers would crucify me."

"That's not the only reason, is it, my child?" Fritz asked. "You liked it. I brought you pleasure like you'd never had."

"That's a lie," Velma said. "I hated it. But I did like the money. The ability to come and go and do as I pleased without having to work or get married to some slob."

Fritz cleared his throat. "Let me tell you about some of the things that Velma liked to—"

"You're stalling, Fritz," 8 said. His lips were tight with anger. "And you don't even know that it's for no reason."

"What do you mean?" Fritz looked over at the grandfather clock in the corner of the room.

"The ambush you had planned for this evening, has been, well, ambushed." 8 saw the flicker of distress ripple across Fritz's face. He continued to turn the screw. "It turns out that while your men were expecting to meet trucks filled with Bugsy and Meyer's hooch, there weren't no hooch. Those trucks were filled with hard guys, harder guys than yours for sure."

"You're lying. How could you know that?"

"I told him, Daddy," Velma said. "I called him and told him earlier. I overheard you talking with Mouse and the others about the details, and I told 8."

"And I, in turn, shared that information with Bugsy earlier today," 8 said. "He was very appreciative."

"But how could you possibly have told him?" Fritz looked from 8 to Velma to Mouse. "Mouse was with you every second." The granite, stern façade of Fritz Hartmann had most definitely been cracked.

"This morning when I came out of my room, he was sleeping in a chair. I went to the telephone and called 8. He didn't answer, but Dottie gave me a connection to reach him. Didn't Mouse tell you that he caught me on the telephone. And that he spoke with 8?"

8 caught movement in the open doorway behind Pearle and he swung his pistol in that direction. As if choreographed, Pearle

swung his gun toward Fritz. Mouse stood there, the pistol looking huge in his tiny hand, the barrel inches from the back of Pearle's head.

"Aha," Fritz said. "It seems that the advantage is ours. Lay down your weapons, gentlemen, and we'll get you a plate. This is turning into a regular Last Supper, isn't it? Or, at the very least, for four of you."

8 wondered if he could shoot Mouse without the man pulling the trigger. Unlikely. Nibbles might have second thoughts about shooting 8, but Hartmann would not. Then he and Pearle would both be dead.

"Why didn't you tell your boss that we spoke on the phone, Mouse? Is it because you're secretly working for Bugsy Siegel?" 8 asked.

"I'm not working for that Jew bastard, and you know it," Mouse said. "You're just trying to cause trouble."

Fritz's eyes flitted to Mouse. "Did you catch Velma on the telephone and then speak with Mr. Ballo?"

Mouse looked sullen but his hand holding the pistol never wavered. "I didn't want to tell because I fell asleep, and she slipped past me. You'd of been pissed. So I just kept quiet."

"We'll deal with that later," Fritz said. He looked back at 8. "Nibbles, if these two gentlemen don't put down their guns by the time I count to three, shoot Mr. 8 Ballo in the head. Mouse, you do the same with his Black friend."

"One," Fritz said.

"Pearle, shoot Fritz on two," 8 said. "I got the rodent."

Fritz hesitated, not sure if he should go to the next number, his confidence shaken.

"Boss, what do you want me to do?" Nibbles asked, a tremor running through his voice.

"Lay down the gun, Mouse, and you live," 8 said down the barrel of his pistol.

"You gonna let your boy Pearle here die, are you?" Mouse asked.

His eyes were flickering wildly in his head.

8 saw the tightening in the eyes of Mouse and knew he was on the verge of pulling the trigger. "Relax, Mouse, think about it." 8 tilted the gun away from the man, holding it out to the side, palm facing him, the barrel pointed at the ceiling. "I'm going to put it down."

"They'll kill us if we surrender our weapons," Pearle said.

"They'll kill us if we don't."

"I'm going to shoot Hartmann in his filthy fucking mouth before I die," Pearle said.

8 saw the tightening in Mouse's eyes and knew he was going to shoot.

And that's when Asta stepped up behind Mouse and cocked the revolver she was holding. "Why don't you lower the gun, little feller," she said.

"Who the heck are you?" Mouse asked, but the gun barrel wavered, then came down.

8 pointed his pistol at Nibbles. "Put the gun down, and you can walk out of here right now."

"The hell he can," Arkady said. "He slashed Peter's throat, and I'm going to kill him."

Nibbles pointed his gun at Arkady. "Shut up, Fairy," he said.

And then several things happened within a split second of each other. Fritz's face exploded in a shower of blood, bone, and gristle. 8 realized that Velma was holding a smoking gun in her hand, a look of triumph and freedom on her face.

Nibbles dropped his gun and raised his hands. Mouse dove to the side. Asta shot into the air where he'd been, the bullet just missing Pearle.

Arkady leaned forward and grasped the gun Hartmann had dropped on the table and turned and shot Nibbles three times in the gut, *bang-bang-bang.*

8 turned his pistol toward Mouse who was on his back on the floor pulling the trigger and wildly shooting in the general

direction of Pearle, somehow missing even from that close range, and then 8 and Pearle shot the little man at the same time, the bullets riddling his body, leaving him like a broken, bleeding child on the ground.

Silence filled the room, and then Fritz Hartmann toppled over backward and crashed to the floor. Nibbles began whimpering and moaning.

Velma walked over and spit on her father. "You fucker," she said.

Asta's face was white as a sheet. She slowly put the gun on the floor at her feet and kicked it away.

"Where'd you get the gun?" 8 asked her, as much to get her out of her own head as anything else.

"Took it off one of the two lumps you left lying out there by the gate," she said.

"You be okay to go and retrieve Marty?" Sirens could be heard just two blocks away. 8 knew that it'd be McGee and the cavalry, come to pick up the pieces. "He's probably out front wondering if it's safe to come in."

Asta nodded and turned to go.

"Hold on," 8 said. He walked over to Arkady and pried the pistol from his fingers. He tossed it on the floor next to Fritz. Then he took the gun from Velma and put it into Mouse's hand, after taking the weapon from his and tossing it in the corner. "Here's what went down. Fritz shot Nibbles for not following orders to kill us, and Mouse missed me and killed Fritz. Then we shot and killed Mouse. Got it?"

Asta nodded, and then turned and left.

Nibbles suddenly took several gasping breaths, his lungs rattling, and then went still.

8 went and grasped Arkady's shoulder. "Got it?" he asked.

Arkady nodded.

"What about me?" Velma asked.

"What about you?" 8 asked.

"I killed my mother. I slept with my father and then killed him. I orphaned myself."

"That seems to be something you're going to have to figure out all by your lonesome," 8 said.

"I set Tomas up to kill that man who was a friend of Bugsy Siegel and had him leave my father's pocketknife sticking out of him." Velma spoke in a monotone. "I wanted my father dead. And I did terrible things to try and make that happen. If I knew it was this easy, I'd of shot him years ago."

"Go out the back," 8 said.

"Are you going to tell the coppers what I did?"

8 wondered about the morality, justice, and honesty of all that. "I don't know," he said. "Best if you're gone when they get here."

Two Weeks Later

8 met Dottie Parker at the Algonquin for coffee. This time it was before the regulars of the Round Table had shown up, a relief for 8 not to have to deal with Benchley's smug demeanor. They were joined by one other, though, and that was Asta Holm.

"I did, of course, read all about it in the *Brooklyn Eagle*," Dottie said as she poured a dark liquid from a flask into her coffee. "But I'd wager that there was quite a bit more to the story, even though it was written by your friend, Mr. Hoffman. What did he call it? 'The Shootout in Bushwick.' Quite catchy, if you ask me."

"Asta, here, was the real hero."

"Do tell, please and thank you," Dottie said.

8 recounted the events of that day and evening in Bushwick some two weeks earlier, holding nothing back. He wondered if she, being a journalist, might work some of it into one of her stories, but it wasn't really her thing. It'd been real and not theater.

"As you can see," 8 said, "without Asta, we'd all have been killed. Velma might've been the only one left standing."

Dottie rewarded Asta with a rare smile. "And for your troubles, you're tasked with looking out for this big... 8... for all of time?"

Asta blushed and looked down at her feet. "I don't know about that. We're not rushing anything."

Dottie looked back at 8. "The newspaper didn't mention anything about Fritz Hartmann fucking his daughter."

8 winced at the hard vulgarity of this truth. "No. We didn't see

any need to expose Velma's secret. If she wants to share it, that's her decision."

"Now, tell me, my dear 8," Dottie said. She took a sip of her coffee. "The story said that the sixteen dead men on the road to Gravesend were Hartmann's men. Did that have anything to do with me convincing Arnie to give that Bugsy Siegel a call on your behalf?"

"An upstanding citizen such as yourself would be better off not knowing the answer to that." 8 smiled broadly at her. "But Fritz is being investigated postmortem for the death of Colleen Brooks and a big fellow named Bull. Seems that once the cook and the butler realized everybody was dead, they had no qualms about spilling their guts. They might be still telling tales to the coppers for all I know."

"Oh, I'm sure your friend, Stephen McGee, has kept you up to date," Dottie said. "I doubt he's any better at keeping secrets than he is about what's in his poker hand."

8 chuckled. McGee, in fact, was still pulling crimes from what remained of Hartmann's hired help and was most likely going to be promoted for his efforts in unveiling the "honest" businessman as just another hoodlum involved in murder, drugs, and many other illegal activities. It probably helped that Hartmann was dead and so unable to point his finger at any of the police brass who'd most likely been taking bribes.

"And what has come of our sweet little Sheba?" Dottie asked.

"Velma?" 8 asked, thinking that sweet may not have been quite the correct word. "A couple of days after the incident, she contacted Pearle and asked him to run her father's legitimate business interests. They sat down with a lawyer and made it all official, and then she disappeared."

Dottie shook her head and poured some more brown liquor into her now empty coffee cup. "Velma gone awry," she said.

"I'm hoping that she'll find a straighter path forward," 8 said. "But who knows?"

"And you've set things straight with that dreadful Bugsy gent?" Dottie asked.

"We came to an understanding."

Dottie nodded. Her eyes suggested that she understood the dead Germans in Gravesend were most likely part of that deal. "And that Russian fellow, the one whose boyfriend was killed, what of him?" she asked.

"Back to Coney Island," 8 said. "I guess. For the living, life goes on."

"That it does, whether we like it or not," Dottie said.

"I'm glad I got to know you," 8 said. "I hope that we can keep in touch."

"I'd like that," Dottie said. "You're a breath of fresh air blowing away the smugness of my usual crowd. If Asta doesn't mind you having a woman as a friend, that is."

"I don't mind at all," Asta said. "And maybe, we might become friends as well."

"All's well that ends well," Dottie said. "It seems that the villains lost once again, or maybe, for the first time."

"I guess the only real victim was Colleen Brooks," Asta said.

"Oh, yes, poor, dear, little Colleen," Dottie said. "All she wanted was money and fame and glory."

"Perhaps she should've settled for happiness," Asta said.

"We're on our way to New Jersey now, to share what we know with her parents," 8 said.

"Mighty brave of you." Dottie shuddered. "To go to New Jersey."

8 had borrowed Pearle's automobile and ferry service to New Jersey. He thought it best to go in person and tell Colleen's parents what had happened to their daughter. Asta had agreed to accompany him when he suggested maybe they'd spend a few nights out in the countryside. It was almost five o'clock when they pulled up in front of the dry goods store the Brooks lived above.

Mrs. Brooks met 8 and Asta at the door with a strained expression on her face. She knew what their visit meant. The newspapers had mentioned Colleen's murder, but there'd been no details. 8's arrival at her front door could only mean they would learn how their daughter had died.

Mrs. Brooks ushered them into the second-floor dwelling above the dry goods store and sent a daughter down to retrieve her husband.

Not a word was spoken until Dan Brooks came into the room and sat down.

8 told them about how Velma had heard the beating, and then seen the dead body, of their daughter, Colleen. How the maid had packed her belongings into pillowcases to be disposed of. And how he, 8 Ballo, had dug up her body in the sunflower bed, only to have it disappear again.

Mr. and Mrs. Brooks sat quietly without speaking. They accepted the details about the death of their daughter at the hands of Fritz Hartmann without a tear. It was almost as if they knew.

8 told them how Fritz had paid for his sins.

The four of them sat in silence for a bit. There was nothing more to be said.

Mrs. Brooks walked them to the door, giving 8 a kiss on the cheek, tears leaking from her eyes, and thanked him for what he'd done.

As 8 and Asta walked to the car, he looked over his shoulder. A curtain moved up on the second floor, and he thought for just a moment that he saw her there in the window. And then she was gone.

About the Author

MATT COST (aka Matthew Langdon Cost) is the highly acclaimed, award-winning author of the Mainely Mystery series. The first book, *Mainely Power*, was selected as the Maine Humanities Council Read ME Fiction Book of 2020. This was followed by *Mainely Fear*, *Mainely Money*, and *Mainely Angst*.

I Am Cuba: Fidel Castro and the Cuban Revolution was his first traditionally published novel. His other historical novels are *Love in a Time of Hate* (August 2021), and *At Every Hazard: Joshua Chamberlain and the Civil War* (August 2022). Cost is also the author of the Clay Wolfe / Port Essex Mysteries, *Wolfe Trap*, *Mind Trap*, *Mouse Trap*, and the latest, *Cosmic Trap*, which was published by Encircle in December, 2022. Cost's love of histories and mysteries is combined in this novel, *Velma Gone Awry*, book one in his new series featuring private eye, 8 Ballo, set in 1920's Brooklyn.

Cost was a history major at Trinity College. He owned a mystery bookstore, a video store, and a gym, before serving a ten-year sentence as a junior high school teacher. In 2014, he was released and he began writing. And that's what he does: he writes histories and mysteries. Cost now lives in Brunswick, Maine, with his wife, Harper. There are four grown children: Brittany, Pearson, Miranda, and Ryan. A chocolate Lab and a basset hound round out the mix. He now spends his days at the computer, writing.

If you enjoyed reading this book,
please consider writing your honest review
and sharing it with other readers.

Many of our Authors are happy to participate in
Book Club and Reader Group discussions.
For more information, contact us at info@encirclepub.com.

Thank you,
Encircle Publications

For news about more exciting new fiction, join us at:

Facebook: www.facebook.com/encirclepub

Instagram: www.instagram.com/encirclepublications

Twitter: twitter.com/encirclepub

Sign up for Encircle Publications newsletter and specials:

eepurl.com/cs8taP